THE COMPLEX

Praise for *The Complex*

"To watch the wily Chopras jostle for dominion—not just over the crumbling walls of their shared home, but over the very historical and moral record of their age—is pure pleasure. Mahajan is, as always, a political anatomist blessed with a comedian's eye for the absurd, and *The Complex* is a singular portrait of a family as riven and fractious—and eternally surprising—as the country that produced it."

MADHURI VIJAY

"This family saga feels like wonderfully told backstories of people you have certainly met at a Delhi wedding, even as it is filled with memorable lines about marriage and the nature of tortured people. This is a tale about family that only an Indian can tell."

MANU JOSEPH

"Brutal, knifesharp, tender—Karan Mahajan packs an entire world of desire, incendiary politics, greed, and transgression into this engrossing tale of a family bartering old myths for new."

NILANJANA ROY

"*The Complex* leaps off the page, comes racing at you, streamlined by Mahajan's style and spurred by his sharp nip. I was amazed at how fast the pages turned. A propertied Punjabi clan, with all of its deadly sins laid bare, generates forces that will frighten and excite the country. Mahajan orchestrates the turbulence with a brilliant eye and a ruthless hand."

RAGHU KARNAD

"Riveting and unputdownable—Shakespearean storytelling. Karan Mahajan's best work yet."

SONIA FALEIRO

“A delicious page-turner about familial jealousy and revenge that, in the Dostoyevskian tradition, doubles as a masterful investigation of the slipperiness of power in a changing and modernizing world. *The Complex* is Mahajan’s most exciting, virtuosic novel yet.”

VAUHINI VARA

“This novel’s rare achievement lies in its masterful portrayal of the intimate relationship between personal lives and political realities. Through the story of a family, it captures the larger movements shaping the nation, revealing how political and social transformations seep into everyday life and quietly shape human choices. The novel seamlessly weaves the intricate power dynamics of the Indian family and the shifting structures of patriarchal authority into its fabric with effortless grace. Embedded deep within the narrative, with great delicacy, are the anguish and disillusionment experienced by those who seek to attain love, one of the most intense human emotions, solely through sensory and corporeal means. Through a powerful mode of storytelling, Karan constructs the intricate connections between a society’s moral upheavals and its political and familial aspirations. The strength, intensity, and momentum of his narrative are such that nothing needs to be pointed out deliberately; everything unfolds with organic necessity. There is a constant sense of danger lurking beneath the story, lending the narrative a palpable, high-stakes intensity that holds the reader in its grip.”

VIVEK SHANBHAG

Also by Karan Mahajan

Family Planning
The Association of Small Bombs

THE COMPLEX

A NOVEL

KARAN MAHAJAN

FOURTH ESTATE · *New Delhi*

First published in India by Fourth Estate 2026
An imprint of HarperCollins *Publishers*
Building 10-A, Gurugram, Haryana – 122002, India
www.harpercollins.co.in

2 4 6 8 10 9 7 5 3 1

P-ISBN: 978-93-6989-748-3
E-ISBN: 978-93-6989-267-9

Typeset in 11 pt/14.2 Sabon LT Std
by HarperCollins *Publishers* India Pvt. Ltd

Printed and bound at
Replika Press Pvt. Ltd.

This book is produced from independently certified FSC® paper to ensure responsible forest management.

*

HarperCollins *Publishers*, Macken House, 39/40 Mayor Street Upper, Dublin 1, D01 C9W8, Ireland

For Shiv Mahajan

A NOTE FROM KARAN MAHAJAN

This is a work of fiction based on the family circumstances of a man I will call "Mohit Chopra."

Before this project, I didn't know Mohit well. We had never met in person and had only communicated twice over email, when I had selected a short story of his for an anthology I was editing. So, when he passed away (quite suddenly, I am told), I was surprised to learn that he had named me in his will as his "literary executor."

This was not a position I was familiar with; his lawyer seemed confused as well. Clearly eager to get me off the phone, she said I should look into Mohit's Gmail account, as per his instructions.

Mohit's password, a generic string of letters and numbers, revealed nothing about the man. And if a prurient part of me had been excited to have access to another's life, I soon found myself swimming in a murk of spam. Then, in the Drafts folder, I came across a striking email.

Addressed to a friend, this unsent message ran to 100,000 words. It was less an email and more a manuscript, and in its endless scroll, it told the story of the rise and fall—and rise—of the Chopra clan; and reading it, I understood why Mohit, a Delhi Punjabi from a similar background as me, might have thought of me as a guardian of his work. My attitude toward Mohit changed. Over the next few years, I became immersed in the story of the Chopras, adding to the manuscript wherever narrative gaps appeared, and acting, I hope, on Mohit's wishes.

Now, years later, this work of creative revision or posthumous collaboration—whatever you'd like to call it—is complete. The email that was never sent has been sent. I hope it does justice to Mohit's vision of the world. It goes out to all of you.

CHAPTER 0

A WEEK AGO, I RECEIVED NEWS THAT MY FATHER WOULD BE released from prison. I had known this was coming—had known his twenty-five-year sentence was concluding—but still the date exploded upon me. I ended the call with my contact at Tihar and sat back in my scaly-walled flat, blinking against the onrush of hot green mulberry leaves outside the window.

In the tall days of summer, family members began to ring my bell.

I hadn't talked to many of them in years, though we all resided in the same ramshackle complex in North Delhi.

"Beta, will your papa live with you?" one uncle asked nervously, clutching the pouch of skin under his jaw. He stood at the threshold of the flat, not stepping inside, his sandals covered in dust.

I hesitated. Then I told him that was the plan—it was my father's property, after all.

"Surely there must be another relation he can temporarily reside with?" he said, sterner now.

I said my brother was in America.

A little later, a cousin with a sleek cobra-like forehead and black curly hair arrived. "Bro, I dialed your mobile ten times," he said. "Please keep it on. It's important. It'll be a huge mess if he comes here. It'll be a tamasha. I don't want that for us, I don't want that for the family. So I hope you'll choose to do what's correct. I know he's not fully in your control, but I'm warning you, bro." He declined my offer of tea.

"We strongly advise you, beta, that your father stays elsewhere." That was my grand-aunt Vibha, the only one who deigned to enter the flat; and it was when she sat down on the burgundy sofa, with its rivers of wheatish discoloration, that I saw how neglected everything was, how unchanged from when I had taken it over at the age of eighteen. I am now forty-four.

I clasped my hands together, eyes following the fantastical vine system in the petrified Kashmiri carpet, so hard with dirt one might have been able to smash it with a hammer. "I understand your issues, Buaji," I said. "But Papa's no longer the man he was. He's old. He's reflected and changed. In jail, they make them do yoga and meditation all day, and he's become spiritual." Lies. "Also, rents these days—" Seeing that Buaji was about to interrupt, I accelerated: "But the most important thing is that he's carried out his sentence to the letter of the law—no bail or clemency was granted. In that sense, justice has been served." Here I was consciously appealing to the memory of the late patriarch of our clan, SP Chopra, one of the framers of India's Constitution and a former Reserve Bank governor. The great SP Chopra had sired nine children with his wife. His six sons' descendants occupied individual flats in this sun-eaten brick complex, along with sundry renters.

Vibha Bua, in her eighties, had a face made for tough irony, with merry incisors she wielded as exclamation points at the end of sentences. But now, sipping tea, she was forced to keep her face hard and serious. She rippled her fading eyebrows. Then she nearly spat out, "If there had been justice, your father would have been hanged."

Evening. I was slouched on one of the old hairy sofa chairs, which reprimanded me with its wooden bones. I peered into the canyon between the two ageless, squat, rough-brick buildings of the complex.

What would it be like for my unstable father to return to this compound covered in pictures of the very man he had killed?

In the intervening years, I had been inside the other flats only half a dozen times, and that too mostly for religious occasions when a cousin in a forgiving mood decided it was time to rehabilitate me, the family black sheep; and it was during these havans, conducted on dhurries laid on top of gray terrazzo, fires mumbling within black iron pots, people's mobiles ringing at odd times before they clumsily answered them, that I would stare at the framed, garlanded photographs of my grand-uncle Laxman adorning the bluish walls.

Laxman Chacha had been a politician—or, rather, a political henchman, a kingmaker. He had had great affection for me and my brother, constantly slipping us bull's-eyes and orange boiled sweets. Before he began his political career, he would take our mother and us to the local temple. He had a long face, small testing eyes, and an emphatic bushy mustache projecting from above his lip. His vigilant upright stance was that of an athlete. "Eat some pershad," he was always saying, handing people the consecrated religious food.

Once, my great-grandfather SP Chopra, the freedom fighter, had been the deity of the family, but now, in Hindu nationalist India, Laxman had replaced SP as the foremost member of the clan.

"Congratulations, Bhai!" a neighbor had greeted me one morning when I was out for a walk in our colony—a colony which is a long blur of green clenched between a main road and train tracks, the peace of the genteel whitewashed bungalows intermittently harrowed by the bawling of an express. "Yesterday I was watching Parliamentary TV," he went on, "and Modiji himself mentioned your Laxman Chacha in his speech! Such an honor."

Did he *really* not know my connection to Laxman Chacha's murderer?

Another time, this same gentleman, who ran a cement company, said, "There's movement in the colony association to name the main road after your uncle." Meaning: the Muslim name—Mir Taqi Mir Marg—would be scrubbed, replaced by Laxman Chopra Marg. "Let us be proud of our heritage as Hindus," he said.

During the prayers, as I sat in a ring of chanting relatives in the complex, my eyes would drift helplessly to the photographs of Laxman Chacha with their brown smut of age.

I would try to look beyond them and make meaning of it all.

But I couldn't.

Say what you would about Laxman Chacha, but he had been exactly what he appeared to be. There was no artifice. He saw the world and he took and took. He never apologized.

Big day coming up, beta.

The message was from my aunt Gita. And before I could respond, more messages poured in.

he committed a crime but then the man he finished also was a criminal.

don't let this family bully u.

It's only your safety I worry about, bache.

I was so overcome by her concern that, at first, I didn't write back.

Thank you :], I finally managed.

Gita Chachi had been a central player in this drama. She is the wife of my father's only brother. After our father's imprisonment, she had helped us immensely, overseeing our daily needs—though I hadn't appreciated it then. I was a fresher in college and full of angry confusion. But, over the years, after Gita Chachi had moved out of the complex, my appreciation for her had grown, and I now sometimes responded to her long emails.

As I typed, I could summon her square, sweet, dimpled face in my mind.

Imagining another's face: Is this why we write?

I have never written, even as an exercise, about my dead mother. Her visage is fading.

If there's an issue let us know, Gita Chachi messaged. *We r very happy his long suffering is coming to an end. God bless.*

It was nice of her, but I knew it was more complicated than that. Before my father shot Laxman, he had threatened to shoot her too.

What had *I* done all these years? Odd jobs, some marketing work, but mostly I had moved my life onto the internet. Beginning in the late '90s, aided by my first asthmatic VSNL dial-up connection, I had made many online friends—through IRC, message boards, and finally Reddit and Twitter.

When Gita Chachi's messages had arrived, I had been writing an email to my Russian friend Lev. Lev and I had known each other for a few years and I was trying to explain to him the story of my family's decline.

Now I found myself typing: *An email is not enough. I'll have to write you an entire book.*

Which, God help me, is what I did instead of escaping from the complex.

—Mohit Chopra

ONE
GITA'S WORLD

CHAPTER 1

THE YEAR GITA "ENCOUNTERED" LAXMAN AS AN ADULT—she didn't like to return there even in her mind—was 1980. It was on her first solo trip to India as a (relative) newlywed. She was happy to be back in Delhi, but it was even more important, she felt, to *project* happiness, given how lackluster things were for her in the US. Her husband Sachin and she had had a dream courtship, mailing each other eloquent letters across continents while he was pursuing his master's in materials engineering at Brooklyn Poly and she was working as an assistant editor in a publishing house in Delhi. But once she got to the US, she found he wasn't the man she'd expected. So effusive in his letters—some were written in spiral shapes, as if his love couldn't be held in straight lines—he was in person taciturn, absent-minded, work obsessed, particular. "Don't put this clock in the kitchen," he told her one day, having just returned from his new job as a packaging engineer at Trident Foods Co. "It's a bedside clock," Sachin went on, his bushy eyebrows lashed together, "it doesn't look nice there."

Gita, who had waited all day to see him, couldn't help herself. "What if I were to retort that it looks *better* here?"

They were in their first flat in America, a small basement-level dwelling in Elmhurst, the building the color of a sky spoiling toward rain, the siding peeling so dramatically that parts of it were bunched like scrolls.

"Gita, please, let's not fight. I'm tired. I've said this before: If you want to rearrange things, you should discuss it with me."

"But this is the first bloody decision I've made in this country!" Gita said.

What was she to do? He had a life beyond these walls, at work. Whereas she was a newlywed housewife in Queens, too afraid to ride the subway with its aura of piss and murder.

In India, she had been an editor. Well, almost an editor—an assistant, on her way up. But here, in the great US of A, upon landing, she had discovered quickly that work experience in the "boonies"—one of those American words that had amused her so much till she had realized it applied to her *nation*—counted for nothing. When Sachin urged her to accept secretarial posts as "a foot in the door," she said with a (she felt) sexy sigh, "Don't make me become a Ramu-Shamu type, darling, come on." Then she had put her hand on his broad chest, felt the resistance of his bouncy thatch of black chest hair, which she had a habit of smoothing and tugging when they made love. Gita did not come from a rich family in India—her father was a bank manager who owed his job to SP Chopra, Sachin's grandfather—but she had attended the best schools and she expected the best for herself. Hence her marriage to a brilliant man from a great family.

Sachin's voice came out in a reluctant choke of desire. "But, Gita, it's not like that here. Here they have dignity of labor no matter *what* you do." He was a short man with strong convictions.

She knew he was right—he was trying to be helpful—but couldn't he tell she was hurt by the rejections? By how the blond Beatle-haired interviewer at the publishing house had questioned her about her bindi and bangles the entire time and then told her she was most suited for a secretarial role and, when she had said she *was* interested, not even called her back? Was she so obviously beneath them? It was nice to be complimented on her English—the interviewer had asked if she had studied at Oxford!—but not entirely.

How to describe this? But that was the problem—Sachin and she loved each other but could apparently *talk* about nothing.

They were good, she knew, when they were quiet together, when they went out to see foreign films at the Thalia or to meet his Indian college friends, a mutual system of comprehension, a double mind making sense of the sights of this new nation: observing the couples shrieking at each other in the streets of Queens; discussing the way Americans insisted on hearing "warder" when Gita and Sachin said "water"; passing crushed bills to the Indian auntie who sold spices out of her cupboard in lower Manhattan; and snickering kindly at the comic bewilderment of the Indian students who, stranded at JFK, having missed their connections, would look up Indian names in the phone book, call, and ask for a place to stay.

And sometimes, in these moments, Sachin would squeeze her hand and apologize for being so stressed about work. "I'm the only Indian in R and D and I need to show these idiots we're smarter than them."

But alone—facing each other—that was harder.

After the first year in New York, things got worse, because they moved to the small, perpetually overcast town of Midland in Michigan, where Sachin's company was headquartered and where there were zero other Indians. Without a surrounding culture, Gita felt they were nothing but strangers with different schedules, energies, interests—people without enough individual excitement in their lives to generate a culture *for* each other.

When Sachin had suggested they take a trip to India together, she had been thrilled. When he had had to cancel because of work, she had not been surprised.

She went ahead on her own, plunging into her past.

"I'm very happy," she told people when they asked her about the US. "But I'm even happier to be home!"

Gita was twenty-nine. She was a compact woman with a bob haircut; mobile, intelligent eyes; and a long nose that extended out a tiny bit at the tip, like the downward snout of a Concorde. When cornered, she turned that nose even farther down, so that it seemed to point to her modest chest. On this first trip home, she was naturally staying with her parents in déclassé Karol Bagh but went soon after arriving to see her in-laws in the Chopra mothership at A-19 Modern Colony. She had known the complex from childhood but now she was coming as Sachin's wife, and the very proportions of the place felt different as she disembarked from the tilting auto, a gunny bag of gifts—Melmac plates, perfumes, dolls—clutched in one hand. She felt strangely naked when she put her palms to the black wrought-iron gates to enter. The two scabby, sooty, sour brick bungalows of the complex sat one in front of the other, their geometry-protractor-shaped windows teary with age and irritated with swiftly moving, watching human shapes. The black iron gate shrieked within its parabolic groove. A balding servant salaamed from the garden, releasing the fair-skin-colored rubber hose in his hand and sending a snake of blackening water into the soil.

The complex had been built by Sachin's grandfather, the great SP Chopra, right after Partition. But now he was dead. Sachin's father—SP's second son—was dead. Sachin's mother was dead. But the rest of the family was close—unlike the country, it had suffered no partition.

In the small pink-hued drawing room with its surprisingly bare floor, Gita encountered a dozen Chopras gathered around SP Chopra's unmarried eighty-year-old sister, Bimla Behnji.

"Come in, come in," the relatives croaked, getting up, their long, proud faces seeming to have leaked down from the photos of the patriarch displayed above them.

Gita touched the feet of the elders. Then the questions came quickly from all sides. How was Sachin doing? What did one cook there? Had Gita taken up a job, the way she had been an editor in Delhi? No, of course not, they said, why bother when one's husband earns so much? And do you do *all* the cleaning yourself? (When she told them about central vacuums that sucked in dirt and mechanized sinks that gobbled up garbage, they were as amazed as she had been.) And what about kids, when will you give us good news? It was only this last question that rankled Gita because Sachin and she had been trying for a year and nothing had happened. *It'll happen when it'll happen*, Sachin's enragingly calm voice came to her—he was calm about everything except his job.

Having another person's voice in your head: That was marriage.

"Soon," Gita said to Vibha, a forty-something aunt of Sachin's whom she liked. "We'll know when the time is right."

Vibha wore a chunky silver watch on her slim wrist. "No one knows when the time is right, isn't it, Bimla Behnji?" she said, her sharp incisors showing.

Bimla Behnji stirred in her chair. Ever since the death of SP Chopra and his wife, Sheela, Bimla had been elevated to the queen bee "elder" of the complex, presiding over its population of thirty Chopras and half a dozen servants. A tall, thin lady, she sat with her feet outstretched louchely on a bamboo stool, her stout maid hovering behind her. Though she had never married, Bimla wore widow's whites—perhaps she wanted people to think she *was* a widow, to attribute to her a more dramatic tragic past. Her hair was dyed and cut in a girlish curved helmet. She had wide, twitching lips and donned round black spectacles. Perpetually at her side was a glass of milk and a card deck, which she cut to play a game of patience.

She was saying something and Gita had to draw closer to hear her.

Bimla repeated, in her gasping voice, "How much does Sachin earn after taxes?"

It was at a wedding three weeks later, in the complex, that Gita ran into Laxman.

CHAPTER 2

"YOU'VE LEFT YOUR HUSBAND IN AMERICA AND COME alone?" Laxman was asking bluffly.

He had materialized next to Gita under the wedding shamiana once Gita had been separated from her parents and brother.

Gita had returned to the complex to attend the wedding of one of Sachin's younger cousins. Someone or the other was always getting married in the enormous clan. SP Chopra's nine kids had had kids of their own—though, thankfully, no more than two apiece—and those kids needed to be floated out into the world like diyas on a river.

Gita smiled in hello and said, "What to tell you, Laxman, it's expensive to fly—"

"Oye, bache, tell the waiter to bring whiskey for your chachiji," Laxman said to a passing nephew.

The tone of the Punjabi man at a wedding; Gita recognized it. Her whole childhood in Delhi appeared to have consisted of such weddings, including those held in this grand Chopra complex, draped in nets of festive light bulbs, where SP Chopra, then alive, had held court in his safari suits and turban, welcoming each person individually, slapping people on their backs and laughing so hard you felt he might never stop, that he might get stuck in one of his own laughs. Overweight, hobbling a little, his mouth puffed and eyes small and folded shut with merriness, he knew everyone, greeted each person with a kind of mirthful disapproval, and somehow found time to talk even to nobodies like Gita and her parents. "What a smart girl," he had said on one occasion, perhaps when she was only ten. "When she's older, she can marry one of my sons." Then, turning to her father, "They're such duffers, nah, Prakashji, someone needs to improve them." Swiveling back to Gita. "Will you teach them? You came first in your class, no?"

In the end, she had married one of his grandsons instead of a son.

"No, not for me," Gita said with a smile, refusing the drink from Laxman.

"The most shocking thing is you're calling her 'chachiji.'" This was another Chopra daughter-in-law in her twenties, Suman, who had sidled up to them, her eyes tiny with mischief and the spiky gold fringe of her black sari afire under the lights.

"Do I have to call her behnji then?" Laxman asked, his teeth showing from under his mustache. Tall, broad, and agile, with a small mouth, he blinked chaotically. Laxman, at thirty-three, was the youngest of SP Chopra's six sons—not much older than Gita. He left his red tongue between his teeth after the witticism, as if to signal it was a witticism. Gita, who had known Laxman, like she had known Sachin, from childhood, noted his stylish white bandhgala with its twist of a rose in a pocket, the thick mustache that accordioned as he smiled, the trim hair. For the first time since she'd known him as a child, he seemed handsome, presentable. His wife's style and touch, perhaps.

"You don't have to make our glamorous American sister-in-law sound so *old*," Suman said.

"There's no hope for me. My glory days are behind me," Gita said, though she was feeling ebullient in her wedding sari, which she was wearing for the first time since her own wedding on this very lawn.

The three of them now shifted under the shamiana, the dewy remnants of the grass trampled in all directions by hundreds of black boots and elaborate sandals while waiters zipped through the gaps with platters of kebabs, the gaps closing as platoons of guests cornered these waiters to sample their smoking wares, the other wedding-goers huddled in tight circles around aromatic smoldering sigris in the cold night or striding with anticipation toward the buffet, as if staring at the silvery lids of the platters would make them snap open and divulge their oily treats ...

Laxman took a squat, chilled glass of whiskey from his nephew and handed it to Gita.

"But I hardly drink," Gita said, grasping the glass.

"Come on!" Laxman said, his eyes flitting toward other relatives coming through the entrance. "Don't make us drink alone! It's a major wedding, after so many years. A daughter of the family is getting married. And it's a tradition in our house to have whiskey on such occasions. Try it at least!"

"I've tried it before," she said.

"Then give me the glass," Laxman clucked. He took hold of her wrist. Surprised, Gita dropped the glass on the lawn. It bounced off a scaly mound of mud without breaking.

"What did you do?" Laxman asked as the liquid seeped between the puzzle pieces of the thirsty winter-cracked earth.

"I'm so sorry," Gita said, now flustered.

Suman laughed bawdily to mask the awkwardness of the situation, her supari breath perfuming the air.

"Anand!" Laxman shouted at his nephew. "Call the waiter again." Then he turned to Gita. "Oh, I see—you don't drink Indian whiskey, is it? Only foreign?"

It's Johnnie Walker, you idiot, Gita wanted to say, but remained quiet, surprised by her own anger.

"Bring me a cognac also," Suman told black-suited Anand huskily.

"See, your sister-in-law drinks," Laxman said, gesturing with his eyes at Suman. "What—you only drink with your American friends? Chalo. I tried the whiskey you brought for your brother-in-law. The brand was good, but when I drank it, I could tell something wasn't OK." He paused, smirking at Suman. "I know the techniques people use; I also used to live abroad." Gita knew he had been posted in the US for two months of training almost a decade back and now oversaw a piddly women's bobby-pin factory in Shahdara. "Instead of bringing two brand-new bottles of whiskey, people take one bottle of whiskey and pour it into two bottles and then add water. And then they give that as a gift here."

"For that you still have to buy two bottles, don't you," Gita said.

"But your husband's a packaging expert," Laxman said, accurately.

Gita said, "You're talking through your hat. We can try that bottle together and see if that's the case."

There was a tense pause. Then Laxman bared his small, bluish teeth and let out his thunderous laugh. "Suman, what did I say—I could get her to drink!"

And then Suman held out her palm and Laxman slapped it.

Gita eventually broke away from Laxman's grasp and searched for her parents and brother. On this trip, she had noticed something strange about friends and relatives—a simultaneous desperation for what she could bring them from America, as well as resentment. When she had told her friend Anamika that she wanted to permanently return to India, Anamika had said, "Gita, you live there, so you see everything in a romantic way, but I guarantee it, if you move back, you'll run away screaming."

Why, Gita had wondered, *is she treating me like an outsider after a mere* three *years?*

Another friend, Vasundhara, had criticized the materialism of Americans and then asked Gita if she had extra forex. You could skip the waitlists for goods like fridges and scooters in socialist India if you paid in foreign exchange. When Gita had said that, unfortunately, Sachin and she were still struggling, rents were high where they lived, a Democrat was in power, taxes had gone up, Vasundhara had said sourly, "I was just asking out of curiosity."

It wasn't all bad, there were plenty of nice, supportive, proud people too, but of course it was the negative interactions that stood out. At these times, Gita remembered a conversation Sachin and she had had before she had left. "They're complexed," Sachin had explained to her. "The whole country is complexed thanks to Nehru's socialist policies."

Gita, who loved home, had said, "We're a young nation. We're growing."

Now she missed Sachin. They had their problems, but he was the only one who could possibly understand what she was feeling, and he was thousands of miles away, in a heavy, pilled sweater, with long, disordered hair, in a big, warm, lonely house in a town that was barely a town, snow-capped houses sparsely dotted all around, and horse pastures beyond.

CHAPTER 3

GITA'S PARENTS ALWAYS SEEMED TO BE ON THE OPPOSITE end of the lawn thronged with liveried, turbaned waiters and wedding-goers; and as the evening progressed, she ran into Laxman again, this time with his wife, Archana, a short, sleepy-looking, lively woman.

"So, is it true that all the maims are ... very fast?" Archana asked Gita.

"Yes, they walk around naked," Gita joked.

"Then you need to keep Sachin away from them," Laxman said.

"Shut up, yaa, they're not all like you," Archana responded. Then to Gita, "Thank you for the Ray-Bans you brought my husband, Gita. You don't know how happy they made him."

"It'll only be forty dollars," Gita said, turning to Laxman.

Laxman looked surprised.

"Just joking!" Gita said with a burp.

It was time for the feras. People began to congregate near the mandap. The pundit intoned his meaningless Sanskrit verses, throwing up memories, for Gita, of childhood boredom rather than of God. Everyone else kept chatting, oblivious to what was going on under the mandap. The wedding-goers could hardly be blamed.

The astrologer had scheduled the wedding for midnight; and as the ritual progressed, even Sukhdev, one of SP's older sons, playing the role of brother to the bride for the ceremony, dozed off on his stool, a spoonful of oil vibrating dangerously in his hand by the fire.

Cold rushed in between flickers of the fire and Gita tightened her pashmina shawl around herself, protecting her inky Banarasi silk sari from the cinders whizzing like miniature glowing kites. She was short of breath. She could appreciate, from here, what an adventure

America had been: the Big Apple, Michigan, road trips, the time she had flirted (innocently) with a handsome Mexican man in a nighttime marketing class (He had a girlfriend! It was innocent!). She was now standing next to her parents and her tall, bespectacled brother—her brother who had a little daughter who was asleep this very minute at home.

How much Gita had enjoyed seeing three-year-old Anjali on this trip, with her habit of pretending she was the "mother" and putting you, her "baby," to sleep!

Gita and Sachin were both good with kids. They had learned this about each other mere days before their marriage, when they had been in the Chopra complex to arrange some details of their wedding, and Sachin's nephew Mohit had been left briefly with them in the drawing room. Mohit had climbed between them on the sofa and had hidden under Gita's shawl because a "bhooth"—a ghost—"was coming." They had all screamed till an irate uncle of Sachin's had come and dressed them down, which made it even funnier.

How much more pleasant it was to think of your husband—your life!—from a distance!

"What, something's funny?" Laxman asked, suddenly appearing beside her.

"No, just watching and trying to remember the steps," Gita said.

"Auntie," Laxman said, turning to Gita's mother, Shanti. "I've told your daughter that now she's part of our family. And if she's part of this family, she should adhere to our traditions: You agree, right?" He seemed drunker; he wasn't quite making sense.

"Of course," Shanti said with her downward smile, her face wrinkled in embarrassment. In her sixties, her skin was loosening like wax on an overused candle. With her hunched high shoulders and slight build and rust-colored sari, she resembled a shriveled bird.

"But, Auntie," Laxman went on, "your daughter has become very American. She doesn't listen. So please teach her."

"Mummy, he wants me to eat meat and drink whiskey," Gita said, trying to sound flippant. She was vegetarian.

"But, Auntie, you tell me, is there anything wrong with this?" Laxman asked. "It's our tradition. It's good for the bones to eat meat. If she wants to have a child, it'll help with that." He grinned at Gita after saying this, and she hated him for it. "We're not bad Hindus. We're Sangathanis like you," he said, referring to the reformist sect of Hinduism to which the Chopras and many Punjabis in Delhi belonged.

Gita peered off to the side, pretended to wave to an acquaintance, and walked off. She moved quickly, even within the tightly wound tube of her sari. She realized her bladder was full. She strode past the mandap's concentric crowds and toward the house. She opened a screen door and went into Bimla Behnji's now-deserted pinkish drawing room. The room smelled of mothballs. A single tattered *National Geographic* lay on a low table, its edges a froth of paper. She immediately felt calmer. Then she heard a careful clicking behind her.

"I was going to the toilet," she said, seeing that it was Laxman who had come in behind her. His face looked grave, pained even.

"This one downstairs isn't working," he said. "I'll show you the one upstairs."

"No need," Gita said.

"I need to use it also," he said, serious, no longer the clowning performer of the wedding.

Gita knew, as she walked up the grimy old stairs, Laxman following her, that she ought to make an excuse and turn around. But even as her tension mounted, she kept climbing, pinching the fabric of her sari to keep it from dragging on the steps. The crowd came to them only as sudden squeaks of music and an oceanic hush.

She walked up quicker.

Then Laxman, his eyes dull with duty, went past her on the landing and opened one of the white-painted doors in the spartan corridor—everything in the house was simple, bare-bones. Still, it was surprising how empty the building was; it had vomited everyone onto the lawn.

"Use the one in this bedroom," he instructed her, leading her into a room with a single boxy bed and a bedside table with a pile of *Reader's Digests* on it. She noticed two large circles on the front of his bandhgala—sweat or spilled alcohol?

"Thank you, Laxman," Gita said. She went quickly around the boxy bed and to the bathroom door and pulled at the silver handle. But the door didn't budge; it was latched at the top. Then, before she could even lift herself on her toes, Laxman's body was around her and he was reaching up for the latch and pushing his crotch into her behind.

"What are you doing, Laxman?"

He was whispering, his breath blaring with drink, into her ear, "Gita, why did you torture me so much?"

"Laxman"—she giggled; why was she giggling?—"Laxman, just let me use the toilet." She slipped out from under his grip. But then, as she turned, her foot hit the side of the boxy bed and she fell lightly backward on it and Laxman reached down and placed his hands on either side of her, tenting his body above hers.

Voices came from outside the door—including the voice, Gita realized, of her friend Anamika's husband.

What would Anamika, that huge gossip, say if she heard about Gita in such a position?

Laxman was slurring his words over her. "But you never even said one word—you never even gave a reason—"

"Please move," Gita said.

"I liked you first, I sent the first proposal from the family—" he went on. "One word at least you could have said!"

A proposal? But this was madness! But of course, when she had been single, eligible, she had been the object of *many* such proposals. Suddenly her father's face swam into view, with its squarish jaw and chunky glasses. Prakash had worked for years as a teller, and then a manager, in a bank established by SP Chopra, but had always thought SP's son Laxman an idiot. She could picture him turning down the proposal in quiet fury—so what if it was the son of the great SP himself!—respecting his daughter too much to even tell her about it.

It was not a time for fathers.

Laxman was kissing her neck. Then he collapsed on her.

CHAPTER 4

GITA WOULD NOT TALK ABOUT THIS INCIDENT FOR YEARS: How could she? She had let it happen, she told herself. She had known he was following her and had let him come up and then had not resisted. Who was to blame but herself?

At least he had not ejaculated inside her, and he had had the decency to leave her alone when she went to the bathroom to clean her sari.

How she had wept in that bathroom!

What she was weeping for was ... well ... what if she had an infection?

What if she became pregnant—from this fool?

What if everyone found out?

"Remembering your own wedding?" Shanti asked, clutching Gita's arm.

Gita had returned to the spot next to her parents and was gazing at the bride and groom as they crouched before the fire. But as she had walked toward them on the grass, her slipper had pressed down on a fold of her sari and it tore a little. Her wedding sari!

"Yes, what a lovely wedding you gave me, Mummy."

"My sweetie," Shanti said. In a strange way, Shanti had always been competitive with her daughter—putting down her looks and so on—till Gita had gotten married. Then their relationship had changed. *Maybe she knew I would enter the same plane of suffering as her*, Gita thought.

"You took a long time in the loo," her dapper brother, Hari, said. Only a lightness in his manner betrayed his drunkenness.

"Bas, they're almost done," Prakash said. He was staring right through the fire, the orange light dancing and dreaming on the lenses of his boxy spectacles, the knot of an ascot scarf showing through his over-buttoned tweed jacket.

CHAPTER 5

OBLIGATIONS DON'T END JUST BECAUSE SOMETHING BAD has happened to you.

Gita needed to go to the complex at A-19 Modern Colony again—for a post-wedding luncheon and then to say goodbye before she returned to the US. She skipped the former, pleading a stomachache, but could not put off the latter, and so she went over one warm winter day, attired in more layers than were required.

She had been feeling very exposed, as if people could see on her skin evidence of the crime she had committed. Going through her wardrobe, she noticed that she owned very provocative clothes, that the lehenga she had worn to the sangeet had exposed too much stomach, especially notable in the winter.

She timed her visit for when she knew—or hoped—Laxman would be at his bobby-pin factory, and was relieved to not see him in that drawing room full of relatives, where the usual hangers-on asked the usual questions.

The deadness of this room. A family in decline. She saw it now and was shocked. *Is this why Sachin keeps away? What will I say to him?*

Nothing—there is nothing to say. You betrayed the love of your life.

"I heard you had *a lot of fun* at the wedding," a voice said. That was Sachin's older brother, Brij. She had walked to the back building and up a flight of covered stairs to the guest area to say goodbye to Brij and his wife, Karishma, who did not live in Delhi and were visiting to attend the wedding.

"No, no, it was nice to see everyone," Gita said, surprised and afraid.

"So you had fun," Brij said again, with his ironic Cheshire-cat grin, his mustache jumping a little. Brij, at thirty-two, was a distortion of his younger brother. He had the same wide-set eyes and an inverted triangle of a face, but, unlike with Sachin, Brij's eyes were coal black and unblinking, instruments of judgment and slyness, so that you had to look at the minute variations in the cast of his thin lips to know what he was thinking. He grew a bushy goatee but the rest of his fair face was furiously and fussily shaved. He was several inches taller than Sachin and had the wide shoulders of an ex-serviceman, which he was: He had been in the air force for several years before he had resigned and started managing a plantation for a paper mill.

Now he and his wife and two kids lived in the middle of a forest in Madhya Pradesh in a British-style bungalow that (Gita had heard) dropped snakes and scorpions on the mosquito netting above the beds, and had no electricity for weeks at a time.

"Oh ho, don't bother her," Karishma suddenly said. A tall, self-contained woman, she had gotten up from her chair to lift an *Archie* comic that her older son, seven-year-old Mohit, had left on the ground.

Gita noted that Mohit had become rather sullen with age. The impish loving child of four years ago was gone. Or was she projecting her own sadness?

"How am I bothering her?" Brij said, raising his voice. "Did she have fun or didn't she?"

A few moments later, Gita followed Karishma to the guest bedroom so she could give one last toy to Karishma's second child, four-year-old Deepak, who was, in his parents' words, "a holy terror" and had been locked up there to play on his own. "I only today noticed it was still in my suitcase, you know how we wrap things up to avoid customs," Gita explained.

Actually, struck by fear the day after the wedding, Gita had frantically looked in her suitcase to see if there were more American gifts she could bestow on the Chopras—to buy their loyalty, as it were, if Laxman ever told anyone what had happened.

But would he? She saw his admonishing face as in a nightmare. "Look what you made me do. Poor Archana. Gita, please don't tell anyone. It was a moment of passion." He had gotten up and was wiping his neck with a towel that had been lying on a chair. "Men need a release."

"Get out," she had said.

"Just remember—Archana and Shilpa and Vaishnavi," he had said, stepping out so she could weep alone.

America. How eager she was to run away. And how little she understood the cargo of poison she would carry wherever she went.

Pain knows no country.

When Karishma and Gita entered the guest bedroom, Deepak was calmly on his belly, drawing scenes of incredible violence—one man shooting another in the face—on torn-out pieces of lined paper. After giving him the tiny American football she had brought, Gita said to Karishma, "Does Laxman force you also to drink whiskey?"

"I don't consume alcoholic substances," Karishma said opaquely. Karishma had a snub nose, a powdery complexion, gleaming solid teeth, darkly knitted eyebrows, and short wispy hair that dangled in hooks at her temples and that she was constantly tucking behind her ears. She smiled often, but without warmth. She was about Gita's age. "Deepak, baby, look at this," Karishma said. She held up the American football, and when Deepak reached for it, snatched it away. She did this two more times and Deepak finally began crying.

"Oh, baby," Gita said.

"Let him cry," Karishma replied. "That's how he'll learn patience."

This struck Gita as cruel. "But ... he's pushy, no?" she said, returning to the subject of Laxman.

"Meaning?" Karishma asked.

"He bullies people."

Karishma hooked a lock of hair behind her ear and emitted a charming, tinkly laugh. "That's just his style. He's like that with everyone, a big boy."

"But with daughters-in-law, it's not ... right, is it?" Gita asked. At that moment, sitting in the Chopra guest room, Gita realized: *Karishma will never be my ally. I'm a fly from the West that buzzes in and out and who she tolerates as an irritant that arrives laden with gifts.* So it was with many other people in Delhi. Once you were abroad, they wrote you out of the family story. She had tried keeping in touch with Karishma and Brij, mailing them long letters from the US, hoping to make up for Sachin's distant relationship with his only brother, a relationship that had grown only more distant after Brij and Sachin's parents had passed away. But Karishma always sent back the shortest missives. "I apologize in advance for the briefness of this letter," Karishma would write in her surprisingly large, jostling handwriting, "but I have been unfortunately busy with Mohit." She would list the minor illnesses Mohit had suffered: diarrhea, a touch of flu. "However, we are all sending you oodles of our love."

Why this desperation to be liked by people who dislike me? Gita wondered.

But as soon as Gita fell silent, Karishma loosened up. Karishma was like a cat who needed to operate on her own terms. She became brusquely friendly and instructed Gita on how to distract Deepak from his tantrum as he paced the room, squealing. "Don't give him bhav," she told Gita. "He just wants attention. You're so intelligent but when it comes to children you have zero common sense."

"Aha ahaaa, aha ahaaa," Gita sang to Deepak, realizing she was making the same twitchy sounds her awkward father made around kids, his dancing arms outstretched like a scarecrow's.

"When you have your own son, you'll learn," Karishma said. "Me—I didn't even like children." Gita could believe it. "But when you have your own children," Karishma said, "everything changes."

CHAPTER 6

NOTHING CHANGED. SACHIN KNEW NOTHING AND SO nothing changed.

Sachin picked her up at the airport, and on the never-ending drive, proudly described the Indian dishes he had managed to cook for himself in her absence.

Long strands of hair fell across the top slope of his prominent Roman nose, and Gita was surprised anew by how short he was—five feet five, lovably so—and, by comparison, how big his hands looked on the gearshift.

She spied a few razor cuts on his cheek. He was a workaholic who did most other things with impatient haste.

The street in Midland, Michigan, was still flat as a map, sentried on the sides by stripped, diseased Dutch elms with fey branches and, beyond, evergreens showing off their multiple belts and pleats of snow.

When Gita disembarked from the car, two of the neighbors, white and middle-aged—always threatening legal action over trees falling across their property lines—were shoveling snow. They waved and came out to ask her about her trip.

Inside, the heat was turned low—an old habit from the energy crisis.

Sachin nuzzled her neck but she refused to make love to him.

He was hurt.

"No, no, I'm having some women's issue—I need to see the gynie," she lied.

"I hope it's a good sign for having a baby," he said.

A day later, secretly, she got tested for disease. Nothing. Thank God.

That evening, she embraced Sachin on the bed.

Their lovemaking was awkward—she couldn't tell who was to blame—but she was relieved.

For the next few months, she threw herself into the project of getting pregnant with such fury that ... well, at first Sachin was flattered, then disquieted, then worried, so much so that, after a year of basal-temperature taking and appointments with the OB-GYN and tests that (frustratingly) announced them "normal" (since there was nothing to do if you were "normal"), Sachin said to Gita, "Darling, why don't you make a plan to go home this year?"

Among Indians, this—a visit again so soon—was the height of generosity.

How had a whole year passed? Gita wondered. What had she done? Cooked meals every day; shopped frequently at Giant Food, the local supermarket; learned to play euchre with the neighbors, Dana and Martha, who had also invited her to her first pajama party, where the neighborhood women sat around with goblets of purple wine and gossiped about their husbands; driven with Sachin to Niagara Falls and Mackinac Island ... it wasn't a bad life, yet under everything she felt a gnawing emptiness, a wish to prove to the world that she was a good person, a good woman, a good wife, a good daughter, that what happened with Laxman was an aberration—even though, of course, no one knew about it. Or did they?

"It'll be nice to go and meet everyone together," Gita said now, sunlight coolly burning her feet on the blue-red carpet in the fall afternoon, threaded vines—vines stitched together by the fingers of Kashmiri craftsmen—lighting up and then dying away: India flashing in and flashing out.

"That's the only issue," Sachin said. "This is the one year I definitely can't." He talked about his projects at work; the pressure put on him to develop a new type of squeezable plastic ketchup bottle for his company, Trident; the way the EPA was constantly interfering by declaring certain plastics carcinogenic so that they had to start all over again.

"Then let's go next year," Gita said.

"I just think ..." Sachin said, "last time ... it made you so happy. And the winter here—"

Happy? Did he know her at all? That same sense of total disconnection, the feeling she had carried on her previous trip, came back to her. "Do you *want* me to go?"

"Arre, why are you taking it the wrong way? Not at all. I'm just worried."

Gita suddenly saw herself as he saw her: a housewife, depressed over the lack of kids, unable to commit to a new career because the kids might come at any minute.

She had turned the encounter with Laxman over and over in her mind thousands of times. What *had* happened? Why did she freeze? Why this inability to fend for herself?

Strangely, she didn't feel that she had betrayed Laxman's wife. She just prayed for Archana, that Archana didn't have to sleep with him.

But the odd thing was that Laxman had the unique reputation in the Chopra clan of being a *pretty decent husband*. The standards were low, of course, in a family of shouters and abusers, but it was said that he rarely raised his voice at Archana or the children and was a doting father.

It was one reason Gita had felt forgiving toward him when he had first come up to her on the lawn during the wedding. *He bullied me as a child*, she had thought, *but he's grown and I'm grown and I'm married to his nephew, and we're all friends.*

Nonsense! No one was friends in any family. It was just another network of power masquerading as a nest of love.

No one in this life loved anyone, she was coming to believe. *It was power all the way down.*

What about you and Sachin?

Sachin had noticed a change in his wife since the day she'd returned to the US. *It's jet lag,* he had thought. *It's loneliness. She needs a job.* Then a visiting relative had mercilessly interrogated her—and Sachin—about their childlessness, and he had watched his wife's mouth tighten.

Is that why she doesn't want to go home?

Is that why I *don't want to go home?*

When Sachin was young, in the crowd of the family, there was a cruel tradition named "jalus" that was in vogue with the Chopras. In this game, a gang of cousins would chase down the youngest one in the vicinity—usually Sachin, already derided for being short—and strip off his pants and underwear, screaming, "We're taking Sachin's jalus," or "taking him on a public procession." How many times had Sachin's pathetic penis been exposed as uncles and aunts—and even his grandfather—sat around cackling in the courtyard? And what about the time on his fourteenth birthday when his cousins had given him "birthday bumps" in a slick of keechad, lifting him by the arms and legs like a human bridge and kicking his butt between every bump, so that he had been unable to shit for a day and had feared that he had fractured his behind?

He hated his violent relatives—Laxman and his brother included—but, strangely, he also felt some affection for them. Hadn't he, after all, done this to his younger cousins in turn?

CHAPTER 7

"DON'T WAIT, COME NOW," GITA'S BROTHER WAS SAYING on the phone. Phone calls were rare, reserved for emergencies or celebrations, and this was an emergency: Her seventy-three-year-old father had had a stroke.

Two years had passed since Gita had declined Sachin's offer to send her to India. She had been working as a secretary for a stonecutting warehouse, and Sachin and she had continued trying for a child. The topic of adoption had been broached. "To adopt here, one of us will need to become a citizen," Sachin had pointed out. "I don't know if I should—there's the land in India."

Would she have to become a citizen of a country she didn't love?

All these considerations were put on hold after her brother's call. She quit her job and booked a ticket to India.

This time, when she landed, on a dry, warm mid-March night, she felt like a stranger. Not because she wasn't Indian—no, no, she was Indian down to her organs—but because, with a sadness, she could see India for what it was: shabby, poor, slow. The men were small and malnourished, badly shaved, scarred. The women were lumpy. The stink of urine rose in one's nose as one stood in the endless line at customs and waited to have one's suitcase prodded.

"Madam, who is this garment for?" a customs agent asked. Gita hadn't taken Sachin's advice of crushing the new (gift) clothes to make them look old. She paid the outrageous duty and went out of the terminal and into the arms of her waiting mother, brother—and father!

"Oh, Daddy, why did you come?"

"I've started feeling better!" he said hoarsely.

In fact, as her brother, Hari, explained in the car, he had shed all his post-stroke symptoms in the last few days.

"Your coming must have done it," Shanti said, squeezing Gita's hand as Delhi honked into polluted life all around them.

They all looked older—her mother and father did. Death traveled equally in all directions. But three years of aging in the US were six years of aging here. Her father appeared thin and brittle in his natty leather-elbowed jacket; her mother kept rubbing one eye under her scratched eyeglasses.

"We pray that this year you have a baby," Shanti said in the car.

"It's good that you're visiting now," her father said, as if he were going to add, *We'll help you now*. Instead, he said, "All the Asian Games madness is over, and we can enjoy Holi together." Then he began to fill her in on all the Indian news events in the past year—that had always been their relationship.

A few days later, when it was time to visit the in-laws, Gita brought her mother along. But if she had thought that having her mother with her would reduce the Chopra family's inquisitiveness about her infertility, she was wrong. In Bimla Behnji's pink drawing room, Bimla silently playing patience, the ten gathered relatives were full of advice.

"Auntie, Gita should see an ayurved," goaty Leela Bua said to Shanti, her bloodshot hazel eyes fully open.

"Yes, why not," Shanti said, her hands folded on her lap, not looking at Gita, who was seated next to her. Shanti always made herself small in the presence of these gigantic Chopra personalities.

Vibha cut in. "Gita, you've tried allopathy—what's the harm in trying this? Laxman is friendly with a famous pahalwan."

"You've never heard of pahalwans?" Leela asked. "They're like vaids. They're bone specialists, but they also deal with other issues. No, no, they're not wrestlers—they're called pahalwans because they used to be specialists for wrestlers in akharas. This pahalwan makes his own balms that are more effective than any medicine you can buy from a chemist. Yes, Laxman can take you."

Gita, sitting on the L-shaped sofa, was horrified to hear Laxman's name in such a context.

More advice poured out. Drink amla sherbet. No, the milk of crushed almonds. Eat ragi. Wash yourself with besan every day.

Visit the Chamundi Shrine in Mysore—that had worked for a family friend. And finally, inject medicated ghee—though Vibha, who was usually direct, wouldn't say where or how to inject it. "Don't take this personally," Vibha said, seeing Gita's eyes filling, "but you must try these things; they're in our heritage; they're made for our bodies. What do you say, Laxman?" she asked as Laxman walked in.

And just like that, Laxman was back in her life.

CHAPTER 8

"NAMASTE, AUNTIE," LAXMAN SAID, BOWING AND touching Shanti's feet, his voice throaty and enthusiastic. Unlike everyone else, Laxman looked trimmer and even younger than before, sweaty in a striped short-sleeve white shirt, khaki pants, and brown sandals.

"Aur, how's Sachin, Gita?" Laxman asked, as if nothing had happened between them.

Had it? It was so many years before! Why was she holding on to it?

She decided she would not be bothered by his presence, even as she stiffened. "Fine," she said.

"You're not going to bring him?" Laxman asked.

An image came to Gita of that cold, secluded top-floor room, held aloft on a tempest of shrill steel music.

"Where does he get a holiday," Gita said in Hindi. The longer she was gone from India, the more she resorted to colloquial Hindi, like someone scrubbing herself desperately with the soil of her country.

Each visit back was harder, as if the soul could reenact the primal loss only so many times before shattering. It would have been better to lose something for good than to lose it every few years.

"But we hear he's doing so well, they *should* give him some kind of holiday, right?" Laxman said.

"Making bottles and all," Vibha said, approvingly.

"Designing them," Gita corrected her. She now delivered what would become a familiar spiel about her husband's work: how, previously, ketchup had come in heavy and expensive and breakable glass bottles; how Sachin and his team had found a way to blow a stable plastic ketchup bottle using a new heat-setting technique; how they'd had to use six layers of plastic to keep oxygen from invading the bottle and drying out the ketchup; how the patent had been successfully registered; but how he had received only a token dollar from the company for his efforts.

Was this her job—to be an emissary for her husband? What about those years in publishing? That was all behind her, drowned in the chasm between America and India.

"He should have come to India for research," Laxman said. "Our ancestors used this design."

"Where did they do this, Laxman?" Gita said with a sigh. And why was Laxman away from work in the middle of the day? Had he heard she was visiting?

"Our gharas. And if you take a look at the bottles the Rajputs used in the seventeenth century—"

"Were they made of plastic, Laxman?" Gita asked with a smirk that could have been charitably interpreted, by an observer, as playful.

"Yes, what kind of comments are you making?" Vibha said to her brother with furious affection.

Laxman got up and stood over Bimla Behnji, his hands on the wood frame of her chair. "Have you had your glass of hot milk, Behnji? No? Where's Lata?" Bimla's maid.

Bimla Behnji, in her eighties, muttered something back.

"Let me call her," Laxman said, and went off to get Lata.

Gita became depressed in this nest of women. Her sadness grew when Laxman's wife, Archana, entered the fray, leading her and Laxman's younger daughter, Shilpa, now seven, by the pinky. "Howdy-doody, Chachi," Shilpa said in a fake American accent, grinning—Laxman's electric mischievous smile. Shilpa was adorable in her tucked-in man's striped shirt, and Gita kissed her on both cheeks and said that if she sat next to her for a while, she would have a special gift for her.

"No need," Archana said.

Tejaswini came in next. This was Sachin's twenty-five-year-old cousin—the one whose wedding Gita had attended, where Laxman had cornered her.

Tejaswini's one-year-old daughter—her second child!—was slung over one of her hunched shoulders. The baby was drooling amiably, with a large, inky birthmark on her forehead. Gita came forward to give the baby a kiss, swooning, but also feeling her own lack, or perceiving herself as lacking through the eyes of the eight other Chopras in the drawing room.

It was hot in the drawing room. The electricity went off. No one seemed to notice. Life went on in the darkness.

This was when an aunt said that Brij and Karishma were returning to Delhi for Brij's posting at the Delhi office of Bijapur Paper Mills, and that, to save money, they would stay at A-19.

"Oh, they didn't tell us," Gita said.

"Brij said he writes letters to Sachin but you don't reply," Archana said.

"That's nonsense," Gita countered. "If anything, I'm always sending *them* letters."

"Chalo, be that as it may," Archana said. "I'm just relating his view."

"And where will they stay?" Gita asked, looking around at the aunts. "I thought the Chopra complex has no vacancies." She smiled to indicate the joke.

"They'll stay with us!" Archana said. "Arre, don't look so shocked, yaar. We all live like this. They're family—isn't it, Vibha Didi? We'll adjust. Laxman has even told Brij that we'll get him a job if he wants to leave Bijapur Paper—he's being treated quite unfairly, poor fellow. His supervisor is a Muslim and has some communal feeling against him."

"I see," Gita said.

"We were telling Gita about Mohan Pahalwanji," Vibha said to Laxman when he returned from calling the maid.

"Well, if you want to discuss your issues, it's better if both husband and wife are present," Laxman said, breathing heavily and sitting down in the pinkish room with its single florid Tanjore painting on the wall.

No taste in this house, Gita thought, strangely out of breath herself. *No sense of style. A village family in a big city.*

Then Laxman said, "But still it might be worthwhile to go—why not? I'm going tomorrow to see Pahalwanji—he's in Kirti Nagar."

"I'm not free tomorrow," Gita said, adding quickly, "I have to meet an old school friend." A lie.

"The problem is that Pahalwanji's leaving for the Kumbh after that," Laxman said.

"You should go, Gita beti," Gita's mother said, finally piping up. "There's no issue, Laxman—she can meet her friend another day. I've also heard great things about Mohanji."

"You've probably listened to his pravachans," Laxman said to Shanti. "Not all pahalwans are like that, but he's a man of religion."

"For years I played them every morning," Shanti said.

"Well, he's stopped doing that now," Laxman said, "to focus only on medicine. He can help more people that way."

Gita felt trapped. "OK, we'll let you know—but I feel bad telling my friend Anamika I can't come."

"Oh ho, what's more important, this Anamika or your child?" Vibha said.

There was silence, broken only by the baby's playful burbling. Gita smiled. But she was burning up. How had her sex life—her sex problems—become public knowledge?

In one sense, it was sweet that everyone was collaborating on her problems, that they cared enough about her as a daughter-in-law to help—but no, Gita knew: No one cared. It was all ego and contempt. Their advice was an overflow of ego, and she was the pool into which their certainties crashed.

CHAPTER 9

THAT NIGHT, AT HER PARENTS' HOME, SHE DEVELOPED A migraine. "Please Mummy, call A-19 and tell them I can't go to this pahalwan or vaid or whatever he's called, I'm not well."

"Oh, my poor little girl," her mother said, bringing Gita a wet towel to press on her head. Shanti was no stranger to intractable, untraceable bodily problems: Once a week, usually on a weekend—the period of maximum work for a woman—her entire body would feel scorched and aflame, as if an evil in-law had poured kerosene on her for not giving enough dowry. Not far from the truth of what had happened to Shanti as a young bride under her late mother-in-law's thumb, Gita thought.

"We'll call him tomorrow—you can call him," Shanti said, "they're your in-laws."

"Mummy, but they're all so pushy!" Gita burst out. Then: "All they want to do is offer advice. None of them actually want to help."

"Shh, my sweet daughter, you're just tired from travel—sleep and tomorrow you'll feel better."

"But I have such a bad headache!"

But the next day, before she could make a call to A-19, Laxman surprised her—and everyone else—by strolling into the Karol Bagh house when the family was at breakfast. Laxman was dressed in smart black pants and a crisp white shirt that made him look like a mid-level babu. "Namaste, namaste," he said, hurriedly glad-handing everyone at the table; asking Gita's brother, Hari, about the insurance business; making charming remarks to Hari's wife about her (disheveled) clothes; even quizzing Anjali, Hari's older daughter, about why she was home from school today, was she unwell? "Sorry I came so early," he said to Gita with unusual courtesy, standing across from where she sat at the dining table. "But I heard Mohan Pahalwanji is free for a consultation in one hour, and I thought I should come now." He turned to her father, Prakash, who was also eating breakfast. "Mohanji is going to the Kumbh tomorrow," he said. Prakash was bashing the top of his boiled egg in a katori with a spoon, but upon hearing the word *Kumbh*, launched into a foggy historical lecture on the reason the religious festival existed, how there were several iterations of the Kumbh, and the way the British had initially tried to clamp down on it. Laxman, obviously hearing nothing of this, turned to Shanti, who was framed in the door to the kitchen. "What a learned man your husband is, Auntie. A gem. That's why your daughter also is a woman of learning," he said, his eyes darting down to Gita's face.

"Don't we have to see the shawl-wallah?" Gita said to her mother, inventing an errand that she hoped Shanti would collude on. But Shanti was now walking barefoot toward the kitchen.

According to Laxman, we need to rush, Gita thought, but now Mother's going to bring out cut-up pears, apples, chikoos, dahi with sugar, whatnot.

When a visitor arrived, Shanti frantically turned herself into the perfect hostess.

At least I'm home, Gita told herself.

It was as if America didn't exist.

No America—no husband—no troubles. If she hadn't gone to America, would any of this have happened? She'd heard it said, more than once, that some of her fertility problems may have come down to the change of diet and air when she immigrated to the US. "People eat a lot of meat there," a sympathetic but slightly scattered female Indian doctor had told her during her first few days in Delhi. This doctor was an acquaintance from Amritsar, with a hunch and a habit of twitching her left shoulder and throwing her dupatta over her back even if it wasn't trailing. "Even the animals there are fed all sorts of chemicals," she said.

"But Doctorji, I'm a vegetarian," Gita had responded.

"But you eat eggs?" the doctor asked.

"Yes. And milk."

"There."

It could be that; it could be anything.

Meanwhile, her flaxen-haired, perpetually winded gynecologist in the US, Dr. Tomlin, had his own theories. Perplexed after years of treating her, he had suggested she be examined by an epidemiologist, since he had heard that genital tuberculosis was "a leading cause of infertility in India"—he had put it like that, as if quoting from a paper.

That's a poor person's disease, Gita had wanted to shout, but she had seen the epidemiologist anyway and submitted to his tests. When the results came back negative, Dr. Tomlin sighed, fiddling with his stethoscope, and said, "The trouble is, women face a far greater range of environmental stresses in a third-world country like India, don't they? An Indian doctor friend—do you know Dr. Vara?—told me that farmers there still spray their fields down with DDT." Theory after theory. No answers. How many more times would she have to sit on a hospital bed, her legs in stirrups and thighs apart as he inserted a cold speculum inside her and cranked it open—as he stuck two fingers within her and palpated her breasts while speaking to her about pesticides in India? During her first visits, a nurse had accompanied him, and he had offered detailed warnings before every invasive step, but now he proceeded as if she were a piece of familiar machinery on which certain switches had to be thrown. And as he failed to cure her, he also seemed to lose interest in her as a person, focusing on her instead as an abstract everywoman from India, destroyed by India rather than ... Laxman.

Was Laxman to blame? But that was a convenient excuse. The problems had preceded him. He had probably come after her because she was a barren bitch. Barren bitch!

Gita, trying to distract herself from Laxman's presence in her house, thought: *Never leave home. Your system goes haywire. You either can't produce—or you produce too much.*

"Beta, I won't be able to come," her mother said, returning from the kitchen. "Anila is visiting in an hour." A cousin from Amritsar. "But you go."

When Gita protested again that she had a headache, Shanti said, "Then it's even better that you see Pahalwanji."

How could her mother be so clueless? *Was* it cluelessness? Was it possible that, under her innocence, Shanti wanted Gita to suffer as much as *she* had as a young bride?

CHAPTER 10

GITA STEELED HERSELF AS SHE GOT IN THE CAR BESIDE Laxman.

"I thought you were going to sit in the back seat like a maharani," Laxman said.

"Hmmm," she said, smiling despite herself—and hating herself for it. A vein in her neck twitched.

He started the smog-blue Fiat, with its reluctant choking sound, the front windows open—no A/Cs in cars here, or in homes. Had she become a first-world snob?

Driving, he asked her about the US, his eyes hidden behind the dark aviators—the same aviators, she realized with a shock, she had gifted him years before.

"America's fine," she said, sitting defensively, her arms folded as she looked away.

He told her he was considering going into business with an Indian in Detroit named Malhotra—did they know him?

She shook her head. "We don't know every Indian in America."

They had pulled onto the colony's main road when she suddenly spoke up, "Stop the car right now."

"Huh, why?" he said, with a small smile on his face.

"I said stop the car. Stop the car or I'll scream bloody murder," she said. Her voice was hoarse and low.

"OK, OK, relax," he said, putting his hand on her knee. She flung it away with force. It struck the ribbed black steering wheel and ricocheted off. But even the slight touch of his hand, the feel of the hair on the back of that hand, the rings on his fingers, which bounced off the steering wheel with lifeless plunks, disgusted her.

He pulled into a narrow street off the main road—the backside of a large gurdwara. "Why are you acting this way with me?" he asked. His voice, astonishingly, was full of hurt.

Gita had practiced this moment in her head so many times. But what came out was: "Haramazade, kameene, you think, you think—" That old stutter, the old habit of tears rising in a crisis.

"But what have I done?" Laxman asked.

He had stopped the car in the middle of the road; no other car would have been able to muscle past.

"Do you have no shame? No concern for your own nephew? What you did was wrong. Forget it, let me out. I'll walk home." She twisted the beaky silver handle of the Fiat door—how flimsy and lousy everything in this country was! Yet the handle made a satisfying click as it pressed down, inciting the invisible machinery of gears and pulleys hidden in the door with its maroon padding. But when she opened the door a crack, he leaned across her and pulled the door back. "Gita, don't do this. What happened between us was a mistake, it's in the past—"

Gita shouted, "I'll tell everyone! I'll disgrace you."

He sputtered, "As if *you* didn't want it!"

And then he was making a shooshing sound and his arms were around her and even as she heaved and wriggled he was nuzzling her neck and saying, "Be calm, be calm, it was nothing," his hands now between her thighs. "I knew you would come back to me, I knew it when I saw you yesterday—"

She shrieked. He backed away, looking tired.

She opened the door and got out. As she turned instinctively toward the car, he leaned toward her open window and said, "Try to tell people, see who's believed."

"Everyone knows what you're like," she said. How was it possible that she was having this conversation in daylight, in the morning—where were the crowds? The hawkers? The hijras? The lost-looking postmen prowling the streets? The loiterers? She had never known one could be this alone in India.

As she walked away from the car, she began to feel an icy panic on her back—as if a frozen pane of glass had been shattered on it. She quickly looked over her shoulder.

The Fiat sat silent, as if the car itself were watching her, plumply malevolent.

Full of doubt, self-hatred, confusion, guilt, she turned suddenly into the white gate of the gurdwara, passing under the hot frosting of golden paint on its ornamented metal arch of twisted vines that seemed taken from a Greek building. The floor beneath her was white-tiled like a bathroom; she quickly took her sandals off and gave them to the attendant, who returned a small scratched plastic token to her. Dizzy in the sun, she moved fast on the egg-colored tiles to keep her feet from burning. She wrapped her sheer dupatta over her head as she went up the stairs into the cool, empty hall of the gurdwara, with its many green rectangular carpets laid parallel and over each other around the central golden dais on which sat the holy book.

She put her forehead on the carpet before the shrine, genuflecting to a god she didn't believe in. She lay prostrated a long time and lost awareness of where she was and was conscious of spiraling through time and space. The only way to stay steady during the fall was to close her eyes. When she made the mistake of opening them, she saw, above her, on the wall, a bat-shaped mark of seepage turning into two eyebrows and then into the hull of a ship. The shape kept somersaulting into newness. It could be anything and everything. She closed her eyes and fell again into a difficult, desperate peace. She was pleading and making quick promises. How had she gotten *here?*

Was it greed—was she being punished for the sin of coveting a great man's lineage: by being sent to this thug instead? She had always wanted to marry into SP Chopra's family: Why? Just because SP had flattered her that one time when she was ten, saying that she was smart and should be a doctor? Or was it her willfulness and frivolousness in the first year of her marriage—postponing kids, applying subtle (and not-so-subtle) pressure on Sachin to move back—was it this that she must atone for? *But I didn't know*, trickled out the thought. *I'm so sorry, I was lost and confused, this was a way of holding on to myself, of not melting into a new continent, I thought refusal* was *my essence.*

The dizziness was receding; the vision was fading.

Across the hall, she gazed at a framed portrait of bearlike, serene Guru Nanak, the glass speckled with reflected white light in one corner—but could focus only on his white beard.

She became conscious of other couples circling the shrine and looking askance at her. *Can they tell I'm mad?* she thought, and with all her power got up only to see, standing behind her: Laxman.

He grinned, his aviators hooked over his top shirt buttons, and she walked right past him and down to the shoe bunker, where she was able, miraculously, to pass the green carrom-striker-like token to the wiry Sikh manning the crevice with its hot scent of ancient leather—and to get her sandals in return.

She was profoundly conscious of the physical world, could see the milky marks left by her toes on the black insoles of her sandals. Had she seen Laxman—or not?

For the next hour, in the furious sun, she walked around the colony, watching the turnover of identical white concrete-box houses, houses built side by side with no style or shape, but comforting nevertheless in their relative sameness, the Punjabi names written in flat black paint on gray frosted glass inserted into the rectangular pillars of the front gates.

When she got back to her parents' house, it was eleven-thirty—plausibly enough time to go see Mohanji and come back.

"Laxman didn't want to have lunch?" Shanti asked, blinking hard behind her spectacles. Her eyes were often irritated in the summers, no one knew why.

"No—he had work." Gita sat down on one of the round-backed horseshoe-shaped upholstered chairs in the drawing room, bowing her head.

"Is it hot outside? Can I bring my bitiya some lassi?"

She nodded gratefully, and Shanti returned a few minutes later with a namkeen-and-sweet lassi. Gita sipped it slowly while looking at the golden tassels of the Pichwai painting on the wall, a neighbor's dog barking obscurely in the background.

"The pahalwan didn't say anything," she told Shanti. "He said nothing is wrong."

CHAPTER 11

GITA COULD TALK TO NO ONE. THE FIRST TIME MIGHT HAVE been his fault—but the second time? No one would believe it.

Her friends were all married and lost within their lives, busy with kids, both pitying her and scolding her for not moving to this stage. Worse, she had learned from their example. When Vasundhara had complained about a relative of her husband who was "bothering" her, her husband had slapped Vasundhara and sent her packing to her parents'.

As for her own parents, she did not want more of their burdensome, unhelpful love and sympathy, did not want to rub imported Nivea cream all over her mother's body when she burned up in sympathy for her daughter.

Then, a few days later, to her own surprise, she found herself speaking to Laxman's older sister, Vibha.

Why the worst instincts about whom to speak to?

She was visiting Vibha as a matter of course—doing the requisite round of relatives. When Gita entered the DDA flat, Vibha, who was in her late forties, was sitting in the stony gray depression that formed the small drawing room area. Vibha was surrounded by tiny papier-mâché bowls filled with namkeen and placed on a low glass-topped coffee table with vaguely Rajasthani or Gujarati ornamental columns between the upper and lower compartments.

Vibha had just bathed; her hair was wet. The fan was on, but not the cooler.

Gita sat down and said, mostly to fill the space, "Vibha Bua, we're thinking of moving back to India. But I wanted your advice." In fact, Gita and Sachin had had no such conversation.

"What advice can I give?" Vibha said.

"As an elder—" Gita began.

"But what would Sachin do here?" Vibha asked. "He's brilliant, a gold medalist from Pilani, let him stay there. Are you the one who wants to come back?"

"I miss my parents, Vibha Bua. I miss our culture."

"You can't get Indian things there?" Vibha asked. "My impression was that Indians there are even more Indian."

"There are no Indians where we live. And, anyway, those who are there are stuck in the past. And we'll also become like that if we stay." Gita fiddled inside a bowl of namkeen for a bite—fried, light yellow, salty bits shaped randomly like the samagri one threw into a havan fire.

Vibha said, "You have to ask yourself where both of you will be happy. Sachin, you know, is very impatient." She brushed her wet strands back. "And here, to succeed, you need patience." Then she said, "Why not come for a year and try it? That way, you'll know."

Gita lied, "That's what we're thinking."

"He's doing so well," Vibha said. "I'm sure his company will give him leave. Maybe he can even set up a tomato sauce plant here. Did you bring it for me?"

"Oh, Buaji, I forgot," Gita said. She had promised, in a letter, to bring her a ketchup bottle prototype.

Vibha shook her head lovingly and stuck out her jaw in a mannish way. "Next time don't forget!" She was a proud custodian of the family's achievements. The walls of the small flat were covered with pictures of SP standing outside newly opened bank branches and of Vibha and her siblings greeting Nehru, Patel, Rajendra Prasad, and Zakir Husain at family weddings. The pictures were a way of projecting beyond the shabbiness of the present. None of the frames were even slightly crooked. It seemed the photos were dusted daily. These were her icons; her father was her god.

The image of Guru Nanak, then SP, and then Laxman, flashed through Gita's mind—a succession, a decline.

"There's another issue I wanted to talk to you about," Gita said suddenly.

"Did Mohan Pahalwanji help?" Vibha asked. "And I hope Laxman didn't force you to take the medicine? He's well-meaning, but men don't understand much."

"Well, it was about that, Vibha Bua," Gita began, haltingly, but even as she spoke, she thought: *This is madness. She is his sister*. "I know Laxman is a loving brother—"

"Did he say something to you? It's his style. He talks a lot. But no one is more well-meaning in this family. Whenever a riot happens anywhere, Laxman is the first to go to see if Hindus are all right."

"No, that's not what I was going to say." Why was it so hard? "But, sometimes, the way he acts with women ... it's not right."

"You mean the Tejaswini thing?" Vibha asked.

What Tejaswini thing?

Before Gita could go on, Vibha said, "People talk too much in this family. He's been nothing but helpful to them."

Gita bowed her head slightly. It was now or never. "He—Laxman tried to kiss me."

Vibha stiffened. Then she started to laugh. "Arre, a kiss? It's 1983! He's just being playful! There's a long tradition in our family. When people come newly, they're always surprised by how rough we are. And isn't the devar always a little playful?"

"But he's my uncle," Gita said. Though they were nearly the same age.

"But basically a devar, no," Vibha said.

"Vibha Bua, he tried to kiss me, he tried—it's very serious."

"I see. Chinku!" she shouted for the servant. "Bring more chai!"

Now the dam broke; Gita found herself speaking again. "I come alone—and—I'm—helpless. And one trusts—one doesn't think—"

Vibha said, "I'm sorry it happened like this. But it's my fault." She shook her head.

"No, how is it yours—these things happen, men are men, but I wanted the guidance of an elder—I don't want to involve Sachin—" Gita said.

Vibha got up. "But it was my stupid idea. You see, Laxman and I had discussed that—if you didn't get pregnant, if there was an issue that even Mohanji couldn't solve, then it would be a good idea for you to try with another man in the family." She said this as if it were perfectly natural, and yet she must have known it was not, because she rushed over it, her eyes fixed on the namkeen bowls as she brought a few bits to her wet open mouth. "I was discussing it with Laxman—and he never suggested it himself, by the way, the idea didn't occur to him or me, in fact the first person who ever suggested it in the family was Brahmpalji"—Sachin's late father—"when another relative was having trouble conceiving. Anyway, I thought about asking Brij, but then we realized ... maybe it's too close if it's the brother. Sachin, we knew, wouldn't agree—"

Gita was too shocked even to be properly angry. Sometimes, when you encounter a bad idea, you can trace its source. But she was so foreign now that even the source—the twisted ideology that lay behind it—was beyond her. *Have I become an American?*

Vibha explained that, by elimination, they had come to Laxman.

As if anticipating Gita's thoughts, Vibha said, "No, of course, we didn't tell Archana. It was the sort of thing one would do completely in private. Of course, Sachin would know." Vibha slapped her forehead, bowing her head in the silence created by the half-bowed servant's entry and exit with his clattering teacups painted with dried rivulets of tea down their sides. "But that idiot, my brother, he can't control himself—"

This is separate! Gita wanted to scream. *He's always been like this!* But her nerve failed her. Who was worse—the idiot brother or the accepting, complicit sister?

Is this how they see me? Gita wondered. *As a baby-making machine? A hitch in their massive scheme of familial expansion?* For the first and only time she felt powerful in her infertility, her body's refusal to do society's bidding. "Vibha Bua, but what should I do?" At the same time, meaningless habitual tears brimmed in her eyes.

"Bas, bas, beta, it's OK, we all go through these things," Vibha said, her eyes darting around anxiously. "I understand why this must be a shock, I meant to tell you about this—but, you know, he's an idiot, that's why Papaji called him Bondu, but he's well-meaning, when I suggested this idea, he meditated on it for a day and only then agreed, it's a sacrifice for him too, it would be his child and it would never know—"

Does this person understand sex? Gita wondered. *Do they disrespect Sachin so much?*

"But the problem is with me, Buaji!" Gita said.

"How do you know that?" Vibha asked. "You yourself said the doctors found nothing wrong."

"But there was no issue with Sachin either," Gita said. "His sperm mortality"—what words were coming out of her mouth! She had meant *motility*!—"his sperm mortality is good."

"Look, Gita," Vibha said, "we only want the best for you. We wouldn't make you do anything you didn't want to. Laxman's being foolish, he doesn't know how to behave with women. I'm angry at him," she said unconvincingly, munching more namkeen. "But please, think about Archana and the kids—"

When she's nervous, she eats, Gita thought.

"And just know, we all will do whatever we can in our powers to help you."

CHAPTER 12

ON THE PLANE BACK TO THE US, GITA FELT INERT. WHEN A baby cried in the crib at the front of the cabin, beneath the projected movie, she didn't offer to help the mother by carrying and shooshing it, as she usually did.

When she had said goodbye to her family at Delhi Airport, that large, airless shed with its many cracked tinted windows, gummy-wheeled carts, and floors still bleeding with a mixture of lemon cleaner and pure mud, she hadn't cried either. She felt she was bidding her parents and brother goodbye one final time; she wanted her eyes to be dry so she could have a real look at them and store their visages in the deep freeze of her brain, to be taken out and examined in the vacuum of life in Midland—a life she needed to embrace as her own.

On the drive home from the airport, she told Sachin, "I don't want to try anymore."

"Did someone say something to you in India?"

"I think we were meant to be without children."

He looked into the distance, into the shivering trees and overhead green metal traffic signs blasted by wind. He said, "If you want me to take citizenship, I can do it."

Then, a month after Gita's return, Sachin said, in reference to a question Gita had asked, "Not that weekend in May, that's the weekend Laxman and Archana are coming."

Gita thought she had misheard. "Anshuman? From New York?"

"No. No. From Delhi. Laxman. He has a business opportunity? He said he'd told you."

In shock, she said nothing.

The monster. I only went to his sister, his promoter—and he, the bastard—he went straight to my husband.

Since returning, she had been fuming. She had finally told Sachin about Vibha's idea—not mentioning Laxman—and he had … laughed! "They're just like that, they're all complexed, leave them behind, this is why I don't want to move back," he'd said, and they'd had a big fight, with Gita responding, "You always promised we'd go back," and him saying, "You're the one who can't handle it, who comes back with a scowl every time," and her shouting, "It's because I'm coming back to you …"

It didn't matter that she'd vowed not to return herself. This talk of "going back" was really a talk of something else—of restoring an Edenic past.

When they'd finally made up, Sachin had said, "I'll speak to Vibha Bua," and she'd mumbled, "No need," and the topic had been put aside.

Why was he so defensive about his family? Gita wondered. Was it just because, after his father had suddenly died, Laxman and Vibha had helped gather funds for his master's in the US?

Now Sachin noted her reaction, furrowed his eyebrows, and went on, "They're going to want the whole works. Apparently, Laxman has business in Detroit or something. Where he found a partner, God only knows—"

Gita said, "He never told me they were coming," though she now recalled a mention of an Indian in Detroit.

"Anyway, what's done is done. Then a few weeks later we have Suresh Mama arriving, so this way the whole summer will pass—"

Sachin paused.

"You know, I don't love him either," Sachin conceded. "But I don't have a choice."

On a weekday, Gita drove to the lapidary lake around which she often took walks—one of the hundreds of smaller unsung lakes in lakey Michigan.

At the edge of the placid, taut, wobbly acre of water, with its evidence of beaver infrastructure projects, she stood barefoot on harsh pebbles, looking in and through the water to the rocks, their green astroturfing of algae, the zebra mussels that had once pricked her cold feet.

She had been born in another country. What would it mean to die here?

This was the fear that united all their immigrant friends.

Sachin's Pilani classmates were always talking about returning to India, though they had never made a move in that direction. Their lives were good in the US. But they were afraid to die here.

Everyone had an intuition that, during one's waning days, the mind would helplessly plummet homeward.

Her mind had always been turned to the past—to India.

"People don't realize," her friend Anamika had told her in India, in the early days of Gita's infertility, when Gita's friends thought they needed to convince their willful friend to join them in motherhood, "but the reason we all need to have children is so that we stop obsessing about the past, about our parents. When you have kids, your love flows downward."

These thoughts glimmered incoherently in her brain as she looked at the swaying water.

Startled by an explosion—a twig or a stone falling into the water—Gita stepped away from the shore.

Gita considered visiting her cousin Anju on the dates Laxman would be here. She'd tell Sachin she had mixed up the dates, present a fait accompli. But when she called Anju, Anju said she would be away, as she had the last five times Gita had tried. Only one relative on this continent, and she's a bloody recluse, Gita thought.

Next, Gita contacted an acquaintance named Jennifer who lived down the street and had recently become an editor at a lifestyle magazine named *Bay City Monthly*, based out of the nearby eponymous city. Jennifer was something of an Indophile—one of the rare Midlandians who had backpacked through the subcontinent—and had asked Gita to contribute a "piece" titled "An Indian's Journey over a Great Ocean to the Great Lakes." Gita, working at the stonecutters', had written and rewritten the article to death till she was in tears—and never submitted it. Now Gita, who was usually afraid to request favors, asked Jennifer if there was an opening at the magazine.

Jennifer said they were looking for a copy editor for a few hours a week: Would she be interested? The pay was low, but they would train her.

"Jennifer Perlin's hired me," Gita told Sachin one evening, exaggerating the extent of her work. Then, quickly, "Laxman's coming in the morning? I won't be able to go."

"Did you have to start on that day itself?" Sachin said, irritably.

"Don't you *want* me to have a job?"

Where had his wife gone? Sachin wondered.

For the first time, he thought about what life might look like without her.

When Sachin had arrived in the US, in 1974, he'd been a shy, grieving young man—his father, a civil engineer at a government-run housing finance company, had died suddenly of a stroke before Sachin had left for his master's. In this new nation, anyway, Sachin had no family to speak of. He was a man without a past. The lack of past, in America, was a kind of freedom. But it meant everything was up to you.

After his master's, the job at Trident had not come easily. When he had applied the first time, for a summer job, he received a cyclostyled letter informing him that there were no vacant positions. He planned to stay on at Brooklyn Poly for his PhD—he had enough credits and had been granted a teaching assistantship—but then, against the wishes of his adviser, he decided to drop out. After all, he'd never even wished to be an engineer, he'd only done it to please his grandfather, the great SP Chopra, who was also dead: Why was he trying to please the dead? He drove cabs for two months in Newark, where you didn't need a green card to become a cabbie, and, bemused and scared, ferried the human cargo of the city behind his tensed back, his eyes and ears and nose absorbing every twitch, perfume, and snore emanating from the back seat, wondering on the one hand what his family might think if they learned he had gone to America to become a mere chauffeur and thinking on the other, *But this is freedom! I could be killed by any of these fast-talking passengers, shot in the back, and I would vanish from the record of the universe: And yet, this is freedom!* His mother would mourn his loss, it was true, but the family was big enough to absorb casualties. Being born into the Chopra clan was no different from being an immigrant here. You were a prized nobody. He had been free from the moment he'd been born. Or, more precisely, from the moment his father had died.

As he drove in the cab at night, his father's mournful face—with the high forehead, gray skin, the large downward eyes and the signature toothbrush mustache giving him a Chaplinesque self-important dignity—this face would flare across the windshield or flash at him from underneath a golf hat, and he would recall the last picture he had of his father, the dead man lying on his back, wrapped in white, mouth open, nose stuffed with cotton, the lines on his forehead like the score of some piece of music that gave a clue to the pattern of his father's thoughts. ... Even then, under that soaring cremation canopy, with his noisy family surrounding him, his engineering mind had been at work, using reality as a springboard to sail into the abstract, and the next thing he knew, his tall and smart air force flying officer brother Brij, in his white kurta, was circling a gigantic but struggling fire, the substances within all evaporating at different rates, the cotton curling and giving off bluish fumes, the skin burning clearly, like cellophane, that beautiful word *cellophane*, an intimation of his life in plastics ahead, and then Brij, handsome Brij, still capable of emotion, was taking a long stick and bashing the charred skull of his father, and then his father's soul was released and loosed into the air, one last substance that burned at its own mysterious rate.

How sweet the letters from Gita had been, arriving in his grad-school cubbyhole at Brooklyn Poly! They had started as missives of condolence for his father, morphed into questions about educational opportunities abroad, and bloomed into romance.

In 1976, blowing all his savings on the flight, he went to India and proposed to her.

"The problem is I don't want to live in the US," she had said coyly as they walked together through Delhi University's campus, where she had studied.

"What's the issue, then?" Sachin told Gita. "I'll move back."

He was still getting used to the sight of her: that delicately bulbed nose, the wide forehead, her small body, the excited eyes that looked away, especially when she was making an important point. Sachin was five feet five, pitiably short, he felt, but she was shorter still and fit in the crook of his arm.

How much of his life, his desperate desire for success, greatness, had been prompted by his shortness?

Is this why he'd gone so far?

On the jungled campus with its thelas of peanut and popcorn sellers, Sachin told Gita the story of his friend Rajesh. Rajesh, a school classmate, had come to the US for his MD-PhD, Sachin said. He had gotten his green card quickly, but then had been sent to Vietnam—to tend to wounded American soldiers near Da Nang.

Are you sure about this? Sachin had asked him before he left. *You can go back to India.*

Look at it this way, Rajesh said. *Everyone said that it would take five years to get a green card. I got it in three months!*

And that, Sachin explained, was the last Sachin had seen of Rajesh, who was killed in one of the most brutal assaults on an American base during the war, his life canceled in a weird parenthesis, a nowhere land between nations.

Gita was greatly moved by the story.

"That's why I'm also not sure about residing there," Sachin said. "I haven't taken a green card, though they're handing them out like candy to Indians."

"You sound so American," she purred.

His blood jumped.

Then Gita and Sachin had considered what their life *here*, in India, would look like. Sachin had inherited a share in some joint lands, but they couldn't be sold, and he had no money. They would have to settle in a room in the complex. "It's a rowdy family," Sachin said. "You only know them as a visitor. They're well-meaning, but rough. You'll have to get used to it—for some years."

Gita could imagine it: sharing a kitchen with six other brides, arguing over eggs and milk. Worst of all, the great SP Chopra—who had once cast a nullifying warm shadow over such bickering—was dead.

Gita said, "Well, maybe America will be an adventure." She brought her hand scandalously close to his on the concrete bench they had settled on. "As long as it's only for a few years."

How much arrogance and confidence this woman had for a girl who comes from a nothing family! he sometimes thought. *So sure of what she wanted! So confident that India was the best of all worlds!*

And who was to say she—or anyone else—was wrong?

Having Gita in his life in the US had extinguished his longing for family, for India. A year after their marriage, when his mother passed away—having developed an infection while undergoing a knee surgery—Gita became, in essence, his closest relative.

But for Gita, he felt, *he* was not enough. In those first years in Midland, she was often lonely, her mind beamed toward India, constantly shooting off letters home, still involved in the controversies of the past, keeping up with friends and family, asking: *When will we move back, when will we move back?*

She was so lonely that he and she had devised, for her, a way of occasionally calling India without *paying* for it—their greatest collaboration. Gita would dial the American operator and say she was trying to reach a gentleman in Delhi named "Keehalji." Then, when Gita's parents answered, Gita would say over and over, "Kee haal hai ji?" while her mother answered in Hindi. Then Gita would return to the operator and say, "Sadly, Mr. Keehalji wasn't available," and so the phone call would be free.

As to her questions to Sachin about when they would repatriate, he'd say, "Arre, you've barely gotten to know this country!"

Or: "When we've saved fifteen thousand dollars."

Or: "We have to think long-term, Gita. If our kids are born here, then they'll have citizenship, and they can more easily go to Harvard or Yale."

He wanted to uphold his promise, but he also enjoyed his work.

When she had turned down that trip to India, he was shocked. But he knew, even then, it wasn't out of love for him. There was something else going on, some problem in India itself.

If India drew her back, it also repelled her.

India was her spouse. What was he?

CHAPTER 13

ON A MAY MORNING, SACHIN DROVE ALONE IN HIS SILVER Pontiac to Detroit Airport to pick up Archana and Laxman. He was still irritable. He worked the more serious job; Gita should have undertaken this nearly two-hour drive.

But as soon as he saw his relatives at baggage claim, with their—five!—heavy, unfashionable, beat-up pleather suitcases and unnecessary sweater vests—two awkward humans—his resentful feelings became diffuse.

He embraced them; saw his own face in Laxman's face.

"Why have you carried so much here?" Sachin asked.

"Because I'm coming after a long time," Laxman said gruffly.

"Gita's not with you?" Archana asked Sachin as they walked through the terminal. It seemed as if Archana had done up her eyes with kohl at the airport bathroom. A tiny woman with a forced swagger, she wore her curly black hair in a clipped bouffant that levitated above her head via a secret network of bobby pins. Laxman's bobby pins, no doubt, Sachin thought.

"She recently started a job," Sachin said glumly, as if to indicate he had no control over her. "She's doing some work for a magazine."

"She's so modest," Archana said. "In Delhi, she never mentioned any of this."

"You know what she's like," Sachin said.

"And what about the sherbet that Vibha Didi gave her?" Laxman asked. "Did it work?" Before Sachin could answer, Laxman said, "Wow, I'd forgotten the size of the fruits here." He pointed at a basket of bananas and apples on a coffee cart even as his eyes followed the breasts of a passing woman.

Sachin wondered, *Do I do this too?* Then he laughed. "The fruit's bigger but it tastes bland."

"And the sherbet?"

"I believe she's drinking it," he said, vaguely, not remembering. Then he said, "Gita's magazine issue is apparently on a deadline the next three days, so she'll be quite busy. But I'll be there." He had even taken a day off from work—an uncharacteristic request, which pained him: He was in the midst of problems with his bottle project. Production on the new plastic bottles had begun at a plant in Flint, an hour away, but, mysteriously, the bottles were developing crystalline stress cracks on the conveyor belt. A colleague thought it might be a glitch in the blow-molding machine—that it wasn't cooling the plastic fast enough—or with the rubber or lubricant on the conveyor, both of which had been selected with glass bottles in mind. All these theories might have been correct—or none. Sachin needed to be on the factory floor to find out, that was the only way to know; and he was nervous. The patent itself should have been his crowning achievement—but he saw now how badly he wanted a real object out in the world, how much he wished to see the red bottles huddled together in symmetrical cities on the long metal racks of grocery stores; or resting noiselessly like cold Siberian sentries, half uniformed in ketchup, within fridges.

The "squish" bottle, as it was called, was his offspring. Like a child—he had actually made this analogy at a meeting—it emerged whole from the blow machine. "It's not like we glue the legs onto a baby after it's born, do we?" he had asked. But the fate of the "squish" bottle was still undecided: It would either be "a turning point or a learning point," a phrase a TamBrahm professor of his at BITS Pilani had favored. Meanwhile Monsanto and Continental were already suing over the patent, trying to claim falsely that they had arrived at the design first, and he was a co-defendant. It was this dull work, browsing legal documents, that he hoped to complete in his bedroom while he was off from his job to host Archana and Laxman.

"You're stuck behind a very slow fellow," Laxman said, as they drove.

"The road is very, very curvy here and they love catching people as they come speeding out of the airport." *He's been here two minutes and he's already pushing me*, Sachin thought. He changed the subject by asking the couple about their kids—he couldn't remember their names. The Chopra family was bloated with people.

"They're very happy with their nani in Ludhiana," Archana said from the back, glancing down at her red nails, apparently bored by everything. One of those people, Sachin thought, who goes places simply to prove they are all equally boring, who wishes to paint the world in her contempt. He knew this because he too had been like this when he had arrived in the US—nine years?—before. His letters to Gita, courting her, had been so knowing about America. As if he had understood anything but his own surging fear.

"Your brother—Amitabh—how's he?" Sachin asked, names and faces coming back to him as the green summer thatch on either side of the highway ignited his mind.

After cursorily answering his question, Archana said, "I see a lot of women are driving. Does Gita drive?"

"Yes. Actually, she's taken the other car right now."

"So she won't be home?" Archana asked, seeming truly shocked, though Sachin had tried explaining this to them.

Laxman was silent.

"She wanted to, but the timing was such—anyway, she's cooked food and I'll make you tea."

"You make tea?" Archana snorted. "We'll see."

When they got to the ranch-style house on Stewart Lane, Archana was overwhelmed. "Wow, this is not a house, this is a mahal. A separate bathroom just to wash your hands? This must have cost a fortune."

"We're renting," Sachin said with a grimace. He had wanted to buy when mortgage rates had briefly dropped, but Gita, who feared getting stuck in the US, had forbidden them from such a radical act of life-rooting.

"And you don't even sit in this drawing room?" Archana went on. "Arre, yaar, you have so much space, think about having some kids." The remark seemed innocent to Sachin.

"Where are we sleeping?" Laxman asked.

Sachin showed them the guest room on the ground floor. "And if you can't find something, just ask me," he said, explaining where the light switches and blankets were.

"OK, headmasterji," Laxman said, in that sarcastic superior Chopra way.

"Yaar, your wife couldn't have taken a few minutes of vacation?" Archana asked, repeating her favorite note, when they sat down to lunch at the long, formal varnished dining table. "We've come all this way around the world."

"She's become a proper American," Laxman said.

"If she's so American, she could have made us pizza!" Archana chortled. Gita had left them several bowls of Indian food—daal and saag paneer—that Sachin had reheated.

Laxman snorted. Then he dug in, eating powerfully, quickly, desperately, eyes blank with satisfaction, licking the daal off his mustache. "Can we have some tea, Bhai?" Laxman asked.

Sachin disappeared into the kitchen and came back a few minutes later with two mugs. Laxman and Archana sat over their empty plates but didn't move to clear them. As he laid the tea down on their place mats, Archana handed him her plate and asked for more rice, and Sachin dutifully retreated into the kitchen again. When he emerged from the kitchen, Laxman said to him, "Bilkul pheeki chai."

"I told you men can't make tea," Archana said. "Let's wait for Gita to make it."

Sachin suppressed a flash of anger. "No, I make it better than her—you want more sugar?"

"There's not enough elaichi," Archana said.

As he entered the kitchen, he heard her shout, "And add more ginger!"

He had been reduced to a servant in his own house. But then, this always happened with Indian guests.

An extreme antsiness overcame Sachin after lunch. "Why don't you take a nap for one hour and I'll wake you up," Sachin said to them.

"No, yaar, we're wide awake," Laxman said. "Let's see this place before it gets dark."

"See the place" in those days meant only one thing—shopping—and he drove to the mall, hoping, almost angrily, resentfully, that he'd run into Gita.

CHAPTER 14

IN FACT, GITA'S "WORK" HAD LASTED ALL OF TWO HOURS IN the morning—using a tattered style guide to painstakingly copyedit a single, awkward article titled "How to Tell a Real (Central Michigan) Woman." Then Jennifer, with her brown bangs and angular, intelligent, no-nonsense face, had told her, "You're free to go, there's no point in you whiling away hours here while we're waiting for the advertisers to confirm this month's copy."

Knowing she wanted to be out of the house—and not serving Laxman—Gita had gotten in touch with Hector, the friend she had made in a nighttime marketing class several years before.

Hector was an elegant Mexican man in his early thirties. He had first befriended Gita in the tiered amphitheater of the classroom by complimenting her on her chiffon saris and by sitting next to her for the rest of the course. At the end of the semester, she had gone out to a bar with Hector and his girlfriend, Molly; since then, she had met them again for drinks every so often—though not for the past year.

She would invite Hector and his girlfriend to coffee or lunch or dinner, she decided; they might even be the source of an interesting story about Midland or Michigan that she could pitch to Jennifer. But when Hector had answered the phone, one of the first things he told Gita was that he and Molly had broken up. "She said I brought up my 'culture' too much," he said.

Though Gita and Hector hadn't spoken in several months, they seemed to pick up where they had left off; she'd always found him easy to talk to. Even on the phone, she could instantly see his clear peeled-almond skin, black hair, iridescent teeth, and wide, boyish smile that made him seem kind and knowable.

"But she was so interested in other cultures," Gita said. The first time they had met, Molly had asked Gita whether she was "a Hindu—or a Buddhu?" and whether "Delhi" was the same as "New

Delhi." "But that must be the other side of the interest, secretly wishing this subject didn't exist."

"Gita, you always analyze situations correctly," Hector said.

"Not always. I got a B in that class—remember?"

"I got a D!" he said, adding that he was no longer working in sales at Dow Chemical—a company which, Gita knew, was the biggest employer in Midland. Instead, he said, he now spent a lot of time at the library browsing business books and talking to people at the career center there. "I have to find a job in two months—or it's back to my father's shoe business." He didn't explain whether he had lost or left the job and she didn't ask.

"There are worse fates, no?" she said.

"Exactly, exactly, there's no place like Mexico," Hector said. "But my father—he's very strict and he'll make me start at a tanning factory. Have you ever smelled a tannery? Even if you mixed all the chemicals at Dow together, you wouldn't be able to create such a smell."

Gita laughed. She said her husband was busy with his family; would he like to meet for a coffee at the bar near where they'd taken the class together?

"Oh, Gita, so classy. A coffee."

"Oh, shut up, you're a foreigner too, you have no right making fun of me."

She drove to meet Hector before lunch, while Sachin went to the airport.

It was illicit enough to be meeting another man at midday, but it felt truly brash to skip out on receiving Laxman at the airport—almost an act of war. *Let people say what they want in India*, she thought. *I live here now. I'm a free woman.* But the thoughts felt like a performance. She drove shakily to the bar and immediately overshot a stop sign; luckily, there was no one at the crosswalk save for one of those gigantic American cat-sized squirrels holding a nut in its claws, the demonic creature scrambling out of the way, its bushy tail rising and falling like a pneumatic lever, the tail shaped like an elongated pine cone and full of sharp, fine hair. A few minutes later, she went the wrong way down a one-way street and had to turn around in someone's driveway, her side-view mirror just barely missing the mailbox with its red salute of metal.

Why did she already feel so guilty? What had she even done?

Hector wasn't at the bar when she arrived. The wait was long and awkward—she sat inside the purposely darkened long room with its greasy, simple, round wooden tables and scuffed concrete floor. Three balding, red-faced men were bent over the bar and occasionally flashed blank stares her way. Smoke rose from the individual ashtrays beside them; they were obviously regulars. It was a balmy summer day, but she did not want to sit on the deck, which was visible from the parkway. She had been to bars before but had never ordered a drink herself, strangely. Would the slow-moving bartender with the checked towelette thrown over his shoulder come to her? What would she order—a screwdriver, a cosmopolitan? She had started to drink on occasion. She looked thirstily at her watch.

A few minutes later, Hector strolled in, charming and warm, giving her a tight hug as she rose to greet him. Close-shaven, he wore an ironed white checked shirt tucked into pleated gray pants with a flawlessly matte leather belt. His hair was gelled into a glinting crown, and he smelled of cologne and a feral, alcoholic aftershave.

"Did you come from a job interview?" she exclaimed.

"I don't bring gifts to interviews, Gita," he said, handing her a small box and smiling again.

"Oh, you didn't need to do this!" she said, blushing as she opened the white box of tiny strawberry-shaped chocolates. He has prepared as if for a date, she realized with fear.

He came back with water for her and a beer for himself. "The coffee is being brewed for you," he said with a wink. "The guy looked shocked when I asked him for coffee—no one in all these years has ever asked him to make a coffee."

"So how is your job search going?" she asked.

"Fine, fine," he said, his jaw tightening. "It's a land of opportunity in Midland." Then he said, "You're not in those wonderful clothes of yours! I always remember that red-and-gold sari you wore."

"You don't like this?" she said, tugging at the shirt over her jeans. "It's from Mexico, actually, this shirt."

"Oh, is it?" he said. "But I prefer the saris!"

They talked a little about Molly, his ex. "She was—how do you say?—a very sweet girl, a very nice person," Hector said, "but her anger—my God, she had a lot of anger!"

"About what?" Gita asked.

"Being a woman."

Gita tensed up.

But then he said, "And she was right. They mistreated her. The problem was that she also refused to leave her job, which, frankly, was the only solution. One has to be realistic. People don't change. Bosses especially don't change." He paused. "You're ready for your coffee?"

"Yes," Gita said, wondering how Sachin might have responded to Molly's complaints, remembering how he had told her at various times to swallow insults lobbed at her by her male interviewers and employers. *That's just how it is*, Sachin would say. *It was tough for me too, with my accent.* He seemed to forget he had studied in the US!

Hector went to the bar and returned with a solid ivory-colored soft-lipped enamel mug full of dun liquid. Then he asked if it was OK if they stepped onto the deck. "It's too black in here," he said.

"Of course," she said. What were the odds that she would be seen by Sachin and Laxman?

Outside, on the rickety planks of the deck, he drew out a cigarette. "You won't take one?"

"I never smoked," Gita said. "Though all the women in my college smoked, mind you. It was very fashionable. I was just a simpleton. I never smoked or drank."

"Congratulations," he said, smiling with the cigarette between his teeth. "You'll have a long life."

"That's the amazing thing about Europe, no?" Gita said, remembering her one trip to Paris and Madrid, accompanying Sachin on business. "Everyone smokes—everywhere. You go to Spain and mothers are lighting cigarettes over their prams."

"People of our kind like to live dangerously," Hector said, connecting himself with Spain.

"You all aren't precious about parenting that way," Gita said. "Kids are allowed to be independent. Here—there's too much fear. The more space people have, the more fear they fill it with. That's why America and the Soviets are so obsessed with each other. Too much space."

"You and your husband," Hector said, "you aren't desirous of children?"

Desirous of children. Hector's charming English. Oddly, the question made her feel warmly toward Hector. An American would never have asked, and an Indian would have freighted the question with menacing curiosity. His question was genuine.

"I don't think it's for us."

He stood right in front of her now, blowing smoke out the side of his mouth, puffing up one cheek. She could smell the smoke on his breath and something more bitter—was he nervous?

"I think you would make a wonderful mother," he said.

CHAPTER 15

THIRTY MINUTES LATER, SHE DROVE HOME, FLUSTERED and afraid beneath her outward calm.

Sachin's boxy silver Pontiac Grand Am was parked in the driveway when she pulled up.

"So sorry," she said, as she came through the door. Laxman and Archana were reclining on the ash-colored La-Z-Boys, watching Phil Donahue on TV in a bored way with Sachin, and sipping Cokes from cans—another exotic treat for Indians: both the can, with its metal coolness, and the American cola, with its perfected sweetness. "I tried to change my work appointment, but—how was your flight?" Gita asked, shuddering a bit from her performed chirpiness. She had worn her flower-patterned "Mexican" shirt precisely because it more closely approximated American professional garb for women: a shirt and pants.

"No issues, no issues," Archana said, getting up and pressing one of her cheeks to Gita's.

Laxman, whose eyes were droopy with jet lag, also gave her a noncommittal hug, which she accepted sideways. How innocent he looked in his tucked-in denim shirt and khaki pants, with his newly-trimmed mustache, and straight, oiled hair! But she was glad to see she felt neither anger nor fear. He was shrunken by these cavernous American surroundings.

"Your husband has been a good host," Archana said, beaming.

"Just a lowly driver," Sachin said.

But Gita immediately intuited the reason for Archana's smile: Sachin had likely paid for a number of items they'd purchased at the mall. This happened on every family visit. Indians were not allowed to bring more than six hundred rupees into the country—a mere forty-six dollars—and were perpetually short on forex, which they asked to "borrow" from Sachin, who, while always tense about money, could not refuse. Then the relatives spent lavishly on Sachin's tab and forgot to pay it back—or as with the gifts Gita doled out in India, occasionally offered compensation in rupees, a useless currency in the US (and the way Sachin treated these rupees, shoving them into old hotel laundry bags and stowing them in his closet, only further convinced Gita that he had no desire to return to India). Now Gita saw three stiff paper bags jutting out from the top level of the shoe-rack by the door. "Ah, Sears and JCPenney. I see Sachin took you to his favorite places."

"What sales!" Archana said. She walked to a bag and pulled out a hideous lime-green sweater. "I got this for Shilpa. It was only five dollars!"

"Yes, this whole country is on sale," Gita said. "That's how they get you to buy more and more."

Archana plopped back down on the La-Z-Boy—there seemed to be no other way of sitting in a La-Z-Boy than with a plop—and said, "Come sit, tell us, what work are you doing?"

Lowering herself on the sofa, Gita glanced quickly at Laxman and then talked about the kind of articles that were featured in *Bay City Monthly*. "Of course, I was an editor so many years ago that I barely remember anything," Gita said, now looking guiltily at Sachin, who appeared neither encouraging nor discouraging as he bit his lips.

"But your English is so good, that's what matters," Laxman responded.

Gita abruptly got up. "I should start preparing dinner." She had learned, from experience, that Indian guests wanted Western food—the Indian food she had left them for lunch had been part of her revenge.

In the kitchen, she boiled pasta, poured salad leaves out of a paper bag, and commenced preparation for a "baked"—the type of lasagna Indians loved. She was still buoyed by that outing with Hector even as she tried to make sense of Laxman's presence here; she was also surprised that he and Archana weren't yet yawning. Usually, guests—eager to make use of every minute in the US, conscious always of the drainage of their socialist incomes—revved around all day only to collapse at 7 or 8 p.m. and wake up at 3 or 4 a.m., when you would hear them prowling around the house and heavily clanging pots and pans in the kitchen to wake you up so you could make them tea. Her mamas, whom she otherwise loved, had been the worst offenders in this regard. Creatures of routine, they needed tea to commence their days—even if the day started at 3 a.m. Having never stepped into kitchens in their entire lives, they were ignorant about implements wielded in that space. "Bitiya?" they would say, knocking on the master bedroom door and entering even before Gita or Sachin had a chance to respond from under the heavy white comforter, mashed over their heads for privacy. "Can you show us where the ginger is? I can't remember." Gita would have given them instructions the night before and they would have purposely forgotten. She then would get up to boil tea, forced to live out the jet lag of her guests.

Why were Indian men so selfish and childlike? she wondered now as she cooked. For all his flaws, her husband was at least resourceful and self-sufficient—had been a better cook than her when they were first married—and though he was clumsy with machines like the lawn mower, he still insisted on muddling through with them, wrestling their levers with all the brute force his slight frame could muster. Yes, she was grateful for his efforts in this department. But for the visiting Indian men, the sight of one of their own working in the kitchen—like a mere servant!—was shocking. Her mamas and even mamis had made Sachin sit with them while Gita prepared the meals.

"No, Gita and I have a system," Sachin would protest.

"What would your late mother have said?" the distressed aunts and uncles would respond. "That she sent you here for higher education and you became a cook? Sit. You work all day."

Thus, lacking an option, Sachin would succumb to this pressure to be "a man" and, at night, Gita, seething from overwork, would scold him in bed for not helping out enough around the house. Then, seeing the tense lines winging out from the groove above his large Roman nose, pity would overwhelm her. He was pressed in on all sides; it turned him into the short, lost elder-younger brother he'd always been. "Don't look so sad," she'd say, kissing him and unbuttoning his shirt. Pity was the only thing that could now drive her to sex with Sachin.

She was thinking this and listlessly stirring the bubbling salted pasta water in the kitchen when Laxman stepped in.

"Can you give me a cup?" he asked, gliding toward her on his socked feet. "A kitchen like this could feed five families."

"Why have you come in here?" Gita snapped.

"Arre." He paused. "I just wanted water—your husband sent me in." He smiled, showing his small, perfect teeth, strange on a man with such elongated features. "And you're OK?"

"They're up there. Wait." And she lifted herself on her toes and opened the cupboard and took out a glass and filled it in the sink.

"You drink straight from the pipes here?" he asked, leaning against the tiled counter and sipping from the glass.

"Yes, the pipes are clean," Gita said.

"Like the water in the spring in Gharam," he said. The Chopra men passed up no opportunity to laud their ancestral village. He took another sip from the glass, then put it down. He started opening the drawers before him, gummy from overuse. "And, wow, a separate drawer for chopsticks. And one for rubber bands. And what's this?" he asked, lifting a rounded ale-colored bottle from the counter.

"Maple syrup," Gita explained. "For pancakes." She focused again on the boiling water, refusing to face him.

"Why does the bottle have a blackie on it?"

"It's Aunt Jemima," she said, gritting her teeth. Tension was flaring through her body, through her lower back and her thighs.

"Then you must make us pancakes," Laxman said, putting the bottle back on the counter and wiping his sticky hands on his pants.

"In fact, Sachin is going to take you to a place where that's a specialty, Mooney's," Gita said. The vast difference between the inner and outer life. What one thought and what one said. They were like two countries riven by an ocean of dark meaning.

"You won't come?" Laxman asked.

"If I have time from work."

"Amazing that you're so busy; you're an American success story." It was half a question.

"No, no, I'm very junior there, I just started. In fact, it's hard to find a job in a small town like this. You take what you can." Then, feeling she was just twittering on, she said, "And how are Karishma and Brij?"

"Very well, very well," Laxman said, sipping from the glass again. "They moved back a few months before."

"I know, you're all staying together," Gita said. "I meant, how are they liking being back? They've lived in jungle rest houses for so many years, it's different from being with the family."

"Yes," Laxman said, pausing thoughtfully. "It's crowded but we enjoy each other's company—it's not just about space."

"I wasn't talking about space," Gita said.

She noticed—or she felt—he had moved closer to her. She flinched and turned around. "It's nice that you're happy here," he said.

Gita smiled thinly, collapsing her lips inward. She returned to meddling with the pasta strands in the volcanic water.

Laxman went on, "You and Sachin are very suited for each other, and I'm very happy to see you have such a beautiful house. That's what Brij always says—the smartest couple in the family."

"Thank you," Gita said, feeling oddly suspended in her own house, as if the floor might give out and she'd find herself, once again, in that room in A-19 with Laxman.

CHAPTER 16

LAXMAN HIMSELF WAS SURPRISED BY HIS PRESENCE IN THE US.

He had come to the US not to see Gita, but to chase a business opportunity. The opportunity came in the form of a man named Vir Malhotra, who lived near Detroit and was thinking of moving home to Delhi and opening a soft-drink business. Laxman, whose own bobby-pin business was in permanent doldrums, had first met Malhotra at the Modern Colony Club after the two had been paired in an impromptu doubles tennis match. Afterward, when they had sat in the club coffee shop with towels horseshoed around their necks, Laxman had flattered him and also peacocked his knowledge about manufacturing in Delhi. "I can easily be your point person if you come here," he had said.

"I really do want to move back, yaar," Malhotra said, shaking his large head. "The problem is my missus. She's used to freedom now and doesn't want to live with her in-laws."

"Show her our house," Laxman said, having already described his triple-decker joint- family to Malhotra. "She'll feel grateful for your setup."

Malhotra laughed. "You really are a man of the soil."

"We're proper Punjabi putturs," Laxman said. Then he told the story of his father's involvement in framing the Indian Constitution and running the Reserve Bank, adding, "His one sadness was that the Congress couldn't win Lahore for us. It was that sixer Mountbatten's fault. He was British but had the mind of a bania, weighing things. He said, if you Indians get Calcutta, the Pakis must get Lahore—as if these cities can be compared!" Laxman moved on to talking about the pickle business SP had set up in Jalandhar. "My nephew Abhay runs it now," he said, eliding the fact that Abhay, while his "nephew," was three years older than him. "But he supplies his pickles mostly to the army. He can give you advice. They have state-of-the-art equipment from Germany," he said, further eliding the squalid fly-ridden sticky floors of the outdated pickle factory, floors on which Abhay had slipped twice, fracturing his hips, so that, at the age of thirty-nine, he walked with a cane. Laxman went on, "I moved to Delhi for my bobby-pin factory, but, to be honest, I'm bored of the business. It's stable and nothing changes. But I have ample space one can employ for another venture."

Laxman took his NRI friend to his factory on a weekend, having had it mopped beforehand, the rusty nonfunctioning rod cutters and conveyor belts cleared of cobwebs and moved to the front to look imposing. But as Laxman drove Malhotra through industrial, garbage-strewn Shahdara in his sky-blue Fiat, Malhotra looked discomfited, and clutched the handgrip above the passenger window. Malhotra had a solid, wide face that never seemed to sweat. He put a white embroidered hanky to his nose and glanced at his heavy silver watch with little gold markings around the black face in lieu of numbers.

In the factory, too, Malhotra was hassled and distracted, but Laxman laid on the charm. "Look, I know things are harder in this country, but imagine the role a person like you can play," Laxman said. "There, in America—you'll just be a company man. Here you can run your own empire. Frankly, this is why I came back." Laxman always fudged the time he'd spent in the US, making it sound like a three-year job he'd given up rather than a two-month apprenticeship in his early twenties that had expired.

"Very true," Malhotra said, his broad face with its perfect skin suddenly full of muscular tension. The lower and upper parts of his face appeared not to be connected; while the lower half emitted a frozen smile, the eyes above were racing with worry. The two of them were sitting in the manager's cabin of the factory, drinking tea.

"Of course, it's also your wife's decision," Laxman said.

"That's the problem," Malhotra said, brightening up.

Malhotra returned to the US. There was no word from him. Then Gita arrived in Delhi.

Laxman had tried not to think about Gita since that night at the wedding. Though he had always been obsessed with women, he had been frightened by how far he had gone. He was a good six inches taller than little Gita, but he had never expected her to succumb so easily. However, he had had a piece of luck—if that's what you wanted to call it.

When he had been sprawled over her on that bed, pleading with her, he and Gita had heard the rowdy voices of two male relatives passing near the door. "Be quiet," Laxman had shushed her. "If you say something, they'll come in."

And that was the moment he had acted.

The next day, he felt dazed and hungover—the hangover didn't vanish for a week. And as he rode his scooter to his bobby-pin factory, his father's words had come back to him: "All my sons—each and every one—is a duffer. But you? You're the stupidest of all of them. You're stupider than these rocks." Laxman had been fourteen when his father had said this; and SP, then in his mid-fifties, had been referring specifically to the flat mineral-flecked rocks in the stream that ran through the mango orchard in Gharam. The two of them had been standing on the riverbank. It was winter. A forbidding fog was rising off the river, a clear stream that was like a piece of cloth being folded and unfolded. Minutes earlier, his father had caught Laxman in a state of half undress with a village girl behind the outhouse. SP had looked away from the girl and taken Laxman by the arm and marched him to the orchard. Then, sitting him down on a rock by the river—the way you might sit a man down for a shave—SP Chopra began to lather his cheek with slaps. They were short, hard blows. "Idiot." You could tell he did not enjoy physical violence; he was not a violent person. "Kambakht!" SP seemed to be grieving something. His youth? His own transgressions? Had there been transgressions?

The day after the dalliance with Gita, Laxman had stopped before a black-and-white age-curled portrait of his father in a corridor of the complex. "I am stupid," he had chided himself.

But a part of him, the part he couldn't control, had grown exhilarated. He had gotten away with something.

He began praying in earnest that day. He vowed to become more involved with his religion, with the Jeev Sangathan. He knew that the most dangerous thing in life is not being caught but rather escaping without consequence: because then you will do it again.

So, some years later, when he had seen Gita again in the complex, he had thought of it as an opportunity for reconciliation—especially important if he were to make a trip to the US. But how could he have predicted Gita's behavior outside the gurdwara? And his own response?

Right after this unfortunate incident, Malhotra seemed to regain enthusiasm about a potential partnership with Laxman. "Remind me, how many square feet is your property?" he asked on the phone from Detroit. Malhotra was profligate with these international calls. Laxman always came running to the one phone in the main drawing room of the complex, summoned by a servant. "And you would rent me a part of it?" Malhotra went on. "Oh, I see—OK, you want to rent out the whole thing. How much would this cost? And is there an option that we could build another floor—let's say if we're partners?"

Laxman was no fool; he wasn't sure about Malhotra either and did his due diligence on him in the colony. On the one hand, the Malhotra family was very wealthy—manufacturers of sports equipment; on the other, the elders of the Malhotra family had twisted themselves into a permanent knot of intrafamilial litigation, and certain segments of the clan had fallen into penury. One of Malhotra's uncles had even spent a few months in jail for his outsize role in a government scam. But Malhotra himself possessed a clean record. He was one of those "good" nondescript sons who had exited the family stage to do his own thing abroad. What was bringing him back now, Malhotra had explained, was that his parents were aging. "Also, the kids are at the right age to settle here—I don't want them to become American." He had two preteen girls who were about the same age as Laxman's kids; this had brought them closer.

On the phone, Malhotra now told Laxman that his wife was the last remaining obstacle. "Look, I myself—I'm more and more convinced to do this," he said, "but I want you to meet Simranpreet.

For her, this is all abstract. She thinks it's one more of my harebrained ideas. And you're so good at convincing people."

"When are you—and she—coming to Delhi again?" Laxman asked.

"She never comes," Malhotra said, clucking his tongue.

"She doesn't want to see her parents?" Laxman asked.

"There are some ... family issues," Malhotra said. "Anyway, your business doesn't bring you to the US?"

"No, not these days," Laxman lied. He certainly couldn't afford a trip to America.

"But—for our venture," Malhotra said, "I think it'll be important to meet in person."

When Laxman didn't offer a quick yes, Malhotra made an offer: He would pay for Laxman's ticket to the US.

This seemed crazy to Laxman but he said, calmly, "No, no need to do it."

"Think about it," Malhotra encouraged him.

"As I said, it's a quite busy time for me with my work," Laxman said, pressing his surprising advantage.

"Look," Malhotra said, "if you're serious—"

"OK, Virji, let me discuss with my wife and associates, and I will get back to you at the earliest."

A free opportunity to visit the US—after ten years! Laxman made a mental map of all the relatives he could stay with, to skip paying for hotels—in LA, Toronto, Chicago, and yes, Midland, which, he had heard, was not far from Detroit.

Now the only impediment was Gita. But Gita was still in India and Laxman knew that, because of the cost of phone calls, it was unlikely that Gita and Sachin had talked.

So Laxman decided to splurge on a phone call to Midland immediately. It was important that he get a yes from Sachin before Gita could make Sachin say no.

CHAPTER 17

SOON AFTER, LAXMAN RECEIVED A PHONE CALL FROM Vibha, asking if he would come by her house. She wanted to add an extension to her ground-floor DDA flat and was hoping that her street-smart younger brother could advise her if it was legal. "Because of your MCD"—Municipal Corporation of Delhi—"connections, I thought, better to ask you first," she said on the phone.

Laxman, used to dropping in on Vibha anyway, went over one Saturday afternoon.

She was alone when he arrived.

"Where is my sweet niece, Aparna—and Anil Bhai?" Laxman asked after her daughter and husband.

"They're in the market," Vibha said absently, leaning forward across the low table to push a bowl of namkeens toward him.

"Why do you send your poor husband out in this heat?"

"Poor nothing! That fellow needs exercise." Then she said, "Accha, I was just talking to Shantiji. How was it taking Gita to Pahalwanji? Was it helpful?"

"We didn't even go; she changed her mind. By the way, I might be going to the US soon. So, I'll see them—Sachin and Gita and, of course, Sharad and Nalini."

"You're going for some work?" she asked.

"A project." Laxman gave a glowing description of his barely hatched scheme.

"So you'll probably stay with Sachin, right?" Vibha asked.

"Yes, unless they've become too American to host us."

Vibha hesitated. "This time, it seems, Gita had a difficult time." Gita had just left for the US. She went on, "She says you tried to—kiss her?" Embarrassed, she laughed. "Is this true?"

Laxman's eyes went dark; then he laughed too. "I just hugged her bye-bye! My God, the things people say about me and all because

I try to help them! Look at me. Do I look like someone who would try such a thing? And we even agreed never to mention the idea—"

"I told her about it," Vibha said.

"I would never have done that."

"I didn't have a choice," Vibha said. "Anyway, she's sensitive. She's had trouble conceiving and she's not used to the family's ways. Please be gentle with her."

"Vibha Didi—do you believe me or her? And here I was trying to help her!"

"I know you're not so innocent," Vibha said with a sly smile.

"I swear on God I did nothing—forget it, I swear on Papaji," he said, holding a coin of skin at his neck.

"Laxman—"

"No, what'll it take for me to be believed?" he asked.

"Then why is she saying this?" Vibha said. "She doesn't strike me as the hysterical type."

Laxman sighed. "She's always disliked me—from childhood. Yes, perhaps I was rough with her when I was younger. I don't deny it. But to hold a grudge all these years later—to slander! And let's say I had done it, would I be so shameless as to go stay with them? Would Sachin have invited me?"

"Does he know?"

"Everyone knows everything," Laxman said. "Gita talks every week to him on the phone when she's here. Now I'm angry. People go away from this country and think they can control us from there. She's never liked my friendship with Brij, that's the other thing, it burns them up—"

"Brij and Sachin—"

"I've done so much to try and bring people together in this family—but this is the result; people don't like it. Gita's upset about her childlessness, OK. But she shouldn't try to sow disunity here."

The more Laxman talked in circles, the less Vibha believed him. She balanced her head on a fist. Laxman rarely brandished his intelligence. The fact that he was doing so now, in the politician's manner he had inherited from Papaji, made her think he did have something to hide. Gita was attractive and Laxman was vital and unafraid—who was to say he hadn't made a pass? All men were suspect, to Vibha, after her own terrible divorce and remarriage years before. But this also made her doubt herself. It was hard to see such things objectively. What made it worse was that Archana and the kids were in the picture—airing the accusation would hurt them the most. In any case, she had said what needed to be said. "Well, it must be a misunderstanding," Vibha said finally, clapping her hands together. "Poor thing, it's difficult for her."

"We only want to ease their burden," Laxman said.

"Maybe we shouldn't try," she said.

"It was your idea, Vibha Didi."

"I was just talking about what they did in families in olden days," she said. "Some people do live without kids."

"I'm not sure how," Laxman said, though he found kids as irritating as the next person.

CHAPTER 18

LAXMAN LEFT VIBHA'S HOUSE IN A RAGE.

When she had explained her idea for how she would renovate her flat, he wasn't able to concentrate. Something about enclosing her veranda with bamboo and fiberglass, building a little metal room for the servant—all straightforwardly illegal but easy for the MCD to overlook. Afterward, he drove to the Jeev Sangathan temple, where he always retreated to cool down. There was no privacy in the flat he now shared with Brij and Karishma and their kids.

The Jeev Sangathan was the Hindu reformist sect to which the Chopra family belonged; SP had been one of its leading lights in Punjab. Laxman had thrown himself into the organization and upkeep of the local temple, which, like most Sangathan temples, was a spartan hall without idols. It was hardly ever used (the Sangathan was against idol worship—so why would a Sangathani visit a temple?). Over time, he had started using the office in the temple as his own private retreat, a place to receive friends, neighborhood gossips, and supplicants; to read the day's papers; to check the accounts for his failing bobby-pin concern.

He walked to the backyard of the temple and spied the pundit snoring in his room with his metal door thrown open. Laxman went to his office and sat down to look over the register of donations made to the mandir. He was distracted again. What had he expected? The real question was: Why had he been so passive in dealing with Gita? Why hadn't he preempted her accusation, spread the first rumors? He should have been more forceful.

Laxman made unintelligible scribbles in the register, trying to bring himself back to the everyday. When he had offered to take Gita to Mohan Pahalwanji, he had meant to put everything behind them. But her hysteria in the car had surprised him, as had his own reaction—leaning in for a consoling kiss. He considered his face now in the long, dull mirror installed on the other side of the room, mainly for couples to freshen up before their impromptu Sangathani weddings, and he smiled wanly. Wasn't there a noble comedy in a man responding to a woman's aggression with a kiss—an offering of nonviolence at the altar of rage? And what was wrong with two people wanting each other? Her prudery was exceptional. In contrast, he had always been grateful to the servant girls of Gharam, who had permitted him his first sexual breakthroughs as a teenager. Those girls seemed to know, better than these upper-class hoity-toity women, that sex wasn't some hushed precious thing. Often they looked away as he rested on top of them in the mango orchard; Laxman would then squeeze the girl's pimpled chin and pull her face toward him and kiss her, turned on by the caste pollution of the action. These girls never protested. They enjoyed his company, teased him, led him on. He didn't hold all the power. And even if he did, that was his appeal: They were consorting with the son of a great man.

What he disliked most about Gita's behavior, her responses, was her automatic assumption of superiority. What did she have to be so high and mighty about? Yes, she lived in America, but that was her husband's doing, not hers.

Laxman snapped the nib of a pencil on the register. A sharp, unpleasant, unfixable feeling. He opened the small, stiff drawers of the desk and fished around for a plastic sharpener he had purloined from his kids (how many sharpeners did they need, exactly?). He got up and went to the empty hall and stood before the painting of the founder of the Sangathan, Guru Harbans Lal, and bowed his head and closed his eyes, muttering the Gayatri Mantra. The pitta dosh was strong in him, he knew; he was trying to cool it down with soft mantras. But waves of heat coursed through him nevertheless.

That night, he told Archana that she would accompany him to the US, though she would have to pay for part of her ticket with her savings from her baking business.

Despite her husband's miserliness, Archana was thrilled—thrilled to have the opportunity to be away from work, family, kids—and her entire body shivered with expectation as she sat up in bed, her arms thrown around her knees. She said, "We can send Vaishnavi and Shilpa to Mataji's in Ludhiana. Though I'm sure Brij and Karishma won't mind taking care of them. And we can ..." she went on.

He didn't tell her why he had invited her—that he needed her for protection.

CHAPTER 19

OF COURSE NOTHING IN LIFE IS FREE: IN A FOLLOW-UP CALL, Malhotra asked Laxman to carry three *extra* suitcases with him. "My man will deliver some carpets to you and he'll show you how to wrap them up with clothes so no one sees. No, no, Bhai, no one will trouble you in America."

Laxman glumly consented. How could he say no?

Arriving at Detroit Airport with this embarrassing cargo of five suitcases, Laxman had been grateful that Gita had absented herself from picking them up. But he also worried that this dramatic gesture on her part was a sign that she had shared the incident with Sachin. *Do you think I would be so shameless that I would come see you?* he imagined saying to Sachin. *But yes, I agree, your wife and I got into a heated argument in Delhi, that was all, I'm sorry if she's trying to now rubbish my reputation.* Then, as they sped through deepening country—dotted here and there with lollipop-like water towers on stilts—toward Midland, he realized they didn't live as close to Detroit as he'd thought. The bewildering size of this country, this freezer of antiseptic smells and brain-dulling openness.

Now, at dinner in Midland, Laxman watched as Archana said to Gita, "Are you thinking of adopting? If so, I know a good ashram—"

Sachin let out a barky low cough of warning.

"Brij and Karishma already told us of one in Bombay," Gita said, looking at Sachin.

"Listen at least," Archana said.

"No need to force them," Laxman responded.

"But you only said we should tell them," Archana said.

"Yaar, let your wife speak," Sachin said, irritably, to Laxman, fingering one of his frequent razor cuts.

Archana now described the ashram, which was partly funded by the Jeev Sangathan. "You see, one issue is that parents never know who the mothers are," she said. "Here, the mothers come when they are expecting and you can even meet them."

"But the women can change their minds in the first three months," Laxman interjected.

"You're jumping ahead, as usual," Archana said. "Anyway, Gita, you can take the baby when it's three months. But you know, they don't want to promote the idea of women giving up their children, so, yes, in the first three months, if the girl changes her mind, then she can keep it. But most of them are too young to be able to do that."

"How young?" Gita asked, politely.

"Oh, fourteen, fifteen, that kind of age," Laxman said. "Might not have husbands."

Gita again had the feeling that the most shameful aspect of life—sex—had been brought into the light for everyone to discuss. "We'll be OK without children," Gita said suddenly, shaking her head.

"You shouldn't think like that," Archana said.

"Why not?" Gita asked sharply. "Don't we have a full existence without them? And, anyway, life is so hard: Why force it on someone against their will?"

The funny thing was that she had believed this sentiment more earnestly *before* she had failed to have kids of her own. The intense desire for kids sprang from failure—not from an inherent obsession with motherhood.

"But why give up like this?" Archana asked, turning to Sachin. "You're so young."

"Gita's right, we're quite happy as is," Sachin said, not looking up from his plate, which was heavy with slabs of baked cheese that looked as if they'd been dipped in blood.

Gita and Sachin had not spoken again about children since that car ride from the airport; and hearing Sachin's reaction, seeing him taking her side, even though he had always appeared to want kids in an uncomplicatedly mild fashion, made Gita feel warmly toward him.

"Oh, I always thought—" Archana said.

Gita said, "See, things here are different: Many people choose not to have kids. There's a whole feature in the latest *Time* magazine about it."

"Yes, there are other things in life," Laxman said.

"I wish you weren't so two-faced!" Archana hissed at Laxman.

Dinner went on at the long rosewood dining table. It became ocean-bottom dark outside, and the sounds of cicadas washed over them in electric waves. It was difficult to recover from this crescendo of argument, so the couples chitchatted now about other relatives. There were always relatives to discuss, a surfeit of people in the Chopra clan, a menu of idiosyncrasies and dysfunctions to choose from. Gita could almost physically see Archana squirreling away this argument about adoption in her mind so that she could transmit it to the gossip-ravenous inhabitants of A-19. *Gita, she's so rude, she's lost her mind, she now attacks anyone who tries to help her.*

At that moment, Gita decided to call Hector again.

CHAPTER 20

BOTH GITA AND HECTOR WERE NERVOUS AT THE BAR, AND it felt like they had exhausted their conversation during that first outing. But when they went outside for a smoke, he smiled, leaned over, and kissed her. Gita found herself kissing him eagerly, nibbling his lower lip.

A few minutes later, she followed him in her car, jumpy, aware that she was driving away not just from the bar but from her life, an idea of herself as a good Indian girl, as one immune to the forces of adultery that smashed through these lonely American lives.

Hector's apartment, not far from downtown, was a cell in a low-slung building with open verandas. It was surprisingly undecorated, like a motel suite—a mismatch with how well turned out he was in person. He obviously concentrated all his energy on his body.

They sat next to each other on his black pleather sofa. When she kissed him again, he asked, "Are you certain, Gita?"

She thought for a second of Archana and Laxman, who were watching TV at her house. Then she nodded.

"I love you, Hector," she said, afterward.

"Easy now," he said with a grin. American slang seemed to come to him most easily at moments of intimacy, like a memory of his private banter with Molly.

As they lay on his bed, Gita told Hector the story of how she'd cheated on the final paper for the marketing class they'd taken together. Instead of writing the assignment herself, she told him, she had panicked and copied an A+ paper her husband had penned for a similar college class. (*Her husband! Did he not have a name?* she thought with a shudder. She could feel the guilt rising.)

"You're the last person I would have thought to do that!" he said.

"But that's not the whole story," she replied. She now told him how, when she got the paper back, it had been given a B. "Though my husband got an A+ for the same paper!" She laughed.

Hector went quiet. Then he said, "It's all about perception. The teacher didn't respect you as much."

"I'm not sure."

"I know, Gita. How one is seen really matters."

That was when she fell actually in love with Hector.

Earlier, she had said "I love you" only as something she felt one was supposed to say after making love; in her mind, sex and love had always been connected. That was why that encounter with Laxman all those years before had been so shattering. It had undone something sacred. Now she felt she was finding her way back to that sacred feeling, even if it was in the most illicit way possible.

In the shower, she had trouble figuring out the faucet. He came into the bathroom to open the hot valve and, leaning into the stall, slipped off his bathrobe and joined her. She did not like sharing a bathroom with another person but accepted his caresses.

"Next time come in a sari," he said when they were out.

"You won't know how to take it off," she said as she dried herself before the long mirror of his bedroom—the bedroom saturated with a cologne-sweat smell that threw her back into her brother Hari's hostel room in Bangalore. "Shit!" she muttered, bringing the towel to her hair. "What did I do?"

"No need to feel bad—"

"No, no, my hair! It's wet! I didn't even think about that. They're going to notice it and wonder."

CHAPTER 21

WHEN SHE GOT BACK HOME IN THE TWILIGHT, LAXMAN, Archana, and Sachin were standing on the tufty, unmowed lawn, chatting with another Indian man in office clothes. Gita didn't recognize him, but this intrusion, on an already strange day, unnerved her.

"Ah, you must be Sachinji's better half," the man said, clasping her hand as she came out of the car. He had a perfect Indian male face, the sort one might see on a frieze in a temple. Flawless skating-rink skin. Large eyes and a broad nose just flat enough not to be obtrusive. Leonine, curly, healthy hair. Wide shoulders and a firm stance in his white shirt and navy-blue pants, an expensive-looking maroon tie with a white snowflake pattern hanging from his thick neck.

"Did you go for a swim or something?" Archana asked.

"No," Gita said with a high laugh. "The salon—I'd had an appointment for weeks and they give you a shampoo afterward."

"Salon. That's the same as a beauty parlor?" Archana asked.

"Yes."

"Your wife is glowing," Archana said, turning to Laxman and Sachin.

"Hardly," Gita said, "the sunset here is always gorgeous—this slanting northern light, the oak trees."

"That's why we came out of the house," the new Indian man said.

The man's name was Malhotra—and he was, it turned out, Laxman's prospective business partner. He had driven an hour and a half from Detroit after leaving work early. "I wanted to see my friend," Malhotra said.

"He means he again wants to be beaten at tennis!" Laxman roared, slapping Malhotra's broad back.

Gita went over to Sachin, who had slipped away from the group to move a shovel that was resting near the front door. She noticed he had wet patches under his armpits and smelled sharply of nerves. "Accha, you should go to Flint tomorrow," she whispered. That was where the bottle plant was located. "I'll stay with them."

"Are you sure?" he said. "They might ask you to drive them to Detroit."

"I'm sure," she said. "I love you."

Malhotra joined them for dinner. Malhotra was a consultant at Arthur Andersen, but his dream, he said—after years of consulting with soft-drink companies in America—was to set up a plant of his own in India. "I didn't know you'd invented this design!" Malhotra said to Sachin as Gita brought out a sample 875 ml bottle to the dinner table. "You must be a rich man!"

Sachin muttered that he had only received a token dollar from his company, which owned the patent. But Gita could tell he was delighted. His self-worth was tied to his work and his invention, and he became silent around his bottle, as if the bottle freed him of the need to prove himself in other ways. He sat lightly rocking on his chair.

"What's it got in it, though—stool?" Archana asked, only half in jest.

"Mustard," Gita said.

"It's old and has been sitting out," Sachin said. "So I wouldn't try it if I were you."

"Wow, and such delicious food!" Malhotra said, digging into the reheated rajma. "Marvelous, just marvelous—you have marvelous relatives," he said to Laxman.

"Mmm," Laxman grunted, not unhappily.

"So you have no desire to go back to India, Sachinji?" Malhotra said. "With your expertise—"

Was this what Laxman was hoping for? Gita wondered. A three-way initiative—with one partner being her *husband*? Could Laxman be so shameless? Why did he need his hands in—on—everything? There he sat, rudely, at the head of the table, a muscular ape mashing his rice with a spoon and mixing it violently with the rajma and making cud-chewing sounds with his mouth open. Not just the mouth—the top button of his shirt was undone as well and an ivy shaft of black hair peeped out. His uncouthness was astonishing.

Sachin deflected the question about moving to India ("Someday," he said) and instead talked about the saturation point Coke and Pepsi were reaching in the US and how they would need to seek new markets in Asia and Africa, a potential threat to other soft-drink makers in those countries.

"But the whole advantage of India," Malhotra reminded Sachin, "is that Coke won't come back there." In the 1970s, Coke had departed from India after refusing to divulge its formula to the socialist government. "That's why I'm drawn particularly to that sector," Malhotra said. "Yes, I've tried Campa and Thums Up, but these are second-class drinks. We need to utilize our own natural flavors—amla, bel, lassi, mango—and carbonate them in the same way. There's a big untapped demand for this."

"But if things liberalize, then Pepsi and Coke will rush right back," Sachin reminded him.

"There's no chance of that under the Congress," Laxman said.

"And your own brother will be able to inform us if anything is about to chage," Malhotra said to Laxman, referring to Bhagat, a former Congress MLA.

"Yes, he can help as needed," Laxman said.

As the evening progressed, Malhotra moved on to a second and then a third glass of whiskey. They relocated to the formal drawing room, where Malhotra became expansive. "You see, Gitaji, the kids are the right age to move back, that's another reason I'm doing this. How old are yours? Ah, I thought they might be at Exeter or Andover? I see. Anyway, the kids are the right age. If I wait too long, they'll be such firangis that I'll have to put them in the American School in Delhi. Then they might as well go to school in America. But at this age they could easily join an Indian school, learn Hindi properly. I'm a Modernite myself and I think they offered me a wonderful education." His accent was becoming more Indian with every sentence.

Gita asked if he had known a Hari Taneja—her brother—at Modern.

"What batch?" Malhotra asked.

When Gita told him, he said, "No, but I'm sure I'll recognize him if I see him. We were a coed school, so we were always looking at the girls, weren't we?" he said, winking at Laxman.

"How much times have changed," Gita said. "My mama said that, in college in Lahore, when girls were first admitted, the boys would sit in the front row and the girls would come in after the lecture started and sit in the back. Then the girls would leave before the lecture ended. He never even saw the girls!"

Archana said, "This cardamom cake you made is tasty, Gita—just missing a little sugar."

Gita glared at her but Archana didn't notice.

"But India changes, it progresses," Malhotra said. "That's what I'm saying, Sachinji. Here—"

Gita suddenly understood what was going on with this bloodless, handsome man: He had been passed over for promotion. His career here had tanked. Gita had seen this with the two other Indian men they knew who had chosen to move back. Rejected by the US, they played up their newfound power in their little suzerainties in a poor country. But this was meant to hide their failure in the first world—the only world that mattered to them. Why else would this guy be clutching at straws—at a man like Laxman?

Sachin asked Malhotra more questions about his consulting work with Tropicana in the US, but Laxman interrupted. "First, hear what Vir has to say about India. It'll be good for you also, Sachin."

Sachin glowered, but again, neither Laxman nor Malhotra appeared to notice.

"I don't have any gyaan," Malhotra said, like a man who in fact has a lot. "But I will say this—we people are the most privileged individuals of our own country. Why are we so afraid of India?"

"What does your wife think?" Gita asked.

"Ah, Gitaji, that's the issue. She doesn't want to move back."

All their shoes were off; they wore socks in the overlit living room, which made the outside feel only darker.

Malhotra explained that his wife was afraid of living with her in-laws.

"But that's a valid issue for us women," Gita said.

"What do you have to complain about?" Archana asked Gita sharply.

Malhotra papered it over. "See, in our family—and especially in hers—there are a lot of disputes. But I'm trying to convince her."

"With us it's the opposite," Sachin said suddenly. "Gita has always wanted to move back more than me. Maybe she and I should divide the distance and live in London."

"Nonsense," Gita said. "You see, Malhotraji, I'd be happy anywhere. I have that capacity. I'll go wherever my husband needs to go for work. But it's true, yes, my parents are in Delhi, they're getting old. That's not a concern for your wife?"

"Ha, as if she loves her parents."

There was something ugly and unseemly about how he criticized his absent wife. Gita had the funny idea now that this monstrous woman was probably just a small Gujarati housewife—one on whom Malhotra had projected his own massive ambivalences.

He was as torn up inside as his face was smooth.

"Don't forget your carpets!" Sachin said as Malhotra began to take his leave.

Sachin and Laxman helped load the carpets into the trunk of Malhotra's sedan.

Before drunkenly lowering himself into the driver's seat, Malhotra invited them all to his home in Detroit for dinner. "You must also come, Gitaji. You'll get along famously with my wife, Simranpreet. Talk some sense into her, please?"

"We will definitely come," Archana said, beaming.

"I really want to make this work," Malhotra said. But it was Sachin's hand he accidentally clasped, not Laxman's, as he said those words.

When Malhotra drove away, Sachin said to Laxman, "Does he have a business interest in carpets too?"

Then, when Gita and he were alone in the bedroom, Sachin—sitting up in a circle of lamplight with a thickly underlined copy of *Future Shock* on the slope of his knees, his new specs low on his nose—said, "You know, if you want to move back, it might not be a bad idea, at first, to explore this venture with Laxman and Malhotra."

Gita glared at him.

"Arre, I was just joking!" Sachin said with a sputtering laugh.

"It's not funny," she said, leaning toward him and giving him a relieved good-night kiss.

CHAPTER 22

GITA NOTICED THAT LAXMAN WAS IN A FOUL MOOD THE next day. She herself was in a foul mood, having stayed home with her guests. She brewed them morning tea and sat with them at the kitchen table as they offered their inane opinions about American culture. But Archana, looking at the onions in their webbing of cloth from the grocery store, said, "Pyaaz tera nakhra," and this made Gita laugh.

Gita drove them to the fancy mall in Saginaw, thirty minutes away. As Laxman and Archana grazed the aisles of Hudson's department store, she got turned on thinking of Hector.

On the car ride back, Archana, sitting in the front with Gita, wanted to know the history of the old stone church they passed; whether the man tending to a hedge in a yard with a long metal tool was a gardener or the homeowner himself; and why, apart from that man, there was not a soul to be seen on the streets. She was, at least, curious about things, Gita thought, even if she made withering comments. "Look at that old lady—she's putting on gloves so she can pick up her dog's shit!"

Laxman, meanwhile, was sullen in the back. "What's this smell?" he asked, sniffing.

"The car is new," Gita said.

"All cars smell like this here," he said. "Archana and I can go to Detroit by train, no?" he asked.

"Arre, we'll take you," Gita said.

"But you both have work," Laxman said.

"Well, I'm curious to meet Malhotra's wife, actually," Gita said. "He made such a houwa out of her."

"Ha," Laxman said.

Two days later, they drove toward Detroit together. Archana and Laxman wore their best clothes, with Laxman dressed in a bulky black suit dotted with dandruff on the shoulders. He had also gelled his thinning hair and was blinking his droopy, off-center eyes (his right one was always apparently a little higher than the left, with the mouth slanting in the opposite direction into a permanent sneer).

"You don't need to dress this formally for dinner in this country," Gita said as they waited by the front door for Sachin to come out.

When Archana asked Gita how long the drive would take, Laxman snapped, "Don't speak so loudly."

"You shut up," Archana said.

On the way there, Laxman and Sachin were quiet, while Gita and Archana gossiped giddily about family members in A-19, Gita turning around in the passenger seat. "And then he fell over, he was so drunk—" They had found a relative they agreed on.

The house they pulled up to in the northern Detroit suburb of Birmingham was an astonishment.

It was a low, two-story brick structure with many wings—a mansion, really. Its wildly landscaped lawn looked teleported from fifteenth-century England, with stone paths, a stone well with a steel bucket hanging over it, and dizzying patches of hydrangeas that were illuminated in flashes by the car's headlights.

Malhotra and his wife, Simranpreet, came to the door. "Call me Cindy," Simranpreet said in a smoky smooth American accent: She was wearing a white dress with white strapped sandals. Malhotra and "Cindy" led them into a living room that was decorated with marvelous Asian chests, vases, and paintings on what seemed to be eggshells. "This is our Oriental living room," Cindy explained. "I hope you don't mind if we sit here. We've made you Chinese food, so we thought this would suit better." She was sinuous and pretty, especially in motion. She was dark, very dark, with stylishly graying hair (though she must have been in her early forties), and had obviously exercised herself into slimness; Gita could see the muscles rippling in her arms as she offered dried lotus root crackers around. "A dear friend brought these over from Hong Kong," Cindy said. She spoke such authoritative accented English that it seemed impossible that the earthy consonants of Hindi or Punjabi had ever lolled on her tongue.

"Suzy and Anna, touch Uncle and Auntie's feet," Malhotra said to his two little daughters, perhaps ten and eight, who had walked into the room. Louche and relaxed, Malhotra wore a glossy shirt with light blue stripes but had rolled up the sleeves.

"Your daughters have American names?" Archana asked. "Jeete raho," she said, blessing both the genuflecting girls.

"No, Auntie, our Indian names are Supriya and Anita," the older one said in an American accent as she bent down mechanically before Laxman's feet. She was all length and no beauty at this time. The younger one, fair and plump, had a slyer face.

"One of our sisters-in-law is named Supriya," Gita said.

"We should also call her Suzy!" Laxman said with a laugh.

Malhotra roared.

As they spread out on a series of divans, Gita was flummoxed: Why would this man wish to leave this perfect castle he had constructed for himself in the West? This wasn't the home of a failure.

"I love your house," Gita said, genuinely, to Cindy, approaching her as she hovered by a chest on which more snacks were kept. "This painting—the Buddha, the subtle rainbow hues—is magnificent."

"You should have heard Val bargaining over it in Hong Kong," Cindy said. Who was Val? "The woman kept saying, 'Are you going to make me a bank crook?'" Cindy said. "I was so confused until I realized she was saying 'bankrupt.' That's the only line of English she knew. We walked away only to come back at the last minute before going to the airport—isn't that right, Val?" she said, turning to Malhotra.

So here, in the US, Vir Malhotra had become Val Malhotra. Gita had heard of such couples who erased their Indianness. She glanced admiringly at Cindy's cinched and belted white-clothed waist. Her slender brown legs were exposed. Turning around on instinct, Gita caught sight of Laxman—sitting on the edge of a leather reading chair, his hands on his thighs—staring at Cindy's legs. He quickly shifted his gaze to a painting.

"You and I are going to be good friends," Gita said, suddenly looping her arm into Cindy's. "You must show me your whole house. You have exquisite taste."

Cindy waved it off with the glassy giggle of a Delhi schoolgirl.

"No—seriously—did you do this all yourself?" Gita asked.

A few minutes later, Cindy was narrating the story of each object in each room. There was, of course, an "Indian" room, but it was all either Rajasthani curios (puppets, toy camels, musician figurines) or authentically scuffed-looking sculptures of Ganesh and Krishan. Cindy said, "You know, I just adore the way they make these blankets in Jaipur. I thought, why not put one on the wall?" As she spoke, her manner relaxed and more Indianisms escaped her mouth. "Beta, what are you doing here?" she asked ten-year-old Suzy, who had wandered in, perhaps to overhear the women. "Tell your sister to go and eat also, nah," she said, her accent breaking again.

So many selves, Gita thought. "Did you do your schooling in Delhi?" she asked as they walked back to the Chinese room.

"Yes, Loreto."

"And college also?"

"Delhi University," Cindy said vaguely.

But these were obviously questions Cindy didn't like answering because, for the rest of the evening, she seemed to keep her distance, fluttering from the well-appointed kitchen—with its massive central island and glass doors looking into the back garden with its shimmering koi pond—to the living room, asking people if she could refresh their drinks and making small talk with Archana and Laxman about how they were liking the Midwest. Gita could hear Archana's accent turning American as she answered Cindy's questions.

These centerless Indians! Gita thought.

The men got up and walked with Malhotra toward the bar, where he showed off his selection of whiskeys as well as a special table which, by lifting a series of flaps, could be transformed into a chessboard, a backgammon set, and a checkers surface. "We had it designed," he said. "We like to play games and drink eggnog when it snows."

"Do you think you'll wish to continue living part of the year here?" Laxman asked. "I can manage affairs from Delhi."

"No. We love this house, but if we relocate to India, we have to do it properly. Still, I wanted you to see this place. Can you understand why my wife is attached to it? And she herself is doing very well at GM. She's a director of market research." He sighed. "The golden handcuffs of America!"

"You can get an even bigger bungalow than this in Modern Colony," Laxman said. "With a full staff also."

"Please talk to her," Malhotra said.

"And she could also start her own business," Laxman said. "Archana runs one," he added, immediately regretting that he had compared Archana's small-time (and occasional) baking business to Cindy's work at an auto manufacturer.

"Tell her that also," Malhotra said, distractedly.

The women, meanwhile, were still talking among themselves in the Chinese room, Archana lounging with her arms spread wide and her butt pressed against one end of the divan—she liked to dramatize her drunkenness. "So you're thinking of moving back?" Archana asked Cindy.

"Oh, God, Val talks about it every bloody year. He imagines we'll get an army of maids if he moves. And also, he doesn't want the girls to become American. To which I say: *Darling, you and I* are *bloody American!*"

"You do sound very American," Archana said in her naughty direct way.

Cindy ignored this. "Why are we so afraid of change? We make these big journeys—we're desperate to set out on them—and when we reach our destinations we want to run back and pretend nothing has changed? Bah!" she almost spat. "You have to look forward. The world is changing. Being Indian isn't what it once was. All over the world we used to be disrespected as people. But here we're liked. They see us the way they see Jews—smart, educated, hardworking. My coworkers in my department in GM—they're mostly Jews, mind you—they call me a 'HinJew.'"

"Or a ThinJew," Archana said with a giggle.

"It doesn't matter to them that I'm a woman. Would this be possible in India? Could my daughters become professionals there?"

Gita said, "But sometimes it seems to me that Americans are much more sexist in their daily lives. They see women as objects—they hire you as a secretary and then all they talk about is your ass." She held up her hand to keep Cindy's response at bay. "I've heard all of Sachin's coworkers talk like this, even the one Mormon in their office. When I looked for a gynie, every single one was a man—whereas we have so many woman doctors in India. And would they ever have a woman president in this country? Whereas we've had Indira Gandhi."

"And look at what *wonderful* things she did for India," Cindy said sarcastically.

"Some of it was needed," Archana said.

"I'm surprised to hear you say that—forcing sterilizations?" Cindy said. "Destroying slums? Throwing opposition members in jail?"

"You get a biased view from here," Archana said.

"That's what people always claim—don't mind my saying—but maybe one closes one's eyes when one is there," Cindy said.

"It wasn't all good and it wasn't all bad," Gita said, being conciliatory.

"Exactly," said Archana.

"But we know Indira didn't become PM because she's a woman," Cindy said. "She's a name."

"Many ladies are becoming professionals now," Archana said. "Most of my friends work."

"I should tell you one thing, about Val," Cindy said, changing the subject. "Though he's sweet, he can be quite moody. I've had to fight with him about everything in this house," she added, laughing. "Of course, once a thing is here, he likes it even more than me." She nodded toward the three men, who were gathered around the game table.

"That sounds familiar to me!" Gita said. "But it seems like his mind is made up about India, but yours is not?"

"It's a life-changing decision," she said. "One can't make it impulsively. And what would we do with all these items?" Cindy swept her arm around the room.

"They'd make you pay for all of it," Gita said, referring to India's customs duties.

"Exactly," Cindy said. "India begins at the airport—the bribes, the cost, the filth. Instead of welcoming people like us back, they want to make us pay for the sin of returning. I've told Val he can handle all of this nonsense."

"Your parents would be happy," Gita said.

"I think they're happier I'm here!" Cindy snorted.

"How come?" Archana asked, gladly playing second fiddle to Gita.

"It's a complicated family situation," Cindy said with another laugh, this one more brittle.

"You have brothers and sisters?" Gita asked.

"I'm an only child—so not that kind of complication," Cindy said, her eyes brightening.

"So your mummy and daddy are all alone?" Archana asked. "That's not correct."

"I must go check on dinner," Cindy said, and got up suddenly and left the room.

"We really interrogated her, yaar," Gita whispered to Archana, who grinned back. An unlikely friendship was developing between them. Gita had never liked Archana before; maybe she didn't like her now, either, but Gita felt she was intelligent. Married to the right man, in the right family, she would have blossomed.

And there was a "Mexican" room! They sat at a long table that appeared to be made from salvaged wood. Around them, on sideboards, lay clusters of huge patterned palm baskets and stick monsters that Cindy explained were from Oaxaca—a riot of primary colors that seemed to both crowd and simplify the world. "This was a door of a Detroit church in the 1800s," Cindy said, knocking on the dining table. "I came across it at a sale at an antique store in Ann Arbor and I immediately phoned Val and told him I was buying it."

"How do you have the energy to do all this?" Gita asked. "With your work?"

Cindy's face crinkled into a smile. "One has to make one's surroundings nice."

Talk finally turned to work. "So the factory's all ready, right?" Malhotra asked Laxman, in his childishly serious way, one eyebrow raised. He had drunk less than the night before.

"Absolutely," Laxman said. "And we can provide you a big service flat to start with."

"Which part of Delhi will this be in?" Sachin asked.

"I will arrange a rental for you in South Extension One," Laxman said. "My role is to make the homecoming as smooth for you and the girls as possible. And my niece is a teacher at DPS RK Puram, so admission won't be a problem." Laxman went on, "I know you have a lot to give up if you leave here, but, honestly—and I tell Sachin this too—India needs people like you. You have the expertise; you love the country. Yes, you might lack a few of the material comforts of America, but you can bring all these appliances with you. I can talk to my brother about the customs issue as well."

"The only thing you must be extra-careful about is the kind of people you deal with," Gita said, looking at Malhotra. Malhotra was seated at the head of the table, and Gita was to his left. "Most Indians are untrustworthy."

Cindy laughed.

"But—" Laxman started.

"I'm not talking about you," Gita said. "But others. Indians become very straightforward after living in the US for years. Also, people in India think nothing of interfering with you and offering advice."

"But that's always been true," Laxman said, grinning. "That's why you have a person like me there. I'll deal with the MCD, the government, the permits."

"I'm also planning to be involved," Cindy said, suddenly. "I'll run the finance side. But I've told Val that if there's any hera-feri"—she said it like a firang—"we'll pack up and go. We don't want to compromise our principles."

Now she began to ask Laxman a series of quick-fire detailed questions, almost as if they were at a board meeting, the Oaxacan figurines a decoy, a distraction. What was the exact demand for soft drinks in India at present? Could Laxman estimate the market? Was the demand seasonal? Wouldn't Campa and Thums Up throw up barriers to entry? What was the market cap of those companies? With interest rates so high in India—and the taxation—would a loan even be worthwhile? Which Indian bank would float it?

So this must be the Cindy of GM, Gita thought. Gita tried to meet Sachin's eyes but he kept slurping the terrible jaundice-colored sweet-corn soup: Food was clearly not one of the Malhotras' strengths.

Laxman, to Gita's surprise, was able to rally back quick replies, even if his insistent name-dropping amounted to little more than bluster. But with each response, Gita reminded herself: *I am going to tell Cindy about Laxman's creepiness.*

Hadn't Laxman considered that she might find ways to avenge herself? But then he had tried to keep her and Sachin from attending this dinner.

Cindy laughed at one of Laxman's answers. "Well, Mr. Chopra, we need to be more specific than that!" She shot a look at Val. "Are you taking notes?"

Gita wondered why Sachin wasn't speaking. As she turned to face him, he flared out his nostrils and made a kind of comical grimace with his face. And she realized it wasn't Laxman whom he found annoying but this interrogating, overly smart woman.

CHAPTER 23

ON THEIR LAST DAY IN MIDLAND, LAXMAN AND ARCHANA asked Gita to take them to an Indian store to buy 220V appliances.

Since the dinner with Cindy and Malhotra, they had been serious and morose.

Gita ended up driving them to Flint, an hour away, where two Indian stores glowered at each other from opposite sides of the same street.

You had to drive an hour from Midland to get anywhere worthwhile.

Once they were in the first store, Raj Electronics, with its smell of stale spices and look of imminent plunder, both Laxman and Archana commented on how second-rate and scratched everything looked.

"I didn't like that Cindy-preet female," Archana said to no one in particular as she strolled the aisles, which bulged with chiffon saris, mixies, ice-cream makers, two-in-ones, TVs, radios, spices, and tea bags: Indian culture boiled down to its most bourgeois essence. "Such attitude, I mean, we're doing business with them—is this a way to question us, in their own house?"

Laxman, meanwhile, was in a state of confusion. He didn't know if he'd succeeded or failed with the Malhotras. And if he had succeeded, did he want to deal with this icy, interfering wife?

More importantly, had Malhotra just used him to smuggle carpets into the US?

This confusion, this oscillation, filled him with nervous energy, and he felt aroused again in Gita's presence, her teasing bob cut and angular, boxy face and expensive perfume. He kept turning to look at her and he didn't care that his stares made Gita shifty.

"But you got along with her, huh?" Archana asked Gita, idly lifting a packet of Marie biscuits.

Gita said, "Well, I thought she was a little pseudo—and what a weird laugh she has!—but obviously she's intelligent."

"You all become a little pseudo in the US," Archana said.

Gita didn't dignify this with a response but walked deeper into the store, seeking comfort in the high-wattage colors of the synthetic saris on sale.

When she turned around, Laxman was having an aggressively friendly conversation with the Gujarati shopkeeper, boasting about the achievements of his father, SP Chopra. It was with these people—not the Vals and Cindys of the world—that Laxman truly belonged.

Soon after, Gita called Cindy, and the two of them became friends. Cindy, of course, had seen right through Laxman, and said on the phone, laughing, "It was as if my legs were having a separate conversation with him," and then, "Oh, forget these louts, tell me, which weekend are you free?"

When Gita and Cindy met for lunch, Cindy apologized for her moments of strange frigidity during that first dinner. "Indians are always trying to place you—where did you go to school, what did your father do, where do you live—and I thought you were also doing that."

Cindy was the first true Indian friend Gita made in the US—and in some ways she was as un- or anti-Indian as could be, a sort of enfant terrible even by the standards of Delhi's rich set. Gita found she could talk to Cindy about anything, and the two women began to meet regularly. The shuttled between each other's houses; and they even took a swimming class for fraidy-cats together. Between Cindy and Hector and her job, Gita felt she had found a footing in this world. But then this, and everything else, was cut short—

CHAPTER 24

"WHY IS GITA COMING BACK AGAIN SO SOON?" KARISHMA was asking Archana and Laxman.

They were all seated in a crowd in the main drawing room of A-19.

"Who?" Laxman asked. Two months had passed since his visit to the US.

"Gita and Sachin," Karishma said. She lowered her head on her tense neck and blinked her eyes slowly at the ground as if rummaging for something behind her lids. She was wearing a green sari, her black hair plastered to her forehead from sweat, and sat upright with her hands on her lap. She always had a strong, alien, uncomfortable posture. "They said in a letter that they're coming for vacation in one month's time," she continued, speaking into the galactic mess of mineral dots on the gray terrazzo floor.

"But Gita was just here!" Laxman exclaimed.

"That's why I was asking," she said.

"They must be considering adoption," Laxman said. "Did they mention this?"

"No," she said.

Laxman regained his composure and began blustering. "I'm sure Sachin's looking for opportunities here. See, Indians go there with big ideas, but they forget that they are, at the end of the day, Indians. The white man is happy if you're his slave, but after a certain point you can't rise ..." But even as he spoke, Laxman was thinking, *I'm far from the center of things. Sachin didn't write to me, and Malhotra has stopped phoning me as well. Why do I fail at everything?* When he bared his small teeth at attractive Karishma, she too looked away.

Since his return to A-19, Laxman had been depressed. The lush guest bedrooms of Midland and Chicago and Toronto had given way to a cramped joint family setup, with Laxman's nuclear family sequestered in an apartment in the back building of the complex along with Brij and Karishma's family. On the second floor, three dark rooms in a row opened out into a shared veranda–drawing room. Laxman and Archana slept in one boxy room; their two daughters in the next room, sharing bunk beds with Brij and Karishma's two boys; and Brij and Karishma themselves in the farthest room. It was like living in a dormitory. The toilet was in bad shape, always wet, humid like the inside of a sick mouth. Water lapsed from the taps in thin, sputtering streams. The flush toiled weakly. One morning Laxman had found a mouse drowned in the pot and wondered if he was hallucinating.

And there was no privacy. Every few nights, Laxman and Archana were woken by the sound of Brij upbraiding Karishma—or worse.

"I'm a good woman!" Karishma had shouted just two nights before, her shrieks followed by thumping, scuffling, creaking, jostling, fumbling, thudding, an applause of coughs from the children's room ... Laxman had swung his feet off his bed. "I can't sleep this way," he'd said to Archana, "and what about the kids? Let me talk to Brij." It was hard to believe this man was little absent-minded Sachin's real brother.

To Laxman's surprise, Archana said, "Sit back down. It's not your business or my business—do you want them to interfere with us?"

Laxman muttered, "I thought you had more compassion than that."

What he meant was: *I thought you and Karishma were best friends*. Since Archana had returned from the US, the two women spent a great deal of time together in the kitchen laughing hysterically and plotting against the men (so Laxman thought, jealously). They were collaborating on a baking business operated out of a neighbor's kitchen. Once Archana had even told Laxman that Karishma was a "prettier" and "smarter" version of herself, the poor thing would have been so "unstimulated" in those small towns and villages where Brij was posted, the men would have all gaped at her.

"You go to sleep," Archana said, now.

And for once, because he was depressed, he complied.

Laxman had always believed that, as the son of a great man, he was destined for greatness. Posted with a cosmetics company in the small town of Saharanpur right after his marriage, he had been reluctant at first to return to Delhi—he was a big man in a small town—but Archana had convinced him otherwise. "You should enter politics," she had said, flattering him when in fact she simply desired to live in a city.

And what had come of that move? After months of buttering up his politician brother, Bhagat, in Delhi, Bhagat had effectively blocked his entrance into the Congress. Laxman's bobby-pin factory never took off and mounds of small matchbox-sized cases were returned, unsold, from the wholesalers. And now Laxman's attempt to snare an Indian businessman in America, with his American dollars, had apparently failed too.

What could he do? He could involve himself with meeting senior committee members of the Sangathan. He could assist in overseeing various schemes at schools and charitable institutions under the Sangathan's auspices ... but what was the point? History was transpiring elsewhere. But where exactly? In the US, where Ronald Reagan was taking his war with the USSR into space? In Punjab, which some of his wife's family had fled for Delhi and Bombay after the militancy began? In the Janata Party, jailed first by Indira and then decimated by elections? In the lumbering industrial houses, which complained about the bureaucracy while cunningly co-opting it? History, he felt, had capital letters when his father was alive. Now was a time of repetition and vagueness. He could have gone into the army if he had wished to be at the burning seam of history, places where the past and future were being rewritten through conflict. But the discipline of the army—the servility to one's seniors—appalled him. Nor was one guaranteed a satisfactory posting.

Laxman's time became filled again with lust. Where there is no History, Desire rushes in. Desire being another way of remaking History.

In the flat, one day, Laxman overheard Karishma asking Brij, "Are Gita and Sachin going to stay with us?"

Laxman was pretending to look at the accounts for his bobby-pin business on the sofa in their rectangular common drawing room. But the numbers on the paper were meaningless. His business was dead.

"Of course, they must stay here," Brij said in his jaunty British way, absently plucking an epaulet on his shirt. "He's my brother, after all."

"We can put mattresses for them out here," Karishma said.

"Nonsense! They can take our room and we can sleep on mattresses here. Or the children can sleep out here. They're our special guests from America!"

Karishma fell silent.

Space closing up. That's what Laxman felt. Like his own throat being squeezed. He kept poring over the yellow crumbling paper on his lap.

CHAPTER 25

AND SO, ONLY TWO MONTHS AFTER THE MEETING OF THE relatives in Michigan, Gita and Sachin came to visit A-19.

Much to everyone's relief, they had decided to stay with Gita's parents. No complicated abacusing of bodies in A-19 would be required to accommodate them.

As Sachin sat talking on the sofa of the Brij-Laxman drawing room, a white cup and saucer of tea on his lap, Laxman was surprised by the change in his face in mere months. He was haggard, his hair uncut and long, the sideburns forming such large Ls that it looked as if he were wearing an aviator's helmet. But if his eyes were tired, his voice was excited, the words pouring out fast. "I know it's crowded but I don't think you people appreciate how nice it is that you all live together," he said, leaning back a little so that the cup clattered. "Seeing you and Archana reminded me how much I miss family. That's why we are visiting. And now I can also see how much more exciting it is to work here."

Has he lost his mind? Laxman thought.

Archana said, slyly, "Accha, that's wonderful news. So you had a change of heart about our poor country?" She posed the question meaningfully to Gita, who had been oddly silent in the itchy crackling bundle of her black-and-white sari, large sunglasses jammed on the top of her head. But Gita, who had had a glazed look about her the entire time, just nodded, with her wide lips slightly open.

"No change of heart," Sachin said. "It's so special for me to see my nephews." He glanced fondly at them. Laxman's and Brij's kids were in a corner of the room, in a state of delirium about a remote-controlled Fisher-Price car their chacha and chachi had brought them, along with cassettes of Simon & Garfunkel songs.

"Then you must live here with us, brother!" Brij exclaimed. He got up dramatically to fling open a window. He wore his signature white pants. His goatee was trimmed neatly against his jawline.

"I'd like to, obviously, someday, but where's the space?" Sachin asked.

"Then build on the roof!" Brij said.

Laxman wanted to kill him.

Brij then started interrogating his younger brother about schools and colleges in the US. He said he kept a scrapbook full of information about "educational institutions all over the world" and wanted to fill in the gaps.

"Oh ho, do you have to do it now?" Karishma asked Brij, coming in with a bowl of namkeen.

"How often do I get to see my brother?" Brij snapped.

"When they're older, you should send Mohit and Deepak abroad!" Sachin said, awkwardly waving at his nephews, who were now ten and seven.

"You know, brother, not all of us can afford that," Brij said.

"They're smart boys—" Sachin began.

"It's just for his personal collection," Karishma said, warning Sachin with her eyes.

What a strange man Brij was! Laxman thought, watching this exchange. Fastidious about dress, sporting an ink-black goatee, he collected all sorts of things: stamps, coins, and now the names, student body sizes, and founding dates of various educational institutions. When he wasn't in a rage at his wife or children, he would bring out his scrapbooks and examine them, stroking the pages with a tenderness otherwise absent from his life.

"You bloody duffers," Brij said to his sons. "Don't get any bloody ideas into your head."

Before Sachin and Gita left, Laxman took Sachin aside. "Everything's OK in the US?" he asked. "If you're having work issues, let me know, I can give you advice."

Sachin kept his eyes on his nephews in the corner. "Nothing like that."

"But if there are, remember we're family—"

"You know, Laxman," Sachin said, "I told you there are no work issues. Why do you keep insisting? People in this family interfere too much."

It was that day that Laxman began to hate Sachin too.

CHAPTER 26

IN FACT, GITA AND SACHIN HAD COME TO INDIA BECAUSE things had become unbearable between them in the US.

It had started when Sachin had discovered a letter from Hector to Gita.

Hector had mailed it to the offices of *Bay City Monthly*, and the magazine had forwarded it to Gita's home address. Something about the envelope, its lightness, the desperate handwriting on the envelope, must have aroused Sachin's suspicions, because he scratched it open.

Sachin's breach had been retroactively justified by the letter's contents:

My Dear Marketing Mistress ...

"I barely know him," Gita insisted when Sachin confronted her in their living room. "He's lonely and has a crush on me."

"So, according to you," Sachin said, sitting down on the sofa, rubbing his large hands together—a small man with a large face and large hands and floppy, healthy hair—"it's all made up."

"If he has mental problems, what can I do?" Gita said.

"Let me speak to him."

"Better to leave such people alone," Gita said, standing before Sachin and shaking her head. "They just want attention—"

"Fuck off!" Sachin roared up from the sofa. "Stop acting. I've met him. I know how you look at him." Sachin had once come out for drinks with Molly and Hector.

"But why would I—"

Sachin held up the letter with its torrent of black inky cursive on nearly translucent paper, bubbles visible where his nib must have burst through the surface with passion. "The guy can barely write English. So this is the kind of man you like? And this is all made up—all the things he says about you, about the visiting relatives, about ... me?" He stood up. "Fuck off, I'm not an idiot."

Gita collapsed on the plump carpet and clutched his feet. "I clasp my hands before you. I really didn't—I promise."

He kicked her in the chest, but more as a gesture than with any real force.

Gita sniffled but was unable to cry.

"You get away from me, you bitch. Get away!"

And he strode off to another wing of the bug-like ranch house.

How little one knows about people one falls in love with! Gita thought, sinking into the carpet. The condition of being in love was itself a kind of passion for the unknown, a coloring-in of the unknown with fantasy. Gita would never have guessed that Hector would write to her at the magazine's office, that he might be foolish or lovelorn enough to pen a love letter at all.

But what had she expected when this had all started?

The next few days were a cycle of recriminations, anger, silences. Sachin started sleeping on the sofa, though Gita had offered him the bedroom, profusely apologizing, trying to think of how to justify it, saying she had been pressured—

"So it did happen?" Sachin asked.

"Not in the way you think," she lied.

Then, at *Bay City*, stealing a moment away from her copyediting, Gita went down to a pay phone on the bricky street corner and called Hector.

"I thought you would feel happy I located a job in Midland," he said moodily. "You can tell him it was a letter for the editor."

"You shouldn't have sent it, Hector—you know that."

"It was delivered to your workplace."

"I'm never going to see you again."

"Gita, you love me," he said.

"Maybe," she said, slamming the phone against its cradle.

Returning from work one day, Sachin's eyes were full of a mysterious angry light. He waited for her to lay the table, then asked, "Was it because I wasn't manly enough for you?"

When Gita looked nonplussed, he repeated it. "I couldn't get you pregnant, so you found a taller brown-looking fellow. Was that your plan? Is that why you were cuddling with me again after all this time?"

And that was when Gita understood the true extent of the damage she'd wrought. Wrapped in her own pain about their childlessness, she had overlooked *his* wounds. "The doctor said there's nothing wrong with you," she said.

"Except I couldn't make you pregnant."

"Sachin, I promise," she said, joining her hands before her.

"Now I know how truly depraved you are. Let the whole world know!"

She feared what he might do next. She feared what *she* had become. How had she transformed from a good Delhi girl into this perpetrator? Suddenly she recalled Laxman's hot eyes in that top-floor room in A-19. Those hot eyes were now her own eyes looking back at Sachin. She was looking at the world through Laxman's eyes.

CHAPTER 27

SACHIN TOLD HER, "I WANT TO GO TO INDIA SOON."

"You should," she said.

"You talk so formally, like an American. *You should*," he mimicked nastily. "And what are *you* going to do?"

She waited.

"No, you're going to come too." He stood close. "I don't give one shit about your second-rate editing job. I want nothing to do with you, but I want you to come with me."

"Have fun in the motherland," Cindy chuckled on the phone to Gita, knowing nothing.

It happened so quickly, after years of planning trips to India together; it happened almost overnight: the calls home, the packing, the gift buying, all of which was left to Gita. Then, on a hot morning, having driven in stuffy silence to Detroit Airport, they took off.

It was their first flight to India together since she had followed him to the US in 1977, a reversal, in fact, of that primary journey—a reversal, Gita thought, sitting in the middle seat, in every sense. On that flight, her first *ever* flight, he had been so sweet and solicitous, letting her have the window seat, lifting the sleepy eyelid of the porthole for her, teaching her how to snap the seat belt and turn on the overhead lights and fans, explaining that they were sitting where they were to be away from the smokers, laughing about the many layers of clothing first-time Indian travelers wore on planes only to be doused in sweat, how his university had "literally begged" Indian students not to bring bistra-bundhs—large bedrolls—when they came to America, that old habit from traveling on Indian trains ... how happy they had been!

But it's only when things are beyond repair that you recognize you'd once been happy. Gita sometimes thought death would be like that too: a long realization of the joy of life. And after that death there would be another death so you would recognize your death too had been joyful. It was a downward staircase of realizations.

Gita did not believe in rebirth. She believed only in increasing stages of regret and longing, the inability to understand what you were experiencing till it was over: seeing one country, for example, from the next.

When she touched her husband's shoulder, he turned his face toward the window, the black window that held a reflection of the two of them, watery, suspended in streaming air.

CHAPTER 28

THEY STAYED NOT AT A-19 BUT WITH GITA'S PARENTS AND brother. This was mainly, it seemed to Gita, because Sachin wanted to be able to deposit her someplace while he went about his business. What was this business? He wasn't always open with her, but soon, to her surprise, he was on a tear through Delhi, reuniting with friends, looking up relatives, poring over land documents ... there seemed to be much to do during this long-overdue homecoming.

And that's what it was: a homecoming. In the Chopra compound, as Gita watched tremulously from the sidelines, Sachin was welcomed back as a conquering hero, a successful engineer, an inventor, a proud descendant of SP Chopra. He wore his loudest Madras prints, he swaggered about, he was impatient with servants and his in-laws, and he puffed his chest out in that short-man way of his. Ram Chacha even threw a party for him at the Modern Colony Club, where a painted sign proclaimed: "HEARTIEST WELCOME TO THE KETCHUP KING!"

Since wounding him, Gita had separated from him and could see him clearly. She understood anew the ways in which he was a younger brother and had depended, almost like a child, on her love. She had been the emotional guide of the relationship, and now, without her, he was looking for other guides.

Family members and "friends"—men who wanted to talk business with Sachin—dropped by the courtyard of her parents' Karol Bagh house. Gita immediately noted the parallel between these fast-talking men and Laxman—how these men were to Sachin what Laxman had been to Malhotra.

"You don't approve of that guy?" Sachin said after one such visit from a friend of a friend who had sketched out big plans for a bottling plant in Maharashtra.

"No, no, of course I do," Gita said, grateful to be addressed at all. Had her parents and brother and brother's family noticed the coldness between husband and wife? But then they hadn't seen Sachin in years, and he was being quite nice to them, referring to her father familiarly as "hazoor." "But won't Laxman be upset if you open a soft-drink business here?" she said.

"Malhotra said they aren't going to pursue it." He paused. "Anyway, I have no desire to move back. This country is fifty years behind." Sachin spoke with American confidence and directness, a directness that seemed all the more discordant in intricate prolix India.

"Of course," Gita said.

At night, in the guest room in her parents' house, Sachin turned threatening again. "I'm going to divorce you. Have you told anyone about what you did? If you tell even one person, I promise I'll immediately divorce you."

"I swear."

"Not even that catty bitch friend of yours, Anamika," he said.

"Godswear."

"*You* can live here," Sachin said. "I've brought you back so you can live here. I see how they all see me. They pity me. They pity us. Have you told them *you're* the one with the problem? Again your mom brought up adoption. Tell her *no*. I don't want a child with you."

She cried a little, just a little, and he turned away in the dark bedroom. It was awful to be so far from someone you loved.

If only he could understand. Hector had not existed—she could see it now. He wasn't real. The smallness of the fling with Hector against the largeness of her life with Sachin ... their families, the two continents ... Hector was like a grain troubling a diamond.

She put her hand on his back and tried to fall asleep.

And when they went to see Sachin's relatives in A-19, Gita was struck anew by the close quarters in which Laxman, Archana, Brij, and Karishma were living.

The shabby shops in the nearby market; the glum black water tankies; the clotheslines savagely crossing the roofs; everything sloping toward death.

Meanwhile, Sachin and Laxman spoke on and on like old friends.

Then Sachin got a surprising, confusing opportunity.

CHAPTER 29

BEFORE SACHIN HAD LEARNED ABOUT GITA'S AFFAIR, HE had been feeling quite relieved.

When Laxman had visited, Sachin's "squish" bottle had been cracking on the conveyor belt. He had been flummoxed by this problem till he had come across a newspaper ad for Ivory Soap that declared, "So soft, it works on a baby's butt." In a moment of insight, Sachin had suggested to the factory manager that the lubricant on the conveyor belt be switched with this soap and—presto!—it had worked.

The revelation of Gita's affair had been like a knife through the chest of a man who has come back exhausted but happy from the battlefield. So *this* is what she'd been doing the whole time he'd been wrapped up with his bottle?

His instinct was to get away from the US, from the site of the crime, of his shame, and in a meeting with his boss, Mike, he had suddenly found himself saying, "Why not look for opportunities to manufacture in India?"

Trident, he knew, was in an intensely cost-cutting-obsessed phase. Its core product—steel cans—was being threatened by the advent of cheap, light aluminum cans. Its attempt to build a resealable can had failed. Executives were now considering a top secret project that would (if implemented correctly) save Trident a whopping $150 million. The project went like this: In 1980, a workers' union at Trident had negotiated a hefty pension package. Trident had agreed. But behind the scenes, executives had put together a computer program to determine which workers were most likely to claim pensions and had started selectively laying them off.

Sachin was proud to be privy to this scheme but also shocked by how immoral he was.

Mike was enthusiastic about the India trip and so Sachin went, taking Gita along. He no longer trusted her to be on her own in the US.

But, in the end, the trip yielded little in terms of business for Trident—the permitting was too complex and expensive for the company to set up a factory in India.

Then Sachin began chatting with his college friend Rishab at a party.

Rishab, a civil engineer, was a famously decent fellow with a pipe-smoking habit. He ran a successful construction company with his brother. "But that business runs itself and I've agreed to take a smaller share," he told Sachin, plucking at his own suspenders. He said he was starting a new business. "The opportunities to build housing for people, especially the poor, in this country are immense. What I would like to do is use the money at my disposal to develop new housing materials."

Sachin said, "It's so strange—that was my father's dream."

"Really?" Rishab said foggily.

"He worked at HUDCO—"

"Yes, yes, of course, I had totally forgotten."

"And he was involved in schemes for prefabricated village housing," Sachin said.

Rishab then began quizzing Sachin on plastic materials that could be blended cheaply with wood. "For our weather patterns here," Rishab said, "we need materials that won't rot."

After a few days of brainstorming together, Rishab said, "Sachin, this is the most excited I've felt about work since we set up that optics lab together in college."

"I've enjoyed it too."

Rishab said, "Think of the difference someone like you can make. You're doing important stuff there, but here you can actually save lives." He then talked about the dilapidated housing he'd encountered during his travels over the country.

As Rishab spoke, Sachin had a glimpse of himself in his first-world castle in Midland while, in India, beggars and their children perished on the street.

Guilt. Is that why he had avoided his homeland for so long? Was India a mirror he hadn't wanted to look into?

"But I'm hardly an expert in housing," Sachin protested.

"You don't need to be. You're an expert in plastics. And you have a sharp mind."

Sachin thought again of his father and his eyes misted: Was it his destiny to complete the work his father had left unfinished upon his sudden death at the age of fifty? Is this where his life had been headed throughout? Was his work with Trident merely a prelude, a polishing of skills before the real work of saving his nation began?

How badly he wanted to do good!

TWO

LAXMAN'S COMPLEX

CHAPTER 30

IN FACT, THINGS BEGAN TO CHANGE IN A-19 AFTER GITA AND Sachin left for the US.

Sachin's talk about returning had set off alarm bells in the complex.

What if they did *move back?* the insecure inhabitants of A-19 wondered. *What about the rest of us?*

Archana told Laxman, "We shouldn't wait."

For some months, Archana had been pushing Laxman to make a decision about housing. One of Laxman's elder brothers, Sukhdev, had moved permanently to Madras to be near his spiritual guru, thus vacating a suite of rooms in the snazzier front building of the family compound. He had left his rooms in terrible shape, refusing even to repair the doors he had dislocated from their hinges with his wrathful slamming. The roof too was sagging and would need reinforcement. After his departure, Laxman's other elder brothers—who, by dint of seniority, already had their own apartments—had told Laxman that if he renovated the rooms, repainted the exteriors, and broke a couple of walls, he could claim this space, on the second floor, as his own private flat. In his depression about his failure in the US, Laxman had refused, but now, egged on by Archana and the threat of Gita and Sachin's return, he agreed to cough up his limited funds. He went to the local State Bank branch and, for the first time, took out from the locker a bundle of cash his father had bequeathed him with a warning to use it only in emergencies—black money from land transactions.

Soon after, Archana and Laxman began speaking to contractors.

Then Laxman received an interesting piece of news.

It happened at the Modern Colony Club.

Ever since Laxman had returned from the US, he had formed a routine with school-and-university-stats-obsessed Brij. On weekdays, after "work"—which for Laxman consisted of whiling time away at the Jeev Sangathan temple—the two men would walk through the robust, old-money greenery of the colony in their shorts, thin racquets plinking against their legs, to play badminton in the club. Then, after a few strenuous sets that involved lots of squeaking Keds and jumping around in the indoor concrete court, they would retire to the club's twitchily tube-lit butterscotch-hued coffee shop to sip nimbu paani.

Sometimes Karishma, who visited the club to play bridge with other women, would join them in the coffee shop as well.

On this particular day, when they sat down, Brij turned to Karishma and said, "Why are you sitting like that? Look at your posture. Are you a lady or a sixer?"

It was true that Karishma sat somewhat mannishly, legs thrown apart, torso leaning backward, so that her small breasts pushed out from under the pink kurti she wore over her white salwar. For a second, she straightened up. Then, instead of offering a retort, she collapsed into herself.

Laxman had been amazed, in the months he'd spent as neighbors with Brij and Karishma, by how compliant she was—then, in other (non-marital) aspects of her life, she projected a blazing and unknowable defiance.

They placed an order for the food, and Brij excused himself to go borrow a volume from the compact dark-paneled club library.

Laxman and Karishma were now alone at the table—a rare occurrence. When a plate of fluffy, large cheese balls arrived—stinking of oil—Laxman pushed the plate toward Karishma, saying, hesitantly, "You're not eating? Have one or two at least."

That wan smile from Karishma—nothing else.

She never spoke to him except in large crowds.

Laxman went on, "And then you complain about how lousy things were in Bhoinda," referring to Brij's previous posting, in a remote village in the wilds of Madhya Pradesh, where he had overseen bamboo-cutting operations in a two-hundred-acre plantation. "You're here, in Delhi, eat and drink and enjoy." He glanced toward the library. "With Brij's job, you're always on the move and you have no idea where you'll get posted next."

"About that, I'm not so worried," Karishma suddenly said, turning her deep black eyes on him.

"What, you like moving? Are you not liking living with your in-laws?"

"No, no, the in-laws are one of the pleasures of being here," Karishma said. There was a mole above her upper lip. Her hair fell forward and around her face, so she had to brush back the moist strands constantly.

Was she being ironic about in-laws? Laxman wondered. He hated not knowing if someone was sly or shy.

By now Brij had emerged from the library, two scratched-looking hardcovers crammed under an armpit, and he was standing by the door of the coffee shop, speaking animatedly to a big-bellied man whose pouchy red eyes looked diseased. This man was a regular at the club to play cards—and was perhaps the most well-liked person in the colony. He even seemed to enjoy cracked Brij's company. (To be liked, you must like others indiscriminately.)

Karishma said, "I don't think we'll move again."

Immediately Laxman was on alert. "Brij is talking about leaving Bijapur Paper again?" Laxman clucked, "He shouldn't act so impulsively." Brij, as Laxman knew, had a habit of submitting his resignation to Bijapur whenever he felt slighted. Luckily for him, none had been accepted. "But if he's burning to do it, there's no issue, we have space here, and he could join me in the bobby-pin business."

Shaking her head the tiniest bit—as if to keep Brij from noting her gestures even from across the room—she said, "No, he's not resigning. But we've decided that Brij will move to the next posting, while the boys and I will stay in Delhi. Their grandparents are here"—Karishma's parents—"but the biggest thing is they're finally in a good school, where they're learning in English." Her eyes flashed toward Brij, whose hand gestures, as he spoke, were becoming more and more crazed, as if he were whipping up an imaginary frond of candy floss. "He hasn't told you?" she asked, quickly.

"He mentioned it," Laxman lied.

Karishma pinched one of her hands with the other. "It's not pukka or anything, but we thought we should try it." Then, looking straight at Laxman: "Actually, please don't tell him I said anything. We're still discussing the issue—I just thought—"

"I will keep your secret," Laxman said. "But eat one cheese ball at least."

That night, in bed, Laxman asked Archana if she knew whether Brij and his family were to be posted out of Delhi.

In the dim room with its gloomy satiny paint, Archana reached behind her and switched off the light. "Where will they go—they've just arrived," she said. "Neither of them want to move anywhere."

"But they have no control over when and where they go," Laxman persisted.

"They'll be stupid to leave now," Archana said. "You don't think they want all these rooms?"

She meant: Since we're moving out soon, they can claim this flat as their own.

Laxman thought: Has Karishma told me a secret that she hasn't shared with Archana?

Then, a few days later, Brij made an announcement at the dinner table.

His training period in Delhi was over, he said, and he was being called back to Bhoinda. "A poacher has been killing elephants in the forest. The roads have been flooded and they can't get any bamboo out. The need my expertise to rectify the issue at the earliest." The kids and Karishma, he said, would stay. "Womenfolk and children will only serve as a distraction," he added, banging a fist on the cheap lacquered deep-brown table that would have been at home in a third-rate Mughlai restaurant. All the people at the table—Laxman, Archana, and the four kids—jumped.

Seven-year-old Deepak, Brij's younger son, started crying. "Don't go, Papa."

Brij turned to Karishma. "I thought you had told him."

Karishma said nothing.

"Papa, but what if you get injured like Sohail Uncle?" A fellow manager who had been trampled by an elephant.

Brij cast his eyes around the table. "What happened to Sohail Uncle was Sohail Uncle's fault," he muttered. "Bugger was using his hunting rifle illegally."

"He's a child," Laxman said.

"When one goes to the heart of the jungle," Brij said, holding up a spoon, "there is always a risk." He put his spoon into a small katori of yogurt.

"It's OK, baba, don't cry," Archana said, coming up to Deepak and touching his small shoulders.

Karishma, however, did not move from her seat.

The next day, Brij began packing up his trunks. He oiled his hunting rifle, and had the servant iron his clothes and buff his boots. Then, a company jeep came to fetch him from the gate of A-19. Its exhaust belched noxious diesel smoke.

As Brij—wearing all white, like an English sahib (only the sola topi was missing)—climbed under the jeep's black fabric canopy, Karishma said to Laxman and Archana, "It was very nice of him to let us stay, it's difficult to be alone on these postings."

To Laxman's amazement, she sounded genuine in her concern for her husband.

CHAPTER 31

WITH BRIJ GONE, A WEIGHT LIFTED OFF THE HOUSEHOLD. Karishma, now free of her husband's tense surveillance, began spending more and more time in the drawing room, where all four kids played freely together after school—impromptu games of rummy, bluff, ludo. At night, if Laxman and Archana were headed out to a social function or a wedding, Archana never neglected to invite Karishma. "You're alone over here and there's a servant who can take care of the children," she would say. "Put on something nice and come with us. You should also make some friends in Delhi."

Karishma often responded, "No, no. You both go and enjoy, what will I do there?"

"Oh ho, are you a young woman or a sati-savitri widow?" Archana asked.

So Laxman, to his own dismay, became the driver of these two females. As he steered his faded blue Fiat to this or that function in South Delhi, Archana sat in the front passenger seat, turning around every few seconds to brightly chat with Karishma, while Karishma, in turn, was bound up in herself in the back, saying little, holding herself awkwardly upright in the center of the long swaying seat, a smile of confusion on her thin lips from Archana's incessant attention. Shifting gears, Laxman glanced into the rearview mirror, with its black rubber lining, and there he caught Karishma's questioning black eyes gazing back at him, the little green bindi on her forehead enhancing the tactility of the brows. Karishma had a brilliant opacity, teeth like individual shields, a taste for flaming red and harsh green saris.

Archana, to his left, kept speaking, issuing endless bulletins from her restless brain, Karishma now bobbing her head up and down and responding with affirmative ohs, which served as rocks for the rapids of Archana's conversation to flow over.

Did Karishma find the talk as oppressive as he did?

But when he looked into the mirror, she did not meet his eye.

CHAPTER 32

IN THE US, GITA AND SACHIN CONTINUED THEIR STANDOFF.

But now there was a wrinkle. In India, Sachin had informally said yes to partnering with his friend Rishab—it was part of the madness of that period, the great rupture in his life caused by Gita's affair. But when he returned to America, reality reasserted itself. His life on this lane with its peacock-fan-shaped Dutch elms was intact. He was "doing well," as people liked to say. He was fond of his pit stops at Freddie's Donuts. He liked his house. He liked his career, the serene, maddening, non-complication of the US. He liked that his work was truly innovative, not just the management of low-level corruption, which is what all work in India amounted to. "But I fear if I stay now," he told his friend Anthony, a Chinese American who had been a classmate at Brooklyn Poly, over the phone, "I'll never go back. What do you think I should do? And it's a rare opportunity to pursue something entirely new. I could never switch lanes like that here." Like Gita, Sachin was an introvert. He didn't have many friends. It was part of their problem as a couple in Michigan.

"As I see it, you're in an unusually flexible position," Anthony—who had four kids!—said. "You don't have kids, so you're not tied to Michigan, and you can always come back."

"I wonder if I'll be able to manage working for myself."

"It's definitely a big pay cut," Anthony agreed. "But you said you have a family home already—and the cost of living is significantly lower."

Then Sachin spoke to Gita.

His large hands were clasped together on his knee, and he looked at her with those keen brown eyes from under his torrential black eyebrows, eyebrows that themselves seemed full of emotion and the turbulence of life, as if to remind her that the sunrise of a clear-eyed gaze was always shadowed by scudding clouds.

"You have to do what's best for you," Gita said, handing him a cup of tea, which he sipped moistly and gratefully.

"What's best for me ... I'm asking for your advice."

His eyes on her. Back to needing her guidance. "You've been a good husband," she said. "I made a mistake. We had so many tough years. And you were my rock, you never complained, I owe you, I love you. You have to do whatever will make you happy." She paused. "Remember, you weren't considering moving back when we first took the trip."

"But that's how things go—one thing leads to another." He looked at her almost accusingly, as if to say: *And this is how we ended up married, you and I. One letter, then two ... then a whole bloody life.*

"Are you sure you'll be OK living with family after all these years?" Gita asked.

"You're asking the wrong question," Sachin said.

She was silent.

"My question was not about whether we'd live with *them*," he said. "I'm asking about India."

"They're one and the same," she said faintly.

"That's not helpful," he said, draining the cup and getting up to put it in the sink.

This was how those twilight conversations went. Gita saw that he was now injured by affection, a hurt child. It was as if all affection were tainted and false.

But really, Sachin was thinking: Could he forgive Gita? What would that forgiveness look like? So much of his introspection happened in his rattling Pontiac, on his drives to work. The gears shifted, the car went silent, a higher speed was achieved. He felt at one with his car, and sometimes he thought the car, which had never betrayed him, was his best friend.

On these drives through Midland, where horse pastures were giving way to malls and motels, Rishab's words rang in his head.

Remember what you always told me? Go there, make your money—but our ultimate responsibility is to this country. It needs us. If people like us go, what future does it have?

But did one *really* owe a country? Sachin wondered. A country didn't have feelings. Did it?

He had studied hard. No one had helped him (well, maybe Vibha and Laxman, when he was leaving, but that was it). Friends and family members had only tried to pull him down. And what could one man do to change the future of a nation?

Then he thought of his grandfather.

He thought about how SP had repeatedly turned down opportunities in the private sector to dedicate himself to the cause of national liberation, how he had taken enormous risks at his bank to siphon funds to freedom fighters even as (out of practicality) he loaned money to British magistrates with his other hand.

And then Sachin thought of Ram Chacha.

Before he had departed for the US this time, Ram had put his hand on his shoulder in the hot, paradisiacal garden of A-19 fumigated by the pollution from the trucks rattling on Mir Taqi Mir Road and said, "You're the star of the family. Come back. We'll welcome you."

"We shouldn't be up here," Karishma was saying to Laxman. Things had progressed quicker than either could have anticipated or even wanted.

It had started when Karishma's younger son, Deepak, seven, fell sick, developing a high fever.

Karishma wasn't, by nature, a worrier, but she'd had no choice but to respond to Deepak's high-pitched whining, bringing him glasses of hot salt water for gargles (though he hated gargling) and dipping towels in a bucket of cold water for compresses. "With such low fever you can easily go to school," Laxman heard her say through her closed bedroom door.

Two days later, she was forced to take back her words.

Deepak's fever had rocketed into the hundreds, and reddish swellings—the telltale sign of mumps—appeared on his jaw.

Laxman watched as a real terror gripped Karishma. She started making frequent, agitated trips down to the main drawing room of the complex to phone doctor-family-friends for medical advice. It was as if her general maternal nonchalance was a cover for deep anxiety.

As the only man in that corner of the house, Laxman took Karishma and Deepak in his car to an allopath and then to his pahalwan (the same pahalwan to whom he had once tried to ferry Gita). The allopath, sitting in a tiny booth full of metal edges and pressing his cold stethoscope into Deepak's chest, scared them all with the idea that an operation may be required, but the pahalwan, who practiced out of a veranda in his home in Kirti Nagar, simply touched the boy's forehead, took his pulse from the neck and the wrist, and prescribed a homemade herbal medicine.

This medicine was so sweet that even from his feverish stupor little Deepak rose over the following days to sip it.

A week later, the swelling subsided; the fever did too. Through a crack in the door, Laxman saw Karishma collapsed next to her son on the bed, a small mountain of towel compresses heaped on the floor.

When she came out of the room a little later, Laxman told her, "Now we should go say thank you to God."

At this time, as it happened, Archana was dealing with a family crisis of her own—her aunt in East Delhi had been diagnosed with stomach cancer, and everyone was flocking toward her house to offer her moral support (and to revel in her bad luck). "You take Karishma and Deepak to the Hanuman Temple," Archana said. "Mona will pick me up when she's coming from Daryaganj."

So, on a Tuesday afternoon, putting his work on hold, Laxman drove Karishma and Deepak out of the house in his Fiat.

Karishma sat next to Laxman—with bony Deepak, who was small for his age, resting between them. Deepak was sucking a bull's-eye, the candy making a repetitive tock-tock sound in his mouth as it alternately bulged out one cheek, then another.

Had Karishma even noticed Laxman's role in healing her son?

"Please convey my regards to Pahalwanji," Karishma said, as the car pulled out of the property gates. But when she put her face into Deepak's brownish hair and inhaled unconsciously, Deepak reared away. "Can you give me more Hriday Shahd, Mama?" he said. Hriday Shahd was the pahalwan's sweet medicine.

"Silly boy," she replied.

They had been planning to visit the Hanuman Mandir in Connaught Place, but as they pulled out of the colony and onto the main road, Laxman said, "One issue, I just realized, is that it's a Tuesday—it'll be so crowded."

"I want to do darshan—" Karishma said.

"Listen to me for a second," he said. "Let's first go to the Jeev Sangathan Mandir. The pundit can bless Deepak personally." He turned to Deepak. "You want to aim samagri at the fire?"

Deepak nodded quickly, considering Laxman with his soft, large, unfocused eyes, the brows knitted as they always were.

To Laxman's surprise, Karishma did not argue. Disentangling her white dupatta from under Deepak, she said, "Chalo, fine." Then: "I wonder if Brij's boss will give him a little vacation." She looked thirstily at a mound of coconuts on a passing cart. She had written to Brij about Deepak's illness when it had seemed serious.

"Now at least there's nothing to worry about," Laxman said.

They pulled into a narrow lane of the colony. The Jeev Sangathan temple sat unfussily between two-story houses. From the outside it looked like a house as well. The three of them walked up the stairs to a narrow, deep hall, its marble floors the color of a thunderstorm. The plump, thin-limbed pundit came in breathlessly from his shack in the back and Karishma touched his feet and instructed Deepak to do the same.

The havan commenced soon after in the hall, and Karishma gazed abstractly into the fire, which combed the air dreamily in thrall to some secret music. *My own family never supports me*, she was thinking. *My mummy and daddy and sister didn't come to help me when Deepak was sick, even though they live only forty minutes away in Ghaziabad. My husband is away and always will be.*

Karishma came from a lower-class family. Her father had been a Central Public Works Department clerk. She had been married into this grand family on the basis of her looks, but felt she had nothing in common with them. It was as if this family were just another portal she had to pass through on her way to death.

She lived deathward.

Deepak was sitting on her lap again but now she gently let him slide forward. It was late August: too hot for prolonged contact. But as she bent her head toward Deepak's, marveling at the tiny white down behind his small ears, she began intoning the mantras mellifluously. "*Bhavna mit jaiye man sae, paap aatyachar kee.*"

Laxman, cross-legged next to her, listened to the notes emerging vertically, tunefully, from her mouth, her eyes half closed. She was devoid here of self-consciousness. He took pleasure in her visage, her eyelids faintly imprinted with red, as if fingers had pressed down on them.

After the havan, the pundit took Deepak by the hand to give him a few marbles lying in a drawer in Laxman's temple office, and Laxman led Karishma on a tour of the complex. Prowling around barefoot, Laxman explained to Karishma how he'd received a donation from a local businessman to build the two semi-pukka rooms for the pundit at the back; how the temple itself had sat half-constructed for five years till another tycoon, a textile exporter, contributed money for the first floor; and how the large hall in which they were presently standing and where they'd conducted the havan was often rented out for birthdays, marriages, and chauthas.

He walked her up to the flat roof of the temple, which looked from one side into a power station full of electric wires and coils, and underneath the wires, dense overgrown grass, as if the electricity were enlivening the grass.

"Why is there a bedroom up here?" Karishma asked, her tongue darting out to catch a drop of sweat at the edge of her lips.

Laxman said, "It's for sadhus and sanyasis."

They were easy with each other as they stood on the rooftop.

Karishma held the door of the room on the roof slightly ajar and said, "Can I open it?"

He nodded.

It was spare, that room. Just: a hard bed that looked like it had been trampled by a million feet—though likely no one had slept on it. A rolled-up cylinder of a dirty white blanket. No pillow. Above the bed, hanging from a nail on the wall, a glossy calendar with a Kali displayed on the front leaf. A toilet attached; and on its wet floor, a plastic mug next to a slowly weeping tap.

"How often does someone use it?" Karishma asked, turning to him.

But before she could finish, he was upon her, holding her awkwardly by the hips, the white door still ajar behind her.

Sachin decided he would speak to his boss at Trident. What's the worst that could happen? he told himself. His mind began to roil with pictures of all the things he could ask for, that he deserved. *Another office. A stipend for research. The position of executive vice president.*

So that's what the "partnership" with Rishab was about, he thought—a desire for more at Trident.

Tall, bespectacled, awkward Mike with his floppy black spectacle straps flowing behind his reddish neck—Mike welcomed Sachin into his vinyl-blinded corner office enthusiastically. But when Sachin raised the subject of his possible return to India, Mike went quiet. Then, nearly biting off the rubber end of the pencil he always held in his hand, Mike said, "I'm not at all surprised. In fact, I'm happy for you. We always wondered when you would go back."

Right then Sachin saw his whole position in the US. He was a permanent interloper. He could be squeezed out of the bottle of America in an instant.

But Mike righted himself. "But we don't let talented people get away so easily."

Things did not go as Laxman had wished.

As soon as he had touched her, Karishma had let out a quick, nervous laugh and expertly shimmied away. Laxman, to his own surprise, had withdrawn too.

Karishma kept laughing. She sounded hysterical. Then she put a hand in her hair, as if to fix it. "My bun," she said. She went into the toilet. "There's no mirror here? My hair is OK, right? We shouldn't be up here. They're waiting."

"What just happened," he said, "I get—"

Why was his confidence so shattered? He'd never been so indecisive before.

"Do you think Deepak is in the front or the back with the pundit?" Karishma asked.

He followed her down. Their elbows knocked into each other. Waves of excitement merged with terror in Laxman. What if Karishma, like Gita, complained to someone? What if she told Archana?

In the main empty hall with its spirals of dust, Deepak was playing marbles with the pundit on the floor. Coming upon Deepak, Karishma ruffled his hair and uttered soothing nothings. Then she thanked the plump trilling pundit, who put his palm on Deepak's head and blessed him.

Laxman was now full of desperate anger. *Let Karishma try to tell people. Just let her. She doesn't know me. I'll deny everything. I'll say she was the one who was sad after Deepak's sickness—and lonely without Brij—and that she threw herself at me; and that when I rejected her, she turned against me. And if my older brothers and sisters try to say something to me, I'll seed rumors about them too. Let them try to torpedo me,* he thought. *I'll detonate this entire fucking family.*

CHAPTER 33

SIX DAYS HAD PASSED. KARISHMA, IN THE BOILING KITCHEN, was examining Archana shrewdly.

The extended family—Laxman's five Delhi-based siblings and their offspring—were going to gather soon for the festival of Raksha Bandhan, and Archana and Karishma had been granted the burdensome honor of hosting the luncheon.

Karishma watched as Archana chided Jatin, the servant. "Arre, donkey, if you don't know how to operate an oven, ask someone."

Jatin laughed dryly in response—he survived the cruelty of his job by being only half present. Much like his mistress.

Despite her needling, Archana entrusted Jatin with baking a complicated chocolate cake. She passed him the round dish that would serve as the base of the cake.

Archana was a sweet, lively, gossipy female with a dour take on things that belied her ultimate optimism. Small and dark with a cloud of curly hair and tired, wise rings emanating from around her eyes, she looked like a nocturnal animal that had stood up one day on its hind legs and kept going. Archana also secretly liked to smoke—Karishma could smell the cigarettes on her breath. Archana had twice climbed to the roof today—to check, she said, on the drying clothes and the level of the water in the tank—but really, Karishma knew, to take a few puffs: an expression of the privacy she otherwise lacked. Karishma never asked her about her smoking or tried to join in. Everyone needed such moments in the cramped Chopra compound. Karishma's moments of privacy came when she was in the weedy garden at the very back of the property. Or when she got five minutes to herself in their neighbor Sarika's kitchen, waiting to take something out of the oven.

It was Archana—who was, in a way, Karishma's mentor in Delhi—who had convinced Karishma to join Sarika and her in their baking enterprise. “The men in this family are misers,” she had said. “It’s important we have some income of our own.” But sometimes the weight of Archana’s company—her desire that the two of them do *everything* together—oppressed Karishma. *It’s as if she wants me to be her maid-in-waiting,* Karishma realized with a shock.

Now, as Archana and she debated the amount of jeera to put into the chicken stew, Karishma smiled.

“You’re very happy,” Archana said. “Excited to see all your tragic uncles?”

“What else is there to look forward to in life?” Karishma said, throwing up her hands.

Karishma had never considered Laxman a sexual possibility—despite his obvious flirtation—but, as soon as he had clumsily tried to touch her, she had realized she had been aware of his desire all along. What would it be like to kiss this crude man? Her husband looked like an innocent boy, which is partly why she had been drawn to him. Brij was fair, his slightly dazed eyes set wide apart, with a sharp chin and an eagle nose—yes, he looked like a fair eagle, defeated, wingless, elegantly resigned. Together they made a stunning, photogenic couple—she had pictured them together on the mandap seconds after they’d been introduced to each other by a family friend. Till then she had not even known, really, that she was special, that the family friend had noticed her in any exceptional way. She had realized then that her looks gave her power, not just with men but with women too. She was noticed even when she felt anonymous.

Brij had proved a lousy lover. He looked so serious, romantic, and earnest when he appeared above her, burying his sharp chin in her breasts and calling her “my Radha” and “my Parvati.” She would giggle, which in turn would quicken his lips into a contemptuous frown.

“What are you laughing at?”

“Nothing, just hurry up,” she’d say, and she would think of all the other earnest men who had courted her, writing her long foolish letters, letters that only ignited her contempt. And she would laugh again.

Brij, for a man who had once been in the defense services, was thin and bony. His hips ground into hers painfully. He had powerful legs from running (he wanted to prove his slight limp couldn't hold him back) and she liked those—she trailed her hands over them as he clumsily rocked into her.

She had wanted their life to be full of romance, but had discovered quickly, upon marriage, that she'd thrown her lot in with a shallow, boastful, silly man—a man who lacked a center and kowtowed to whomever happened to be the most powerful person in his vicinity, adopting that man's mannerisms and laughing at his jokes, only to turn violent against her in private over small matters like the degree to which his military boots were buffed.

Physically and emotionally, Laxman was Brij's opposite. Laxman had a terrifying solidity—he was like a chunk of rough-hewn wood thrown into the middle of a pristine room. He wasn't in the armed services but was a natural athlete with sinuous arms; he seemed incapable of indirection. He had flirted with her shamelessly from the start. Seeing that Archana didn't seem to mind—and enjoying the attention herself—Karishma had, in her own quiet way, flirted back.

It was hard to say if the Rakhi lunch was a success, since, as usual, Laxman's elder brothers—Bhagat, Ram, and Hans—were in such a rush to eat. They wanted the food served on the table *immediately*; and Archana and Karishma became so hassled by the multiple requests that they, in turn, started shrieking at Jatin, thus establishing that it was the servant, not them, who was at fault for the delay. Laxman, too, wandered into the kitchen and gruffly shouted at Jatin, who started sputtering back, his acne-scarred face turning red. Archana, the circles around her eyes pronounced, said to Laxman, "What's the point of you coming and standing in here? Get out and ask the guests if they want more Rooh Afza."

The talk in the drawing room was focused on Laxman's flat in progress and the rudeness of the laborers, who refused to salaam anyone. Laxman told his relatives how expensive it was all proving to be. "For everything, they quote double the market price." He promised to have the contractor "sort out" the rude laborers.

"Is the food coming?" Ram Bhai, SP's third oldest son, bellowed toward the kitchen. "Bimla Behnji eats at exactly one-thirty!" Bimla was sitting on a sofa chair, her legs stretched on another plastic chair. Four playing cards were laid out in a wobbly row on the lumpy red arm of the sofa chair—the start of a game of patience.

"Bas, they're bringing it," Laxman said, trying to draw them back into his commentary about the construction.

Meanwhile, Ajay, Laxman's nephew, had gotten up, saying he wanted a glass of milk. "Just one warm glass," he repeated, biting his thin lips in a nervous tic in which he pulled down all the muscles on the left side of his face from the cheek to the neck, so that his black mustache also flexed to the left momentarily. Then he seemed to sleepwalk toward the kitchen, where he could be heard asking, "Arre, yaar, do you have Bournvita or Horlicks?"

In the drawing room, Ajay's wife, Suman, cracked a crude joke, her laughter invading the room like a blast of forced sunlight. With her large teeth and charming, disappearing eyes, she always covered up for Ajay's strange unemotional antsiness. Then the room smelled of supari—Vibha had opened her silver box and was offering it around.

"But let the food be laid at least!" Laxman said. "We'll eat this in a relaxed way after lunch."

"You be quiet!" Vibha said with gruff affection. "You have no idea what's happening in the kitchen."

"Yes, you'll remain a donkey," Ram muttered.

More laughter and cackling. All of the men's brown wrists were shiny with rakhis. The rakhis looked like golden growths or exotic, spiky caterpillars wrapped many times around their hairy arms. The sofas in the drawing room had been pushed back as far as possible and the rosewood chairs usually attached to the dining table had been littered all over the room and occupied by the adults. The kids came running in and out of the rooms, roguish grins aflame on their faces. Laxman's younger daughter, Shilpa, fair with impish, tulip-like ears, was clearly the leader of the gang. *Like me*, Laxman thought, neutrally. The other girls—Vaishnavi and Smriti and Manjuri—sat shrieking in a corner over a pile of cards.

So many centers to this gathering, Laxman thought. Not like in their childhood, when everyone coalesced around Papaji, watching him lean back on the sofa in one of his bland crinkled khaki shirts—a tribute to the simplicity and socialism of the era, but without the outright self-abasement of rough khadi, which declared you a Nehruvian or Gandhian, Nehru and Gandhi being two men whom Papaji (and therefore his children) mistrusted. At such a gathering, Papaji would sit on the sofa, a paper plate full of crumbling Black Forest cake held toward his chest, the fork currying the soft substance as he talked, laughing, his hands hyperactive over the plate, his jaw powerful and chin pressed forward, with sweet laughter flowing around him, the children cross-legged at his feet and his eyes suddenly falling on this or that child—*And what do we think of Sukhdev's recent medal in tennis?* he might ask. *Should we force him to coach all of you?*—and Sukhdev would blush as everyone marveled at their father's memory ... Papaji, who passed in and out of their lives in a blur of politics, the perpetual chief guest, feted by the family, the family indulging him with plates of food, and who, despite his peripheral daily presence—that of a general rather than a platoon commander—seemed to know everything that happened in his household.

Am I romanticizing things? Laxman worried, trying to recall the beating he had once received from his father in Gharam after he had been caught running around with a village girl. But then he thought: *To hell with it! So I romanticize! What else is love?* All around him now were men who were like smashed pieces of the great man. *Together*, Laxman realized, *we add up to less than our father.* At this point at a luncheon, Father would have jocularly asked one of his kids to refill his plate even though he was unwell—diabetic, gout-ridden, a heart patient—and though he knew that his long-suffering, always-pregnant wife, crocheting in the corner with her blue cataract-clouded eyes the color of a high-altitude lake, would disapprove. Papaji would even look at her guiltily, and the kids liked this guilty look, because it made the great old fat statesman seem like a boy—yes, that's what he was, Laxman thought, an eternal energetic boy, blessed with restless youth—younger than any of these soggy, gray defeated men around me—even me.

Laxman felt tired. The food had been laid on the dining table finally, and there was a great Chopra panic toward the buffet, followed by sudden sounds of mastication, kids being ordered around, criticisms being aired, a special meal on a special plate being brought to Bimla Behnji. Then Lata, Bimla's dwarflike maid and foot-lady, always at her side in her black-and-gray sari with a striped pallu, brought Bimla her dentures, which Bimla plopped in her mouth before staring at the food on her plate through her thick bifocals, with their fossils of fog.

She seems to be examining every grain of rice for germs, Laxman thought groggily, suddenly catching Karishma's eyes as he swiveled around.

"Are you not going to eat?" Karishma was asking Ram.

But she bypassed Laxman.

People sat scraping at their plates in the fan-swept but humid drawing room. The kids were sent to the dining table with curry-swirled empty plates to bring back seconds for the adults.

Even Karishma and Archana were allowed to sit down and eat, their bodies hunched with tiredness, their hair frazzled.

That was when the discussion turned to Gita and Sachin.

"So, have our American relatives given any further indication about whether they're moving back?" Vibha asked.

"We've not heard, but we're always the last people to know, Buaji," Karishma said. She used a scrap of chapati to make absorptive circles on the crazed surface of her plate.

Laxman said, "It won't happen, take my word. They have too much there to give it up. But if it happens, it'll happen whenever Gita's in the mood."

Vibha agreed. "When Gita was here, she was asking if there were opportunities for Sachin in India. She hasn't fully adjusted to life there—she finds it quite boring, she was saying. And it's tough without help, no? Could you have done this lunch without help?"

Karishma ignored this rebuke.

Archana piped up, "But there she was saying the opposite."

"Meaning?" Laxman asked.

"That she'll go wherever Sachin wants to go."

"That's all talk," Laxman said. "We saw it all with our own eyes, Vibha Didi," he went on. "*He* picked us up from the airport. *He* cooked us food. Poor guy had no say in anything. And, as we learned from one of their neighbors, the custom in America is to buy your house. The way mortgages work, it's cheaper than paying rent, and at the end you own a house. But she didn't want him to buy a house, so they could move back."

"Do you think they'll be able to adjust to living here?" Karishma asked. "I mean—in the complex. If they move here."

As Karishma asked more questions about Gita, Laxman thought: Was Karishma panicked by the thought of Gita and Sachin returning to the complex, claiming their share of their property? Was she threatened by Gita? Then, he thought: Of course she is. Gita with her perfect English and distant manners is always putting us down. She didn't join the rough-and-tumble of the family, hadn't even let Laxman tug her wrist like a brother. Instead, year after year she returned from America laden with expensive gifts that she knew no one could repay—that were meant to establish her supremacy over everyone—and then she complained about how hot everyone's houses were. How could Karishma, a beautiful but simple woman, stand up to this Delhi dame?

He felt protective now toward Karishma, who was gaunt and without a real protector in this house, bony on her chair, pink bangles lined up on her left wrist, bangles she kept pressing back up toward her elbow, her fingers outstretched delicately over her plate as if it were a harmonium rather than a battlefield of food ... a woman with two kids, her husband posted thousands of kilometers away. Of course, the appearance of a savvy, Americanized lady would disrupt Karishma's life. What if Gita and Sachin wanted one of these rooms in A-19 for themselves? It wasn't a problem for him: He was moving to his new flat. But would Karishma and her kids be crammed back into a single room?

"Anyway, they won't live here with us in A-19," Archana said.

"Why do you say that?" Laxman asked.

"It's beneath them."

At this, Laxman bristled. "They won't find a better address."

"We can take a bet," Archana said.

Vibha said, "Chalo, whatever it is, I'm sure they'll inform us. I didn't raise this topic so we could gamble on it! I just thought you all were likely to know. Anyway, people who go abroad always say they'll come back."

Suddenly, she had a sensation that the family was about to be swept away from its foundations.

It had much to do with her own history.

CHAPTER 34

VIBHA WAS RECALLING THE TRAGEDY OF HER FIRST marriage. Married off to an Indian doctor in 1959, she had moved to London only to discover that her new husband, Ravi, already had a wife in the city.

Ravi didn't wait long to tell her. It was the night that Vibha and he arrived in London, haggard from their two-day honeymoon in Jaipur, where an overenthusiastic bearer woke them every morning at six with bed-tea. Then, on a connecting flight from Cairo, they had dozed, their heads forming a tent against the propeller roar, and now, in Earl's Court, the street below empty save for murmuring students and a chestnut seller with a scratchy voice, they stayed awake into the night. Ravi showed her around the sparse, drafty top-floor flat and plugged in the three-bar fire. Then he began speaking to her in a businesslike way, a tone she'd never detected before in his arsenal of charm.

"I suppose, dear, we might as well discuss the issue at hand," he said. Casually he brought up the fact that he was already married to a woman in England, Margaret, a nurse. "I can only be half a husband," he declared. "I owe a responsibility to this woman. You see, when I was lonely and sad in this new country, she was of great ... assistance ... to me, and I am like a father to her two children. No, let me finish. You see, there was no circumstance in which I could inform my family in Amritsar about her. People there don't understand these distances—the new world you and I inhabit." Ravi was a tall man with aristocratically weather-beaten skin. He stooped more and more as he spoke, clutching the daggers of hair at the back of his neck, one eye twitching a little, the whites embroidered with rivulets of red, even as his voice remained deliberate. "You must realize, Vibha, it was a very difficult circumstance for me. When a man is cast away from home, he needs an anchor to keep his ship in port."

Vibha stood on her toes. Swaddled in several hand-knit pullovers, she reached up and touched his face.

Ravi looked as if he were going to sneeze but then relaxed.

He grew sleepy, like a boy. Drowsily, in bed, he kept speaking and she shushed him and stroked his hair.

In the morning, he woke full of energy and said, "I won't see her. I don't know why I told you. It's long over. It was a marriage of convenience. You know Count Leo Tolstoy? On the night he and his wife were married, he told her everything about his past. Everything."

But what about the children? Vibha wondered. Then she extinguished the thought.

Three days passed. Nothing more was said of this subject and, because it had been spoken of so late in the night, it acquired the quality of a memory from transit, experienced nowhere. Ravi once again became the gallant man who had patiently showed her how to make love on their wedding night while relatives giggled outside and parroted raucous sex noises. He laughed heartily now at her Indianisms and on Sunday took her by the hand into the streets to name the flowers growing in boxes on the windowsills, damp and fresh and pouring downward, their tendrils caught in the teeth of the sooty brick.

Then, one windy and dry day—the pavements heaving up dead leaves and blowing grit into the eyes—Ravi came home from the hospital where he worked looking tense and withdrawn.

"Would you like a shoulder massage, Maikyaji?" she asked. She had been hoping good behavior could make the nightmarish conversation evaporate.

"You judge me, don't you?" he snapped. "You think I'm a coward. Why couldn't I simply tell them, isn't it? Well, you don't know my family. My father is a very traditional person. If your dear Papaji had taken the time to investigate, if he didn't have eight other children to marry off, he would have seen it instantly."

"Don't say anything about Papaji," she growled. She loved her father, was proud of his role in the freedom struggle, the fact that he had retired as the governor of the Reserve Bank of India.

Ravi hadn't even heard her. "My father brought a great deal of pressure to bear on me to get married," he said. "My mother, frail in the best of times, perversely worried about *his* health and made it seem *he* might have died if I didn't go ahead with the proposal. So, you see, one's hands were tied. And then I met you and I thought: *Ah, this is a modern woman, educated, well-spoken, from a great family, she is likely to understand.* Don't cry."

She cried some more. She was thinking about how disappointed her father would be. He had gently warned her against marrying a man who lived abroad, but she had been adamant. She was a great lover of her family, of her boisterous brothers—no one had expected her to leave India. But the converse of this love of family was a need to discover herself.

Ravi started skulking around the flat, his black shoes gleaming brilliantly—he wore a scuffed pair at the hospital, he'd told her, and changed out of them when he left. "I knew it," he said. "No one understands." That night, he drove off in his Morris to his other family.

It was Vibha's first night in England alone. Ravi had left the three-bar fire going in the kitchen and a pile of shillings on the table for the meter, otherwise she would have frozen. She lit a candle and by the familiar wavering light at the waxy kitchen table wrote a letter home. The letterhead said: "THE LONDON HOSPITAL."

She composed the letter in her cramped but polite slanting cursive. The letter was as deliberate in its form as Ravi was in his tone of voice. "I believe I have had a relapse of my bronchial infection in Jaipur," she wrote to her father. Ravi, being a doctor, had suggested she go home immediately and get fresh air in South India before it became too damp and cold in London. "Ravi says he can purchase a ticket on the Anchor Line. Better for me to make the arduous journey before I am with child, he says."

It took three weeks for the letter to reach India; another month for the reply to come back. But Vibha's father, traditional himself, wrote to Ravi instead of to Vibha. And when Ravi returned one night to the flat—he now spent only the first half of the week with Vibha—he waved the reply, written on the cheapest, lightest onionskin, to save postage, at her. "Bronchial infection, is it? Come here. Come here!"

He lowered himself onto the green, woolly, pilled reading chair. She came close. Ravi peered up at her through the circle of lamplight. His voluminous eyes, with their English rationalism, seemed to press into all parts of her, like they were the cold ovals of stethoscopes. His eyelids were ash gray; his dense eyebrow hairs were quilled upward. "Any phlegm? Cough for me." Then, before she could do so, he abruptly waved her away. "Cowardice! You couldn't say to my bloody face you were unhappy?"

Vibha, marveling at his hypocrisy, drew back. "I ..."

He went on, "And here I was mistaking you for a modern woman! Don't you see, I'm not just living half the week elsewhere but am also giving *you* freedom to do what *you* want for that time. And see it from Margie's perspective. She's agreed to share me with you out of *deference* to my culture. When she could have easily said no and thrown a fit, as you have. But you see, these English women, they're practical, not entitled, like you upper-class Indian behnjis." A sneer distorted his face. Vibha thought, *He's going to kill me. This is how husband-wife murders happen, it is this kind of hate that does it—two people alone in a place where they know no one and are free.*

But before Ravi left for the hospital the next morning, he kissed her on the head. Then he led her to the bedroom, and they made love methodically in the sunlight, as they often did on the days he was home. Vibha, greedy for affection, accepted it as a mark of his dedication to her. At the end, he said, "I'll write your daddy today, OK, I'll tell him everything's well, your sickness is homesickness and that's that." He smiled and kissed her on the head again, as if he were already living in that solved future.

Yet, as soon as he left the flat, with its rippled floors and grimy lace curtains and unpainted window shutters—a flat she occupied in fear for much of the week, too frightened even to go out and greet the milkman—she started packing her suitcase. She was crying. With each object she put in it, she understood that her life as she had known it was ending, that what she was doing now was even more irreversible than the vows of marriage. She was throwing herself across a line, the line of being a woman without a husband—a nobody, unprotected—and, just as Ravi had smiled at the vision of their contented future, she wept for her future self. She knew what the future held for her. It was exactly out of a desire for a future that she had pressed for a match with this doctor living abroad. She had thought of marriage as a way to move through space at a speed India would not allow—oh, how much she had looked forward to Big Ben, Stratford-upon-Avon, the Tower of London, the Peacock Throne, "heather" and "gorse" and "marsh" and "moors," the chance to leave her teeming family behind for a while, and on top of that there was Ravi's collected, reserved, British style and charm, such an antidote to her uncouth siblings ... yes, it was an arranged match, but she had felt truly known; had felt that he was picking her for their life together because she was special, not just because she was the daughter of a famous man; and they had made each other laugh with a reference to Gandhi's obsession with bodily functions and she had loved that boyish gap in his front teeth, had dreamed about it. But of course it was this very charm that allowed Ravi to imagine he could maintain two wives, two selves; what he had seen in her was not her intelligence, she thought now, but her pliability—why else would he have been reckless with someone from a famous family, when he could have found a nobody who might have been grateful for even half or a quarter or a fifth of an Indian doctor? But perhaps, Vibha thought, this was another aspect of his greed and charm and acquisitiveness, perhaps he had forgotten when he saw her that he had an English wife. He was a divided person, *he really was two people*, and sometimes, when he was home with her in their hot-water flat (small, as befitting a half marriage), Ravi would appreciate her cooking, would laugh and joke with her in Punjabi; he was a great mimic of distant relatives of hers, people he knew he could mock without hurting her, the voices bursting through his gray reserve (no, he wasn't two people, he was many, the acting and balancing had destroyed his center, he could be invaded by anyone or anything), the Punjabi that of an exile, inflected with villagey phrases that made her laugh. "What's so bloody funny?" he would say with affectionate cocked eyebrows before launching, almost as a response, into the squawking Punjabi voice of a family friend. It was as if a switch were being thrown—the serious doting doctor and the crazed mimic—and it was the same at the midpoint of the week, when, the night before heading to Margaret's, he was seized by a coldness, his body flung about by chills as he lay next to her. It was as if he were remembering Margaret and the kids and his awesome pileup of responsibilities, aspects of life he had forgotten with Vibha. *Perhaps this is why he married me*, Vibha thought, still packing, *because in fact he wanted to start anew, he saw me as a chance to be young again, to continue the life he had always wanted, one that got sidetracked by this English virago*. She was now very angry at Margaret. *How dare she never show her face here, that bitch! She and I have more in common than most women, and she knows I am new here, whereas she has lived here her entire life and she probably spends the days with him at the hospital. Doesn't she owe me a visit?*

But Margaret remained an enigma. And it occurred to Vibha that Margaret could very well have directed Ravi into this sham marriage, that Margaret might have even explained to him the type of Indian lady who'd be most accommodating—Vibha could see them having a measured conversation over flower-patterned teacups. "Well, you see, darling, there's nothing to be done, is there?" Margaret would have said. "Quite right," Ravi would have replied, sipping the weak tea. And then Vibha thought: *No, no, this is wrong, these images are false, how can I be sure Margaret even knew about my marriage before Ravi returned from India, handcuffed to me?* And now Vibha felt that she could guess why Ravi became so cold toward her during certain weeks. These must have been the weeks when Margaret was raging at him, belittling him for his cowardice, overturning the imaginary teacups in fury, asking how he could be so spineless—didn't he live four thousand miles from home, and, given the distance, and the fact that he had money, power, status, and the awesome validation of British citizenship, what could his supposedly traditional family in Amritsar have done to him? "You surely can't think your grand old father would stoop to suicide, now, do you?" Margaret would have said, and suddenly Vibha was fully in Margaret's head, speaking her voice, feeling her curvy white pale body from the inside, the body sagging at the center but with blue eyes burning at the world, a woman all the way around, not boyish and wiry like Vibha, a carrier of children, yes, Vibha was inside this other woman and crying and packing and she thought, *I'm losing my mind, I am doubled now too. I now have the gift or the curse of being inside everyone, like my husband does, and it is because I can't bear to be inside my own self—I'll be anyone but me. I'll even be my enemy, Margaret, because in fact we are one.*

CHAPTER 35

SHE LEFT THE FLAT AND SOMEHOW, USING AN A-TO-Z MAP, walked to her uncle Harish's place, several miles away. But, when she showed up at the iron gate of his decaying semi-detached Victorian, dressed in a red sari and a camel-hair coat, carrying a neat little suitcase with an ivory handle, she was no longer the weeping bride who had fled her sanctuary. The journey had forced her into composure. Even as Harish Uncle opened the door, she couldn't project despair or fear, and when she told him what had happened, his expression locked into place. "You mustn't bring this to me, no, no, no," he said. "How can I help you, beta? I myself, I was never married, you must sort this out between the two of you." He was one of those doting third-cousin-ish father figures, a bachelor with wispy hair growing out of his ears, white and curly like pubic strands, his glasses hanging from a cord around his neck. He was shrinking with every year. He sat at the edge of his cigar-scented sofa with its dirty white lace cover. "Beti, what would your papa think?"

And Vibha thought, *He's not heard me*. Now Harish Uncle began droning on about how good Indian boys got entrapped in such relationships, these maims really knew how to blackmail them, there was a reason the Britishers ruled us for so long, you think enslaving one Indian is so difficult? "Our chaps," he said, "they're so innocent, earnest, dutiful, and the maims can never find men like that in their own country. Moreover, these chaps are emotional and not buttoned up, no, these maims throw themselves at our boys, what chance do the poor chaps even have? And your papa, think of what he'll say if you leave—he'll scold me, he'll say, 'You bloody fellow, you're supposed to be her guardian, and you allowed her to just run away ...'"

The disadvantage of being the child of a famous man: All of her Papaji's henchmen feared him. Topmost in their minds was the desire to please him. *This man*, Vibha thought, *has a false idea of my father in his head. My father is more liberal and loving than twenty fathers combined. Doesn't everyone say the Chopra girls are like boys, tough and individualistic and educated, and didn't he agree to send me four thousand miles away?* She became angry on behalf of her father. *How dare you speak for him*, she wanted to shout, *I am his daughter, not you*, and now she was angry not just at this soggy, hairy specimen but at all men. *Go to hell, all of you*, she thought, but a layer of tiredness slipped over her again and she started to cry.

Harish was off the sofa, coming toward her with his awkward hands and hunched back, saying, "Beti, what will crying solve?" She thought, *He hates all of us, hates our tears, this is why he's a bachelor*, and suddenly she was lit up with warmth toward Ravi, toward his neat way of expressing himself, of taking his tie off every evening and folding it just so and placing it on the dressing table, his hands open at his sides as he talked about his day at the hospital—she was in love with Ravi.

I'm going mad, she thought. She wiped her tears and said, "Thank you, Uncle."

"I understand," he said. "It's hard to be in a new place. It takes time to adjust." He went on, "It's a big shock, how free people are here. Do you mind if I light a cigar? And you can imagine when I came here, it was a different time, I mean, these chaps were still our rulers, but of course they treat you differently once you're here—especially in London, they're very liberal and courteous and curious, they want to know all about you. But it's all very well to treat a few of us nicely when you're enslaving a nation, isn't it?"

"But we're independent now," Vibha said.

"Quite right, quite right," he said, puffing on his cigar.

Vibha returned to her flat, unpacked the suitcase, and made Ravi a nice meal.

She lasted a year. But when she thought later of what one year meant against an entire life, it was nothing. She had almost accepted half a life *as* her life.

Every day with Ravi was new. Every day was unpredictable. And yet every day, when it reached its conclusion, could be recalled only as an accumulation of signs: grayness, clouds, rain, milkman, flower seller, greengrocer, baker, the tramp at the bus stop who yelled about the deaths at the Somme.

India had been the opposite: a daily external extreme churning, a chaos of relatives and servants—but a place, too, of inner peace, a kind of boredom and security, the kind that had made her eager for an adventure in another country.

Vibha missed home. She put her head against the crosshatched windowpane, absorbing the cold through her temple.

One warm morning, when she opened the tiny window in the bedroom, it simply fell out, along with its wooden frame, into the dirty alley between the backs of the houses.

She read in the papers about Sophia Loren's husband, accused of bigamy, but could not connect the story with her own condition, did not feel that English laws applied to her. Nor had she been able to bring herself to investigate Margaret. This was because all white women of a certain age in London *were* Margaret. Suspicion made her peer at each one of them, noticing their teeth, their noses, their lips, their low-cut blouses, their fashionably belt-cinched waists. How could she compete with them?

At home, she sometimes touched herself while imagining Ravi with one of them—only to pull her hand away.

She didn't want the revelation of the true Margaret to take away a city full of her playthings.

These thoughts came and went in flashes. She told herself that her perversions were brought on by loneliness—the desire for friendship, the kind of bond she had formed with only one person in London, the landlady's daughter, Abby, who, like Vibha, had been a competitive badminton player in school.

"And how alike we really are!" Abby had said, pressing Vibha's hands as they chatted by the staircase.

Abby seemed to know about Ravi's other wife, because she never mentioned his prolonged absences. This knowledge sat heavily between them, preventing them from progressing further; they were always stuck on the ground floor of friendship, expressing admiration for each other's existence without making the slightest attempt to penetrate to the truth, their friendship little more than a series of chirps of affirmation.

The flat was not without clues about where Margaret might live—receipts, faded prescriptions for the kids (two boys, she had learned). But every time Vibha took the tube and got within a few blocks of Margaret's possible address, in Islington, she turned around.

In this way, Margaret helped her discover the city, develop confidence, learn to be alone.

"When you came, you were like a mouse," Ravi was saying. "A small freezing mouse. Do you want to go to the theater?"

She nodded.

In the dark of the matinée, he held her hand. She let it lie limp but did not pull it away.

At home, he was distracted. He took off his tie. Then, for the first time in months, he bent down and passionately kissed her. She resisted, but then her mouth sagged open and they lay in the bed together, close to the repaired window with its fresh, harsh eye on the back-alley.

"I want us to have a child," he whispered into her neck, nestling his hooked nose there.

"Hullo?" Ravi said. "Anyone home?"

"I don't want to," Vibha finally replied, her eyes scanning the pressed-tin ceiling.

"But why, darling?"

"I don't want to bring more sadness into the world."

Ravi got up on his elbows. "Vibha. It's not what you think it is. Margaret's a good person. She was widowed and I used to comfort her. Then ... love ... developed." He paused. "The love has been dead for years. When I met you, I was trying to escape her. But how can I? I'm incapable of leaving anyone or anything, of moving on."

You left India, she almost said. But what was the point?

"It's the children. That's why I've stayed." He stroked her sides. "That's why I want us to have one of our own. Half of you, half of me. Think of how sweet he'll be. How much we'll adore him. It's a different kind of love one has for kids."

He kissed her on the cheek.

"I don't want to," she said again, covering her eyes with an arm.

Night after night now, the building would come alive with the sound of Ravi's trotting footsteps approaching the fourth floor.

Then the good doctor, placing his black valise on the carpet, would crouch down beside his intransigent wife—usually knitting in a chair—and say to her, "Will the Duchess of York consent to make love to her humble servant tonight?"

"No."

"May I serve the Queen of Sheba the crêpes suzette I brought home especially from Veeraswamy?"

"Give it to your other wife."

But, to her surprise, he was starting to make her laugh again. Northern summer light swamped the flat in the evenings.

A man who likes a project, she thought. He brought home a suitcase of clothes. She anticipated his arrivals with dread. She had carefully calibrated a routine—cooking, shopping, walking, playing cards and badminton with Abby—and now it was crumbling.

Nevertheless, she could feel her resistance giving too, and she was frightened. Then, one night, Ravi was crouching on the floor next to her and stroking her thigh as she read in the green chair, when she said, "Will you take me to meet Margaret?" How many months it had taken her to ask this question!

Ravi startled. He was still in his gray work suit; his brown hat lay on the carpet. "Why would you want that? Of course, that can be arranged," he said. "Of course, that can, yes ..." He seemed to be speaking to himself.

"I propose we meet halfway between India House and the House of Commoners," Vibha said, purposely misstating the latter.

"It's a joke to you?" Ravi asked.

Her mouth tightened.

"You have to understand, Vibha, once I open that door—that's the issue," Ravi was saying.

For three days, she didn't hear from him and was in suspense. She mopped the floors, dusted the fronts of the cabinets, beat the sofa with her palm.

The door groaned. It was Ravi. He stood in the frame, hunched and weary, his black doctor's bag under one arm. "She is amenable to it. She says you can come to our—to her—place, but not to expect any grand cooking." He seemed older, broken, a man caught between two lives, two wives. And what she felt for him, even as she said, "Very good," was not pity but contempt.

The next morning, Ravi was unwell. He had evidently caught a bad cold and began coughing into the kitchen sink. "Not there!" Vibha found herself shouting. "I just cleaned all those dishes!"

He glanced sideways at her from over the crack-spidered sink, eyes bulging as he coughed some more.

"Just do it on the side!"

"I'm sick, Vibha—"

"Move!"

She felt, again, that unbearable contempt for him.

For the next two days, they fought. When he called her fat and uptight, she taunted him for not having gotten her pregnant the first months they'd made love in England. "Is that why you brought me here, because you couldn't get your English screw pregnant?"

"Listen to the words coming out of your mouth," he said.

Suddenly, she was on the landing. She had run out of the flat, slamming the door behind her.

As she came down the stairs, the door to Abby's flat opened.

"It's not all right, what's happening with you," Abby whispered. "I'll help you."

It was the day she was to meet Margaret.

But Vibha was on a bus to the airport.

Abby had helped Vibha sell her gold wedding bangles and purchase a ticket.

The flight plunged through never-ending clouds.

In Delhi, her father, broad-shouldered and upright in his tight study, was shocked to see her.

But when Vibha started crying and told him the whole story, he said, "Oh, my bitiya, this is my mistake, you've run all this way—"

"No, Papaji, it's my fault," Vibha said, clumsily trying to clear her eyes with the back of a hand. "I should have known." How had her life come to this?

"How could you have known, bitiya?" he said. And then, "You know, when my first wife passed, I was only twenty, and I didn't want to remarry, I didn't think life could start again, and I was angry that my father had pressurized me, but then I went ahead—and look at things now. I have you and all of my children. So, at your age, there's no reason to be despairing."

Men always take the occasion of a woman's sadness to launch into reveries. She didn't mind. She got so little time alone with him. It was only tragedy that had brought them closer. She was, for a second, almost grateful for it: She had lost a husband but gained a father.

After a discreet back-and-forth with Ravi's family in Amritsar, the marriage was annulled under the pretext that it hadn't been consummated.

A few months later, she was married off again—to an older, widowed, mid-level railway official with a weak heart. She had no idea how much diligence was done. It was understood that she had to go back into the world, even if it was as damaged goods. And so the shambles of London gave way to the shambles of India—a more lower-middle-class existence than she'd ever imagined, a union with a man she had nothing in common with and who, strangely, had no interest in her famous family and instead asked her questions about England, as if she had been there for her studies rather than for a wreck of a marriage.

Was that really me in England? she sometimes wondered, remembering the first night Ravi had spoken to her about Margaret, and how that conversation itself had seemed like a dream. A dream upon a dream upon a dream: her life. There was, however, one sobering, bracing dose of reality: Ravi.

Ravi never vanished. Ravi kept writing to her for years. He said he loved her deeply. In the letters, he was apologetic and morose, he wanted her to see his position, asked how she was, how her daughter, Aparna, was growing, and so on. He wanted Vibha to forgive him from afar. He wanted India to forgive him for marrying a British woman.

She never replied.

Was she happier now? Vibha wondered in that packed drawing room. *Yes, I suppose I am*, Vibha thought. But that marriage had divided her life into before and after, and she had never recovered.

So many feelings and eras existed at once in this room in the complex. Old paint on the wall, mere powder in places—paint chosen by her father and never recoated. Old black switches, the wires running in covered plaster rails along the walls. To live in this house was to live inside their father's mind: half village, half city.

And when Vibha thought about people returning to the house, she could think of only one reason: failure. Sadness. But she did not air this as a theory for Gita and Sachin's potential return. It did not fit with the tone of the conversation. In fact, the split between her inner self—compassionate and knowing—and her outer manner—gruff and bright—had only widened with the years. *The last time I was myself was with Ravi*, she thought. *Then he took that self away.*

The mood in the drawing room lightened. Archana and Karishma collected plates from the guests, though a few of the ladies had the sense to deposit them in the kitchen themselves. Then Jatin brought in a steaming silver bowl of gajar ka halwa and a plate almost fully annexed by chocolate cake. He had not burned it, after all.

CHAPTER 36

BRIJ ANNOUNCED VIA POST THAT HE WAS RETURNING IN A week to Delhi on vacation, and so Laxman put Karishma out of his mind and focused on having the renovations to his new flat finished.

Then, on a Sunday, when Laxman was heading out to the temple for a special havan, Archana said, "Can you stop by the tailor's on the way back and pick up the blouse I gave him?"

"Fine," Laxman said. "But tell him it should be ready when I arrive."

"Karishma, do you also have to get something picked up?" Archana asked.

They were all in the drawing room.

"Actually, I need to *give* him something," Karishma said, knitting on a sofa, her eyes on the clanking silver needles.

"Do this—explain it to Laxman and he'll give it," Archana said.

"I'm not sure he's capable of understanding," Karishma said.

"Men don't have common sense about clothes," Archana said, laughing dryly.

Laxman, in the drawing room, hands on his hips, had had enough of this bonhomie. All four kids were away at the Modern Colony Club, where they had cycled to play table tennis and badminton.

"Laxman, just take her to the tailor with you," Archana suddenly said.

Turning unnecessarily to Karishma, she added, "Laxman can take you and he'll drop you back."

"But the prayers at the temple start in thirty minutes," Laxman said.

"You know the pundit will wait for you," Archana clucked. "Who else even goes?"

"Don't worry if it'll interrupt puja," Karishma said.

"You women should make up your mind," Laxman growled.

Then, amazingly, she agreed to go with him.

In the car, Laxman and Karishma both perspired. It was pure, hot, sweaty late summer, the worst time of the year—the monsoons giving way to the retreating monsoons, as Deepak's geography textbooks had reminded Karishma. She spoke fast now about any subject that came into her head—Rakhi; Gharam; the colony's attempt to demolish the little illegal chai shop with the Thums Up sign painted on it. Then, unable to help herself, she said, "Do you really think Sachin will choose to live in A-19?"

Laxman grimaced. "If you keep obsessing, Karishma, they will come back. What are you so worried about? That they'll take your rooms?"

"No."

"I didn't mean it like that," Laxman said.

Karishma said, "Didn't we miss the turn for the tailor?"

"Oh," he said, "yes. But I'm late, and the pundit will keep people waiting if I don't go. It's OK if we go there first?" he asked.

Karishma crinkled the blue plastic bag full of rough fabric on her lap. Then she nodded.

They passed the scaffolding of the massive Krishna Bhagwan Mandir that was being built on the artery that divided "Old" Modern Colony and "New" Modern Colony. (Modern Colony was once considered an extension of the city, but even the extensions had extensions—that's what this city was like.)

The rickety bamboo rods of the scaffold, laid crosswise over the ghost of the temple, bristled with plastic, tarpaulin shreds, jute rope. "I never understand how people build things," Karishma said, with true wonder. Her gaze fixed, as they passed, on the tense foot of a worker who was standing on a knobby length of bamboo scaffolding fifty feet in the air. He appeared to be resting with his forehead on a beam in front of him. His body was limp but his feet were tightly curled around the bottom rod. Then it became clear that he was shouting to someone on the road below. Down there, only a few meters from Laxman's car, women were carrying baskets of gravel to a recess in the building. Their saris were the color of the landscape from which they'd fled—greens, maroons, soil. The man above kept shouting. It occurred to Karishma that she had never been on an elevation in the colony—never higher than two floors in this huddle of gated houses. The most open vista she had encountered, surprisingly, had been from that balcony in the Jeev Sangathan Mandir that looked over fields requisitioned for a power plant.

So much of this colony had been mere fields in the 1960s and '70s—Yamuna marshlands. Now it was dense with mansions and bungalows.

"Is it legal to make something this high in the colony?" she asked Laxman, eyes on the half-built temple complex.

There were all sorts of rules to preserve Delhi's shrinking water table.

Laxman laughed darkly. "Does God need to worry about laws?" Now he launched into a long story about the corruption of the man who was funding the Krishna Bhagwan Mandir—how this man had also tried, a decade ago, to grab the leadership of the Colony Association and preferentially allot land to people who *already* owned property elsewhere in Delhi, "when of course," Laxman explained, "the idea was that New Modern Colony was for people who had *no other place* to call home. But history is easily forgotten. People forget how we came here after Partition with nothing, how difficult it was for people like us."

She was struck by the use of the word *us*. *Your family*, she wanted to say, *didn't suffer in 1947—your papa seemed to know what was coming and had transferred his accounts to Delhi.*

Karishma was not as impressed by Papaji's achievements as the others were. She felt he had been buoyed by history rather than affecting it—that, ultimately, he had been a profit-obsessed banker.

that the loans he had given to freedom fighters had been part of a larger investment in a future he could see coming.

But she knew not to push that button in this family.

She pressed her back into the sagging fabric of the Fiat's seat and yawned.

Karishma and Laxman left their slippers at the Jeev Sangathan temple door, which was framed with rough, unvarnished timber, and entered the narrow smoky hall. The pundit sat behind his cast-iron havan kund on a short wooden stool—more like the sort of low table on which joss sticks were displayed in houses. The havan kund lay in a depression carved out of the cheap gray marble.

Across from the pundit sat a graying man and a graying woman; his back erect, hers hunched; the man's wrist covered in fresh red threads. There was no one else at this "public" Sunday ceremony.

"Are we early?" Karishma asked Laxman.

Laxman didn't answer. This was actually a larger gathering than normal. Jeev Sangathanis were so lazy! They interpreted the sect's permissiveness as an excuse to do nothing. Or they branched out into other, more ornate sects: His sister Gaurika had joined a satsang; his brothers Rattan and Sukhdev, perhaps missing the comforting figurehead of their father, had vanished into a guru's cult and were now proselytizing other family members—and even *he*, Laxman, kept two idols of Krishan on his table in his office. But this was part of the generosity of the Sangathan: It didn't frown upon anything. Yet this caused others to frown upon it.

At various points in the previous decade, Laxman had been enticed to join the Hindu nationalist RSS but had felt that he owed it to his father to watch over the embers of the Sangathan.

The pundit continued chanting but then smiled at them and levered his hands, inviting them to come sit. The air was fragrant with burning samagri. The seated couple who was already there turned around too. Karishma saw that they were the Puris, a rich couple from the colony. Everyone namasted, and then the Puris turned around and went back to prayer.

Karishma and Laxman sat cross-legged on the left side of the havan kund, Laxman careful to keep his distance from Karishma. He knew what the Puris would be thinking. But as he chanted the mantras, he fell into a trance. *What do Karishma and I have in common?* he thought. *We both care for Archana.*

After the fire had died down and the pundit put boondi in all of their outstretched palms, the Puris and Karishma and Laxman stood up in the hall to chat, their bare feet enhancing their intimacy. The Puris said they had been wishing to come regularly, as Laxman had so kindly suggested (they were all friends from morning walks in the colony), but one thing or the other had gotten in the way till now. "Actually till last week only," Mrs. Puri explained, "we were in Switzerland, Jungfrau and Geneva and all those places, and, you won't believe, we were in a cable car five thousand feet high—"

At this Mr. Puri smiled dryly and said, "My wife didn't want to climb the stairs."

Karishma saw he was gallant and well-mannered.

Mrs. Puri said, "Quiet, he acts like we're still twenty."

Mr. Puri smiled again. He had thin lips and prominent gums; the subtle smile really became him; even the gray in his hairs seemed to be dotted at even intervals ... yes, he was such a contrast to his dowdy, dark, hunched wife, Karishma thought.

Mrs. Puri now launched into a long story about how their cable car had stalled halfway to the mountain, just dangling over the valley. "We could see these giant pipes below, what do you call them, darling, aquaducks?"

"Aque*ducts*," Mr. Puri said. *Of course*, Karishma thought, *he's an ex-army fellow*, and she noticed he was examining her with his regiment-inspecting eyes, muting his interest, just as she was—*Are servicemen my type now?* she wondered—and meanwhile Mrs. Puri's story went on and on, but the long and short of it was that their cable car had finally gotten moving after twenty-five minutes of being up there, and disaster had been averted.

"All I could think of was I had to go to the bathroom," Mrs. Puri said.

Laxman roared at this comment.

Maybe he should be with this lady, Karishma thought, standing in this huddle in the hall, *if he finds her so funny, this ugly old maid. He has never laughed at any of my jokes.*

Meanwhile Mr. Puri's gaze on her grew both more misty and intense, as if he were hoarding photographs of her in the back of his mind.

Suddenly Laxman said, "Of course, you've met my niece-in-law Karishma—"

"Of course, of course," Mrs. Puri said.

"My husband also used to be in defense—in the air force, the Tuskers Squadron," Karishma said.

"Yes, of course, Brij," Mr. Puri said. "I've played billiards with him in the club."

Laxman said, "I'm trying to make more of my family members come to the mandir and Karishma's son has been sick, which is why we thought to come and make an offering to God."

"We also came to thank God after the cable car only," Mrs. Puri said.

"He's fine now," Karishma added.

"Still, one can never say enough prayers where the life of a child is concerned," Laxman said, brushing aside her comment.

Karishma bit her lip and glanced at handsome Mr. Puri. He was like a film star—rich, he paid casual elegant visits to Switzerland, but then she became conscious of Mrs. Puri's shrewd measuring gaze on her, and so she smiled blandly, turning herself into the stupid doll, the adjunct to conversation she had been taught to be.

"And Punditji has such a beautiful voice," Mrs. Puri said, smiling toward the pundit, who was sweeping dirt from the corners of the temple theatrically and wiping his forehead with the end of his saffron dhoti.

The pundit came toward them and said, "Accha, Laxmanji, I have to go get some milk from Mother Dairy. Is that OK? It'll take me just twenty minutes."

"Yes, we'll be here," Laxman said.

Really, Karishma thought.

After the pundit left, Laxman laughed. "Oh, our bhole-bhale Punditji! I've never seen a man of God as restless as him."

The Puris laughed too.

Mrs. Puri said, "He has a good heart but he should have been in business."

"Or a beat constable," Karishma said. But Laxman didn't laugh at this joke either and the Puris only offered polite smiles and Karishma was irritated.

Husband and wife were smiling identically now. Mrs. Puri had taken on her husband's mannerisms, Karishma noticed. It was as if Mrs. Puri were trying to possess Mr. Puri by merging them into one person.

"They're also human beings, after all," Mrs. Puri said about the pundit, with all the class disdain her tiny frame could muster.

"And after a havan in such heat—even I want to get out," Laxman said.

"Go outside—in this month?" asked Mrs. Puri.

"Well, he is something of a prisoner in this place," Laxman said. "We have a guard, but he's turned out to be an unreliable fellow—"

"I thought you said Punditji was always going away to his village," Karishma said, and Laxman shot her a slightly baleful glance, as if he didn't want this known.

"That's only when *I'm* here to watch," he said curtly.

She stood quietly next to Laxman as he talked now about the problems with the Sangathan. She even nodded in agreement. *We have barely touched*, Karishma thought, *and we are acting like a married couple; perhaps this is what all love devolves into anyway, irritation; perhaps irritation is the goal of love, and what I have with Brij is normal; the more irritated you are, the more intimate you are.*

Interrupting his stories, Laxman made a pitch for funds for the Sangathan, how great it would be if each family in the colony gave even Rs 500 or 1,000, because, as you two know, you are good people, the Sangathan, which did so much to bring Hindus together in Punjab, is suffering, it hasn't been able to keep up—

"Well, it had that split in the 1920s, right," Mr. Puri said, "and it became dominated by shopkeepers and became anti-political and pro-British, and that's when the RSS swooped in and filled the political vacuum."

A learned man, Karishma thought, blushing.

"That's only one part of the story," Laxman said. "There were also many great freedom fighters in the Sangathan."

"And your father," Karishma added.

"These splits happen," Laxman said. "But the issue is really that the Sangathan's assets were left behind in Lahore and therefore we never recovered. And after Tilak Ram and Harbansji"—he swept his arm to indicate the paintings of these founders of the Jeev Sangathan on the wall—"we haven't had good leaders."

Karishma suddenly noticed the framed photograph of SP, full-cheeked but dour, with a ropy mustache, in a suit, staring angrily downward from the wall: How had she missed it the first time? But then she lived in a world where that picture, like that of Mao in China, was hung on every wall. She had stopped seeing it.

CHAPTER 37

ONCE THE PURIS HAD DRIVEN AWAY, KARISHMA ASKED Laxman, in the hall, "You think they'll donate anything?"

Laxman frowned. "The rich never part with their money."

"That's how they remain rich," Karishma said.

He put his hand on her arm. "I need to check something upstairs."

"I'll wait down here," she said.

He removed his hand and walked toward the stairwell—that narrow column of bluish paint. Then Laxman heard steps behind him. He turned around.

"I remembered the view!" she said.

They came to the balcony together. But the sun was so harsh that there was no vista at all—no way of looking without having your eyebrows and eyes flooded with sweat.

"Bloody fellow doesn't clean," Laxman said. He shouted for the part-time guard: "Ramu! Ramu! Come up!"

It was such a raw animal sound that Karishma started. She was standing against the unevenly painted outside wall of the room on the roof, under a small parapet that cast a gutter-width of black shade over the bright powdery limestone floor. Her bare feet burned the second she'd come up, but, strangely, she'd almost looked forward to that feeling as she had ascended the incrementally warming steps. It brought back memories of running—almost skimming—over hot courtyards with her cousins, of not knowing when the pain in her dry soles might rise to a physical screech.

Laxman leaned over the balcony and shouted again for the part-time guard, pressing his powerful hands down on the low wall of the roof. *The whole colony will hear!* she thought. But then these Chopra men—with the exception of her demented husband—were unusually uncouth. Her eyes passed over Laxman's flat buttocks under his navy-blue pants. The material of the pants was soft and smooth. For a rough man, he was quite a dandy. No stray threads emerged from the unused belt loops.

"It's too hot here," he said, and, turning from the balcony, walked to the door of the room, pushing it open with the heel of his hand.

The floor was pleasurably cold under Karishma's feet as she entered. Laxman turned on the overhead fan and wind slapped their faces and tousled the sheet on the bed in uncomfortable, uneven waves. She reached instinctively to tuck one end of the flapping sheet under the thin loaf of the mattress. Laxman switched on the light and then turned it off to test it. "Good," he said. "It's working." He opened the toilet door and sniffed and closed it and latched it—the smell of naphthalene came tumbling in from the small cube of wet tiles.

She was sitting on the side of the bed, her bare feet dangling down.

"No one ever uses this room," Laxman said, then he sat down next to her on the bed and kissed her.

"Of course you got the wrong thing," Archana said to Laxman in their bedroom later that day. "You could have looked to see if he'd done any work on this kameez you picked up."

"You just told me to pick it up," Laxman said.

"If you'd shown it to Karishma, she would have told you."

"Is it my fault or the tailor's?" Laxman asked.

Karishma could hear this conversation through their closed door as she lingered in the small landing outside the kitchen. *He's ruder to her now*, she thought. *If he's going to treat her badly, I must stop this. I don't want blood on my hands.*

CHAPTER 38

SOON AFTER LAXMAN AND KARISHMA'S TRYST, BRIJ returned home for his brief vacation.

"You can't lay dinner like this," he scolded Karishma on his second night in A-19. "Set down the napkins and smooth them. Yes, like this." He fussily folded one napkin into a triangle like a cartoon sailor's hat and placed it symmetrically beside his fork, looking blankly at Laxman, who was sitting diagonally across.

Karishma got up from her seat and went to the head of the table and started folding the other napkins, but Brij again raised his voice. "Neatly! Neatly! And forks and spoons shouldn't be arranged in this haphazard manner. Kindly switch them."

"Arre, enough!" Laxman said, with a laugh, his small teeth showing. "It's not like you need a fork to eat rice!"

Brij fixed his hooded eyes on Laxman. "It's important that things be done in the correct manner, regardless of the result."

"Bas, darling, I've done it," Karishma said harshly, sitting down again.

Brij ignored this and began talking about leaving Bijapur Paper. "I've written letters to all my seniors informing them of the corruption in the lower ranks of the company," he said. "No one has done more work to cultivate the forest than me."

"But you know they won't accept your resignation," Laxman said, noisily cleaning his fingers by putting all of them in his mouth.

"They'll convince you to stay," Archana said to Brij. "They don't let good people go that easily."

Karishma appreciated Archana's ability to harness Brij's idiocy with flattery.

As everyone in the family knew, Brij loved resigning. He had lasted a mere seven years in the air force before impulsively quitting, and at Bijapur Paper he had chafed from the start about how inefficiently the business was run, and how little respect he received as a former squadron leader in the air force. "Anyway, Sachin says I can earn ten times that amount in America." Sachin and he were more in touch now than they had been in a decade.

"But that's a different world," Karishma said.

"You don't want to go there?" he said, grinning. "At first you used to bug me every day—'Tell him to get you a job there, why don't we go there ...?' Now you've turned into a great patriot?"

She was quiet.

Then, three days into his vacation, Brij did go ahead and mailed yet another resignation to Bijapur's Delhi office.

He was simply bargaining, in his mind, for a higher salary. The business had been founded, after all, by a close friend of SP Chopra.

Nevertheless, family members wondered: *What would the outcome be? Was he really stupid enough to give up a good job? Why did he act so foolishly—his father hadn't been like that. Must be his cracked mother's genes ...*

A week later, a thick rectangular envelope arrived at the house via registered post. Brij tore it open eagerly. Then bile rose in his throat. "We are grateful for your exceptional service," the letter said, "and hereby accept your request."

Brij's hands tightened around the paper. He had misread the mood of Bijapur Paper, which was now being run by the son of the former owner, who didn't hold Papaji in as much respect as the previous generation.

And so, all of a sudden, Brij was out of a job.

"I had only one home, bloody Bijapur, and even *that* wasn't a home to me," Brij complained to Karishma that night in a rare moment of honesty in their bedroom—a dark chamber with only one set of frosted windows over the bed, opaque glass that gazed into the drawing-cum-dining room, draining light rather than bringing it in.

Conversation easily carried through these hazy portals; they kept their voices low. "So this is how the buggers treat people for years of service," Brij went on.

Karishma knew she should be worried that this man would once again be at the center of her life, but she was thinking instead of Laxman's gravelly cement-grinding voice. Then the image of Mr. Puri and his handsome face flashed through her mind—a moment in the temple when his tiny tongue had darted out to lick a corner of his lips. "But, darling, you're the one who gave the resignation," Karishma said.

"Yes. But come on, man, what way of behaving is this? At least tell a fellow face-to-face, give him options."

"So send them another letter and tell them you weren't serious," Karishma said.

"That's not how life works," he said. Then he started laughing. "Not serious? By God!" He was coughing; his strange phlegmy barking wouldn't stop.

"Darling, are you OK?" Karishma asked angrily. "Should I bring some water for you?"

"Not serious!" he said through a fusillade of coughs.

"Darling!" she snapped, examining her nails.

He lay back on the bed, silent. Then he got to his feet and went out of the room.

He thought about writing to his brother. But pride, as it always had, held him back.

CHAPTER 39

BRIJ BEGAN THREATENING TO MOVE HIS NUCLEAR FAMILY to the ancestral village of Gharam in Punjab. "It'll be good to be back near one's roots, isn't it?" he said to Karishma, verbally caressing the word *roots*.

"And where will your sons study?" Karishma asked. Gharam was a backwater—an actual village.

"You're talking as if I'm moving us to the bleddy jungle again!" Brij said, his mouth permanently twisted into a grin. "Where did Dadaji get educated?" He paused. "There!"

"But it was a different time, Brij," Karishma said, casting her eyes around the living room, where she was sitting with her husband and the boys.

Brij was undeterred. "The Gharam Fort still has the school where Dadaji was educated. Boys," he said, turning to Mohit and Deepak, who were squeezed together on a sofa, "you don't want to study in a fort?"

Mohit looked away, embarrassed, but Deepak fixed his father with his set-apart eyes—eyes so much like Brij's but lacking their slyness, Karishma thought.

"Will it be like studying in the NDA, Papa?" Deepak asked.

"Yes!" Brij said. "Exactly!"

"Please reason with him," Karishma said on a Sunday morning to Laxman. It was one of the only moments of privacy they'd had together since they'd made love—and it wasn't even that private: They were out for a morning walk along with Archana. Brij was away at the club, playing badminton.

Archana, of course, had totally claimed Karishma for herself as they strolled into the massing heat that morning, her lithe torso and frizzy head of hair turned almost completely toward Karishma, her body electric with gestures, eyes never on the road ahead of her.

"Watch there," Karishma said. "You'll fall—there's a guddha."

"Yah, yah," Archana said, sidestepping it as if it were a pause in the conversation, not the road.

Laxman walked behind them, stopping occasionally to namaste colony residents out for their constitutionals and to take their palms between his in a warm gesture of familiarity. Still, Karishma felt, there was something stilted about his speech and posture.

It was only when Archana was pulled aside by an acquaintance—an out-of-town friend who'd spied her from across the street—that Karishma had a chance to speak to Laxman. "What'll happen to me and the boys if we move to Gharam?" she asked.

"But Brij might be at peace there," Laxman said blankly.

They had stopped on the unpaved perimeter of mud that ran around the manicured park—a perimeter that was left as such because it clutched several eucalypti in its clammy soil.

"And the boys' education—" Karishma said.

"You and the boys should stay here," Laxman said, as if this were the easiest thing in the world. With his hands on his hips, he swiveled, eyes brightening, to wave at another resident ambling by.

"He won't let us," she began. "If he could find some work here ..."

"I could give him a role in the Jeev Sangathan," Laxman said with a shy smile. But he stopped smiling when Karishma wrinkled her forehead.

Laxman wondered: *Does she not know that my bobby-pin business is in the doldrums?* That *this* was why he'd been spending more time on the Sangathan and even trying to take over the leadership of the Residents' Welfare Association?

Finally, Laxman said, "Don't worry so much, I'll talk to him. We won't let your husband rot away in a village."

But Laxman had no solution; and, suffering from headaches, he went one day to see his doctor, Mohan Pahalwan, the traditional healer who had cured Deepak and who would have cured Gita had she not thrown her hissy fit outside the gurdwara.

The sixty-something white-bearded bonesetter took Laxman's pulse in the veranda of his decrepit Kirti Nagar home and asked whether something had been bothering him.

"There's a lot of employee turnover at the factory," Laxman said.

The pahalwan nodded gravely, then asked after Deepak.

"Mohanji, you performed a miracle on him," Laxman said. "My niece-in-law was very grateful. Of course, the boy wants your Hriday Shahd every day now!"

"He's a child, he wants sweet things," the pahalwan said, moving gingerly around the shady, dusty veranda of his house and tightening the caps on his brown bottles full of murky liquid and adjusting piles of gauze on the shelves. On the walls hung framed white posters with quotes from Shelley and Keats—Mohanji had been a professor of English in Jharkhand while continuing the family line of bonesetting and Ayurveda. Yet he was not comfortable in English and spoke an accented Hindi that swung, often in the course of a sentence, between extreme UPite formality and Bihari jauntiness, his smile full of extravagantly crooked teeth, two vulpine molars jutting out of the upper gums like stalactites, completing the look of mischievous but inclusive conspiratorial boyishness.

Mohanji found the bottle he'd been looking for, inhaled, and said, "Arre, Laxman sahb, one should have one teaspoon of Hriday Shahd with lemon and hot water every day: It contains twenty different herbs which are in our shastras. Some of them are herbs that Hanumanji went to get from the mountain to cure Ram."

"I don't understand how you can do it all from here," Laxman said.

Mohan Pahalwan was the official masseuse and doctor of several famous politicians yet lived modestly with his ancient mother on the ground floor of this old house. He rode a scooter, the sides of which were pitifully tied up with string to prevent the fingernail-pink panels from falling off like the flaps of a box. Laxman had seen Pahalwanji on the road in his flowing saffron kurta on the pink scooter, twisting the knobs with his bony wrists, his white beard resting on his left arm and his chest sashed with the strap of a khadi satchel—a sight to behold.

"It's thanks to God," the pahalwan said, "and my respected mother, who has been taking care of me for fifty years." The pahalwan, Laxman noticed, always revised his age upward. The wrestling genes had been bred out of him over several generations, it seemed.

"I'm only sad about one thing," Laxman said. "That, apart from a few enlightened people, the public don't know about your balms."

Mohanji smiled his molar smile. "See, Laxmanji, I have neither the time nor the means. I'm one person. Those people who know of my practice, I help them as much as I can. And those who don't know, they'll also come eventually. Our people always come back to tradition."

Laxman said, without conviction, "Yes, you're saying the right thing."

"And you tell me, Laxmanji, is everything OK in your family?" the pahalwan asked, suddenly serious. In a swift motion he was at Laxman's side, sitting on a low stool, faintly humming a tune.

How can I tell him? Laxman thought. *There is no way: This is a private love.*

Love. The word sent a shock up the back of his spine and into his head. And then the headache that had brought him here suddenly vanished, and Laxman said, brightly, "Everyone's fine. I'll take your medicine and I'm confident everything will be cured." And now the dilapidation that had seemed to him so depressing moments earlier began to shimmer with life. In the yard, a white cat with brown spots on its spine sashayed noiselessly, throwing an ageless green glance at him. The upstairs neighbor, a lady with tumbling rolls around her sari-clad stomach, appeared in the yard behind a curtain of white clothes, taking the clips off the line. Beyond the low property wall, a man pushed his cart of smoked peanuts with sudden jerks. "What I'm wondering, Pahalwanji," Laxman said, "is why you don't sell this medicine in stores. That's the way to reach people."

The pahalwan laughed. "I can barely make enough for your large family. How will I make it for the masses?"

"But it won't happen just by sitting here!" Laxman said. "If you put it in stores, it won't just benefit you or the people who are taking the medicines; it'll also increase our own respect for our traditions." He got up. "Look at what the British did to us. They ruled us by the sword and they brought us their culture by force. But when we people seek to return to our own tradition, we're passive. We say, 'Whatever happens will happen, it's up to God's wishes.'" Laxman added, "What you need is a business partner."

"At my age," the pahalwan said. Acting shy in the face of flattery, he started puttering around with his bottles again, none of which were labeled. Laxman wanted to ask how he even kept track of his potions but resisted. The pahalwan had a thin, long, powerful nose. He was myopic and wore ineffective thick bifocals; his sense of smell must have been overdeveloped.

"But, Pahalwanji," Laxman went on, "it's about our Sanskriti, our tradition. Our country is full of great men like you, but their learning is never brought to the public. Meanwhile, these men who were trained in the British way, the Western way"—an image of Sachin came to his mind—"they know how to make money and they control the economy."

"Nehru set it up like that," the pahalwan said, warming to the concept.

The mention of Nehru—SP's great enemy—stirred Laxman. "Nehru was an intelligent, educated man but a zero when it came to tradition. He studied in Britain and became a Britisher himself, and I don't want to say such things in front of a man of your sensibilities, but he also only loved British women."

"But his father believed in Ayurveda—he even set up a dispensary in Allahabad."

"No, Pahalwanji, maybe once upon a time, but my family, we knew the Nehrus very well," Laxman said, making much of this up. "By the time Nehru was growing up, they had become one hundred percent British—we even stayed at their house in Allahabad. Even when there was Indian food made in the house, they ate with a fork and knife. That's why the British liked him so much as the prime minister. It is this country's misfortune and shame that his family has ruled us since Independence. The British at least knew they were in a foreign country; they brought their learnings but didn't try to wipe ours away or convert us all to Christianity. Whereas Nehru was Indian and therefore thought he had a right to suppress everything Indian. And during Partition, he would take one Muslim over ten Hindus," Laxman went on, feeling angry now at his elder brother Bhagat, who had flattered Nehru's daughter, Indira Gandhi, into elevating him to an MLA. "Nehru did so much to promote Western medicine, opening many institutes—but look, despite tens of proposals over the years, he refused to set up a ministry for our traditional systems—whether in maths or science or medicine." He paused. "Tell me, Pahalwanji, do you approve of this idea? Would you like your medicine to be produced on a large scale? If you give your blessing, then from tomorrow itself we can start making it at my factory. I'll sit at your feet and learn all about it—I'll read the granths and the shastras. What could be better—a doctor and a patient, a true believer!—in business. I can tell you what the patients will like, and I have experience with accounting and packaging."

The pahalwan, hunched on the stool, pressed his hands into his beard and cheeks. He looked like a bored schoolboy, except he was not blinking.

More energy surged through Laxman.

"Yes, I can see it," Laxman said. "Mohanji Pahalwan Balms and Medicines."

The pahalwan changed the subject.

Afterward, Laxman felt as if he had been drunk, and that he should put this scheme out of his head; the pahalwan had not been interested.

But a day later, to his surprise, he received a call from the pahalwan in the complex's main drawing room. "Laxmanji," the pahalwan said, "this business idea you brought up, tell me more about it."

Laxman was sitting on a chair in a dank corridor a few feet away from his aunt, Bimla Behnji, who occupied her own chair silently, her head covered with a rumpled white cotton dupatta, her knitting needle piercing upward through layers of yarn.

The pahalwan wanted to know where in the country the demand would be highest.

"I'll have to research this," Laxman said.

"Then please do," the pahalwan responded. "We can't rush into business with vague ideas. And how would you want the stakes divided? Is your whole factory available?"

CHAPTER 40

LAXMAN WANTED TO SPEAK TO BRIJ. BUT FIRST HE WAS engulfed by chaos: It was time for Laxman and Archana and family to move into their own flat in the complex—the renovation was complete. With much mutual shouting and panic, they packed up their two rooms; three servants maneuvered the chests, chairs, and dressing table down the stairs of one building and up the stairs of another.

Karishma and Brij helped by staying out of the way.

Then, suddenly, Laxman was in his own space. A new home. Two bedrooms. A bathroom.

Laxman missed being in the same quarters with Karishma, but it was also divine to possess a corner that was all his; to rest on a private balcony that peered into the pink bluster of a bougainvillea bush reeling upward from the calming green of the front garden, so gorgeously maintained by Laxman's older brothers. The weather on the front side of the property itself felt different. The building was older and draftier and there was a greater density of foliage and flowers here despite (or because of) the absence of the towering gulmohar tree that stamped the other side's courtyard with shadow. One felt closer, too, to the urban rush of Delhi, because the low wall was only a few feet away from the gurgling gigantic artery of Mir Taqi Mir Road.

The first night that they moved into their new flat, he felt loving toward Archana—they shared a sense of mutual achievement—and she, too, lovingly pressed herself against him in the bed.

That weekend, Laxman went to see Brij. Laxman had lived in this flat for seven years; now he was just a visitor.

Brij had already established himself the king of his new space. He sat in a bathrobe on the sofa, his hairless white legs with bluish streaks spread apart, a newspaper held stiffly before his hidden face.

Karishma came in and out of the drawing room, organizing tea for Laxman and Brij.

Laxman told Brij he had a business idea for him and that they should discuss it before he went to the Sangathan for the puja.

"You go every Sunday, is it?" Brij asked, scratching his beard.

"Yes. In fact, Karishma also came once," Laxman blurted out.

Karishma had sat down and was pouring tea from a kettle into cups.

Brij put his hand up regally to indicate she'd filled his enough.

"So, you've finally started to have some respect for God, is it?" Brij said to his wife, showing his perfect teeth, one single tooth brighter than the others on account of its fakeness.

She mumbled something about Deepak's health.

"Your family used to worship snakes," Brij said to Karishma. "Forest-type creatures. Anyway, I told you Deepak would be fine. These things happen. He's a strong boy, sporty. Feed him chyavanprash every day. And cod liver oil. We had it every week when we were young. It tasted bad but we didn't fall ill."

"In fact, this is what I wanted to talk to you about," Laxman said. And now he began to tell him, in a slightly exaggerated manner, about how he felt there was a real market for ayurvedic balms in India, how the pahalwan was on board, and how, in any case, since he was looking to exit the female vanity space, this would be a good way to put the factory and its heavy machinery, such as the labeling press, to good use.

"But how can I help?" Brij asked. "Karishma and I are already in agreement about Gharam. The children can do the schooling at the fort or in Patiala, and then we'll admit them to a hostel like Sanawar"—Karishma looked on glumly—"and Rattan Tau has indicated that we can be provided with a tractor. Remember that small plot behind the house? We'll cultivate it and live off it. And I can take over the overseeing of the mosambi orchards, so there'll be no need for this manager chap, Dharmendar, who has been cheating us. In fact, I told Rattan Tau, I'll take over all of Dharmendar's responsibilities. Why have an outsider do it?"

Had Tau really agreed to this? Laxman wondered. But this was madness—this bitter, crazy man taking control of the joint income from the orchards. "But you have all this space here," Laxman said.

"We'll rent this out—what's the big problem?" Brij said.

"No one in the family will agree to that," Karishma cut in.

"If they see money in it, then—" Brij rubbed his fingers together as a gesture of lucre.

"If you move from here, I'm sure Sachin and Gita will take these rooms," Laxman said.

"Good!" Brij said. "Then let them come. Let them also enjoy living in this zoo!"

"Why not delay a little bit?" Laxman asked. "I need a partner. Archana has agreed to help, and if Karishma—if you can handle some rudimentary accounts—you can also be employed by the family business."

Laxman had already sketched out a plan in his mind that was practical commercially and sexually. In fact, he had never felt so creative in his life. Karishma and he would oversee the "soft" aspects of the business—accounts, purchasing, dealing with suppliers, and so on—from an office near the complex, while Brij, with his zest for discipline and mortification of the flesh, could strut about the grease-blackened factory in shirtsleeves. Archana, he planned to distract by giving her money for a tailoring business she could set up in the servants' quarters.

Having a single goal—time alone with Karishma—was making him generous elsewhere. He was becoming his best self.

"I've seen Abhay's pickle business in Jalandhar," Brij said. "It's a constant struggle. There are nonstop inspections. And they're dependent on defense contracts."

"Which is why a person like you would be helpful."

"You think the air force would ever buy ayurvedic balms?" he said with a dry laugh, lifting a Marie biscuit from a silver tray streaked brown. He cracked the biscuit between his teeth before placing the remaining half down on his saucer. "Don't take this the wrong way," he said, clearly *hoping* it would be taken the wrong way, "but I don't believe in this jadi-bootiyan business."

"Brij, listen at least," Karishma hissed.

"I'm stating my point of view," Brij said. "These defense people are hoity-toity." As a recent retiree, he was both a representative and a credible critic of the defense forces: their best enemy.

Nevertheless, in the following days, Laxman continued to work on Brij with real energy. "Come and at least meet Pahalwanji," he told Brij when they ran into each other in Bimla Behnji's drawing room. "And think about property values in Delhi—you'll be giving up a huge asset here. More importantly, the stars are in alignment—you are free, I am free, the market is wide open. I've done an analysis, and the other day when I spoke on the phone to the astrologer in Samana, he also told me this was the most auspicious period in years to go into business. And think about how much money you'll save here—boarding schools cost an arm and a leg."

The astrologer in Samana whom Laxman had phoned was the grandson of the astrologer who had shaped SP Chopra's life and, therefore, that of the entire family. When SP was born in the late 1800s, the astrologer, Shivshankar Trivedi, who lived with the family, leading a small team of Brahmins, had told SP's father, Hari Lal, that the boy had been born at one of the chanciest nexuses of the stars—the abhukt mul—a sign under which the historical figures Kans and Tulsidas had also been born. According to this alignment, the astrologer said, if Hari saw his son's face, he would die immediately. However, if precautions were taken, the boy would grow into epochal greatness. And so, at the word of this astrologer, SP, a mere twelve hours old, had been exiled to a household of Rajput peasants who lived on the other side of a ravine full of large, smooth stones speckled with gray and brown minerals ... peasants who had sometimes worked SP's parents' lands as sharecroppers.

Growing up in Delhi himself, Laxman always thought that such an exile, which his father had endured till the age of eight, at which point he was gradually repatriated into his birth family—living first with his grandmother in Patiala, then in a special quarter built at the back of the Gharam house so that his father would avoid running into him, before being finally presented to Hari Lal after Hari had propitiated a hundred Brahmins with a feast—Laxman had always thought such an exile would be an embittering experience. But SP's point of view as an adult was different: He considered himself blessed. "I had two families," he stressed. And then: "Another child in my position—what do you think the family would have done to him? They would have killed him or given him away for adoption. You have to remember: I wasn't the firstborn; they could have easily floated me away on a basket in the khud, like Kans." Moreover, the eight years with the Rajput couple, Sita and Chhotu, had given him a taste for peasant life: days spent herding cows with thin sticks of discarded firewood; throwing stones into vivid, clear pools full of tadpoles, which looked like spreading dots of ink; slapping together cow-dung patties for the hearth; and sucking mangoes that had been carelessly tossed on the ground by the benign broad trees. These experiences formed him. SP laughed when he narrated these stories to his rapt children on the veranda of the Gharam house many years later. He was surrounded, as an adult, at all times by an audience—a man who thrived on an audience. *Was he ever alone?* Laxman wondered now, walking back to his own flat from Bimla Behn's drawing room.

"In fact, when my mother came to take me back the first time from Sita and Chhotu's," SP had recalled in the veranda, "I was angry. 'Who are these rich Chopras trying to steal me from my family?' I asked. And when I was returned to the big Gharam house, my mother would bribe me with sweets and horse rides, but I would still run back to the farm." Finally, the shehzada, the little prince—the only surviving child after the premature death of his older brother from cholera—was installed again into the life of the landowner. But he never forgot his foster parents, their easy relationship with the land, or the way they cared for him, Sita's daughter-in-law even breastfeeding him after he had been exiled from his own mother's lap by the astrologers.

"Can we go meet Sita and Chhotu?" the kids and grandkids once asked SP in the veranda.

SP rotated a pair of binoculars on the green table hammered together from rough planks, nails jutting out at intervals. "They're no more," he said.

At that age, we didn't think to ask about Sita and Chhotu's children, Laxman thought now, climbing the stairs to his flat. *Later, we learned that their two sons, like true Rajputs, had enlisted in the army and had been killed fighting for the British in Gallipoli.*

Sita and Chhotu bore the grief bravely. The loss of SP, their foster child, had been a warning shot.

Half statesman, half villager—this is the stock I emerged from, Laxman thought, stomping around his new home in socks. But what was stranger still was that, after all of SP's years in the Jeev Sangathan, a reaction to the Brahminic control and orthodoxy exerted by the sinister exiling astrologers, SP, in his late middle age, returned fervently to astrology. As with many of Papaji's decisions, Laxman thought, it wasn't explained to them. Instead, one day, quite suddenly, the hunchbacked, kind, half-deaf astrologer—son of the exiling Shivshankar Trivedi—began appearing at their meals in Gharam, his large, shaved, black-spotted chin jutting out; his mustache long and drooping at the sides; the whites of his eyes so clear and unblemished that he appeared blind. He wore a perfectly pressed black kurta and was served on a silver thali since he did not eat chicken, unlike the defiantly non-vegetarian Chopra clan.

The kids knew he was an important man because Papaji, for all his socializing at night, rarely let outsiders join family lunches.

Why did the astrologer appear then? Laxman wondered now as he summoned up the past. *Was it simply that, having lost his parents, having fallen out with his thieving, backward uncles over property in Punjab, Papaji longed for a surviving piece of his past?*

Yes, what was going on then? But I was only a child, and when you are a child, you have no sense of your father's troubles. Perhaps it was after Vibha's marriage to Ravi in England exploded that Papaji decided he needed an external authority to certify the speedy weddings of his children. Bhim Trivedi, the astrologer, took out mahurats for each of us and we got married at odd hours—midnight, 3 p.m., on rainy but auspicious nights. Even while we participated in minimalist Jeev Sangathani havans, we became used to the directions of astrologers, most of us lining up in the musty old Gharam house after meals, the astrologer with the large fierce chin and kindly eyes examining us on the rectangular wooden bench that had been built around the brick fireplace, with its black memories of a thousand fires. Some of us, like Abhay, became fanatical devotees of Bhim Trivedi. Papaji, a vein in his neck twitching as he watched us, seemed to tacitly encourage this return to his past. Perhaps, Laxman thought now, *he had had his first intimation of death. Yes, this is actually when the astrologer came into our lives,* Laxman remembered now, *after Papaji's first heart attack*.

But astrology couldn't save him, no matter how much zeal he brought to it.

Bhim Trivedi had told SP, as he entered his fifties, to avoid cities that began with the English letter "K"—"Your chances of passing are very high in such a city," he said.

"K ...? K ...? K ...?" SP said out loud, later, as he sat with his brood of sons and daughters, some of them married, in the Gharam house. Then he laughed. "Karnal? But everyone from there comes to visit me *here*!" At the time, Kanpur—where he would die—was still widely spelt as "Cawnpore"; and SP had not realized that this city would become a center of so much of his business upon retirement: He was on the board of the Swadeshi Bank, of Jeev Sangathani schools, and of a large charitable institute that had formerly resettled Partition refugees and now worked for the education of widows and orphaned girls. And as his work began to take him frequently to Kanpur, he found there was no way to ask the committees to convene elsewhere on account of an astrologer's hunch. But SP tried to make his trips to Kanpur as brief as possible, arriving one morning, staying at his eldest son Rattan's house (Rattan was then posted in Kanpur), and jetting out the next day, splurging on airfare to abet his swift getaways. At the start of these plane rides, he prayed out loud as the rickety Cessna, its windows rippled with UP heat, seemed to claw the earth with its desperate small black rubber tires before sailing off.

But what kept him in Kanpur, finally—what killed him—was not a train or a plane or a car—but a doctor.

The arrogance of science! Laxman thought, still pacing his flat, depressed by the excess space, which seemed empty not just of humans but of meaning, making him long again for the extreme density represented by his father's reign, the pre-big-bang state of SP's empire when everyone and everything was crushed together. And his thoughts turned again to the great man's death.

The year was 1973. Laxman wasn't in Kanpur then but he had constructed the scene in his mind. On the morning of that unspeakable day, SP—then in his seventies—came out of the bath in Rattan's house in Kanpur, sweating and out of breath. His bearer asked if he wanted a rest, and SP shouted at him to bring him his clothes instead: He had a morning meeting at Allahabad Bank and despised lateness of any kind, though he knew that two of his fellow board members would waltz in twenty minutes after the meeting began, offering no apologies. They were, of course, not the businessmen on the board but rather the retired bureaucrats who had risen above such earthly matters as punctuality while they luxuriated in the lap of government, which existed as a sort of rotting heaven suspended six feet over the reality of the country.

Despite having played an active role in the Indian state in the 1940s, SP had come to hate the government. He was increasingly enamored of the private sector, which, he felt, freed up individuals' energies. If he'd had his druthers, he would have eradicated the bureaucracy altogether, replacing it with a council of elders (helmed by himself, of course!).

When he arrived in the boardroom that morning, the room done up in the dark hues of power and coffins, the first person to take note of his pallor was Dr. Harpreet Singh—the only doctor on the board. "SPji, are you OK? You're looking tired. Did you not sleep well? It's not good that you're sweating so much at this hour."

"You've been outside, it's hot," SP said.

"But your face is flowing like a river! How long has this been happening?"

When SP refused to answer, Dr. Singh said, "If you've been this way for more than an hour, we should take you to the hospital—it's not good for a heart patient."

"If I go to the hospital," SP said, "I know what you'll do: You'll make me give up my favorite foods." He pointedly broke off a piece of matthee lying on a plate and placed it in his mouth. He hated being told he couldn't eat oily food.

But then his breathing grew more labored and another board member, Sardar Kishan Jeet, said, "Look, SP Bhai, listen to our friend Harpreetji—he saved my wife's life when she had a heart attack."

"Let's first finish the meeting, please," SP said.

"But Jindal and Arun haven't even reached," Kishan said.

"And you're acting surprised?" SP asked. "We can start without them." He was panting now.

"Arre, Suresh, bring water for sahb," Dr. Singh said to the bearer, who was standing by the door in a turban with a long tail, looking on in a droll manner.

By the time the bearer returned—after a great clanging of vessels in the adjacent pantry—Dr. Singh had gotten SP to his feet. "My God, man, don't be this stubborn. You Chopras are tough, but if we don't go now, you might have a heart attack here. Have you been eating uncooked vegetables, as I said?"

"Never!" SP said, grinning mischievously even as his breath grew shorter.

"Come on," Dr. Singh said.

"No hospital!" SP shouted. (Looking across the years, Laxman could feel his father's panic: his fear of dying in a city that began with "K"; his inability to admit, through all the layers of contradiction that made him a man—peasant, landowner, banker, freedom fighter, Hindu reformer, orthodox believer—that an astrologer's prophecy was driving him.)

"Don't worry, yaar," the doctor said, one hand under SP's armpit. "I'll specially bring you ladoos while you're on your deathbed. Arre, Jeth Ram, you're just standing there, call the driver."

But even as SP staggered about faintly on his feet, sweating through his tight white shirt, he kept shouting, "If you take me to the hospital, I swear on God—"

The doctor finally had no choice but to accede to SP's demands: He instructed the driver to take SP not to the hospital but to his—the doctor's—house.

From the house, Dr. Singh phoned Rattan's servant and, finding that Rattan, a deputy general manager at Canara Bank, was out of town, told the servant to inform SP's children about their father's worsening health. He then made SP lie down on the hard bed of the guest bedroom and unbuttoned his shirt, revealing a soaked white vest.

"Now listen very carefully to me," Dr. Singh snapped, walking about the room in his chappals, his royal-blue turban loosely folded on his small head, a mound rather than a wrap. "I'm giving you two tablets. Take them right now and then three more times today. And remember, I've already done you a favor of following your wishes and bringing you here instead of the hospital, though a doctor must never listen to his patient. I'm adhering to your wishes because I respect you and because I'm your friend"—he spoke partly to the easily impressed audience of his two young twin Sikh grandsons, both eight years old, who had come out of their room (holding a torn kite between them) to look at this felled ox of a statesman—"but one thing you must do: You have to cancel your flight. You're in absolutely no state to fly for a few days."

SP tried raising himself from the bed in protest. But when he tried speaking, his eyes bulged.

Dr. Singh, who had the reddish eyes of a drunk (he had two whiskeys every night and woke up hungover, in a foul mood), screeched, "Good God, man—you want to die up in the air? Is that the way you want to go? Then go. Die in the clouds. No one will be able to help you, and the only thing those pilots will care about is how to get to Delhi as quickly as possible to offload your corpse. Whereas here you're among friends, your children are coming—Rattan has already canceled his work in Bathinda and is driving back, and Rupvati, your favorite, is also arriving soon." This was a running joke among SP's friends: how he was attached to his fair, pretty, and widowed distant-cousin, Rupvati, who often acted as his hostess in Gharam, where SP held court for much of the year, far away from hospitals and doctors. This was the first time the joke had been openly aired before its subject.

"You've talked a lot, now at least give me the medicine," SP growled, finally, gasping. Noisily wiping his brow, his chest wide and large under the vest, he sat up in the bed to wash down the pills with a tumbler of water. "Ahh, see?" SP said. "Now I'm OK. Already better. So I won't need to cancel the flight. After one hour of resting here, receiving your beautiful wife's hospitality"—the two Sikh boys tittered, having sat down on cane stools—"I'll be revived."

"Ji, I can't understand what your desperation is to get on this plane," Dr. Singh said. "From what I know, you're a retired man. Is there really something so serious awaiting you in Delhi that you can't reschedule? Honestly, you're not behaving like a former Reserve Bank Governor—but like a little boy!" At this, the little boys with pink lips and judas tied down with blue and yellow handkerchiefs respectively, fell silent. Calling someone a boy was a grave charge.

Laxman wondered with the hindsight of years: *Why wouldn't Papaji just say it—why wouldn't he give Dr. Singh the true reason for his desperation to leave this "K" city? Papaji was not a man who was ashamed or who apologized for earthiness or his embrace of tradition—he had earned enough credit as a reformer to indulge a few eccentricities. But, at that time,* Laxman realized, *we were still close to British rule. Their opinions dominated our lives; imaginary white men glared over our shoulders. And perhaps SP felt*—so Laxman thought—*that admitting the prophecy out loud would loosen a barrage of arguments from the angry doctor, that furious jinn of rationality in his tumbling turban. Or perhaps something deeper was going on—SP had been reduced, in the moments before death, with death rushing to meet him, to the young boy who, one day on his farm, at the age of seven, was suddenly brought back to the large mansion of his "real" parents, realizing his childhood so far was a lie, an ersatz life, a biding of time, that nothing was stable and permanent; in fact, later, it was this feeling that had kept him on the go, on the run, one step ahead of a life that may reveal itself to be a false floor, and perhaps SP felt it now again, the feeling that this huge life itself, dense with dramas and peopled by his own offspring, had been a distraction from the longer, truer experience of death. Perhaps he said nothing because he* wanted *to die. SP stopped reading the astrologer's warning as a remedy and took it as the release it was meant to be.*

By the time Rattan arrived from his meeting in Bathinda, driving at top speed in his Ambassador, SP had expired of a massive heart attack. He had been sitting half-upright on the bed and sipping tea from a cup and saucer balanced on his stomach when the convulsion came. The cup and saucer jumped up from his belly and smashed onto the floor, the tea arcing into a puddle by the old wooden frame of the bed. Then SP rolled into the hot liquid with a sigh.

Dr. Singh had stepped out at that moment for a smoke and a shot of whiskey. He came running in when he heard his grandsons screaming.

CHAPTER 41

SINCE THEN, LAXMAN AND HIS SIBLINGS HAD HATED THAT doctor—they had cut themselves off from Dr. Singh's family. They had felt—perhaps rightly—that, left to his own devices, SP would have driven out of the city right after the meeting, that his death would have been averted.

We would have kept him out of "K" cities forever, Laxman thought now, lighting a joss stick before a portrait of his father, the only thing he had hung so far on the wall of his new flat. *And he would have lived forever.*

After SP's death there had been an even greater effusion of enthusiasm in the family for astrology and superstition and fasts. But that enthusiasm, like all others, had steadied or muddled over time. Apart from his nephew Abhay, only Laxman, with his simultaneous love of the Jeev Sangathan and of his father, had remained on SP's path, consulting the astrologer and also partaking of ayurvedic remedies when possible. If there was a lesson to be learned from his father's death, it was this: *Allopathic Western doctors couldn't save you.*

Brij listened to all this. Then he opened his eyes. "Do you know what the annual fee for Sanawar is?" he asked Laxman.

Talking to Brij was like speaking into a void.

Laxman said he had no idea.

Brij quoted an extravagant figure. "I learned about it today. Karishma makes fun of my scrapbooks but she's right that they are out of date. Chalo, if you're so insistent, let's go and meet your pahalwan. What's the harm in it?"

Laxman was a little tense during the meeting in the pahalwan's veranda, because both Brij and Mohanji were odd men, and he had no idea how their oddness might interact.

But when the two men met, they discovered they had lived in Calcutta and Bangalore at slightly overlapping times, and were soon deep in conversation.

"You didn't tell me he was an English professor!" Brij said on the car ride back, gripping the handle above the window. "A truly learned man!"

A few days later, when Laxman invited the pahalwan over to his new kitchen to demonstrate the cooking of potions, Brij joined them and even relished the gingery taste of the potion that the pahalwan stewed in a pot. "I'm in good health—but one could always be healthier!" he said, licking the spoon as the pahalwan consulted a large saffron-cloth-covered granth on the countertop, moving a finger over the fine but fading Sanskrit instructions.

But after the pahalwan left, Brij said to Laxman, "It's all very good, but frankly, as I said, I can't see any future in it. The overheads will be too high."

Brij left for Gharam to investigate the idea of moving the family there and of becoming the overseer of the joint lands.

But what happened in Gharam was a mystery, because Brij returned a week later with a sullen, fixed expression and said only that he had taken a look at the lands and found they were barren and underwatered because of the current caretaker, Dharmendar. "And to make them fertile again will require a Herculean effort. I'm not a servant that *I'm* going to take that responsibility." He went on, "And Dharmendar is cheating Rattan Tau, who is a good man but too trusting."

Laxman knew how to read between the lines. Clearly Rattan Bhaiya—most certainly not a good man, with his ferocious, sadistic temper—had insulted Brij, and Brij had come running back.

And so the decision was made: Brij and his family would stay in Delhi.

They commenced their balm venture.

CHAPTER 42

THE COMPLEX SAT RIGHT NEXT TO A SMALL GALLERY OF shops—a chemist, a stationer, a halwaii. This gallery was owned by the family, though the tenants paid only nominal, ancient rent. A travel agency had just shut down and a small office was available there. It was this space that Laxman and Co. took over.

Responsibilities were divvied up. Brij, with his yen for physical labor, would oversee the former bobby-pin factory in Shahdara, which would be repurposed to manufacture balms, the last of the black bobby pins carted away in slinking mounds on the backs of rickshaws. He also started driving around in the family's jointly owned jeep to the teeming markets on the outskirts of the city, acquiring herbs at cheap rates and introducing himself to potential stockists.

Laxman took on the responsibility of getting the finances in order and putting together program notes to submit to the Ministry of Industries. Here, Bhagat Bhaiya's Congress connections were helpful; the application was expedited.

Laxman, it was also decided, would direct the finances from the office near the complex—that way the women could join him part-time while being near the kids.

Karishma would handle the accounting, and Archana would liaise with suppliers and customers.

In the tight cubic office, which had a front of glass, Laxman sat at a desk that was at right angles to the door, facing a wall, so that passersby would see his profile. Archana sat at a desk near the door, her back to the road, and Karishma sat across from her, near the far wall of the room, facing the front door. Laxman was in the middle, swiveling his head between the two women.

This is how the whole family came to know of the strange triangle.

Or, no, they didn't know, but they gossiped, how could they not?

Sensing trouble ahead, Laxman's older brother, Ram Bhai, tried to discourage Laxman from embarking on the joint venture. "There are always issues that come up when money is involved—and Brij, he's an unpredictable type."

Laxman nodded, as if agreeing. He was standing in the manicured lawn, his brother's domain, and he wanted to show a bare minimum of respect before defying him. "The problem, Bhaiya," Laxman said, "is that the bobby-pin business is not profitable anymore. But I don't want to stay in this balm business forever either. Brij asked me for help, and this will allow him to become settled after leaving Bijapur. After one or two years, I'll exit."

"No one leaves a business like that," Ram said with a jeering smile, his hands on his hips, oblivious to his permanent floating crown of October mosquitoes.

Laxman slapped one dead on his own arm, creating a surprisingly large smear of blood. "See, Ram Bhai, you're right, and so I'll be careful. But, unfortunately, I've given my word."

Ram looked on sarcastically. "We all know what Bondu's word is good for."

Laxman's hatred of his brothers was growing but he would never speak back. That was one lesson his father had instilled in him: Rank mattered.

Laxman had, as per an earlier plan, tried to convince Archana to initiate another business—such as tailoring—but there was no question, in Archana's mind, of sitting out this exciting enterprise while Karishma, Laxman, and Brij all dedicated themselves to it. "We may be no longer living together," Archana said one evening at the Modern Colony Club to Laxman and Karishma, "but in a sense we're even closer now. And Karishma and I have always worked well together—there was never a problem when we ran the kitchen jointly, was there? So why will there be one now? It's really you men," she said, pointing a finger at Laxman, "with your big egos, who have issues. But Karishma and I will keep us all together, isn't it? Anyway, it's good you and Brij will be in separate areas—you'll have your own domains, which men like. But it isn't like that for us, is it, Karishma? We women like being together."

Karishma smiled with her mouth closed, pushing a long, dangling question mark of hair behind one ear.

In fact, no matter what Laxman tried, Archana refused even momentarily to vacate their mutual office near the complex. When he offered to send her on a free trip to Benares—she had always wished to buy Banarasi silks in bulk and sell them at a markup in Delhi—she put it off; when he requested that she visit the factory to see if Brij needed help, she said, "I get a headache from all the fumes there." Then, looking straight at Karishma, across the tiny box of the office, she added, "Only a tough air-force man like your husband can survive there." Laxman had to apply great effort to keep from glancing at Karishma. He noted jealously that she suffered from no such problem. Lost in her accounts, her smoggy black eyes were half-closed, and with her charming left-handed grip she made finicky tick marks on the page. It was only when Archana needed to go to the toilet—in Brij's nearby flat; there wasn't one attached to the office—that they had a moment to look at each other with the curious heaviness of people who are hoarding a secret between them.

Yet how lovely those moments were! Karishma would look down at her papers and then swing her eyes up warmly, and he would glance at her without blinking, careful not to mist his eyes with visible emotion. Or she might yawn and get up from her chair and pass by his desk to fiddle with a pile of papers in the glass casing of the metal cabinet, turning her back to him and feeling his glance rake little shivers up her spine. He had to exert all his will to not get up and embrace her.

Or: If she were sitting, he might rise up from his desk, and place a paper on her table, muttering a few meaningless financial words but really only finding an excuse to brush his hand against hers. They were two prisoners making shy progress toward each other in a jail.

"The accounts aren't too complicated, I hope?" he said one day to Karishma from his chair, putting his newly acquired gold-rimmed glasses low on his nose. Archana was within earshot.

"It's not like there's money pouring in," Karishma said, not looking up except suddenly, at the very end—a flicker of warmth. A few shops—mostly dispensaries connected to temples—had started selling Mohanji's bottles, which had been laboriously hand-labeled by Brij at the factory. Their logo was a wrestler with obscenely bulging muscles, underneath the words: "MOHANJI PAHALWAN BALMS."

"The tax regime is unfavorable," Laxman said.

A few seconds later, Karishma got up to go to the toilet in the complex.

"I also have to go use the bathroom," Laxman told Archana.

Archana considered them both with kohl-weary eyes. As if for the first time, Laxman saw that the top half of Archana's upper teeth were striped with red from paan.

As Karishma and Laxman went through the gate of the complex and then up the covered pistachio-green stairwell to Karishma's flat, she snapped, "Have you lost your mind?"

"Nothing will happen," he said. And then, as she stood a step above him, he clasped her legs. She wriggled, but his grip was powerful and he pulled himself up to her step and brought his nose to her neck.

"Laxman, not here," she breathed. "The servants."

He kept pressing his face into her neck; she felt his dense stubble on her collarbones; and now his lips were tracing upwards toward hers and he was pressing himself into her.

"Move!" she hissed suddenly, pushing him with her hands and immediately using those hands to smooth out her kameez and adjust her gauzy dupatta, which had become knotted as it had been pinned behind her on the wall of the stairwell.

They walked up the last few steps side by side. Karishma said nothing. She was radiant with anger. She went into the flat and straight to the toilet; Laxman took a farther flight up to use the other toilet and was surprised to see the door locked. Then he remembered: It had been turned into a servants' bathroom three years before. Flustered, he went back down. He considered waiting for Karishma at the landing in front of her flat's front door but thought better of it and returned to the office, mildly frazzled, running his hands through his thin hair and patting his mustache thoughtfully.

He was also angry: He had done so much for her!

"You've come very quickly—where's Karishma?" Archana asked.

"It was only number one. She's still in the toilet."

Archana put a paperweight on a pile of documents on her table, the edges of the papers still flapping in the fan breeze. She looked mildly harassed in her black outfit. "These accounts you were asking Karishma about—I also examined them. It looks like we're going to have to put a lot of our own money into the business."

"Don't take tension, yaar."

"I didn't know you had this much income at your disposal," she said quickly.

He coughed. "These days there's a lot coming in from the orchards." The common land.

"But earlier you said you put it all in savings and life insurance?"

"Not all of it, obviously," Laxman said. He knew he was being accused of the ultimate marital crime of withholding money, which she could have used to purchase better clothes for herself and the children and to acquire modern fittings for their flat. "It's left over from the construction also," he said.

"Which you told me went over budget." She was now leaning forward, her small head cradled in her small palms, her frizzy hair encircling her face. She was coolest when interrogating him; she thrived on directness and confrontation, traits Laxman had valued in a wife in a joint setup where one was always being called to defend oneself against bullies while taking care not to accidentally insult elders.

Archana glanced at the clock on the far wall, above Karishma's chair. Perhaps she was wondering where Karishma was.

"When you start a business, you have to put down an initial investment—we'll earn it back," Laxman said. "Plus, there's the money from shutting down the bobby-pin business—outstanding dues from the shops, tax write-offs for those machines."

"Then you should note it in these documents," Archana said.

"Stop being smart," he barked, the muscles in his neck tensing up. He had no desire to tell her the truth—that he had skimmed donations from the Jeev Sangathan.

CHAPTER 43

THE NEXT DAY, KARISHMA AND LAXMAN WERE ALONE IN the office for once. But this time, Karishma's jaw was set tight and she refused to look up. Instead, she made savage notes on the wafery translucent sheet in front of her, somehow avoiding nicking the paper. Laxman got up to adjust the knob of the fan and came closer to her. "I hope this cools your anger a little bit," he said.

She kept staring at the paper. He was about to speak further when she said, "Don't you dare treat me like this. Is this how you treat women in the family?"

He put his hands in his pocket. Anyone viewing them from outside the office would have seen two individuals—one sitting, one standing—at a safe distance from each other, engaged in dispassionate business chitchat. Laxman always carried this self-surveilling double consciousness with him when he was in the office or the complex, performing as if on a stage. He had learned to separate his words from his physical gestures, to create two distinct, unrelated streams of emotion that could flow side by side: one private, one public. With his tongue, he felt the back of one of his sharp canines.

"Do you realize how many sacrifices I've made for you?" he growled.

"We all know you've done this many times," Karishma said.

Was she talking about Gita? Did she somehow know? "Karishma," he said. It was a warning to keep her voice low.

"It's not like your wife's coming back in a rush," Karishma said of Archana. "And even if she came, she wouldn't hear. And anyway she probably knows everything. She looks at me these days like I'm an untouchable."

"She knows nothing," Laxman said. "I guarantee it."

"It would be the only way a woman could live with you," she said.

Laxman fiddled with the fan knob again. "It's loose—that bloody electrician." Then the electricity suddenly clicked off, the room sighed into darkness, and the fan overhead began a death spiral. "Chalo, that solves the fan problem."

"Unless you blew the fuse," she said. Even when she was angry, there was an undercurrent of flirtation and irony to her voice. She was wearing a low-cut blouse and had two overlapping gold chains around her neck. Her lipstick was alarmingly bright. *She has come prepared to fight with me*, Laxman thought. *Which is why she's looking her best. What does she want?*

He felt again that he was trapped in some eternal game of purposeful miscommunication—of willful misdirection—with the women he knew, both sides sending a blast of signals meant to confuse the other party into submission or at least throw them off-balance. Yet the pleasure lay in letting these emotional winds take him, to not resist, to know that it was pointless to analyze or fight back. *We are first and foremost physical beings. Talk is just an instrument of confusion.*

If he could have, he would have grabbed her even more violently than he had on the stairs—to assert that talk was meaningless.

Surging with power and self-regard, he went back to his table and sat down. "We need to go together somewhere," he said in the hot office, rotating the date stamper before pressing it into the plush blue mini-carpeting of the stamp pad and bringing it down with plunging violence on a piece of paper destined for the Ministry of Industries.

"And how will you arrange that?" she asked, biting her lip and then using her hands to pick the skin around her thumbs, shifting nervously from one hand to the other.

"You act as if I didn't arrange this whole business for you."

Karishma looked over her shoulder for signs of Archana.

"She's not fond of work," Laxman said. "She's probably got a 'headache.'"

This made Karishma laugh. "I know," she said. "Her smoke breaks always got longer and longer when we were cooking together."

"She still smokes?" Laxman asked.

"You never kiss your wife or what?" she said.

They looked away from each other.

At that moment the fan came on again; the milky tube light began its spidery clicking and sputtering. "Believe me, I've tried," he said. He put his head back on the pleather office chair and placed his hands behind his head. They were both softly laughing now. Anyone glimpsing them from the outside would have seen two people having a gala time in each other's company. They were enjoying it so much in fact—especially now that the fan was cooling their sweat—that even their double consciousness, which haunted them at most moments, vanished.

CHAPTER 44

THE PRODUCTION OF BALMS WENT AHEAD. THE DOZEN workers in the factory grew more and more skilled at evaporating the mixtures in the pans to create decoctions. The pahalwan visited the factory weekly, burying clay pots full of herbs in the tiny yard. And Brij designed increasingly intricate colorful labels, showing Laxman the options.

In the office, meanwhile, Laxman, Archana, and Karishma fell into a rhythm of paperwork. Laxman would work alone in the office in the mornings, while the women were away at their baking business with their friend Sarika; after lunch, they would join him. At least he wasn't tortured by Karishma *all day*.

One afternoon, Laxman walked into the office where Karishma and Archana were sitting and said, "There is an emergency situation." He told them the company was behind on its permit applications and an inspection of the factory could happen any day. "Karishma, did you submit the safety certification?" he asked her.

Karishma began to rifle through her schoolgirlishly neat pile of papers.

"That's what I thought," he sighed.

Laxman sat down, wiping his brow with the towel he always slung over his chair. "We're in big bloody trouble. But the man we have to see about permits is there today, in his office in Sheikh Sarai—that's who I was just speaking to on the phone. The problem is I don't understand the papers—Karishma is the expert."

"Can you invite the man for tea?" Archana asked.

Laxman made a dismissive gesture with his wrist. "Here? He'll never come. They want people like us to fall at their feet. He's one of those arrogant IAS types. When are Lekha and Sujeet coming?" he asked Archana. These were relatives of hers expected for late-afternoon tea.

"Ten minutes."

"Shit." Then, "Do this: You go ahead with tea—I'll take Karishma in the car. Can you come?" he said, turning to Karishma.

Flustered, Karishma said, "I have to just tell Jatin."

"Is it really that urgent?" Archana asked, and at that moment Laxman felt that she knew and that, instead of fighting the affair, she was quietly giving up. He was sorry for her, almost angry on her behalf.

"Believe me," Laxman said, "I'm not exactly burning to go myself—traffic will be bad. But what choice do we have? Karishma—can you collect your papers?"

But Karishma was already up, whipping her sapphire dupatta over her kameez and spreading the papers on the table the way a gambler might deal a pack of cards. "Do you need the corporate certificate also?" she asked.

"Bring everything," he said.

Laxman and Karishma were in the car, sailing along Mir Taqi Mir Road before Laxman U-turned toward Central Delhi.

"So, where are you taking me?" Karishma asked in a slightly bored, masculine way.

The words hit Laxman like a wave of drowning cold air. He smiled, his ears sticking out and tensing as they did when he grimaced.

"What? You think you can make a fool out of me the way you made a fool out of your wife?" Karishma asked, thrusting a (Laxman-manufactured) pin into her dense hair, which had been knotted up at the back instead of dangling behind her ears in its beguiling hooks.

"I'm not making up the story about the paperwork," he whispered.

Slanting sideways toward him, Karishma curled her legs up on the long car seat. "I see—at four p.m. on a Thursday, someone will accept paperwork from us?"

"Put your legs down," he hissed.

"What are you afraid of?" she said, refusing to shift. "You think all the people on the road know you?"

She was acting crazy. They were only five minutes from home, at a crossing on the main road over the railway tracks. But, yes, this was one of the oddest things about intersections that sat near your house—no matter how many times you sped through them, you almost never encountered acquaintances; the heart of the city had grown so dense that it flooded every street with strangers.

"And why will this 'official' help you?" Karishma asked, yawning, and lazily putting her feet back down into her slippers and straightening up.

"I'm one hundred percent serious," Laxman said, revving the car on Mir Taqi Mir Road. Why was he feeling so angry? Because she had fooled *him* with her performance in the office more than he had fooled *her*? In his mind's eye, he saw her nervously shuffling the papers at her desk and rising up like a shouted-at secretary, and now he experienced another gust of sympathy for his wife, who would have been so distraught and confused had she known the extent of their connivance in the office. His acting, he felt, was necessary; Karishma's was heartless and over the top.

He took a left and they rose up Ring Road, with the railway tracks glinting and zagging perpendicularly underneath. Then the colony fell behind them.

CHAPTER 45

AS LAXMAN DROVE, KARISHMA SAID AGAIN, "WHERE ARE we going? The Maurya or the Taj? Choose a good place, because everyone's going to talk about it."

"I've heard enough from you today," he snapped. He now felt brutal and stiff, glued to his roaring machine, overly familiar with its burps and shudders as he thumped the Fiat's sideways gears.

"Are you going to get a new car or will you drive this old Fiat forever?" Karishma asked, trailing her right hand over his hand on the steering wheel.

He neither offered a response nor pushed her away. He could never understand her moods. Her voice was sweet, her lips were full and pressed together, and the corners of her radiant black eyes crinkled with smile lines.

Then she turned away with a flounce, putting her head against the window. "Fine. Do this. Take a right here and let's go to your favorite brothel on GB Road."

He said, "Is this a way for a woman to talk?"

"Or maybe you should just take me back to that room above the temple, which is the only place you can get hard."

This time he was so shocked he didn't reply.

Minutes later, they were strolling side by side in Connaught Place, promenading among the afternoon shoppers like a couple, though they were both careful not to touch the other in a familiar way. Laxman spasmed in and out of tension, running his hands through his thinning hair. The large colonial complex, with its curving corridors and plaster facades, was crowded with nearly recognizable faces. He would shortsightedly grimace at an approaching stranger in *hello*, his head and neck going tight, only for the tension to dissipate as he turned toward Karishma and heard her voice with its upward lilt, saw a flash of her perfect teeth, smelled her citrusy perfume.

It had been her idea to come here; he had had no desire to be caught in a public place patrolled by the middle class. But when she had told him, in the car, that there was nothing more she would rather do than have a cold coffee together at the Indian Coffee House, he had acquiesced. His own idea had been to take her to a deserted corner of the Ridge, which, he could tell from her mood, would have backfired. And acceding in this way, taking the car where she directed it, made him burn up even further. He was not in control—and he liked it.

He only feared now, as they sashayed down the dirt-rangolied Art Deco corridors, that *he*—unable to keep his hands off her hips or her behind—would be the one to accidentally expose them.

We are in CP visiting an ayurvedic company, he imagined telling acquaintances if they ran into them. Or: *We are finding a new stockist.*

They stepped around footpath sellers hawking cigarettes and magazines and chooran. "This has no health properties," Laxman said to Karishma, pointing to a silvery, braided packet of chooran and realizing then that there was only one way for people to interpret the sight of a man and woman in a market together in the mid-afternoon. "But that's the problem with the government," Laxman went on, "they certify everything and so no one trusts anything."

Karishma said, "I've always wanted to come here in a happy mood. When you grow up in small towns, CP is the very idea of glamour, and it's remained that way for me, even with all these other markets that are opening. But Brij is in a bad mood whenever he's near a shop—it's as if he knows that, once he's in a market, someone or the other will take his money—and we always fight when we come here. Once," she continued, "he hit me here, on the cheek, in broad daylight"—how calmly she said this, as if these were the simple wages of marriage—"and Mohit was so afraid that he ran away and when I went after him, I also got lost." She smiled at the memory. "So I wanted to come back here to enjoy myself. Oh, look—here's that lovely bookstore!"

They went into the chaotic and stuffy aisles of the decidedly unlovely Galgotia & Sons, where, by the front shelf of books, a couple of management-trainee types in semi-translucent banyan-revealing white shirts and elastic black ties were holding up thick business guides before them, their chins sunk toward their chests, their hair hard with brilliantine, the brilliantine only enhancing a sense of cheapness, the strands releasing no real luster, bits of dandruff dotting the partings—the hair of people who spend too much time indoors.

"I hardly ever read," Karishma said, as they walked past these mannequin-like men. "But I find bookstores very relaxing."

When's the last time I read a book? Laxman wondered now, panicking. "Yes, they're peaceful, like libraries," he agreed. Then, embarrassed by the obviousness of this, he walked over to the biography section. After thumbing through the titles for a few seconds, he nearly shouted, "They don't have a copy of *Memories of a Patriot*!" SP's autobiography.

Laxman marched to the front of the store. "You're Galgotiaji, right?" Karishma overheard him saying to the silent mustachioed proprietor. "Namaste, I'm Laxman Chopra. I believe my family knew your family from Lahore days ..."

Madness, Karishma thought, shrinking into the back of the store as she listened to this conversation. *On the one hand, he's nervous about coming to CP and being exposed; on the other, when it comes to their dead father, these Chopra men drop their genetic pants wherever they can!*

Galgotia listened impassively to Laxman and then burst out, "Of course, of course, who doesn't know SPji! You live in Modern Colony, correct? In fact, your aunt Vibha—accha, she's your sister?—she comes almost every month with her daughter, Aparna, and she buys her one Agatha Christie or Thomas Hardy each time."

When Laxman raised the issue of *Memories of a Patriot*, Galgotia said, "Yes, your sister has also informed us. But the publisher has lots of distribution issues." Galgotia had a still, long face with one twitchy eye and a brushy reddish-black mustache.

"Then I'll talk to the publishers," Laxman said.

Karishma continued lingering in the back, pincering out a black pocket-size Penguin edition from its tight array, the edges of the pages turning into a powdery blur as she turned them with her fingers. She had always had the ambition to be creative—to paint, to design clothes—but could never graduate beyond the romantic notion of the artist as genius to the gritty dailiness and boredom of *being* an artist, as one of her college friends had.

There were two arthritic fans in this humid store, with its acres of rotting moldy paper. The dust on the books hadn't shifted in years; it was a graveyard. Now the door opened and younger, noisier shoppers came in: three college students, two boys and a girl. Karishma watched. The three students were all clearly in love with each other to various degrees, but were disguising it with levity, their laughter and high spirits tragically taking each of them further into themselves rather than connecting them with the others, each locked up in his or her joke, so that none knew what the other really felt and instead got lost in a thicket of witty, meaningless signals. They were on familiar terms with Galgotia, greeting him cursorily before continuing their jocular one-upmanship and burrowing through the aisles for some French-sounding author they had asked the shop owner about. Karishma backed toward a shelf, holding a Somerset Maugham novel open before her but glancing at them. She had never, as a girl or even a woman, had such open freedom with men; even now, unchaperoned groupings seemed to her vaguely illicit, too obviously drenched in carnality. Yet as drops of sweat slicked her back in the humid store, she was full of amusement and pity. The girl, while dark and plump, had a pleasant face with alert, clear eyes. She wore the half-Western clothes of the lefty jholawali—kameez over jeans—and she had done what all women do: worked hard, like an artist, to highlight the assets she possessed or had been told she possessed. Her eyelashes were long and painstakingly curled, and she wore a star-shaped silver stud in her nose and earrings in her tiny, pert chikoo-like ears. The boys, meanwhile, were still boys—simultaneously rowdy and sheepish, secretly despising each other, the one with the bulkier body more comfortable in his skin, standing heavily on his two feet, while the other boy, lanky, with ungainly long legs, fidgeted awkwardly near the girl, who looked away from him to the burlier boy. The burly boy, in turn, soaked in the attention from the girl but ignored both his companions.

By now, Laxman had come to join her by the Penguin alcove with its orange-black covers, and she felt closer to him and more affectionate than she had ever felt before; but when she smiled openly at him, she could feel the gaze of the shopkeeper following her. *He must think I'm his wife*, she thought, and was filled with a dizzying pleasure—the pleasure of *not* being seen, of being cast into a role and turned *into* a wife: more an anonymous appendage than a person.

"Did you find anything good to read?" Laxman asked.

"No," she said, "let's leave."

CHAPTER 46

AS IF IN A TRANCE, THE TWO LOVERS CONTINUED CIRCLING the market, which was even more packed now with twilight crowds. The sounds of traffic lapped at Laxman's and Karishma's feet the way an ocean punctuates the quiet of a beach. Bats with mechanical-looking veined wings sailed down from the parapets of the walkways. A few tube lights clicked on. With every minute, Laxman thought, Archana's suspicion must be growing—but neither he nor Karishma stopped moving, the market tempting them with its endless portals to disappear into.

They came to the Indian Coffee House. The front door was framed by two large potted palms, and the insides of the establishment were obscured by a brutally tinted door. A bearer held the door open for them and they went in.

They sat across from each other on the first floor, at the back, watching the fans with their long stems bear down from the high ceilings like lazy, rotating eyes. Fingering the flimsy menus with their crinkled and torn plastic coverings, they handed them back to the ancient, sharp-beaked waiter in his uncomfortable bandhgala and turban. They ordered cold coffees. They had never sat across from each other like this. Laxman was nervous. He was aware suddenly of his scarred skin, the creeping thicket of stubble on his cheeks, the two moles on his neck (supposedly auspicious, but this is what everyone said about ugly features), the way his hairline was receding even as he made it recede farther by pushing back the thin strands atop his head.

Karishma pinched her lips together and put her hands facedown on the table. Her neck was bent but she straightened it—a tall, splendid woman—and she craned around and touched her collarbones in that way that she often did when taking control of a situation.

"Do you think our business is proceeding as you'd expected?" Laxman asked.

"I have zero expectations," Karishma said, putting her teeth over her lower lip.

Laxman went on, "I'm worried, frankly—because how can we compete with Dabur or Zandu or Hamdard? These people have been making balms for fifty, sixty years and they've cornered the market." It hurt him to look straight at Karishma. Again he felt pity for Archana.

"What story are you going to tell people when you go home?" Karishma asked.

Laxman smoothed the hair on his left arm with his right hand. "We were at the government office and the official kept us waiting—they always do."

The bearer brought their tall cold coffees on a silver tray.

Welcoming this reprieve, Laxman sucked in the barely melted vanilla ice cream through his straw and made an involuntary "aaah" sound at the end.

"You think they'll believe it?" she asked. Her eyes danced with mischief.

"They won't have a choice," he said.

"Good," she said. "Then we can relax."

She began to pepper him now with questions. What had he been like as a boy? How had he and Brij and Sachin gotten along? Unlike him, she was not afraid to introduce her spouse or children into the conversation. She apparently saw no contradiction between the affair and her family, saw the dalliance as a continuation of the family, as opposed to a negation, a point from which to consider her "real" life.

"And did you love Archana when you first married her?" she asked.

He found himself saying, "Like yours, it was an arranged marriage, and you know how she is, she's only for herself and she's very stubborn. Anyone else's ideas she instantly puts down." He immediately felt bad after he had spoken.

Karishma slurped her coffee, looking impassively into the frozen eddies of milk and ice cream in the narrow glass frosted on the sides with condensation.

"So, you never loved her," she said, as if calculating something.

He nodded "no," but then felt ashamed again. What was the need to disparage his wife—given that he already had Karishma? But he felt vulnerable sitting across from her. This was a training one did not receive in the Chopra family—how to be alone with another person in a serious way. Even if you found yourself in a one-on-one conference in the bustling clan, one of the two people would be restlessly pacing around. Movement was the hallmark of the family, a hundred eyes dancing in the background, watching you.

"Archana is a very good mother, though," he said. "And generally a good partner."

Karishma's eyes flared open; he could see black storm clouds in her irises. "When men say such things—that's when I can get angry. You don't think a woman needs love?" She almost spat into her coffee. "I've seen it all from day one: You never gave Archana any love. Why do you think she reacts to you this way and keeps herself busy with her friends and all these hobbies? Because she knows you're not for her, that your eyes are turned on every woman but her."

Laxman gripped his emptied coffee glass with both hands, unsure where this was going.

"I'm just saying this because I know how you'll be with me," Karishma said, slumping forward on the table and pulling back two strands of hair that had come down on her forehead from her dense bun. "Especially if we have a love affair. That's why it's better for me to keep my distance."

Love affair! He was electrified. "Wow, you'd think you did not just an MA but a PhD in psychology!"

"Don't be saarci with me," she said. "You know I'm right." She straightened up again, proudly. He tried to x-ray his way through her clothes, imagining his hands closing on one of her unusual, upturned, large-nippled breasts.

"Are we going to eat something also?" Karishma asked.

As they munched on fries and chicken patties a few moments later, the gold rings on Karishma's fingers glowing with oil, she said, "You're very quiet—you don't have any questions about me."

Laxman crisscrossed his hands together and cracked his knuckles. "No, it's not like that." But he was, again, taken aback. Finally he said, "When did you first know that you ... liked me?"

"Typical," she said. "Exactly the question a man like you would ask first!"

"But you asked me to ask!" he said.

"And you're only capable of asking a question about me that's actually about you!"

"I knew I shouldn't have opened my mouth," he said with a smile.

"Except to eat these fries—eat more," she said, pushing the plate toward him. He thought of the first time they'd had a moment together at the club, how he'd been the one prodding her to eat. She had become more confident. Was *he* the cause?

Over the next few minutes, their banter crescendoed in tense climaxes only to fall apart in mutual conspiratorial smiles and silences. He started to become comfortable with this rhythm and to see that she was leading him somewhere, with a series of secret challenges, challenges that were both serious and jesting—a way to maintain and also publicly enunciate the tension they felt inside. He was impressed and surprised by her boldness. Who *was* this woman? How come he hadn't noticed this aspect of her personality before? But then he had mistaken her wide-eyed response to his advances as a species of shyness or self-protection, of holding one's self erect and reserved in the face of a man's onslaughts. Yet she had known very well what was going on—she had obviously known from the start—and had been weighing the consequences, dipping in one toe, then the next, into the murk of this affair ... what if *she*, not he, were the instigator of the affair? The thought made him soar up instantly into an erection.

She had power. He was not exploiting anyone—no, the exploitation, if that's what you wanted to call it, was mutual. He had found his equal.

Now he began to jealously worry that she, too, might have done something like this before—pretty women like her rarely escaped the attentions of men when they were young and growing into womanhood. He thought involuntarily of one of his village conquests—Ritu—and he thought he saw the ghost of that village girl's expressions in Karishma's and wondered: *Am I drawn to Karishma because she looks like Ritu?* These village women either reacted to advances by fully retreating into themselves, frightened of all men, or by becoming sexually bold, wild-eyed with lust, seeking to repeat the secret family liaisons through which they'd come of age. So, no, his question to Karishma had been in earnest. He actually did wish to know if she had started to conceive of him as a sexual possibility at the same time, or even before, he had.

"Did the other men in Bijapur Paper treat you all right?" he asked when he realized no answer to his previous question was forthcoming.

"What do you mean?" she said.

There had been rumors, he wanted to say, but then stopped. *These, of course, are the sort of rumors that will soon be spread about us*, he thought.

"I just wanted to know how the wives of senior officials are treated," he said.

She looked at him with confusion, eyebrows knit, sending that familiar tilak of tension up above the bridge of her nose. A glimmer of sexual recognition passed over her face, and she smirked. "It was a hard life. I'm glad it's over, though I could never say that to Brij—"

"Even though it was *his* idea to resign?"

"I didn't want him to blame me," she said.

"You were right to stay in Delhi without him," Laxman said.

"But it wasn't good for his career, it didn't look good before his seniors that the wife and children are far away, but what choice did I have? Moving every year—"

"I saw how you lived in Orissa," he said.

"And that was a comparatively *good* posting. When I look back at the last ten years, I can't believe how many of the states in this country I've seen."

"At least that's interesting," Laxman ventured.

She shook her head. "Why? It's a sad, poor country. The farther you go from the cities, the worse it is. And it's getting filthier every year. It's smart of those people—Sachin and Gita and Sharad and Nalini—that they went abroad."

"We've only been independent for thirty-six years," Laxman said with a smile, a smile that, for the first time today, seemed to him to fit naturally on his face. "Give it some time."

"Till then, the poor will live like animals," Karishma said. "And the Congress will continue doing nothing."

Laxman sighed. He wanted to criticize the Congress too, but felt an ache of loyalty toward his Congress MLA brother, Bhagat.

She went on, "And Nehru was an absolute nincompoop and had no idea how to use the army strategically. If he'd given orders earlier, all this 1962 nonsense could have been avoided."

"This is why I stay away from politics and focus on what I can control: the Jeev Sangathan, Mohanji Balms, family."

"Don't take this the wrong way," Karishma said, suddenly lighting up, "but I think you would make a very good politician—and that you will be powerful. Of all the people in the family, you have the personality most suited to it."

"Shamelessness, you mean," he said with another smile.

She waved it away, smiling too. "Yes. But also strength. And a way with people. I mean, you have more friends than—"

Stop this flattery, he wanted to say. *You'll make me fall deeply in love with you.*

"I've actually talked to Bhagat Bhai," he said. "But there isn't another constituency to run from. And if I was serious, Archana and I would have to move to another small town. And Archana—you know how much she hates small towns, even more than you do." Then he said, "But I don't think I could ever do it. Politics corrupts the politician."

It was getting dark. They had to leave, but they spent a few more minutes talking in the maroon colonial chamber, with its burning sconces giving off the soft orange glow of socialist India. They were discussing sundry things now—the colony, family gossip—but it felt good. Laxman's desire to touch her had gone away. They were friends; and when he led her to the car later, he held open the door for her gallantly and she got in with a tinkling, pleased laugh, swatting away a trapped mosquito that flew out.

CHAPTER 47

ARCHANA WAS SKITTISH AND MEEK AS SHE BROUGHT IN casseroles from their new private kitchen. She wouldn't meet Laxman's eyes as he gazed at her from the dinner table. Her shoulders had collapsed inward, making her look smaller than usual (the way she curled up into herself when she smoked, a posture Laxman remembered from the first years of their marriage, except that at those moments she had possessed a kind of gleeful conspiratorial expression, as if her body itself were a hand closing around the lit cigarette). "Sujeet and Lekha—is their financial situation better?" he asked.

Before she could answer, eight-year-old Shilpa said, "Sujeet Uncle showed us four separate magic tricks."

"Only this dumb one thought they were magic," Vaishnavi scoffed. She was twelve and blessed with her mother's curly hair.

"When did I say that?" Shilpa asked.

"Ha!" Vaishnavi said. "For two hours afterward, Papa, Shilpa was eating my head, asking how did Sujeet Uncle get magical powers."

Eating my head, Laxman thought. One of his phrases.

It occurred to Laxman that one reason he loved Karishma so much was that—unlike the masculine Chopra women, his sisters and aunts and daughters—she was tough *and* feminine, both aspects exerting themselves by turns, as in Laxman and her combative crescendoing conversations, so that there seemed at all times to be two Karishmas, an excess of personhood. But perhaps Karishma's toughness was an act, just as the femininity of the Chopra women felt like an act.

"What tricks did he show?" Laxman asked.

Vaishnavi described two card tricks that involved making all the aces appear together at the center of the pack.

"If you know how to do it, show us," Laxman said.

"Right now?" Vaishnavi asked.

"Yes, right now," Shilpa said, playing the imperious sidekick to her father.

Vaishnavi got up to bring a pack of cards.

"More daal?" Archana asked Laxman, dully.

"You were right—this business is proving tougher than I realized," Laxman said. "The whole afternoon was wasted. They gave us such a runaround: We ended up in an office near Connaught Place and then they wanted the document notarized again, and you should have seen Karishma, she was being so sharp with those guys, the way she can be. I had to tell her, look, what you need is tact, this tone won't work, this isn't the air force or Bijapur." And what *had* they done? They had not touched, had they? He shook his head and became, in the process, aware of how he was obviously overacting. His stomach fluttered. "You didn't tell me how Lekha is—how's her mother?"

Archana's answer was mumbled and negligible.

The pressure in his head was not leavened by the way Vaishnavi was now noisily dealing out a pack of cards.

"I told you she didn't know how to do it!" Shilpa shrieked a few seconds later.

"Accha, bachu, what about this ace?" Vaishnavi said, holding up the ace of clubs.

"Enough!" Laxman finally shouted.

They were stunned into silence; he didn't often shout at them.

Vaishnavi got up and stormed into her room—she had her own room now!

When Shilpa jeered at Vaishnavi's failure to perform the card trick, Laxman told her to get lost from the dining room too.

"There's no need to be so bad-tempered," Archana said.

"It's comments like that that put me in a bad mood."

"I can always sense your moods," she said. "I'm afraid of them."

"I was out all day, I had to drive, it was hot and that sister-in-law—"

"Niece-in-law," Archana said, softly.

"She was no help, complaining, complaining. I hadn't realized she was such a princess! This is probably why Brij was happy to be posted in MP without her."

"You must have not been behaving properly," Archana said.

"Again, you trust anyone but me."

"She never talks that way with me," Archana said. "She's a straightforward person and says what she thinks." She went on. "And if this business is going to make you dislike your family members, leave it."

He laughed. "Two weeks ago at the club you said the opposite—how nice it is to be close—"

"I didn't start the business," Archana reminded him.

Flicking a handful of rice back into his plate, Laxman rose up. "No matter what I do, you're bloody ungrateful."

"You're the one who's come back in a bad mood!" she shouted as he retreated to the bedroom, where, ignoring her voice, he picked up a file from the bedside table and began, for the first time in the day, to properly work.

CHAPTER 48

KARISHMA WAS HAVING HER OWN CONFRONTATION WITH her nuclear family.

When Karishma had entered her flat, Brij had glowered at her from his perch on the sofa chair. "You spent a lot of time at the office today," he said.

He would have driven by the glass cube of the office upon his return from the factory; he would have seen it was empty.

Karishma said, "I wasn't in the office—I had gone to see Manjuri Auntie." A lady who lived down the street. "And you know when she starts talking ..."

"Hi, Mummy," Deepak said, coming out of the boys' room and hugging her by the waist.

"What's this you're holding in your hand?" she asked. Something spiky was pressed against her hips.

A shuttlecock.

Mohit and Deepak had been playing badminton on the roof.

"I've told you so many times, beta," Karishma said, "play anywhere, but not there: The fence is rusted and you can fall down."

"Yes, you should have informed your mother," Brij said, getting up to decant some whiskey into a glass lying on the sideboard. Then, scoffing, "You should have couriered the message to her, since she is never here."

As the night wore on, Brij got drunker and drunker, making ludicrous statements about national events from his sofa perch and then at the dinner table. "And these bloody fellows in the printing shop," Brij went on, "they have no idea about quality and finishing. How crookedly they stamp logos onto paper! I had to show them myself," he said, boasting to his sons, who, knowing their father's temper, nodded vigorously in response. But when Mohit asked if he could read out a poem he had written for a class, Brij steamrolled right over him, continuing his emphatic monologue, which had now taken him down the road of impugning the integrity of the field marshal of the army.

"Brij, your son wrote a poem for you," Karishma said.

"Perhaps I have heard his comment? And I decided this is not the time nor the place?"

Karishma frowned.

Brij went on, "I do the tough labor, I slave in the factory, I sweat all day, I toil among the laborers."

"You and also us," Karishma said.

"Beta, pass the roti," Brij said to Mohit, before continuing his raging. "You call that work? Sitting in a cool office all day with your boyfriend and girlfriend."

"Brij."

"Talking and gossiping, all of you, like ladies," Brij said.

"Mohit and Deepak, you go inside."

"No, stay," Brij said. "Are you excited that your Rupvati Chachi is coming to live with us?" Brij asked.

"What?" Karishma asked.

"Just like air rushes in to fill a vacuum, Rupvati Chachi has heard that Archana and Laxman's room is empty and is coming to fill it," Brij said. That room had, in fact, been recently allocated to Mohit.

Rupvati "Chachi" was an elderly, religious spinster in her seventies whose relationship to the Chopra family no one could completely ascertain. She was (maybe?) some kind of younger cousin of the great SP Chopra, and he had been very fond of her, and so had let her run his household in Gharam, and that was all that mattered. Since SP's death, she had lived with various Chopra families as a "state guest," passed around like a radioactive package from one household to the next because she was notoriously critical, unhelpful, nosy, gossipy, miserly, and generally useless in the kitchen, though she was always around to offer pious bons mots and could, for certain families, serve as a bumbling babysitter.

She had been living for several years with SP's oldest son, Rattan, in the ancestral home of Gharam. But Rattan Tau had apparently kicked her out.

"Has she given a date?" Karishma asked, even as she relaxed a little, understanding the source of his anger. "Of course she can take ... Archana's old room. But who'll cover her expenses?" Then she put her hand on her face. Her anxieties had returned. What if Gita and Sachin moved back too—would there be any space left for her and her family?

Brij shrugged. Then he took a stick of butter from the butter dish and rubbed it on his roti like he was putting out a cigarette.

CHAPTER 49

THERE WAS NO END TO CROWDS IN THE PROPERTY. ONE crowd departed; another formed. Within what seemed like hours rather than days to Karishma, bumbling old (but not as old as she looked) Rupvati arrived in A-19, taking kabza of the corner room with her three large trunks and bistra-bundh. "No need to touch my feet," Rupvati said repeatedly to Mohit and Deepak—who, in fact, deeply suspicious of the pious lady, with her oiled double-braided white hair, were doing no such thing. A fair woman, she was plump, with an egg-shaped paunch and close-set eyes, eyes that made her look alternately sly and daft, and she played her radio constantly.

"Why was Papaji so fond of her?" Karishma asked Laxman and Archana in the office.

"He had a soft spot for people who were slightly lost," Laxman answered.

"And she behaved very differently around Papaji," Archana recalled. "When he died, her true self came out."

Regardless, with Rupvati's presence, it had become harder for Laxman and Karishma to organize their trysts.

So they cooked up a clumsy scheme. One Sunday, freshly showered and in a white kurta, Laxman ambled up to Brij and Karishma's and invited them and the boys to visit the temple with him. "It's a very auspicious day, and I want the pundit to bless the boys." Archana, he explained, had taken Shilpa and Vaishnavi to sitar lessons.

Brij said, "Why do you hold the puja so late in the day, yaar?" He had taken a run at dawn and showered and changed into his bathrobe.

"So we can encourage the lazy people of this colony to come," Laxman said, showing his small teeth from under his projecting mustache.

For a moment it looked as if Brij—who wished to be seen as pious—might join them. Then Brij said to Karishma, "I've just changed. You and the boys go. But remember, Karishma, you have to help Mohit with his homework tonight."

A few minutes later, Deepak and Mohit and Karishma entered Laxman's Fiat.

Mohit—whom Karishma seated in the front, next to Laxman—made awkward, halting conversation with his uncle. Deepak, in the back with his mother, looked sourly out of the window.

"Wipe the rotten expression off your face," Karishma said to Deepak. "You're going to greet God. Is this the face you want to show him?"

"And afterward you'll get sweet pershad," Laxman said from the front.

"Headmistress Ma'am says sweets are bad for the teeth," Deepak replied, his breath hot. He had inherited his father's unfocused brown eyes. Three prominent, fetching black dots—birthmarks—studded his left cheek, as if to draw attention to the unusual fairness of his skin, a feature he shared with his mother.

"This is not just any old sweet," Karishma said, "it's pershad."

"Ma'am says that we should trust science, not super-tuition," Deepak said, confident in his malapropism.

"Ma'am, Ma'am," Mohit bleated in imitation from the front. At ten, Mohit was three years older than Deepak and was five inches taller. A beanpole with a thin, long face and a crooked nose that hung over crooked teeth, his black eyes were often full of earnest intensity. Even now, mimicking his brother, he did not look malicious.

"Mummy, see, Mohit is troubling me again."

"Complain to your Ma'am, then, OK?" Karishma said.

Laxman slowed down the car in front of a strip of shops on the colony's main road.

"What's here?" Karishma asked.

"They both got such good report cards that I wanted to get them gifts," Laxman said.

The window of a toy store shimmered before them.

"But, Mummy, won't we be late for the havan?" Deepak asked.

Karishma noticed that Deepak did not address himself to his uncle, and she was flooded with guilt, then rage. "Look at the ungrateful boys I've raised," she spat. "Laxman Chacha's taking you to a toy shop, at least show him the respect of going in with him."

"But, Mummy, you only said we should pray first!" Deepak said.

Laxman and Mohit were already out of the car.

Karishma slapped Deepak. His face became smeary with tears and then he unlocked the door and stepped into the hazy, forgiving winter light. Karishma remained in the car, even as Deepak looked back to see if his mother would join him.

But Karishma did not stir. She did not feel pity or remorse for her action: That was not her way. She acted when it was time to act—that was that. She had a remarkable ability to keep the future out of her head. She did not occupy herself with what *might* happen in the room above the temple. But then a cold tingling rang like a bell through her body, and she cranked open the window and inhaled the dusty, flat winter air. A zealous cleaner was beating the sidewalk with a jangling jhadu, and clouds of sepia dust rose at regular intervals on the road. Karishma's right nostril was slightly blocked, and she closed the left one with a finger too—the one that was sucking in the atmosphere—trying to force breath out of the blocked passage instead. It was as inelegant as a car attempting to rev itself up. Then she shut both her nostrils with her fingers at the same time, trying to see if she became lightheaded—a game she had played in her childhood and that had helped her when she started swimming (she only breathed on one side of her freestyle).

On the road before her walked slight men wearing thick, flimsy spectacles, their hands loosely clasped behind their backs, long khaki trousers flowing past their ankles—shopkeepers, maybe. They didn't notice her in the car, which trapped heat within its alloyed surfaces. Even the cracked-open windows didn't help, and she was suddenly flooded by an image of Laxman on top of her in the back seat, his hands pushing her hands down, herself resisting with a kiss ...

She did not need the boys. Yes, she loved them, but that was different from necessity. She was ashamed to have such thoughts but was also proud of her honesty. She tended toward the harshest truths about herself and other humans.

Karishma's intuitions were often correct. When a family friend in Amritsar had told her that she was going to set her up with a handsome qualified Chopra boy, she had thought, *A famous family, but I'm sure he is the stupidest and meanest of the whole bunch*. She had been right. When Laxman became friendly with her, she had thought, *Like uncles when I was growing up, he wants to put his fingers in my mouth*. Right again.

But she was confounded by Archana. Archana seemed to know what was happening but kept her cards close to her chest—as if for a single triumphant ultimatum. Sometimes Karishma wondered if she had slept with Laxman—had waded further into the murk of the affair—to goad Archana into issuing this demand. But Archana kept silently smoking on the roof of A-19, watching, calculating, understanding, building toward an obscure goal; and now, as Karishma thought about Archana's evasiveness and elusiveness, she became antsy and wanted nothing more than to dig her fingernails into Laxman's strong, hairy back and to feel him inside her.

Sex was a response to confusion and doubt. It was the most certain thing in the world. She rolled up the window. She finally took a breath.

CHAPTER 50

WHEN THEY PULLED UP AT THE TEMPLE, LAXMAN SAID TO Mohit, "Now, you and Deepak play cricket in the park while your mummy and I go pray, OK?"

Will God ever forgive us? Karishma wondered.

Laxman had bought the boys a bat and a tennis ball and he pointed to the small municipal park across from the temple.

"But, Chacha, I thought the pundit was going to give us pershad," Deepak said as he emerged from the car. His whining lacked its insistent droning power. The bribe had worked, casting him into confusion. Still, a part of Deepak understood that one could not completely shed a performance one had earlier committed to; credibility required continuity.

"First you say Ma'am doesn't want you to eat pershad," Mohit responded to his younger brother, "and then you say you want it. Mummy, he's being a silly brat!"

"Is Deepak afraid you'll beat him at cricket?" Laxman asked.

"I'm an all-rounder," Deepak blustered.

Mohit scoffed.

"Come, I'll show you," Deepak said. "Mummy, didn't I tell you that Sir said I'm better than Mohit at sports even though *he's* bigger?"

"Sir shouldn't be saying these things," Karishma said with a slight laugh, meeting Laxman's pleased eyes in the rearview mirror for a second.

"He's lying, Mummy," Mohit said. "He says whatever he feels like."

"You're afraid," Deepak said, spitting his words out of the window.

Suddenly, Karishma heard herself shouting, "Enough! You both get out and go play or Laxman Chacha is going to confiscate your bat. Now, come on, what do we say? 'Thank you, Laxman Chacha.'"

"No need," Laxman said.

"Thank you, Laxman Chacha," the boys said in that chiming, singing way of children that instantly makes their gratitude sound insincere.

Karishma and Laxman deposited the boys at the threshold of the park and watched them rotate through the rusty turnstile into the barren square. Then, Karishma and Laxman climbed the steps to the temple.

Laxman told Karishma to wait in the temple office. He himself walked to the back.

The pundit, in his dhoti, was bending over and pressing mounds of earth into the flower bed with his hands and groaning, "Hari Om," every time his body creaked upright. He brought up a strand of his dhoti to wipe his forehead.

Laxman felt a constriction in his throat, and then he said to the pundit, "Mohit and Deepak have come, Punditji."

"Ah, Deepak, my sweet friend Deepak," the pundit said. "How is his health?"

"Fit, ji. In fact, they're playing cricket in the park, and they both said, 'Call Punditji, we know he's a great cricketer,'" Laxman said.

The pundit had been a first-class Ranji cricketer in his youth.

"How will I play?" the pundit said. "But I'll say hello to them."

"If you can play a little bit with them, that'll be nice for them—they were asking after you. And I have some work here with Karishmaji—the accounts for our business—and it'll be good if the boys are distracted."

"I'll say hello to Karishmaji also," the pundit said.

"And I told Mohit you'll teach him how to deliver a googly."

The pundit knew what was going on. Laxman knew that the pundit knew. It was all in the pundit's blemished, yellowed eyes, with their pretentions toward wise blindness. The pundit pursed his lips, as if to say something. But then he laughed. "I'd be honored. I also want exercise. My paunch is growing bigger."

"Don't bowl too hard at them, Punditji!" Laxman said.

"I only do what the one upstairs tells me to do," the pundit said in a self-mocking way.

Hiking up his dhoti, he walked to the front, greeted Karishma in the office, and was gone.

Karishma and Laxman immediately headed upstairs. Neither commented on the danger. But when they got there—to the filthy room, with its toxic scent of paint and naphthalene balls—and took off their clothes and lay down on the hard single bed together, Karishma said, "What are we doing?" She stroked his penis absently, even as she looked away, forming the inner side of a spoon. "What's the point of this." His fingers were inside her. She kept talking as he moved his fingers. "We're going to get caught, and that will be the end of it, and Brij will kill you."

"You want him to kill me," he said.

"The boys know," she said. "The pundit knows. You have no shame." She betrayed no passion in her voice even as her body buckled, her hand around his cock. "Soon everyone will know."

"They can go to hell," he hissed.

"You realize?" Karishma said. "Brij will never die. When he was in the air force, I would pray that his plane would crash. But he would never even get slightly hurt—not even when he parachuted out onto rocks."

She started stroking him faster.

"What do you think he's thinking now?" Laxman asked.

She said, "He's thinking of what he'll do to us. But, oh, no, it won't be when you expect it. He'll walk right into this room."

"No!" he said, coming to climax.

"Now put your hand here," she said, closing her eyes and focusing, for once, on herself.

CHAPTER 51

SOON AFTER THIS VISIT WITH DEEPAK AND MOHIT, LAXMAN went to the temple alone and called the pundit aside. In an understated way, looking at the floor, Laxman accused him of overcharging for joss sticks and samagri and the like—things that Laxman had known about for a long time but had never bothered to bring up. "Punditji, it's not a big thing, but for a man of God ..."

"I did nothing," the pundit said. "On the soul of Ram."

"It gives me no pleasure—" Laxman went on.

The pundit said, "Even if I had done something, what difference would such a small sum make? I've been loyal. And there are my children, my wife ..."

Laxman told the pundit that he would reconsider.

Four days later, he fired him.

He gave the pundit a week to pack up and leave. Then the temple was padlocked. No one in the Central Jeev Sangathan Association was informed. Laxman posted a handwritten sign on the metal door saying that the pundit was out of town and the building was shut for renovation till further notice. This was how the most intense period of his life began.

At first it was impossible to find a way for Karishma and him to converge at the temple without raising antennae in the family. Then they hit upon a solution. In the winters, Karishma liked taking evening walks, but Brij did not, preferring to play badminton indoors at the club. Archana and Karishma sometimes took their evening strolls together, but Karishma began altering her timing so that she would head out for her constitutional in the early afternoon or the very late evening. At these times, Laxman, citing a meeting at the Sangathan or with a wholesaler or the pahalwan, would drive over to the temple. Arriving there, he'd wait under the portraits of Guru Harbans Lal and Tilak Ram and his father, pacing the floor in his bare feet, excited and melancholy. He did not do well in empty spaces. He liked bustle—a trait inherited from his hyperactive father. He would walk to the back and open the metal door that led to the pundit's now-empty quarters, checking the corners for mice droppings or cockroaches. The floors were unfinished earth. The cabin had been shoddily built, its ceiling bulging downward. When the pundit had left, he had taken everything with him—even the simple cane furniture that Laxman had installed. There was nothing Laxman could do to retrieve it. He felt guilty. He had liked the lazy pundit; they had been synchronized in various ways, the pundit happily playing the role of passive pawn in Laxman's schemes. Yet what choice had Laxman had? He was entering the most important phase of his life, the only time he'd had the opportunity to make meaning on his own terms. Could you put a rupee value on that? Surely the gods would understand?

And so *what* if he *was* found out? He would wear the scandal proudly, like a badge, strutting about like a man sentenced for killing someone everyone agreed was evil. When you were condemned fiercely, it was because everyone wanted what you had; and he saw the lives around him now as terrible tight cells of repression, meant to slowly asphyxiate the passionate souls of those who had been randomly roped together by marriage. He knew he was not alone in the physical aversion he felt toward his wife (or she for him). Marriage was a device to produce children, but it brought little pleasure to the adults. The future—not the present—was what mattered to the god of marriage. This was the strange thing about ancient civilizations; they were the ones most obsessed with the future and with children; this is *why* they had survived. Whereas Laxman's great discovery had been the present, the burning-up of time for one's own edification and pleasure.

He realized now, as he waited for Karishma, that the closing of the temple, the firing of the pundit, was a prelude to something else: He was falling out of his religion.

Once upon a time, Laxman realized, the gods had lived on earth like mere humans. But when artists painted them or encoded them in bronze or stone, they became immortal. These gods—men and women—had enjoyed lifetimes full of ardor and war but now cast their long shadow of morality over future generations, denying them, through their images, the pleasure they themselves had experienced. *What made a god? The experience of pleasure. And the denial of the same pleasure to those who followed.*

He thought of Ram and his gorgeous wife, Sita; he pondered the Pandavas and their shared dalliances with Draupadi. Did *these* people lead moral lives? Didn't Yudhishthir gamble away his wife? Didn't Krishan consort with gopis? Why weren't these models—rather than warnings?

His eyes fell on the pictures of the reformers on the walls of the temple. These reformers had been right to refute idols; they had understood and feared their seductive power. But now Laxman saw that the Sangathan favored a lessening of life—a desiccation, a decoction, all pleasure consigned to the fire. The fire was cleansing, but it was also pure, boring, fundamental. He understood now that the Sangathan was a poor fit for someone of his temperament, but also why, for this reason, his own father, with his huge appetites, must have been drawn to it. The more sensual you are, the more severe you desire your religion to be. You want to be held in check. That is, until you want to be free.

These thoughts bothered him for days; they didn't come linearly or clearly; and in any case his belief in the Sangathan had never been absolutist—he had always visited Sanatani temples and, on his morning walks, often prayed to the ornate marble Hanuman installed under a canopy near the colony park. But he was like a man who, waking one day, realizes that the circumstances of his life, the particularities of his identity, are just that: particularities, a random accoutrement of culture that can be shrugged off if it doesn't fit him.

He had an urge to read *The Kama Sutra*, which he knew only as a "dirty" book; he wanted to see the famed temples in Khajuraho.

And when he was with Karishma on that bed, both of them expressing their pleasure openly, he pressed his closed eyelids and his nose to every part of her.

"You like this old woman's body?" she said. "Even when you have all your nineteen-year-old prostitutes to chase around?"

"You're more turned on by them than I am," he said.

"Nonsense. I know men. I'm in my last days as a woman. Then my skin will start to shrivel and sag. You'll have no use for me."

"Why not enjoy it now, then?" he said, kissing her again.

She placed a hand on her collarbone, as if wanting to assess the temperature of the words bubbling out from her throat. "The future matters more to us women," she said. "We lose power as we grow older; you gain power."

"Nonsense." He kissed her on the outside of her thigh. "I like this depression here. It feels like the bed of a lake."

"Don't tickle me," she said. "Soon this will all be gone. And you will find someone younger. Like Rohini." She began listing all the younger attractive brides in the family. "And maybe you'll bring her here too—when it's dark." Her left hand was between her legs; she had learned to give herself pleasure. Her talking was always proportional to the amount of pleasure she was receiving. They had reached a plane of trust and neutrality.

And sometimes afterward, lying together, time running out, hearing the blind rush of bats outside the window, she would talk about what she actually wanted from the future, one downy arm thrown over her breasts in a gesture of modesty that only highlighted her total nakedness. "I would like to disappear," she said once. "To be totally alone. To have no people around me. To have no responsibility. No mother, father, children, husband—to just be on my own, on a hill, for three months. Surrounded by fog."

"I see," Laxman said. "Like a true devi."

"Don't look jealous," she said. "If you behave, I might even invite you."

CHAPTER 52

GITA HEARD OF THE SCANDAL IN THE COMPLEX IN A LETTER. She had come home from work earlier than her husband and torn open the mail. It was from Prabha, Bhagat's wife.

> *I thought you should know about the latest developments in A-19, as a family member and as Sachin's good wife. I know Sachin prefers to not have an involvement with such issues but I believe this could have the mightiest consequences—for, e.g., with the property—down the line. Hence this letter.*
>
> *As you are aware, Brij, Karishma, Archana, and Laxman have entered into business partnership together.*

She knew this, yes, yes, Sachin and she had even exchanged a few terse words about the space the business was being run from, whether Sachin should press for his share, and he'd said, "Do you want us to look like monsters who are demanding things from abroad?"

She read on.

> *Anyway, Karishma and Laxman were seen nearly holding hands outside a chemist's shop by Vicky and then ...*

She stopped. She was thinking: *That bastard, Laxman.*

What had happened was (uncharacteristic for Prabha) exactly what Prabha had said: Karishma and Laxman had been seen together.

Talk in the family about Karishma and Laxman, of course, had been brewing for some time; men and women who weren't married were rarely so friendly; and Prabha was an especially persuasive and persistent gossip on the subject of illicit love.

Besides, as long as one person in the family, Prabha, could be blamed as the source of the gossip, everyone else merrily amplified it, even as they pretended to criticize the person spreading the rumor, which itself was a form of spreading the rumor.

But rumors are normal in large families. The problem acquired graver dimensions when a thirty-something second-cousin bachelor relative saw Karishma and Laxman standing close to each other in a chemist's shop near the temple.

It was one of the few lapses of secrecy Karishma and Laxman had suffered that winter.

Karishma had been having a headache at the temple and Laxman had gallantly offered to fetch her Crocin. "It'll take me one minute to go to the market," he had said.

"I need to walk in that direction anyway," she had responded—to keep up the pretense that she was out on an evening walk.

"You sit and take a rest," he said.

"I'll walk a few steps behind," Karishma insisted.

He hadn't liked the idea, but it had worked and then they had done it again a few times—even, on that one fateful day, entering the chemist's together, which is where they were spotted by Vicky, the second cousin, who was buying fly-bitten silver-deckled mithai across the street.

Vicky was a straightforward business type, a chartered accountant who favored dark Terylene shirts and had been boarding with Laxman's brother, Ram, in the complex. When the subject of Laxman and Karishma had been raised at a small family gathering, he had said, "Prabha Tai's not lying—I also saw them together."

"What kind of nonsense are you talking?" another relative had said, though Vicky had already shared this juicy tidbit with her and she had been equally appalled.

Still, Vicky couldn't stop himself. "Yaar, I told you: They were in the chemist's—I was across the street at that Balram Di Hatti."

"It must have been someone else," Ram interjected.

"No, Tayaji, it was them only."

That was all it took.

A-19—and the colony—was abuzz with the news of what Vicky had seen with his own two eyes.

Laxman first heard about the sighting when Ram showed up at his doorstep. "Didn't I advise you not to do business with your relatives?" Ram asked, eyes volcanic and hot. "Is there any respect left in you for your father's name? And what about your own wife? Your children?"

"Bhaiya, nothing happened, this is sheer gossip," Laxman said, twisting his hands.

"Shut up," Ram said. Then he turned away and stomped back to his own flat, kicking away twigs with his splayed feet.

When Laxman walked to the office, he found Karishma there already.

"We'll have to stop meeting for some time," he said. He filled her in on Vicky's accusation.

Karishma's face became pinched.

"But the key thing is, don't do anything, don't say anything," Laxman said. "It'll pass. In the meantime, you go for your walks, I'll go for my meetings. If we change our routine, people will become more suspicious."

She nodded her head sorrowfully. "I knew this would happen," she said.

CHAPTER 53

THAT EVENING, BRIJ ENTERED THE HOUSE RANTING. "HOW dare that bloody fool Vicky go spread rumors about my best friend and my wife! Does he not understand friendship between men and women?"

Karishma, who had been sewing on the sofa chair, said, "I agree."

"What kind of village family is this?"

"Keep your voice down—the boys and Rupvati Chachi are in the other room."

"Let them also hear!" Brij roared. "We've—you've—done nothing wrong."

Then, suddenly, he walked to the dining table, pulled out a dining chair, climbed onto it, and took his Ishapore 2A1 hunting rifle down from where it was proudly displayed atop a bookshelf. "I'll show that bastard Vicky," he said, lips turned downward at the ends.

"Brij, no!" Karishma said.

The boys came out of their room.

"Go back!" Karishma told them. Then, to Brij, "Listen, I'll go talk to Ram Bhaiya. Vicky wasn't wrong, Laxman and I were there—"

"And what century do these buggers live in?" Brij raged. "Do they not know that you and I and Archana and Laxman work together—in the *medicos sector*?"

He stormed down the stairs.

Karishma panicked. For years she had been planning to remove the bullets from his dormant rifle but hadn't—why? Did she secretly want him to turn the gun on her? Surprisingly, it would have been only the first murder in this bad-tempered family. Despite the verbal violence endemic to the Chopras, physical conflict was almost nonexistent (save for the regular roughhousing, which no one saw as conflict). But this unspoken agreement about physical harm licensed the most brutal forms of verbal abuse. Brij was, of course, one of the few hitters in the family. What if he shot someone now?

She decided not to follow him down.

Instead, scrambling to the kitchen, she dispatched Jatin to go inform Ram and his wife, Usha, that Brij was rushing toward their house with a gun. "Go from the back side," she told Jatin—though she was not confident he would make it before Brij.

Jatin's readiness to act was a reminder that everyone in the household was in solidarity with her against Brij's anger.

Deepak came out of his room and hugged Karishma. He looked frightened.

"It's OK, my baby," Karishma said. "Papa's just gone to talk to Vicky Bhaiya, because he's causing a dispute in the family."

Why hadn't he just *hit* her? But he never acted the way she expected. Operating on a deranged but consistent inner logic, he was bent on showing the world that he was ungovernable. *You think this will turn me against my wife and Laxman? Ha! I'll shoot you instead.*

Her younger son's warm body was a balm, and she was cognizant, suddenly, of how little time she'd been spending with her boys.

"Why are they trying to dishonor Mummy?" Deepak asked, his long lashes flecked with tears.

"Baby, it's like this, when people start doing well in life, especially from a small place like our little office in A-Block Market, no one likes it. They all thought we were idiots for starting this business and now that everyone is buying our balms, they're bad-mouthing us."

"I'll kill anyone who dishonors my mummy," Deepak responded.

Brij stood knocking on the door of Ram's house. "Ram Bhaiya, open for one minute. I have no issue with you—but I want to speak to your guest, Vicky. A civil discussion I want to have."

"Don't bang the door!" Ram shouted. "I'm coming."

Ram appeared at the threshold in a dressing gown. But before Brij could even speak, Ram, who was in his early fifties, with a long, mournful face and small glistening teeth, said, "What is this nonsense—coming here with a gun? Do you have any shame? In broad daylight?" He reiterated his favorite theme. "You don't care about your grandfather's name? And what would your father have said? Is this why he sent you to the air force? Put it down!"

The servants loitering near the gate had walked down the driveway to have a look.

Brij said, "But I want to speak to Vicky—"

"You're acting as if Vicky is always here," Ram spat.

"Beta, will you have some water?" Usha asked, materializing behind him. She was a small woman with a slightly open mouth and frozen eyes.

Hearing Usha's feminine voice, all of Brij's genetic training asserted itself, and he found himself placing the heavy rifle down by his side, the barrel pointed toward the marble floor. "Thank you, Chachiji," he said, accepting the water from her.

"Live long," she said, though her eyes were open and burning.

"Come in, come in," Ram said irritably. He beckoned Brij to a sofa. "Now, why are you letting some idle chatter bother you? Vicky didn't say anything, but you know how people talk and spread things here."

"Where is he, Chachaji?" Brij asked, his goatee wet with droplets of water.

"Vicky?" Ram replied. "He's at work."

"I don't know what bloody work that bloody fool does."

Usha added, "Beta, Vicky's just come from a small town; he doesn't even know who you are; how could he have seen anything?"

"He saw correctly," Brij said. "They were together." (At that moment, his head clearing, Brij became aware of the truth. He had known even prior to Vicky's accusation that something was afoot between Laxman and Karishma, but he hadn't respected Karishma enough to think her capable of an affair, and had anyway been glad to have her out of his hair.) He glugged down the water and gestured for the waiting servant boy to bring him more. "Chacha and Chachi, look: We're in the medical business and we have to run such errands at the chemist's. Now, I don't know which village in Haryana this Vicky fellow hails from, but if he can't accept how we live in the big city, he should jolly well go back. I'm not going to shut down *my business*"—he was apoplectic again—"because of some *fucking villager.*"

Ram nodded.

Then Usha said, "And, beta, tell me, how are the boys doing?"

CHAPTER 54

"I COULDN'T BELIEVE MY EYES," GITA TOLD SACHIN AS SHE handed him the letter from Prabha.

"Let me sit down at least," he said. He had just come in from the snow and she had machine-gunned him with information.

"But ... didn't I tell you it was a bad idea?" she asked, referring to Brij's partnership with Laxman.

"Bloody third-rate cursive handwriting," Sachin said, sitting on the sofa. "She writes like a doctor filling out a prescription. What's this here?" He pointed to a liquid-stained blue-inked word that was draining out of itself. Couldn't he see? Gita wondered. It was the bomb site of one of her tears—from when she'd first read it at the dinner table. How hard her heart had beat as she'd read the letter!

He placed the creased letter next to him on the pleather sofa. "So, both the sons of Brahmpal are cuckolds, is it?"

She was impressed he knew the word.

"If we believe this," he said, "then people have to believe things about us too."

"No one knows anything."

He raised his eyebrows. "Really?"

"I swear on my mother," she said.

"Not Cindy, not Anamika? Not Martha?"

"No," she said.

"Women talk."

Was this why he really wanted to leave the US? Gita wondered. To get away from the ground on which the rumor could be born? Where Hector might return? Trident had given him a bonus and had said they were working on creating a "juicy" new position for him—but, to Gita's surprise, Sachin had remained pessimistic. She, too, had been uneasily awaiting another letter from Hector. He had done it once, why couldn't he do it again? She always came home early to snatch up the mail, and when she walked through bricky downtown, she kept scanning the streets for his springy stride and his big shawl scarves.

Sachin relaxed. “Do you think Prabha is right?”

Gita shook her head. “I don’t know if it’s an affair.” Then quickly, “Laxman is so crude with women.”

“But my sister-in-law is no innocent lamb. She dresses so provocatively.” Gita had seen Sachin sizing up Karishma’s sometimes-exposed belly.

“She needs attention because your brother treats her so badly,” Gita said.

Sachin didn’t like criticizing his brother but he also did not disagree. “What should we do? Do you want me to say something?”

She said, “No, what can you do?” She paused. “Maybe you can write a letter to Brij.” Then: “But I don’t know what would be gained.” She went on, “I just feel bad for Karishma. In these situations, the woman is always blamed. I’m sure they think she seduced Laxman, when I can guarantee it’s the opposite.”

Suddenly, Sachin snorted. “Do you think she’d have such pity for you?”

CHAPTER 55

SOON AFTER THE BLOWUP, LAXMAN APPROACHED BRIJ IN the factory. "I'm very saddened by what's happened," Laxman said to Brij. "I fully accept the blame for the rumors. It's a problem of the way the office is set up; I should have had better sense about how people would talk and behave—they're all small-minded. So, it might be good for me to divest from the business." He didn't tell Brij he had been scolded by Ram.

"Once these people start a rumor, it's bloody difficult to squash it," Brij said as they paced the factory floor together. "If Ram Bhaiya wasn't in the picture, quite honestly, I'd give that Vicky guy a few tight slaps, which is what he deserves for disrespecting his elders. But times have changed, Laxman, haan? Youngsters believe they can say anything to anyone these days. Imagine you and me—we would never have been so rude." Brij paused to shout desultorily at a worker who wasn't efficiently turning his pestle to ground the herbs. The floor of the factory was slick with spilled herbal juices. The two men walked now with great care—as one might on a ship in a storm, the ground feeling unreal—between the sooty vibrating heavy metal machines. Flies dove into sticky puddles, committing happy suicide. The workers' toilet had still not been fully built. There was no real place for the workers to go number two—and certainly no place for them to wash their hands. They had been instructed to wear their crinkly plastic gloves at all times, but few used them. Laxman was surprised by the growing disorder of the factory. It did not comport with Brij's spick-and-span image. But then again, perhaps the armed services trained you to discipline and finesse your body even as the surroundings degraded, grew bloody. Brij was a uniformed officer in a miasmic theater of war.

Laxman said, "So, what do you think of my proposal? I discussed it with Archana and I can sell you my share."

"My friend, you'll let one setback deter you?" Brij said with a smirk. "You would have never survived the air force."

"It's a question of all of our honors, Bhai," Laxman said.

Brij snorted. "The person who has been most dishonored is my wife. Poor thing—she's very upset."

"Maybe she shouldn't work there for some time, then," Laxman said.

"So, if Vicky lies, you'll punish *her*?" Brij asked.

Laxman went quiet, pursing his lips.

Then suddenly, as if nothing had been said before, Brij changed the subject. "Accha, one thing I wanted to ask you about, Laxman. Since Rupvati Chachi has moved in with us, I've been thinking of building an extra set of rooms on the roof—for the boys. But my liquidity is low. Is there a chance you can advance me a loan?"

CHAPTER 56

SO THIS BECAME THE ARRANGEMENT. LAXMAN WAS FORCED to advance Brij more and more zero-interest loans. In return, things could go on as before.

When Karishma came to the office, Laxman saw she had a black blemish—a bruise—on the corner of her left eye; and the eyelid, too, seemed curled up into itself.

Archana didn't comment on it. Nor did Laxman.

The atmosphere in the office became sour. A sense of hysteria entered the space. Laxman could see a deadness in Archana's eyes when she looked at Karishma, but then Archana would cover it up with quick nasty jokes about the "other side" of the compound—how Ram Chacha dressed or the embarrassing way Usha's relatives spoke about money in public—and Karishma would smile in sympathy. It was as if, having accidentally led Laxman into the affair, it was now Archana's duty to cheer him and his mistress up. But the humor, when it came, was more like the memory of humor, a moon or planet glimpsed on its dark side, and the jokes were not funny, and Laxman and Karishma laughed anyway, and more discomfort darkened the small room, and Archana apparently felt obligated to go on, clawing around for targets in the family, lobbing grenades at everyone except Karishma and Laxman.

At home, it was worse: Archana wouldn't meet Laxman's eyes.

Laxman said, "You're angry at me."

"No, I was just thinking—I don't deserve you," Archana said, tearing up.

"What kind of talk is that, darling?"

"You're so smart, so well-liked—what do I add? Sometimes I think I should take vanvas."

"Have you been smoking?" he said as he drew close.

"I stopped five years ago." Then she said, "These people only want to tear you down. It's because you're strong. You've handled all this with such strength. You aren't even upset." She started crying. "Sometimes I think my work in this life is done."

Her makeup had melted into a delicious quivering mess.

"No, darling, you're just tired," Laxman said.

He put his arm around her as they sat on the bed. But he couldn't go further. It would feel like cheating on Karishma.

CHAPTER 57

LAXMAN'S SIBLINGS AGREED THAT HE NEEDED TO BE brought under control. Vibha was chosen to speak to him.

But, before she could phone him, he showed up at her house. He sat down without preamble, his eyebrows raised in high, angular mountains. "The way the youngsters in this family behave—it's a matter of great sadness. There used to be respect for elders. Now a guy like Vicky can go around saying anything to all and sundry."

"Yes, times have changed," she conceded.

"A lafanga that Vicky is," Laxman said. "I never liked him." He touched his head. "Look at how much the business suffered because of his one comment."

Vibha considered him. With every year, he looked more like their wonderful, dead father. What a man their father had been—above such things. He would have had many opportunities to seduce women. Instead, he had focused on the future of the nation.

"First Gita, now this," Laxman was saying. "I'm disgusted. The end goal of these people is that our family falls apart."

"But, Laxman, does Karishma have to work with you?" Vibha finally asked.

Laxman was ready. "But, Didi, you're acting as if *I* have *any* control! *Her* husband wants *her* to work, *she* wants to work ... you tell me, should I punish her for something that isn't true? We were at the chemist's, I've said that's true—but that's what our business is! We're in the medicos business! I mean—"

"Next time send someone else," Vibha said.

Laxman's face was wet with tears. "You don't know how much of my blood and sweat and money I've poured into this venture. The success of traditional medicine matters for the future of our country. We can't let outsiders destroy it—"

Looking at his wet, emotional face, it came to Vibha, unbidden: *He's in love with Karishma.*

She had not believed it was an affair. A flirtation ... yes, like with Gita. As Laxman talked, Vibha became nervous. "It's just that the well has been poisoned," she tried again.

"But, Didi, as I said, Brij and Karishma, they're most eager to proceed with the business. If they had said, 'No, let's wash our hands of this venture,' I'd understand. In my view, the matter is closed. It was humiliating for them, for Archana, for the children. Why humiliate them further?"

Vibha started again.

"With due respect," he said, "you're my sister, not my father."

After Laxman left, Vibha got up and rearranged the photographs of her heavy-jowled father on the wall. But one photo remained off-center and she found herself filling with rage.

CHAPTER 58

AFTER VICKY'S SIGHTING, KARISHMA AND LAXMAN COULD no longer meet at the temple.

Laxman began receiving messages from the Jeev Sangathan Association and a few of the Sangathanis in the colony who used to visit the mandir—the Puris, for instance—and he told them simply that he was looking for another pundit and in the meantime was planning to have the place painted and renovated, sincerest apologies for the inconvenience.

But then Mr. Puri came to see him at his office in the market. Puri was wearing one of his expensive blank white shirts, the glossy surface glowing unevenly with light. Archana and Karishma looked on as Laxman got up to greet the unexpected visitor.

Puri wanted to know what was being done to reopen the mandir. He said he had a good pundit who could fill in for the time being.

"It's unfortunately closed for renovation," Laxman said again.

"But the work hasn't yet started, no?" Puri asked.

"It was supposed to begin soon," Karishma said. She had spoken up only so that the lean Mr. Puri would look her way; and suddenly she wondered if he had come to look at *her*.

(If asked, Puri would have denied it, but it was true—news of the affair had increased his fascination for Karishma. The affair had opened up new sexual possibilities for the whole colony.)

Puri glanced at her, then said to Laxman, "But even if it's being renovated, we can do havans upstairs, at least." He took a seat.

Archana got up to order tea from a nearby stall, but Puri refused.

"We're going to drink some anyway," Archana said.

"I must not," Puri said. "Diabetes."

"Without sugar, then," Archana said. "Our relatives from the US brought a very nice sugar-free ... sugar."

Karishma admired Mr. Puri in profile as he and Laxman razzed each other with laughter, clasping hands. *What a selfish person I am. Do I care about anyone—even my children? No. Only myself.* It was as if a bottomless trapdoor had opened with that thought. Where did the door lead—to a kind of hell? She was now outside herself, examining herself with fear and even admiration: Where had she come from? How, as the daughter of a minor PWD official, had she become so ferociously self-centered and depraved?

To her surprise, she had not been ashamed about how the affair had been made public. Though she had acted appalled and distraught, on a certain level, she was proud. She wanted everyone to know Laxman was her protector.

When Puri got up, Archana repeated, "Stay for tea, at least," and Puri said, "No, no, I was only dropping in," and Laxman said, "Tomorrow let's go, I'll show you the plans and maybe we can have your pundit come over, but you know how bureaucratic the Sangathan has become," and Puri said, "Don't worry, I'll handle it," and then the meeting was over.

Soon after that, the control of the temple slipped from Laxman to Puri, with Laxman finding himself strangely eager to let it go, to let someone else have control of a dying sect that he himself no longer believed in.

CHAPTER 59

BRIJ INDICATED THAT HE WOULD NEED ANOTHER RS. 50,000 in a couple of months. Lacking access to the Sangathan donations, Laxman began seeking other avenues for cash, which led him, in a roundabout way, into politics.

"You here, Laxman sahb?" a high-pitched male voice asked. "Tell me, how are things?"

Laxman pretended he had run into the man, when it was in fact exactly whom he had come to see.

It was now late June 1984. For the last week, Laxman had been frequenting the new Krishna Bhagwan Mandir—the three-story half-acre Sanatani temple complex in the colony that had been built over three years and had only recently been freed from its jail of bamboo scaffolding. It was this temple that Laxman and Karishma had passed on their first visit to the Jeev Sangathan temple together, and that Laxman had criticized to Karishma for the corruption of its trustees.

In the halls of this gigantic rocket-shaped marble edifice, Laxman would linger before the statues of Ram and Sita and Hanuman, the foreheads of these marble majesties bright with tilaks, the marigolds around their necks emitting a shrill, swirling scent which he inhaled deeply. He would buy a packet of pershad and chadao it on the murtis; and would take the consecrated orange boondi pershad back home and offer it from soft wallets of newspaper to his fellow morning walkers.

Now he said, "How wonderful to see you in person, Kapoor sahib!"

Mr. Kapoor, a rich businessman who ran a toilet fixtures empire, was the founder of the temple. Short, dark, pockmarked, and compact, his shirt pocket was creased with clipped-on heavy golden pens, and his fingers were ringed with age-dulled rubies. He wore a white safari suit.

After a few moments of hushed chitchat, the two men shifted to the open-air landing outside the massive hall and began talking about the trusteeship of the Jeev Sangathan temple. Kapoor wanted to know if it was true that Laxman was no longer managing it. "But you were doing remarkable work there," Kapoor said.

Was Kapoor's curiosity earnest? Laxman wondered. But Kapoor blinked his small red-runed eyes so often that one couldn't tell the speed of his thoughts. "You run a temple, Sir, so you know," Laxman said. "I had been doing it for too many years and it's a full-time job, and anyway our balm business is growing. Plus, the Jeev Sangathan Association wants us to rotate leadership. And it's such hard work to collect donations." Then Laxman added, "But you've built something very monumental here."

"We've erected this big mahal," Kapoor said with a sigh, shaking his head, "but let's see if people come."

"Whenever I drive by, there's a line of cars outside," Laxman said.

"People come when someone dies—for chauthas and memorials." Kapoor smiled, showing his small, yellow, widely spaced teeth; and behind them a tongue spackled with unhealthy white. "There's a crowd on Tuesdays, but otherwise you have to always convince our people to come."

"Do what the Muslims do, then, put up loudspeakers," Laxman said.

This was meant to be a joke, but Kapoor took it seriously. "We wanted to, but then the neighborhood people complained."

"Classic," Laxman said. "This is the problem with us Hindus—there's no unity."

Soon the two men had moved on to talking about political developments in the country, echoing the talking points of the Hindu Right: the forced mass conversions of thousands of Hindus in Tamil Nadu to Islam; the fact that millions of Muslims were pouring into India daily from the black swamp of Bangladesh; how the Sikhs in Punjab were beating their chests for their own nation, Khalistan, and driving Hindus out of Punjab with terrorism; and how Laxman, in fact, knew several Hindu families that had relocated from Punjab to Bombay. "What difference did Operation Blue Star make?" Laxman asked, referring to Indira Gandhi's audacious storming that month of the Golden Temple to flush out militants sheltering there. "It's made the sardars even angrier."

"But this is exactly what we're talking about, Laxman sahb. The sardars would have remained angry whether or not Indira stormed the temple! I'm not a big lover of that lady"—Kapoor was a member of the Hindu nationalist Trishul People's Party, the TPP, which strongly opposed the "secular" Congress Party and its dictatorial leader, Indira Gandhi—"but in this instance she did the right thing. It's important for us to show that we Hindus are capable of using force, that we won't let this nation fall into bits and pieces."

Laxman was loyal to Hindus. But he was also loyal to Sikhs, who were, in his opinion, a subsect of Hindus. He had many Sikh friends.

Kapoor went on. "But, yes, it's true that, by overseeing Operation Blue Star, Indira is going to lose the Sikh vote to us."

"So, there was some advantage!" Laxman said, boyishly clasping Kapoor's large hands.

"Exactly!" Kapoor roared in response.

Over the following weeks, the two men began meeting occasionally, repairing for their discussions to Kapoor's office on the ground floor of the temple complex. Kapoor paid a reciprocal visit to Laxman's office in Modern Colony and applied several of his balms experimentally on his arms, eventually ordering a dozen cartons for his temple's dispensary.

And in his own office, Kapoor began to tell Laxman about the TPP and its ideology and why a man like Laxman—with his impeccable Punjabi Hindu pedigree—ought to consider joining. "I know your brother Bhagat has been a Congress MLA for years," Kapoor said, holding up his hand as if to say, *let me finish,* "but your father was first and foremost a leader of Hindus. Look at his involvement in the Jeev Sangathan and the RSS. And if there's a real party of Hindus—a party of your father's ideology—it's the TPP. Right now, Indira is talking a lot about Hindus because it's good for her vote bank. But tomorrow, when the mullahs start shouting for dispensations, she'll drop everything for them."

Laxman, eager primarily for new avenues for cash, said he'd be interested. The TPP was a new, minor, untested party, but access to its supporters could be useful for business. The TPP's grassroots organization, the RSS, had local branches—shakhas—all over the country, and these branches provided health services and would no doubt welcome Mohanji's balms. In fact, Laxman knew that the two leaders of the TPP, Mangal Das and Santosh Kumar, often visited Mohanji for medical advice.

Kapoor laid his disproportionately large hands on his white-painted table and went on, "But it's not like everything is peaceful within the TPP. Mangal Das—he wants to make the party more secular, like the Congress, to make it grow nationally. But the issue there is that the RSS"—from which many party workers were drawn—"doesn't like that its planks are being ignored. And while I admire and respect Mangal Das—he's one of our greatest orators and poets—I personally think we should be uniting Hindus instead of chasing the Muslim vote. We need to address the conversions in Tamil Nadu. We need to be shouting to rebuild the Ram temple. Which is another reason bringing a man like you into the party, with your family name—well, it'll make us look good as well!"

Laxman smiled.

But, before any date could be set for Laxman to come to one of the organizing committee meetings with Mangal Das and Santosh Kumar, Laxman's life—and everyone else's—was interrupted by a national event.

CHAPTER 60

HE HEARD IT ON THE PHONE FROM A FRIEND: INDIA'S PRIME minister, Indira Gandhi, had been assassinated.

The rest was chaos.

The story emerged in fragments as the day went on: That October morning, the PM was walking across her lawn in her saffron sari when her two Sikh bodyguards had opened fire on her. What had happened to the bodyguards? They had been apparently shot dead or apprehended. And Indira? She was driven by her secretary to the hospital, her corpse cradled in the arms of her Italian daughter-in-law.

Laxman was shocked to feel real grief about the death of a woman he hated.

How deep India lived in his soul!

Then, All India Radio interrupted its programming with menacingly meaningless music, and shops began to shutter.

The next day, Indira's supporters and others unleashed a wave of massive anti-Sikh riots.

Laxman had heard rumors about the baying crowds that had gathered near AIIMS Hospital, where Indira had been declared dead, but he was surprised, the following afternoon, to come to the gate of *his* own house and see large groups of men trudging by—the sort of crowds he'd never witnessed foaming through the posh colony, with its bungalows and neatly bisected roads. At the front of the mob of fifty-odd men were two freshly bathed fellows in white kurtas, their foreheads smeared with tilaks, running shoes adorning their feet, stubble growing out from the ends of their careful mustaches, as if they hadn't had time to shave since the murder of their leader. Behind them, in the anarchic jhund, men—boys, really—of all ages, eight to thirty years old, were toting jerry cans filled with stinking kerosene and clutching rags that might have been used to clean the houses of the rich. Some looked like mere villagers. Others, twirling pieces of sariya and cricket bats and sticks and knives, had the nourished looks of shopkeepers. Everyone in the crowd was chatting animatedly till the short but broad man at the front stopped to consult a piece of paper. "Wait!" he shouted. "OK, we will go right over here. Ready the matches." Some of the boys waved their sticks and cans menacingly at Laxman as they passed.

"Go inside!" Laxman shouted at the servants who had gathered behind him to watch.

Laxman shuddered. He hoped that the man with the paper had not been directing the mob to the home of his sardar friend Harbir.

Laxman went back into the property and up the stairs of the front building to see his brother Bhagat, who had been close to Indira. He found Bhagat lying on his bed, which was covered with half-read newspapers—Bhagat seemed almost to float on a carpet of disintegrating paper, never moving.

When Laxman told Bhagat about what he had seen on the road, Bhagat responded, "Here?" with a look of surprise that Laxman wasn't sure was genuine.

"Do you know which Congress person might be leading the mob?" Laxman asked. "I'm worried they'll accidentally burn our office."

"It's not the Congress's doing," Bhagat said, making a *phew* sound. "These are spontaneous, uncontrollable forces." He wiped something from under his glasses with his two fingers, as if to signal his grief over Indira.

"But their leader was reading a list—someone must be organizing them, no?" Laxman asked.

"Laxman, take my word, you like being a hero, but in this case, stay out of it. In our country, riots are natural reactions, and like all natural reactions, they also will pass."

CHAPTER 61

LEAVING BHAGAT, LAXMAN CAME DOWN THE STAIRS AND got into his Fiat. He drove toward Harbir's house. When he turned onto the road that abutted the Krishna Bhagwan Mandir, he witnessed something astonishing. All manner of objects had been dragged into the street, where they were serenely and unevenly on fire: a floral sofa (weeping its white cottony innards); framed portraits; a TV. And next to this instant pyre, a burly, tall man in a T-shirt grabbed a thirty-something Sikh by his black, healthy beard and led him toward the flames. Two other men—more like boys, again—hit the Sikh triumphantly on his back with metal rods. The Sikh—was he one of the local shopkeepers? A scooterist who they had pulled off a vehicle?—somehow didn't double over from the blows, even as his white shirt bloomed red and then black. Then another slight man with a sooty face, in a vest, came running from a shack with a car tire in his arms, and smashed it down on the Sikh's head, trying to garland him in it. But the tire bounced off the Sikh's large pink turban even as the Sikh's neck buckled and he fell to the ground. The burly T-shirted man shouted something and then he and the other men held a brief discussion around the body of the supine Sikh.

To Laxman, driving slowly, it all seemed make-believe, especially as all the Sikh could say in response to being beaten was "oye naheen"—as if he were having a civil argument with his attackers.

The four men now pinned the Sikh down, tearing off his turban. Then the man in the vest slipped the tire around the Sikh's neck and pushed him into the bonfire of objects, where the Sikh's orbit of rubber quickly caught fire.

With a final splash of kerosene, they sent the Sikh up in flames.

The Sikh screamed and danced within the glittering flames. The men, meanwhile, began scooping up from the fire some of the looted objects that hadn't yet burned: a radio, a sewing machine, an orphaned drawer. Right then, Laxman realized more screams were emanating from behind the small marketplace on his right—the marketplace he frequented to get watches repaired and buy tandoori chicken. Smoke slanted up mournfully from the top of the toy shop from which he had, months earlier, purchased toys for Deepak and Mohit.

At the next intersection, the road was blocked by two burnt taxis. Three men—servant types, Laxman thought—stood at the only opening between the cars and flagged him down. Laxman had no choice but to stop.

Shining an unnecessary flashlight in his face through his window, they motioned for him to open it.

"Jai Shri Ram," Laxman said, as he rolled down the window. "Bhaisahb, I'm with you," he went on. "I was going to join the freedom fighters up ahead."

"What's that?" one of the men asked, still flashing the torch at Laxman's forehead. The man had absurdly sharp and crooked teeth hoarded in a proud mouth.

"Abey, he's just old," the other said. "That's a wrinkle on his forehead. From tension."

They were looking, Laxman realized with a shock, for a telltale turban line that would confirm he was a Sikh who had undone his turban to hide his identity.

"Jai Shri Ram," they said, and moved aside.

CHAPTER 62

HARBIR'S HOUSE HAD NOT BURNED—YET—BUT ALL ITS residents had fled, and by evening, Laxman was filled with great resolve to protect the colony. He wanted to organize a nighttime patrol.

But when he walked to his office to hunt down the phone numbers of other members of the Colony Association, Karishma, who was idling in the garden, said, "You're more worried about the sardars than your family or children?"

In the months since they'd been seen at the chemist's, Karishma and Laxman had started meeting every two weeks at an inn that lay along the road to Karishma's parents' home in Ghaziabad. Karishma would head out to visit them in a taxi, and Laxman, leaving the office on an "errand," would intercept her midway at the inn. Then they would go up and lounge in the seedy room with its plump curtains, complaining about their spouses. But in the last month, with her parents out of town, Karishma had been unable to make an excuse for a long visit; and a slight distance had opened up between them.

Now Karishma went on, "What will anyone gain from your heropanti? You think these goondas are going to care whether you're a sardar or not? They'll just see that you're rich, in a car, and they'll want the car. You're from a big city, where there are a lot of policemen and ministers, so you don't know what riots are like. It's the one day in the year these people can have fun."

"And what will we do if they attack here?" Laxman asked, pressing his fingers to his temples.

"The family name is written in the front. They know that a Congress MLA lives here."

Laxman tugged at his lower lip. "It sounds like you're worried about me."

"Believe it or not, I'm actually worried about our *children*," Karishma said.

This was one of the strangest aspects of the affair, for Laxman: her almost maternal concern for his family, *his* wife. It was as if she needed to act this way to cancel her guilt. Or: as if she had joined with him so fully that she felt she was the matriarch of a joint clan.

Laxman proceeded with his plan and made the calls. Archana, who had many Sikh friends, encouraged him in this, saying that they could offer A-19 as a safe haven to fleeing Sikhs.

Together, the members of the Colony Association decided they would take turns driving out into the colony, two at a time, to guard the streets at night. "My wife will be standing near our gate to give coffee and tea to everyone who goes on patrol," Laxman told them on the phone. "It's our duty to protect our sardar friends."

As evening came, Laxman and Brij positioned themselves by the gate of the complex. The air was tangy with smoke—a never-ending Diwali—and you could hear solitary motorcycles tearing down the main road, perhaps identifying targets for mobs to attack.

"What is this I hear you're doing?" Bhagat said to Laxman with a sigh, emerging from his house into the twilight, his kurta crumpled from his daylong lounging. "Don't get involved. The police will hundred percent come. They'll handle it."

"Bhaiya, people are already on their way for our patrol," Laxman said.

Bhagat put his hands behind his back and stuck his neck out. "Be careful. These angry mobs can be ... quite unreasonable." Then he vanished back inside.

By 11 p.m., it was Laxman's turn to patrol the dark colony. Brij joined Laxman in the car. Brij had brought his rifle and was dressed in his old blue air-force fatigues.

"That gun even work?" Laxman asked, as if he had been unaware of its existence, its central role in the affair blowup.

Brij nodded.

Laxman drove them down the familiar, dark streets, past the boxy mansions behind low walls thatched with bougainvillea and sentried by Partition-era mulberries and Ashokas. The streetlights were off. Laxman had never felt so immersed in his environment—a network of small roads he knew as well as he knew himself. They passed a block thick with sleep, the street watched over by a thousand dusty broad leaves, and came upon a two-story house that was black and burnt. It belonged to a family called the Bedis. Laxman and Brij got out, opened the gate to the house, and walked in through the smashed glass door of the front veranda, screaming, "Hello! Hello!" No one stirred within. The flavor of smoke hurt their throats, and they both saw the congealed black pools of blood on the terrazzo. Either the Bedi family had fled or Laxman and Brij had come too late. "If we see any sardar name boards, we should rip them out," Laxman said as they got back in the car.

"Forget that, we won't even allow the buggers to get that far," Brij said. Having seen the blood, he was now operating at his full childish seriousness.

On another narrow colony road, their headlights illuminated a gaunt, long-haired man who was running in noisy hawai chappals down the street with a metal rod in his hands. Shouting through the car window, Laxman raced the Fiat to catch up with him. As the Fiat jerkily slowed next to the man, the rifle, angled in Brij's lap out of the window, suddenly fell over, pointing at Laxman. "Careful!" Laxman spat.

"I'll shoot the bloody bastard, stop the car!" Brij said.

"Yaar, wait, wait," Laxman said.

But Brij had already jumped out of the moving car and was pointing his gun, shouting, "Stop," and the running man panicked and dropped his rod, and Brij caught up with him and smacked his head hard with the gun's butt. The man instantly fell to the ground.

Laxman leapt out of the car and started slapping the groaning man on his head.

"Saale, what do you think you were doing?" Brij said, gritting his teeth, the tendons on his neck dancing. "Is this your father's colony? Where are the others?"

On his back and wailing, the man pressed his hands together. "Sahb, I'm a servant, I was running away, I was protecting myself."

"Then why do you have this rod?" Brij asked.

Laxman had backed off. He was impressed by Brij's reflexes and strength.

Once blood was pouring satisfyingly from the rioter's forehead, gelling into the crevices along his nose, Brij, too, stopped hitting him.

Then, leaving him on the street, Laxman and Brij got back into the car and drove off—triumphant, silent, bonded in their violence—to A-19.

CHAPTER 63

LATER, LAXMAN WOULD UNDERSTAND, SUBCONSCIOUSLY, that what he had really wanted to do was *participate* in the violence—but that his atavistic love of the colony, of which his father had been a founder, had kept him from joining the riot.

It was important to be clear, when they got home, that they had chased down "a dangerous, armed rioter." Karishma and Archana were waiting for them in the garden of the complex, huddled in sweaters, on chairs, surrounded by a knot of servants. Everyone cooed over the two men for their heroics. Even Ram Bhaiya, after barking at a drunk servant, said to Laxman and Brij, "I heard that there was looting near Anand Park but the private guards in front of people's houses wouldn't help." The fact that Ram had suspended his default sarcasm must have meant that he was quietly impressed, Laxman thought.

"People are cowards," Brij said, taking a chair and gratefully sipping a glass of water a servant had brought him.

"They don't all have guns," Karishma said. But before Brij could rebuke her, she said, "I mean, that's why it was a good idea you took one."

In the office the next day, Karishma said to Laxman, "I'm just glad he didn't use that gun. My heart always starts racing when he brings it down from the wall, that's why I've even tried hiding it. I didn't want him to shoot *you*."

"Have a little faith, yaar."

So this was the reason she hadn't wanted him to go?

After three days, the riots ended. Sikhs all over the city had been murdered, with entire slums gutted. But most of the Sikhs in the colony escaped unharmed—even if a few lost their homes to arson and looting.

CHAPTER 64

AT A SMALL MEETING OF THE TOP BRASS OF THE TPP, Mr. Kapoor crowed about Laxman's heroism. "Thanks to him, not one hair on a sardar's head was touched in Modern Colony," Kapoor said.

From being anti-Sikh, the TPP had jumped to being pro-Sikh, since it gave them a political opening.

The TPP president, Mangal Das, said to Laxman, "You're upholding the great legacy of your father with your bravery." He lisped a little. In his fifties, Mangal Das looked like a sensual frog, froth forming at the end of his perfectly weighed sentences, the mouth measuring out each syllable the way a halwaii doles out rasgullas. "This is the way your family members protected the Hindu areas of Lahore in Partition."

"Yes, two of my uncles were in the RSS," Laxman said, "and made bombs that they would throw into the Muslim localities. Other people would go on patrol with kuttas." This is where his own inspiration for a colony patrol had come from.

Like the other men at this gathering, Laxman was seated on a concave bone-white rattan chair in Kapoor's gloomy courtyard. Laxman did not mention—did not feel he had to mention—that he had been a mere newborn during Partition and remembered little about it.

"And your father's contributions to Hinduism—to the Jeev Sangathan—we all know about that," the party secretary Santosh Kumar said quickly, in his reedy, encouraging-schoolteacher voice. "Without him, the freedom fighters would have had no funds to fight. And as you know, the RSS was partly founded at the Jeev Sangathan headquarters at Hanuman Road in Delhi." Tall and balding, in his early fifties, Santosh had a bushy mustache and watchful, intelligent eyes.

Mangal Das and Santosh Kumar were the complementary figures at the heart of the TPP. Mangal was a pleasure-loving, pakora-nosed, squat, half-drunk man who was the party's supreme orator—a man who could rain down opprobrium on his opponents with the utmost humor and poetry. Santosh Kumar was the doer, the man who connected the various factions of the TPP and RSS.

Now all the men started talking about the political situation in the country.

"We both tried to intervene with Narasimha Rao"—the Congress home minister—"to stop the killing," Santosh Kumar said, pointing to Mangal.

"But he's neither a man nor a lion," Mangal Das said, punning on the home minister's name. He paused. "This kind of rioting and looting—I never thought I'd see it again after Partition. Imagine, Laxman sahb, how your father, who did so much to make Punjab a part of India, would feel if he knew this was how we Hindus were treating Sikhs, who are our brothers. That is a link that must never be broken."

"Riot or no riot," Santosh said, "it'll be an uphill battle for us in this coming election. By dying in this way, Indiraji, God bless her, has become a martyr. People sympathize with her."

National elections had been called in two months' time.

"Don't people see that she herself was responsible for the situation?" Laxman asked.

"You're a cultivated man, Laxmanji," Santosh said with his half smile and irony-delighting eyes, his cheeks rising toward his eyebrows. "But most people think the riots were a great thing, a very enjoyable spectacle. They don't know the history of Bhindranwale and all that. Luckily, we have Mangalji here. He'll explain it to people. He can hypnotize anyone."

"He makes it sound like I'll put them in a coma!" Mangal said.

"But you can see, you've come to us in a moment of need," Santosh said. "We recently suffered losses in Jammu and in Delhi. But we think this can be reversed by strong campaigning, especially in Delhi. And the truth is that many Punjabis—and even Sangathanis!—have moved away from us, and you could help us bring them back into the fold. We want to be the party for all Hindus."

"All Indians," Mangal reminded him.

Laxman, cognizant of the hierarchies in the family, went to see Bhagat Bhaiya—to seek his blessings about entering politics: Bhagat, who many years ago had *prevented* Laxman from joining the Congress.

Bhagat, on his bed of paper, said, "I wish you the greatest success. As you know, I too think that Hindus are being left behind in this country. But I must warn you, as your elder brother, as someone with knowledge of politics, this is an unfortunate time to be joining the TPP. If you look at the poll results from Jammu and Delhi, even their foot soldiers in the RSS have deserted them."

"That's just talk," Laxman said. "Mangal and Santosh—these people grew up in the RSS."

Bhagat smiled, his lips open in a small O.

Laxman went on, "We're more worried about the sympathy vote for Indiraji."

Bhagat said, "That of course there will be. I mean, look at how brutally she was gunned down. But that's not the issue," he went on. "The issue is there already is a party of Hindus. It's the Congress."

So, Laxman—who'd previously had no political experience—ended up assisting the TPP in campaigning in the elections that were held in December 1984, two months after Indira's assassination. He worked tirelessly, doing what he did best: glad-handing men and women from his own class; visiting the homes of the rich and powerful in the colony; impressing upon them the importance of moving beyond the corruption and minority appeasement of the Congress. To high-ranking members of the Jeev Sangathan he made the case that the Sangathan could gain greater tax benefits if they had a few TPP MPs in Parliament supporting Hindu organizations. "We have become refugees in our own land," he said, solemnly.

He became enamored particularly with Santosh Kumar. Though Santosh, at fifty-seven, harked back to the glories of ancient India and the Vedas in his talk, he was, in other ways, modernity itself: No man like him had ever existed before, a man willing to harness every available technology and idea in the service of the old.

After a month of electioneering, the poll results came in. Indira's son, Rajiv, had won the largest election mandate in Indian history—over 400 seats. Meanwhile, the TPP, which less than ten years before had been part of a ruling coalition, was reduced to a mere 2 seats in Parliament out of 543. Mangal Das, the lion of the TPP, lost his Lok Sabha seat in Lucknow, though he managed to scrape his way through to the Rajya Sabha from another constituency.

Shocked, Laxman attended a postmortem meeting of the TPP's top brass in Kapoor's courtyard.

The meeting turned out to be smaller than Laxman had expected—there were only twenty men (and one woman) present. Santosh, with his bushy mustache and arms behind his back, now went about upbraiding each of these men in his sharp, schoolteacherly way. "What kind of party are we if we let Hindus vote for a party that is *against* Hindus?" he asked one downcast publicity worker. "No, Sir, your messaging was not good."

Laxman, sitting next to Kapoor, waited tensely for Santosh's wrath to turn on him. Instead, Santosh looked right through him, his mustache jumping, and moved on to wagging his finger at the next apparatchik.

Afterward, as the crestfallen men streamed out—they hadn't even been offered tea—Santosh asked Laxman to stay behind with Mangal and Kapoor.

Laxman sat very still.

"What do you make of what happened, Laxmanji?" Santosh asked. "You're a newcomer, you can see these things clearly."

Laxman had thought he would say, "We didn't play the Hindu card correctly," but instead he found himself saying, "Our time hasn't come."

"Can you elaborate?" Santosh said.

"We are a Hindu nation. The bedrock of this country is Hinduism. When you see a red dot on a stone you know it's Hanuman. We might not win today but we will win someday." And as he spoke, he found he believed it. After years of seeking it, conviction—real conviction, not opportunism—had come to Laxman. He had a lump in his throat. *It has happened. I have become my father.*

"Precisely! We're a party of Hindus!" Santosh said. "Why were we seeking the endorsement of mullahs and sardars!"

Mangal Das, his eyes red from drink, sat bent forward in his chair, saying nothing.

As the night went on, Santosh outlined a new vision for the party. "When such moments occur, you have to take the bull by the horns." He laughed. "The holy cow by the horns. You have to come out of the fire, cleansed. We've had many moments of defeat before and we've always emerged strong. We have the entire country—all the Hindus—at our side. Why are we so ashamed of it?" Then Santosh turned to Laxman. "I am going to ask you to help us more. We need more new ferocious blood like you. Tell me, Laxmanji, are you ready to be part of a renaissance in this country?"

"I am," Laxman said.

"Very good, very good," Santosh said. "We will make it happen."

Thus, the loss in the 1984 elections proved a boon to Laxman's personal ambitions. After the defeat, much of the old guard of the TPP was retired, and even Mangal Das, perceived as a moderate, was forced out as party president, replaced by his old friend Santosh Kumar. And Santosh, of course, had taken a liking to Laxman. Overnight, he turned Laxman into his right-hand man.

CHAPTER 65

IT WAS AT THIS TIME OF TUMULT, IN MAY 1985, THAT GITA AND Sachin moved back to India. They were, by now, familiar with Laxman's story. How he had joined the TPP; how it had suffered massive losses in the election; how he had been promoted (despite, or because of, the loss), and was now active in Delhi politics, where the TPP had gained a foothold. "Whatever you say about that guy," Sachin said, "you have to give him credit. They've erected a major statue of Papaji by the lakeside in Bhopal—that's Santosh Kumar's constituency. Rajmata Scindia herself graced it."

Gita was taken aback. "You support a party of Hindus?"

"I just think Hindus are left behind," Sachin said. "Did the Congress ever celebrate Papaji?"

Your spouse could always surprise you.

They sold their things in a garage sale and shipped the rest, with Sachin rubbing melted chocolate onto their washing machine to make it look old, to avoid customs duties.

But where there should have been excitement about his new modular housing venture with his friend Rishab, there was a bitterness in Sachin's heart. He had been betrayed first by Gita, then Trident, which had finally offered him a promotion, but one that he felt was overdue—and had already been granted to a white colleague whose role in the ketchup bottle project had been ceremonial. "Fuckers only saw me as hired help, as labor," he told her. "When it comes to seniority, forget it, it's whites for whites."

Gita wanted to remind him that Trident had also been very good to him. Yes, there had been isolated incidents—his managers, for example, had tried to christen him "Sasha," till he had started purposely mispronouncing *their* names in turn—but otherwise they'd showered him with perks, and much of the pressure he'd felt had been self-applied.

It was nothing like what Blacks or women faced, she felt.

Still, Gita was grateful he was beginning to blame the company and the country for his unhappiness—and not her—and so she said, "They don't see India as real competition," and that was that.

Gita herself had given up trying to affect fate one way or the other. Nevertheless, she now felt a certain tenderness toward her life in Michigan. She went door-to-door and hugged her neighbors goodbye on the suburban street, promising they would return. But deep down she knew she would forget that place, that it would be an interlude, a gap—not a real part of the story of her life.

With an optimist's faith in signs, she told herself: *And maybe things will change for Sachin and me in India, maybe we'll even have a child—*

No matter how much she gave up on the idea, the longing didn't go away.

One of the strange things about people who travel so much is that even they forget that they are the same people no matter where they go, that immigration does not lead to rebirth. It simply multiplies disappointments, gives you a new start with the same lousy material.

The flight this time was more relaxed than the previous trip. They felt the exultation of having pulled off something big. "I can't believe we did that," he said. "We're mad."

"*You're* mad." Then she said, "But there's nothing saner than going home."

Gita and Sachin had decided to live in A-19. It was what Sachin wanted. "And this is why I wished to invest in property in America," Sachin had clucked. "We just don't have enough savings to buy our own place in Delhi." Gita, chastened by her affair, had not argued with him. As Brij himself had suggested to his brother, there was space to build on the roof. But, till they had sized up the space and settled on an architect and contractor, they had opted to stay in a temporary rental in Defence Colony arranged by Sachin's business partner, Rishab.

On a boiling day in May, they were welcomed to this rental the way one is always welcomed to India: The flat hadn't been dusted; the cleaner had failed to come; and most of the taps weren't working.

Still, it was a place to rest.

After the obligatory calls to relatives, and hiring a cook and a cleaner, Sachin immediately started commuting to the office in ITO that Rishab and he had rented.

Then Gita and Sachin visited A-19 to look into building on the roof.

That was when they learned that Brij had started his own construction—on that very site.

CHAPTER 66

TO LIVE IN THE COMPLEX WAS TO BE INSECURE; IT WAS TO know that real estate was fate; it was one's life.

SP Chopra had been a great man but, for some reason, none of his children had succeeded financially.

People sometimes said it was because the man himself had been too great, casting too big a shadow; others blamed the placidity of his wife—forgetting, of course, that she had done all the labor of raising the kids herself.

Regardless of the cause, the lack of success made everyone fixated on their shares, shares that were not clearly demarcated and could be acquired only through haggling or seniority—or a grab.

This is what Brij had done right before Sachin had come back.

The strange thing was, he had not wanted to. He had been forced into it.

It had started when Karishma received the news via post that Gita and Sachin were definitely returning.

Sachin was taking a job with some kind of construction-related company; Gita and he would be renting a flat for a while in Defence Colony. But they would eventually build on the roof of the complex.

"Where else will they live?" Brij said to Rupvati Chachi after he had read the letter from Sachin about his plans.

All other permissible spaces in the complex had been built up.

Overhearing this, Karishma said, "But I thought *we* were going to build on the roof."

This fiction had been kept up for the past year. Brij had been accepting sizable loans from Laxman, supposedly to build an annex on the roof for his sons. But Brij had done nothing.

Where was the money going? Karishma often wondered. But if she questioned him too much about this, he lashed out at her physically; and she had learned to keep away from the subject, to let it remain a transaction between the two men, Laxman and Brij.

Karishma had not worried or obsessed about property before, but as the affair had gone on, she had become more melancholy about her sons' prospects.

Ever since the scandal of the "sighting," it was obvious that her children knew about the affair. They avoided her; their hugs and smiles were noncommittal, confused, distant. In turn, she avoided them too. One evening at dinner, Karishma had seen Mohit shivering, snot pouring through the estuary above his lips. When she had offered to take him to the doctor, he had said, "No need, Mummy, I've almost finished a full week's course."

A full week of antibiotics?

He had been sick for a *week*?

How had he not told her, how had she not seen?

How different this was from the time she had palpitated over Deepak's fever!

Yet she did not act. Instead she withdrew, spending more and more time in the office.

She might have ruined their childhoods, but she could save their futures.

In the office, Karishma now told Laxman what she had learned.

"And what's going to happen to all the money I've been loaning him?" Laxman asked.

Karishma shook her head and looked down at the fine print of the government document before her, the cyclostyled paper thin as fabric, edged in with tearaway sides.

Laxman said, "This is utter foolishness! I want you all to live properly. You can't stay in those two rooms forever—the boys are so grown now."

"And after their marriages, where will they go?" Karishma asked.

"I'll go speak to him," Laxman said.

In the factory, when Laxman cornered Brij about Sachin's plans, Brij protested, "But I didn't think they were actually going to *build*."

"You know your brother says what he means," Laxman said. "He's an American."

Brij was silent. They were sitting in the supervisor's cabin in the factory.

Laxman said, "I'm not saying you should build something immediately. But we know you're planning to, so why not start a little bit of the work, so they can't take over the whole area? You know they'll build a palace—three or four bedrooms, two floors, and the construction will last for years. Think about Mohit, his studies." Laxman knew Brij had a soft spot for Mohit.

Brij sighed.

"What?" Laxman asked.

"I thought these loans were without strings," Brij said.

Laxman said, "They are, but if you aren't going to use the money, I'll need it back."

As Laxman's political stature had grown—and more and more contracts for balms poured in from Hindu nationalists—Brij's position had become weaker. What could he do?

In fact, though he had used the pretext of construction to secure money from Laxman, Brij had a different private idea of what he would do with the money he was storing in bags in his Godrej almirah and also squirreling into a mutual fund account: He would send his kids abroad. Though he personally despised all those Indians who fled India and insisted on calling themselves Indians (Like his brother: What had he done for this nation? Apart from becoming soft?), he wished for nothing more for his kids: for Mohit and Deepak to escape this country and avoid the cascading disappointments that Brij himself had endured.

Brij, for all his failures, his carapace of glittering resentment, still contained a few sparks of compassion.

Ever since Sachin had moved to the US in 1974, Brij and Sachin had exchanged polite letters every six months. These letters contained little more than the occasional photo and birthday wishes and answers to Sachin's casual questions about how the mango trees on their joint lands were doing; whether Bimla Behnji's arthritis was better; whether Karishma and Brij would like to come visit them in the US, they could even pay for one ticket. But once he received the loan, Brij began to ask Sachin, in his letters, about how much education in the US would cost; whether Sachin could send him clippings for ads for colleges; whether it was easier to be admitted if you did schooling in the US or in India; did international students receive funding—Brij said again that he was asking for his "scrapbook." But as the answers came back, Brij began to calculate how to invest the loan from Laxman—which came with no written terms—so it might grow into something that could eventually rocket his son Mohit across the planet.

His eldest son, growing into his teens, was intelligent. Intelligence was so rare in the family that Brij did not want to waste it. Though it pained him to admit it, he saw himself in his son. This made it hard for him to look directly at Mohit: He could only, in a sense, do it from an angle. When he came face-to-face with Mohit—with Mohit's black and straight Central Asian eyebrows, his crooked nose—Brij was filled with shame and he retreated. Mohit, he could tell, was aware of this shame too. *But if only Mohit knew how much I worry about him.*

Brij himself had not been cut out for the defense services; he had been forced into it by his father, Brahmpal, who had also forced Sachin into engineering. Yes, Brij had been sporty, but his disposition had always been bookish, scholarly: He would have made a better professor than a pilot. Aspiring to write autobiographies like Ved Mehta, he had in fact taken careful notes about his NDA training in Poona, only to lose the diary when a batch mate of his (a jovial boy named Ryan, who later revealed a streak of recklessness that led to quick promotions and then a stupid heroic death in a border skirmish with Pakistan) had discovered the journal, read it out loud to the others in the long mosquito-netted dormitory, and then fallen silent as their instructor entered the room, tearing the notebook from Ryan's hands, saying, "What is this nonsense," Ryan stoically *not* telling on Brij and pretending the notebook was *his*, already acting like a self-sacrificing platoon commander, and for this (false) transgression, Ryan was punished physically for a week, forced to rise even before the dawn call and run extra laps around the field—one lap sprinting, the next one walking, a famously tiring technique—and being denied a biscuit with his morning tea ... yes, Ryan had accepted it all without complaint and he never made fun of Brij again but nor did they become friends. *What did he want me to do*, Brij wondered, *reveal myself as the author—when he was the one who stole the notebook from me?*

Brij was in the air force for himself. He had only one desire when he entered: to get out alive. And, like Hemingway, he would write a book about his heroics—or his failures. He would coldly watch and observe, owing no one anything.

But the air force did not allow this self to flourish. It broke him into service, erasing selfhood.

When he finally resigned, in 1978, he was, of course, no longer the person who had entered. He had given away nearly a decade of his life to a cause he did not believe in.

He joined a family friend's paper mill, but that was no better: the same distant postings, the same hardships. He returned to Delhi, but there was no peace or privacy in the joint family, and he was constantly pulled into schemes—like this bloody balm business—against his will, to make money. Once his cawing aunt Rupvati arrived from Gharam to live with them, all delicate thought became impossible. Every day, he put down his imaginary pen.

His children were now the only way to make something good of his life. But even then, a part of him revolted. No one had helped *him*: Why should his children have this privilege? Wasn't it better that they be prepared for the cruelty of the real world rather than be mollycoddled? But then he would catch a sideways glimpse of Mohit—*my son Mohit, my reflection!*—and all these rational considerations would melt.

If Mohit escaped, then he—Brij—might too.

What would a successful version of himself look like?

He did not discuss these ideas with his wife; he did not respect her intellect, did not think she would endorse his wish to send Mohit abroad. Karishma had a short-term outlook. Even when he was in the air force, all she'd cared about was where the boys and she would be most comfortable, not which postings would lead to the quickest promotions and therefore the most *long-term* comfort; and in kowtowing to her, mostly out of melancholy and a secret drive for self-destruction, he had wrecked his career. For this, she took zero responsibility. Karishma saw him, he'd always felt, through a sheet of glass. Even when he punched through it, she flinched and then reconstructed that glassy aura around herself. Had he ever known real love? He understood now that what had happened at the outset—wildly chasing Karishma after he was introduced to her—had been infatuation, a need for self-erasure after another arranged match had rejected him. So, Brij had thrown himself into his obsession with Karishma, who had been thrilled (he thought) and a little alarmed (he could see now) by his reckless courting. She would never have encountered such passion in a man—even *he* had been impressed and frightened by his zeal, all the unspent emotion breaking through his air-force reserve, the strict posture concealing a person willing to humiliate himself for love the way his fellow cadets humiliated themselves before their instructors. He would be, he thought, a servant of love, of this woman. The idea of individual devotion greatly appealed to him. It was a *pleasurable* way to erase the self: It would lift him out of the pungent restlessness of the air-force barracks and send him sailing upward into a heaven full of sex, cuddling, delight; and could he have found a more beautiful woman to concentrate his passions on? But he mistook Karishma's shyness as a sign of hidden depths—when her personality turned out to be exactly what it appeared to be, nothing more, nothing less: She was glassy, tentative, watchful, careful, selfish, dispassionate, and even anti-intellectual. But if he had actually read her letters rather than inhaled them, he would have known her words were the runes and recordings of a dry soul—a trickle of a personality flowing stubbornly across a massive desert to a destination only she could surmise, with the husband as a hindrance, a rock to flow around.

The disillusionment with his wife took a few months to set in, when they were on a posting in Agra. That was when he understood a crucial fact of life: *People are exactly who they say they are.* Only our projections blind us to their reality. But what would life be without such projections, such dangerous overflow? And so mistaking people for something they were not—imbuing them with transcendent qualities—was a symptom of living, of being alive.

Karishma, on the other hand (he knew), bore no illusions. She approached every situation with ruthless clarity—it was almost a religion with her, the stripping away of romance, of sentimentality. Just as Brij had been infatuated with Karishma, Brij would go on to become infatuated, as a friend and fan, with seniors and colleagues in the air force. But Karishma cut them down in private or remained rudely diffident in their presence when they came over to Brij and Karishma's house for dinner. "He makes eyes at me," she would say about a vice marshal, and Brij would respond, "Let him, yaar—he's human, no?" and she'd say, "You wouldn't care if I became a mistress of one of your commanders?" and he'd say, "Don't say such obscene things," and she'd say, "I know, in the end, only your promotions matter to you," and he'd say, "You think you see things so clearly, Madam, but I have to inform you that your windshield is fogged: Why would I have taken *this* posting if only my career mattered? *You* matter to me, *your* happiness matters to me," and she would do that stubborn, glassy thing with her jaw that drove him to rage and made him hit her ... it was his overflow coming across a wall. He couldn't accept such ghastly certainty about things, the shutting down of possibility. Worse, she was often *right* about people—snipping away the gaudy ribbons of novelty around this or that fatuous new friend—so that *he*, too, would be infected by her judgment, and the friendship would wither on the vine. She was the principle of reality that destroys your fun. He resented her for it. He also respected her for it.

The trouble, of course, was that his illusions about *her* had fallen away as well. The thing about marriage is that it forces you to see at least one person in your life clearly. And as he saw her clearly, he saw also the flaws in himself that had driven him to choose her: his impulsiveness; the tidal rush of his moods; the pleasure of falling headlong into joy or despair till you could no longer remember what had brought you there, you were rappelling on a rope in a cave without a flashlight, your legs swinging above unseen ground, an updraft tickling the soles of your feet ... thanks to Karishma he could see this all objectively, and he tried to change himself. But as his career in the air force flailed, his willpower drained.

All he could do, in the end, was be himself. And see his wife clearly. And hate her. And hate himself.

(It did not occur to him that the person who Karishma became in his presence might have something to do with how *he* acted; *his* verbal and physical lashings; *his* unpredictability; *his* miserliness; *his* impatience with the sheer fact of another person, her differing intelligence and interests. She had been perfect in his mind, and when she turned out not to be perfect, he had revolted.)

Karishma knew too that she disappointed him, and though she understood (with her ruthless clarity) that Brij's behavior had little to do with her, she still felt bad about herself, put herself down, retreated more readily into hesitation—which was also, for some reason, the state in which men saw her as most attractive, even mysterious and radiant, the light still blazing out from under a gaze that had been turned down, as if in grief.

So now Brij put his hopes in Mohit, as he had once poured his hopes into Karishma. This set Mohit up for failure. And things between father and son were not easy. When Mohit brought home report cards laddered with B+s instead of As and A+s—70s instead of 80s—Brij would give him tight, instant slaps; Karishma would rush out to protect him, and Brij would push her away violently—he could do whatever he wanted now that she was openly having an affair—and then Deepak too would run out of the bedroom to grab his crying mother's feet to console her; elderly Rupvati Chachi also emerging from her room and saying, "Stop it, stop it," and then Mohit would turn to Rupvati and to his mother and say, "I deserve it, Mummy, I didn't study hard enough"; and then he would disappear into his room, his face stained with tears.

Here the fates of Brij's two sons diverged. During this time, Deepak, free from all pressure and supervision of his father, began to thrive, developing friendships with other boys in the colony, playing cricket every afternoon in the park, honing his talent for tennis, and generally accepting even his mother's affair as a kind of mystery of adult life that it was better not to think about, or rather to drown out with heavy activity and heavy music—Def Leppard, Metallica, Iron Maiden—that he began to blast from his two-in-one.

Mohit, meanwhile, stayed at home, brooding—brooding that would erupt into action when he came of age, bringing the family down with him—

Or rather, with me, your hidden narrator.

That night, after Laxman buttonholed Brij in the factory about the construction, Brij was divided over how to act, and violently shoved Karishma during a fight. She fell on the bedroom floor and he kicked her. The next day, he asked his factory workers to come to his house with a Tempo full of bricks and to cart them up to the roof. When nosy Rupvati Chachi asked what was going on, Brij said, "We're just storing some things from the factory."

CHAPTER 67

DROPPING IN FOR TEA AT BRIJ'S, GITA AND SACHIN WERE shocked to hear that Brij had started work on the roof.

"But you're the one who suggested building there to us," said Sachin calmly, thinking it was a misunderstanding. He was still new to the caprices of the complex.

"Brother, things have changed," Brij said. "Rupvati Chachi has moved in, the boys are growing up, our needs have increased. And since you don't have offspring, you can perhaps be more flexible."

"But we wrote about all this in our letters," Gita sputtered, as if words uttered from the US could have any meaning here, as if language were a stable international currency.

"There must have been a misunderstanding," Brij said. "There are other places to build in the complex."

"There are no places," Sachin said.

"What about the servants' quarters?" Karishma said, pouring a thin stream of tea from the cozied kettle into Gita's cup.

This could only be taken as an insult, Gita knew. The servants' quarters—a two-story structure in a state of immense dilapidation—abutted the building that housed Brij and his family. The bottom floor was a storage shed. The two floors above the shed—though Gita and Sachin had never been inside—were dingy, with small transom windows. From these open windows came the miasmic smells of shit and piss—there had never been proper plumbing for the poor servants—as well as the electric, teeth-chattering sound of sewing machines.

"And where will the servants go?" Gita finally said. "This is nonsense." But Sachin put a hand on her arm.

"Come, come, I'll show you what we've done," Brij said.

Up on the roof, he led them to an immense pile of bricks—more like a pyre—in the middle of the blistered limestone floor. "See, this is where we'll put the room for Mohit," Brij said. "When he's married, he can live here."

When they went down, Gita said again, "Brij, this isn't fair, you and Sachin have an equal share."

"You were in the States for so long." Brij paused, feeling his beard with the underside of a finger. "If you want," Brij said, "we can bring this issue up with the trust. Laxman said he's happy to mediate."

Gita snorted.

"You have an issue with Laxman?" Brij asked.

"No issue," Gita said. "Except he's your business partner."

"Control your wife," Brij said to Sachin.

Right then, Mohit walked in from his room, which was separated from the drawing room by a wall with a pane of frosted glass incongruously installed there. Of average height but gangly, now twelve, he hunched his shoulders as he approached them.

"Wow, you've started to shave!" Gita said, immediately changing gears.

"But he doesn't study," Brij said. "Did you do your revisions for your maths exam?"

As Mohit bent down to touch her feet, Gita said, "Oh ho, don't be silly! We don't believe in this stuff."

"OK, Chachi," Mohit said.

"Wow, and his voice has totally broken," Gita said.

"It's been broken for many years," Karishma said proudly.

"And where's your brother?" Gita asked Mohit.

"Oh, Chachi, he's gone to play cricket in the park."

"You didn't go?" Gita asked.

Mohit shrugged his shoulders and grinned, showing his vulpine, conical, overlapping teeth. "I have to study."

Then Mohit, who appeared to have come out of his room only to defuse the tension between the adults, vanished back into the flat. Loud, antagonizing rock and roll—Gita recognized the Rolling Stones—began to pour out of his room, and Brij raised himself from his chair and bellowed, his face red, "Turn that off!" When the music didn't subside, he nodded his head at Karishma, who, like a servant, got up quickly and rat-tat-tatted on the frosted pane. The music shrank to a whimper before vanishing altogether.

Sachin's voice finally came out in a hurt choke.

"What was that?" Brij asked.

"Come, Gita," he was saying, "let's go."

CHAPTER 68

"WHY DIDN'T YOU SAY ANYTHING MORE TO HIM?" GITA asked her husband when they left.

Sachin shook his head ruefully, his floppy hair drenched with sweat.

In the driveway, Gita convinced Sachin to talk to Ram Bhaiya and Bhagat Bhaiya, who had encouraged Sachin's return.

But when Gita and Sachin strolled over to their respective flats, she was surprised by their reactions. "Perhaps they're right, you were in America a long time," Ram said with a big afternoon yawn, fanning out his hand over his mouth without actually covering it. "What did Laxman say?"

Bhagat said, "The issue is between you brothers. Anyway, Laxman said you wanted to build something very large there, which would not be right." Then he added, "Why not consider the servants' quarters?"

Gita and Sachin protested, but the message was clear: Laxman was now in charge.

How had this happened? Gita wondered. How had the worst person in the family become its doyen?

Or was this the fate of all groups? That power accrued to the person with the most energy, regardless of whether that energy was good or evil?

"I can't forcibly remove their bricks," Sachin said later, when they were back in their rental.

"No," she said.

"And I don't want to get stuck in the courts."

"True," Gita said. "But we can't back down. If there's one thing I've understood about your family, it's this: You can't back down." How strange that she was arguing for them to live in the complex! But it wasn't about the complex. It was about her personhood, the need again to be whole in the face of bullies. Strength had come to Gita in India. It was the strength she had been hoarding in the US—which had crazily zagged out in all directions, into the affair with Hector, into her longing for India—a strength Laxman had tried to sap from her but that he had simply suppressed till, like greenery at the site of a nuclear disaster, it came back doubly strong.

A day later, returning to A-19, they reluctantly toured the servants' quarters.

As they had known, it was in terrible shape. Climbing up a spiral staircase, they opened the whitish door of the quarter to find themselves in a dank space that smelled like a bachelor haunt, with its residue of smoke, sweat, piss, liquor, weed. A series of cells with badly fitted doors were set off from a narrow corridor; the corridor itself was crisscrossed with three clotheslines, festooned with cheap men's underwear. Gita and Sachin had to duck under the lines to pass through. Below the mildewed, seepage-softened walls ran open gutters. Through a half-open door, Gita glimpsed a blanket on the floor and a rippled poster of a starlet on the wall. Two male servants with rough towels around their necks walked by, doffing their heads and grimacing cursorily.

"Namaste," Gita said, before they did.

"Namaste, Memsahib," they both mumbled, looking away.

One friendly older cook with a neat mustache stopped to ask them about America—he followed American politics in the papers.

But the blankness in the eyes of the other servants suggested embarrassment and anger at having their only sanctum violated.

"Their lives are hard enough already," Sachin said afterward, overwhelmed. But he was feeling grateful for Gita's strength.

A few days later, an architect who was also a family friend told them, "The reason they're all telling you to build in the quarter is simple: It's going to fall down." Bhim Nath, the architect, then talked about how he had once been inside and had been shocked by the sagging ceiling beams. "When the servants' quarters was built, the contractor cheated your family and put in substandard materials. The ceiling doesn't have enough iron rods. It's just luck that it hasn't collapsed. You'll be doing everyone a favor by renovating it."

CHAPTER 69

THE CONSTRUCTION LASTED FOUR MONTHS.

The eight servants were unhoused. From their communal barracks they were sent to live on the landings and in the kitchens of the family members they worked for. From now on, when they wanted to meet, they would have to gather in front of the gates, the last joint space available for them.

Gita, who was in charge of the renovation as Sachin settled into his new job with Rishab, tried not to think about this. Instead, she focused on their plans. The small monastic cells would be demolished to create a large drawing-dining room; and at the far end there would be a square kitchen. The old storage area above would boast two bedrooms and two bathrooms.

Their flat would be linked to Rupvati Chachi's room, which of course would be linked to Brij's house and the rest of the complex.

Laxman was often in his office, on the phone, when Gita went to the nearby market to consider the cost of construction materials. He would beckon Gita in with a finger, and then she felt she had no choice but to enter that fishbowl of an office and endure interrogations from Laxman, Karishma, and Archana.

"How many more months will this take?" Laxman would ask.

"It is happening on schedule."

"Tell the contractor that the laborers' children shouldn't be playing here."

"Fine, Laxman."

Is Karishma really sleeping with him? she would wonder, looking around the office.

She remembered that night in Midland when she had read Prabha's letter, the letter that had informed her of the Karishma–Laxman liaison. She remembered how Sachin had initially refused to believe it. And she remembered something else: the way the letter had released her from the trap of her shame—she wasn't alone!—and the way she had turned to Sachin a day later and said, with certainty, "We must go back to India."

One day, the contractor, a rotund man with a huge scar on his neck, said, "Madam, whenever you're not here, Laxman sahb tells us to stop—that we're making too much noise, that he'll report us."

"People are very interfering in this family," she said.

"I tell him that I have orders, but then he starts threatening me: 'This is illegal, I'll have your license confiscated.'"

"Who is he to say anything?" Gita said.

Then she saw Laxman striding toward her, his face distended.

"I just saw they're breaking a wall. That's not legal."

Gita said, "Laxman, this I don't know, but—"

"Then your husband should know," Laxman said.

"Laxman, please."

"You can't just start breaking parts of this house willy-nilly!"

"Arre, Brij only told us to build here," Gita said.

"To renovate! You people are breaking."

"Stop shouting, Laxman."

"You're the one who's shouting," he said.

And suddenly they were both shouting at each other, erupting in the courtyard.

"You have no right to speak to me this way!" Gita screeched.

As he raised his voice in return, standing inches from her, Gita opened the door to the stairway that led to Karishma and Brij's flat. She slammed the door behind her. Climbing up the stairs, she knocked on Rupvati Chachi's bedroom door and entered. Rupvati Chachi sat on a chair, knitting. Gita collapsed on Rupvati's bed.

Rupvati Chachi was an irritating person, but she was also neutral territory and fond of Gita; Gita often used her bedroom as a sarai during the day, when she needed a break from supervising the construction.

"What happened?" Rupvati asked. "Servants were fighting?"

"Nothing, Chachi, just the heat."

But Gita lay on the bed, her head pounding, near tears.

When she recovered, she walked up to Brij's roof.

She saw that Brij's pile of bricks was untouched.

Going down later, Gita ran into Brij in the driveway.

"There's been a slight delay," Brij told Gita, without shame.

CHAPTER 70

A FEW DAYS LATER, WHEN SHE WAS IN THE QUARTER, checking in on the five workers etching out the frames for the windows, a man showed up at the door, carrying a register under one armpit and holding a battered egg-yellow scooter helmet in the other hand. "Is Mr. Sachin Chopra here?" he asked. He was short, plump, bald, bigheaded, and bearded. He wore a brown shirt over his black pants.

"He's at work at this time—you are?" Gita asked.

"Madam," he said, "I'm with the MCD."

"What is that?" Gita asked, though she knew it stood for the Municipal Corporation of Delhi.

"Madam, you don't know the MCD?" He laughed. "Well. This is something you should have known before you started; your architect should have contacted us. This work that's happening here—you did it *without* the MCD?" He was pointing to the laborers in her drawing room.

"What can I tell you, ji, my husband handled all of this," Gita lied, "and he's not home." Had their architect not taken the requisite permissions?

"You're Mrs. Chopra?" the man asked.

She nodded noncommittally.

"How long has this work been going on?" he asked, pulling out the register and holding a pen over it.

"But who are you—and who sent you?" Gita asked.

"Madam, I'm Aggarwal from the MCD. I'm an engineer. For all these matters, one needs permission from the municipality—"

"But my husband has taken all the permissions," Gita said.

"If you can show me the papers and the plans, I can check."

It was a warm winter day. The man stood on the landing atop the curving concrete spiral staircase. He could see past Gita to the chaos of the construction site, to the five workers barking at one another in their sharp, phlegmy voices, voices trained to carry over the vast voids of construction sites and scaffolds, but impossible to turn off even for these smaller projects.

"Who sent you?" Gita asked again.

"Madam, it's our job. But if you don't have the plans, let me speak to the architect." He looked at her balefully from under his thick eyebrows, which had been clearly plastered upward like paused black flames from hours in the velvety humid enclosure of the cushioned scooter helmet.

"He's not here."

"Really?" Aggarwal said. "One of your relatives said he saw him come here. Madam, this is a very serious matter."

Gita said, "Ji, I'm just a housewife."

"Till we're shown the plans, you'll have to stop the construction."

"Then we will," she said.

And she closed the door on him.

Gita walked down her stairs and out of the compound. Laxman, Archana, and Karishma were in the office as usual when Gita stepped in.

"Laxman, I have a question for you." Suddenly, Gita felt an incredible tightness in her chest.

Laxman looked bemused.

"Did you talk to the MCD man who just came?" Gita asked.

A look of suppressed rage passed over his face. "Oh, yes, I saw him, he was asking where your house was."

"And why did you send him?" Gita asked. "You have no right to interfere."

"We didn't," Laxman said through gritted teeth. "How dare you accuse me." He stopped. "In this family, you may not know, but we handle all matters *internally*. But this guy was hanging around for hours outside and wanted to meet you."

"Then you could have told him we weren't there."

"We don't lie in this family," he said.

Gita looked at all three of them—Archana, Laxman, Karishma. "Very rich, coming from you." Then she stormed out.

Over the phone, the architect told them he hadn't, in fact, taken the permissions. "Gitaji and Sachinji, I was only trying to save you headaches. The MCD would have demanded big bribes, and frankly they don't need to be involved in internal renovations in the back of a complex. Someone must have told them about it, otherwise they never would have come for such a minor matter."

We should have told him what kind of complex it was, Gita thought.

But before Gita and Sachin could react, another scandal shook the complex.

When everyone received their mail the next day, they found within it an envelope that contained a chit:

Lacks Man, Stop sexploiting your dotter ***Curries Ma,*** the letter said, in badly spaced typescript.

CHAPTER 71

"I DIDN'T SEND IT, I PROMISE."

Gita was so hysterical that Sachin said, "It almost seems like someone with legal training has done it, since they've avoided the actual names."

"Yes, exactly. If I'd have done it, it would have been paragraphs, pages." She was laughing and crying. How badly she had wanted to shame Laxman. But like this?

The house was again in an uproar. People stood in knots in the driveway of the complex, chatting. When Gita came over to supervise construction, she had a sense that relatives were either avoiding her or looking at her with admiring, bright, sly eyes, as if to say: *You did it, we never thought anyone would, we've all wished to.*

But Gita, who had done no such thing, ignored them all. Instead, she waited till she knew Karishma would be alone in her flat and rang the bell.

"Hello, Gita," Karishma said as the servant led her in.

"Karishma, whatever you might think of me," Gita started, "I would never have done it." Then she said, "I have nothing but love and respect for *you*. In fact, I worry about you. Because he tried it with me too. You may not believe me. But it's the truth."

Karishma's face hardened.

"If he's forcing you, tell me—"

"Get out!" Karishma shouted. "Get out."

Gita felt now that she had made a true mistake. And, in fact, she had. Soon after, the MCD came and demolished a part of their renovation.

Rooms that had taken four months to put up were brought down in eight hours. Gita watched as the workers turned on their own work with a fury that only comes from a particular mix of intimacy and disappointment. Though they never got to inhabit these palaces, they at least took pride in building them; and so to have spent months laboring and hammering and carrying stones for something that was half mirage felt like an arbitrary penal punishment, like they were prisoners forced into the repetitive labor of gathering and breaking stones because the warden lacked anything productive for them to do. And perhaps this was why, despite a buffet of months when they could have been shirking work, this was when workers began to fall sick. Two of the older ones, graying and gaunt, vomited down the side of the building, only to be revived by nimbu paani (in the special steel tumblers reserved for servants). It was more humid now but also, Gita thought, they had likely been drinking. Demolition did not require the sober precision of construction. Another worker dropped a large chunk of concrete on his foot; Gita sent him immediately to a nearby government hospital in an auto.

At the end of it, Gita and Sachin's flat, originally meant to be a three-bedroom place, was reduced to 550 square feet, with only enough room for a single bedroom, a kitchenette, one toilet, and a small drawing-cum-dining room.

The irony was not lost on Sachin that—as he designed modular housing prototypes at his new job with Rishab—his own house had been dismembered.

As for Karishma, after Gita had left her flat, a memory had come to her.

It was a memory of Gita on a visit to India, looking very American and guileless and saying, "Does Laxman force you also to drink whiskey?"

Is that when I became interested in Laxman? Karishma thought.

Is that why I did it? Am I really so jealous and bottomless?

Am I always a second choice?

She had made a mistake. For the second time in her life, she had chosen the wrong man.

The person who had sent the letter sat silently in her own house, brooding over what she had done.

Then, as she always did, Vibha got up to straighten the portrait of her father.

CHAPTER 72

VIBHA HAD NOT EXPECTED TO ACT THIS WAY.

Her entire life had been dedicated to the cause of the family, but the open affair, the property drama, her brother's shameless role in it, had loosened something in her.

Growing increasingly incensed by Laxman's bullying behavior, she had typed out chit after chit and mailed them.

The addresses of her relatives were easy: They all had the same address.

She felt exhilarated for a moment but then shame took over.

I've failed you, Papaji, she thought, weeping about the direction her life had taken.

Gita never figured out who sent it; she would never have guessed it was Vibha. But it was comforting, in a perverse way, to know that there were others chafing against Laxman's reign.

The letter ripped down the veil of politeness and indirection that hung over interactions in the family. Karishma, Brij, Laxman, and Archana would no longer speak to her; she wouldn't speak to them. That suited her fine. It made the complex bearable.

Sachin, somehow, as a man, as a member of the clan, was spared excommunication. He still went to the drawing room and touched Bimla Behnji's feet and talked to people about his new job, which was going well.

His partner Rishab had been fantastically helpful through Sachin's family-related ups and downs. In fact, when Rishab had heard about the dispute, he had counseled Gita and Sachin, and phoned lawyers on their behalf. He had allowed Sachin flexibility with work hours.

"That's the thing about India," Gita said to Sachin. "Even if family doesn't behave like family, there are so many friends who do."

Gita and Sachin were now outcasts in the complex. But then a subtle change occurred.

Their flat was a mere 550 square feet but flowered exotically with electronic goods from America—a Panasonic TV, a Sony music system, a fat Westinghouse fridge, a Whirlpool A/C—and these were a source of fascination to the teenagers and preteens in the complex, who came over to pop cassettes into the Sony or to watch DD shows on the TV.

Mohit and Deepak were the most frequent visitors, slipping through Rupvati's room to their chacha and chachi's, where they knew they would be indulged with treats. "Come over here, you rascal, you're getting too smart," Gita would say, and then thirteen-year-old Mohit would let Chachi run her hand through his frizzy gelled hair, feeling how it faded into soft fur at the top of his spine. "See, you're a teenager but you'll always be my little bacha," she would say, and then suddenly, in the middle of this petting, in the middle of Mohit's easy submission, she would realize what she was doing: She was standing in for the missing mother. He was here not to fiddle with their stereo but to be renewed through adult eyes. Even her soft rebukes, delivered the right way, were a form of attention, of saying to a child: *I see you.*

One day, Gita asked Mohit casually, "So, where are Mummy and Papa? Is Papa going to the club?"

Mohit said, "They've gone to the factory, Chachi."

"Together?"

"Yes, Chachi." The slightly cracking voice of an adolescent.

Was he lying? Besides, if he knew his mother was with Laxman, would he really tell her? As far as Gita could tell, the anonymous letter had changed nothing.

And do you know when your papa will complete his construction? she wanted to add.

She decided it was wrong of her to ask. She stopped.

That day, she became truly close to Mohit.

CHAPTER 73

THEN, ONE DAY, GITA RECEIVED A SURPRISE VISIT FROM Rishab.

"I was just driving by," he told Gita, "and I wanted to give you this mithai and a card for my niece's wedding myself."

Gita sat Rishab down on one of the La-Z-Boys—so huge and bizarre in this tiny Delhi drawing room—and insisted he have tea.

"Thank you," Rishab said. "And do you mind if I smoke my pipe?"

It turned out Rishab had come with an agenda. "Gita, I hope you won't mind my saying this, but I don't know who else to turn to. You know I respect Sachin more than anyone else in the world—almost as much as my mother, who, let's face it, was the brains of my family. But one issue we're having. Has he told you?"

She looked on, curious, thinking how much Rishab reminded her of her own decent brother. Rishab went on, "You know how Sachin is such a brilliant person? Well, one difficulty is that he is very impatient with all the employees. These chaps are from tier-two cities, from second-rate colleges … they have to be trained. But he blows up at them."

"Moving back here has been much more stressful than either of us thought," Gita reminded him.

"I agree," Rishab said. "That's why I opened my life to you. I understand it. But … to be honest, I don't know how to deal with this problem. When I talk to him, he says, 'Rishab, you accept a lower standard for everything.' I try to explain that India is like that—you need patience. And what's the difference between a small bribe for a government employee and a tip you are forced to give everywhere you spend money in a country like America?"

Gita was feeling annoyed on her husband's behalf. Why was she being involved?

"Look," Rishab said, loading up his pipe. "You know I wouldn't come to you if it wasn't a serious problem. All our employees are threatening to resign. I suspect he will listen to you."

When Sachin returned from work, Gita said, "Guess who came by," and she filled him in.

"That's classic Rishab, he won't complain to my face."

"But, Sachoo, there is some truth to what he's saying."

Sachin looked on.

"Even with the servant and driver—" Gita said.

Suddenly he started shouting. "Do you know how it feels! To know you're good at what you're doing and to be constantly told you're the idiot! They don't listen to a word I say! They say one thing and do another! I'm just some idiot from America!" He went on and on, his face reddening.

After he was done, she joined her hands in mock apology. "Please leave me out of this. I'm just the messenger."

You really are an ugly American, she muttered under her breath, wondering now if this was how she had behaved in 1980, when she had come back on that first visit.

But the visit from Rishab had been a sign of things to come. One day, Rishab simply stopped appearing at the office. Sachin could not get Rishab on the phone again, and when he drove to Rishab's house, the guard said he wasn't home.

Their partnership was over.

Sachin was now alone in their two-room office in ITO with a skeleton staff of two employees; Rishab had paid the rent for the month and did not demand back payment, which was characteristically decent of him.

"Don't worry," Sachin told Gita, bitterly. "I'm not going to leave your beloved India. I don't want to go begging back to Trident."

It was at this time that Gita finally got a job of her own.

Gita had initially considered jobs in publishing, only to realize—from talking to Mohit—that she was most invigorated by the company of kids that age. So, when her friend Vasundhara had told her about an opening for the position of counselor at a new school, she had taken the teachers' exam and dutifully applied.

When she was rejected, she was downcast—all the old doubts about wasting her life and her career reemerged.

But then, writing an overdue letter to Cindy in the US, she vowed not to repeat the mistake she'd made in America—the mistake of accepting premature defeat.

Two tries later, she had the job.

Sachin, too, gradually underwent a change in his career.

The modular housing enterprise was kaput; he didn't know enough about that world to proceed on his own. Nevertheless, soon after the "breakup" with Rishab, Sachin was filled with hard determination, the kind that had enabled him to succeed as an orphan in the US. Freed from Rishab's prefabricated attitudes toward the country, he began studying India on his own, scouting opportunities in the sector he knew best: plastic packaging. He learned the regulations. He walked through Delhi's markets and noticed how people used plastic bags to carry milk and then, working from there, calculated the demand for plastic bottles and Tetra Paks. When he could, he visited bureaucrats and was more than willing to throw around his grandfather's name.

Soon after, he began placing calls to all his business contacts in the US, exploiting his years of connections to see if any of them might be interested in setting up operations in India, especially since certain rules about foreign investment were now being relaxed.

Within a year, he got his first client: Trident.

And this was how his iconic squish bottle came to India.

(It was only years in the future, when Sachin visited his ancestral home in Gharam and saw the ditches and irrigation canals filled with plastic bottles—crushed and grimy and glittering and endless—that he understood what he'd done, the kind of causeway he'd built between the two countries. And his life, which had changed so many times, would change again.)

THREE

MY PROTEST

CHAPTER 74

IN SEPTEMBER 1990—FIVE YEARS AFTER SACHIN AND GITA'S return—the family came apart.

It began with Mohit's participation in the anti-affirmative action protests sweeping the country. Mohit was now seventeen, a fresher in college.

Gita had just returned to A-19 from her work at St. Xavier's School when she heard that Mohit had been grievously injured at a protest and was in the hospital.

She phoned Sachin at his office. "Should we go there?" she asked. "Or will Karishma get angry?"

What had happened was this: A month earlier, in August, India's prime minister, V. P. Singh, had undertaken a controversial, populist move, pressing into law the Mandal Commission Report, which gave twenty-seven percent reservations in government jobs to OBCs. Government jobs were one of the few paths to security and upward mobility; and so the upper-caste students—the majority of college students—responded with fury to this affirmative action. As a friend had put it to Mohit: "Twenty-two-point-five percent of these jobs are already reserved for untouchables. Now they want to reserve fifty percent. What's going to be left for us? Is it our fault that we were born upper caste? V. P. Singh is just appeasing minorities to garner their votes."

In Brij's house, too, there was surprising agreement on this issue.

The coddling of minorities, Brij felt, had gone too far. Whenever he could, he would quote a newspaper interview he'd read with a rising rustic politician who supported the implementation of the quotas.

"But would you go to a doctor who got in on reservation?" a journalist asked the politician.

"No, Bhaiya," the politician responded. "I'd go to America."

The politician was being facetious, but Brij chose to interpret it literally.

Soon after the implementation of the Mandal Commission Report, protests had erupted. Mohit joined them. The upper-caste students shut down colleges, blocked buses, demonstrated in front of hospitals and major intersections, and sat on traffic islands polishing shoes (as an indication of what would become of them), stopping motorists and chatting with them. How could merit, the students asked, the one source of "fairness" in an unfair country, be stripped from them? (The lower-caste students, if anyone noticed them, huddled silently in the college canteens, their very silence exposing their previously only guessed-at castes.)

Nevertheless, though Brij supported the protest, he was not happy with his son's participation in it. For all Brij's strict drill sergeant patrolling of his son's education over the years, he had failed to turn Mohit into a stellar student. Instead, in class 11 and 12, Mohit had started to boldly rebel, whiling away long hours at the club, playing squash and table tennis, coming back with his clothes stinking of smoke, and interfering whenever Brij tried to discipline Karishma—what did the boy understand of his parents' relationship? Did Mohit know the humiliations Brij had suffered to collect loans to send Mohit abroad? But now Brij did not feel warmly enough toward his firstborn to grant him his wish of being freed from his father's gravitational pull. No, Mohit would remain under Brij's command till he learned to obey, and so now Brij's strategy, as Mohit had progressed stumblingly toward college, doing worse and worse in class 12 but wanting money to treat his friends and buy rock cassettes, was to make Mohit aware of the money that *he*, Brij, possessed, while withholding it so that Mohit often stormed off in a rage at being denied even minimal pocket money, shouting, "This is why I don't study, I live in the house of a fateecher," and when Karishma tried to intercede on his behalf, Brij would say, with all the force of someone who feels permanently wronged, "Enough from you, he has to learn the value of money: Is there one thing he's achieved? Let him not think that if he goes on like this, we'll support him," and what hurt Brij later, when he turned his mind to the subject of his older son in the privacy of his dark-wood-paneled bedroom, was that he knew Mohit was *smart*, that he was verbally and mathematically gifted, but was throwing it all away in an act of revolt against the very circumstances—Laxman's support—that made Brij flush with funds to spend on Mohit.

And Brij knew, too, that Mohit's rage in public was directed only at his parents. With his Sachin Chacha and Gita Chachi, he could be polite, giving, observant. It had also come back to Brij, via the double-agent Rupvati of course, that Mohit sometimes went over to his chacha and chachi's and asked them about college in the US, was it expensive, what would Chacha recommend, should one go for graduation or for postgraduation, and yet when Brij raised the issue of Mohit's future with Mohit, he would shout back, "Why do you care, I'll manage it, and it's not like *you* went to college," and Brij would get up from his sofa-chair in the drawing room, ears burning, and shout, "That's exactly why, you duffer! Do you want to be like me? Fine, we'll send you into the armed services, we'll turn you into a man," and he would perhaps even have acted on this threat had Karishma not literally thrown herself at his feet and begged him not to sacrifice their oldest child.

Then, one day, when Mohit was in class 12, Laxman (always a third party in all of Karishma and Brij's conversations) had asked Brij, "How are Mohit's studies? He's in the school cricket team, no? You know, I'm on friendly terms with the vice chancellor of DU." Laxman was glowing with power. The TPP had done very well in the 1989 elections—winning eighty-three more seats than in the previous election—and was supporting V. P. Singh's coalition from the outside, though the party was ambivalent about the Mandal Report.

That was the thing about having Laxman in their lives, Brij thought; though he created problems, he also solved them, and this was partly how, through hera-feri—a crooked use of the sports quota—Mohit (who, at the end of the day, *did* care where he got in, the frightened academically inclined boy still underlying the tense rebel) had gained admission to Hansraj College for history, where he was a fresher when the protests erupted all over Delhi.

The difficulty of having gotten Mohit into Hansraj now further inflamed Brij's sense of grievance. How dare his son willingly throw it all away by shouting, "V. P. Singh! Hai! Hai!" on the street, blackening his own face (and thus the family's) with boot polish and sitting on crossings, pretending to clean shoes, throwing himself in front of buses?

"Everyone's doing it, Papa," Mohit explained at a heated family dinner conference. "Even the college principal is encouraging us. He calls us in the morning and scolds us for bunking classes, but in the evening he talks to us about how this is all a political ploy by V. P. Singh against Devi Lal—"

"Devi Lal, Shavi Lal," Brij said. "You've hardly started to shave and you're talking about politics. Take my advice: Stay out of it. Stay on the sidelines. *Observe*. One can never guess how the government will behave. You want to be smashed by a lathi? You know what a lathi feels like? It's nothing like being hit by a stick. And I'll tell you, these police buggers seem to be on your side right now, but one student kills a policewallah or chucks a rock at them and you'll see how quickly they forget—they'll throw you all in a thana, and then don't come begging to me or your chacha to let you out—"

"He's right, beta," Karishma said, mashing rice on a plate with her hands. She was always ravenous at mealtimes—a change that had come over her after the affair had commenced.

"You think the revolution won't happen without you?" Brij continued. "Many big things have happened in this country without you."

"This is probably what elders said about the freedom struggle also," Mohit replied.

"Are you listening to your brother, Deepak?" Brij said. "He gets thirty marks in history and now he's an expert!"

Deepak, fifteen, sitting across from Brij, snickered. Mohit didn't respond. Mohit was forgiving of his brother—he doted on him and protected him. He understood that, in order to survive, Deepak needed to act in certain ways around their parents. He did not begrudge him. In any case, Deepak's behavior wouldn't alter Mohit's circumstances. Unlike the other Chopra men in the complex, Mohit knew how to concentrate his rage. "And then you people ask why OBCs and lower castes are taking over," Mohit said, changing tack and appealing to his father's elitist instincts. "*They* at least stand up for themselves." He pushed his plate forward theatrically, but the performance didn't quite come off. "So, don't blame me when I don't get into the IAS."

"Maybe if you were studying instead of bunking—" Brij began.

"It's not bloody fucking bunking!" Mohit said. "Everyone is doing it! All the schools and colleges are closed! And our princi said they didn't even close for the fucking freedom struggle!"

"Young man," Brij said, teeth gritted. "You will NOT. USE. THAT KIND OF ... UNPARLIAMENTARY LANGUAGE ... AT THE DINNER TABLE!"

"Screw you, man."

Brij leapt up from his chair and slapped Mohit so hard on the cheek that Mohit's flimsy dining chair tipped over and he fell backward, bashing his head against the edge of the sideboard that served as a bar.

"Abuser!" Mohit shouted, eyes streaming as he lay crumpled on the ground. If Brij had learned the art of physical overreaction, his son had learned how to powerfully project victimhood. "Asshole!"

"Oh, my baby!" Karishma said.

"You also shut up!" Mohit said, getting up and walking over to his shared room.

CHAPTER 75

A FEW DAYS LATER, THE PROTESTS DID TAKE A TURN FOR the worse. This was partly because V. P. Singh pulled off a masterstroke: He secretly promised he'd extend the reservations to Jats, the caste from which most of the police force was drawn. Now the police saw no reason to indulge these simpering, entitled college kids; and they hit back with force at the swarming protesters, bringing on brutal lathi charges and raining back stones from police stations that were under attack.

At a meeting of the protest organizing committee, in a brick alcove of Ramjas College, numerous students suggested next steps. Mohit was there, too, among the twenty activists. As a "sportsman," he had become close friends with the political types.

One said, "We should lie down in a long line on Ring Road for a full week."

Another said, "What about a hunger strike—going without food for eight, nine days? Fasting to death?"

"Abe yaar, have you ever gone one second without eating!"

"Would drinking water be allowed?" another asked.

After much debate in this vein, the students concurred on the idea of a hunger strike—it would be very Gandhian.

Yet at this crucial moment of action, when Mohit could have volunteered himself and his body to the cause, his courage deserted him. He let others speak.

The person who had asked about the ethics of water-drinking was the first person to volunteer himself for the strike, a boy named Anshul Tripathi.

Five other boys and two girls agreed to join him.

For the next four days, these boys and girls sat on scratched plastic chairs on a makeshift dais on the recently renamed "Mandal Chowk" crossing of Delhi University. They chatted freely with friends at first, but then a sympathetic medical student advised them to conserve their energies, and they fell silent. Closing their eyes in the drenching September sun, they hummed tunes and projected wretchedness, absorbing the attentions of the crowds.

For all their apparent heroism, they were secretly taking shifts to wolf down food—dal chawal—in the hostel room appointed as the headquarters of the organizing committee. Mohit supplied these meals—a mere chaprasi to the cause—and he now felt deceived, punished for his earnestness. Had he known they were going to cheat, he would have thrown *his* hat into the ring too, but then he had always been slow in such matters, unable to read the intentions of others, the ways in which they said one thing sincerely and did the opposite in the next instant, and for a second, he was proud of the uprightness that had filtered down to him from his air force-trained father. Then he remembered what a sadistic failed husk of a man his father was.

Of the eight students on strike, only one refused the secret meals and took sips of juice or tea instead: Anshul Tripathi. By the third day of the strike, Tripathi really was going gaunt. Tripathi, at twenty or twenty-one or whatever age he was, already looked like a grown man—with his windshield forehead, his thick mustache, frizzy hair falling on either side in wings from a center parting, sleekly slanting nose that ended in large nostrils, the worry grooves on his forehead like lines of angry text for his followers to interpret—a tall, thin, nervy lad who occasionally smeared Brahminic ash on his forehead. Perhaps he had worn the ash even before the strike—but Mohit hadn't noticed. Yes, Anshul looked more and more like those serious, starved Brahmins one saw haunting the roadsides with silver begging bowls and staffs, but dressed spiffily in dhotis and possessing the pride and dignity of Brahmins nevertheless …

At that moment, sitting in the headquarters with Anshul, Mohit realized—with a kind of shock—that he *believed* in caste. He had grown up without caste as a subject of conversation. Punjabi, Jeev Sangathani—these were more solid identities than caste in Delhi, and he had even failed to wring from his father the true caste that they, the Chopras, belonged to.

"It's the Chopra beraderi," is all Brij said.

"But are we Vaishyas?" Mohit asked.

"Yes, yes, Vaishya, Kayasth, whatever you want to say—we've had lawyers and scholars in our family"—it was as if even his father didn't know about their caste or didn't want to, and a few times Mohit had even entertained the suspicion that *they* might belong to a backward caste, since they were traditional agriculturalists. But then he'd suppressed it.

Now, in the filthy hostel room headquarters—war-torn with cigarette butts, browned teacups, Old Monk bottles, and overlapping unfinished posters on the floor—Anshul told Mohit that his father was a railway clerk. He had grown up with little money. "And this is partly because I have four elder sisters."

So he was the miracle son.

Mohit sympathized. "I also come from a large family."

"A government job is imperative for me," Anshul said. "Without it, I'm finished. But what does the government care about a person like me? I'm not an important vote bank, unlike the backward castes."

It was still two years before the markets would burst open, bringing in a torrent of foreign investment and private-sector jobs.

For the first time, Mohit considered his own future. He never had. The aura of his famous great-grandfather, the great SP Chopra, had protected him. Now, he realized with something like surprise, that his great-grandfather, the mascot of his life, whom he had never met, was dead: had been dead for nearly twenty years. In his mind's eye, the family complex crumbled. He was afraid. But then, like bulletins from the present, the faces of his politician uncles, Bhagat Chacha and Laxman Chacha, came swooping in—those emissaries of possibility.

"You'll get into politics," Mohit consoled Anshul.

"It's not written in my fate," Anshul said.

Fate. It was about to knock them both flat on their backs.

CHAPTER 76

THE TRAGEDY OCCURRED ONE SATURDAY AFTERNOON outside Swaminathan College in South Delhi, not far from where Mohit lived—near Nehru Place. The student protests at this time were waning. The hunger strike had failed to move V. P. Singh or garner the requisite attention in the press, and the students had decided to make a large concentrated push outside Swaminathan.

That morning, Anshul showed up at the HQ with a jerry can of kerosene.

"Ah, you're ready to break your hunger strike with something tasty," Mohit said. "Does kerosene count as veg?"

"Always jokes with this one," Anshul said. Then he added, "It's for drama." He held up a reddish-black box of matches. "Some fireworks."

"Be careful," said Neha, another activist and hunger striker. "If you put too much kerosene on the V. P. effigy, you'll get burned too."

"It would have been better to set the effigies up like a mini-Dussehra, side by side, in one place," Sakshi—who had also participated in the hunger strike—said. "Still, if we burn them in the middle of the road, the police won't be able to stop us."

The police were now a constant, tense presence at the protests, parading in riot gear and forming cordons around the chanting students. Mohit knew that, perversely, this riled up the students further. What you wanted, really, was someone on a human scale to be angry at—not the abstractions of quotas or caste maneuvers.

"Just don't pour the kerosene on yourself, OK?" Mohit said to Anshul.

CHAPTER 77

THEY WENT TO SWAMINATHAN COLLEGE IN THE LATE morning. But the turnout outside the campus—the roads haphazardly paved with discarded student election posters—was thin. A hundred-odd students had gathered desultorily by three large pyres of leaves and posters that had been lit on the partially-blocked-off road, so that one felt one had happened upon the aftermath of a riot.

Twenty policemen in battered helmets milled about, carrying sticks.

But the initial impression of sparseness was deceptive. By noon, dozens of other groups of students showed up on hijacked DTC buses and the demonstration swelled. A female student, hidden somewhere near the gates of the college, led a "Mandal Commission, down, down!" chant on a megaphone, the words echoing back from Mohit's mouth as he reveled in the energy of the crowd, the familiar faces, the foreheads painted with tricolors, the furiously sketched signs held aloft. It was the first time in his life that Mohit had recognized the power of oratory, poetry, and painting to move people. The marginal figure of the artist—a type that clashed with his own brand of sporty pragmatism—had become central to the revolution.

Now the students blocked the entire road; and the policemen, whose numbers had also swelled, formed a semicircle around the chanting crowds.

Mohit, Anshul, Neha, and Sakshi were at the center of this proudly peaceful protest. Then a stink of gasoline hitched itself to Mohit's nose—but there were no vehicles about. He turned around to see Anshul shouting and pouring the kerosene from the jerry can over his head and laughing, as others clapped in encouragement.

It was the happiest Mohit had ever seen Anshul, as if he were a child bathing in the first rain of the season.

"V. P. Singh! Hai! Hai!" Anshul chanted and, catching Mohit's eyes, handed him the plastic container of kerosene, as if he'd anointed Mohit as his successor.

The can sloshed in Mohit's hands; a little kerosene wet his left fingers.

Mohit gratefully passed it on to another boy. Then Mohit raised his sticky hand and shouted loudly, "Mandal Commission, down, down!"

There was no center to this crowd of a thousand students; many were coalescing around the tiny woman with the megaphone. Then Anshul gained height; someone had brought him a couple of empty Thums Up crates, and he climbed up on them and tried to shout over the crowd. He held a box of matches over his head. Then he lit a match and went up in flames.

CHAPTER 78

MOHIT WAS LOOKING STRAIGHT AT ANSHUL AS IT happened but couldn't grasp what he was seeing. Then Anshul fell off the crate in a flush of fire, and a terrible heat roared up toward all their faces—the intoxicating burnt-earth smell of kerosene. The students jostled and the crowd grew tighter around the burning boy on the tarred road, and Neha and Sakshi and Mohit struggled not to fall right onto Anshul, who was screaming, eyes curdled shut by the fire that was eating him alive. The police rushed in, and Mohit, unthinking—or thinking, remembering his father's bravery in the air force—Mohit tore off his T-shirt and threw it on Anshul as Anshul rolled about on the ground, but somehow, in doing so, Mohit got his hands confused, he meant to put the shirt down with his right hand (innocent of kerosene) but used his left hand instead, and there, suddenly, in front of his face, furling out from his own hand, was a hot flag of fire.

He screamed, but after a few seconds it didn't hurt, and then his head was bashed onto the ground; he was being attacked or killed in a stampede.

When he came to, he realized that two large policemen had thrown their shirts on him and on Anshul.

Mohit smelled burned milk. "I'm fine," he shouted, though he wasn't.

Louder screams came from the megaphone. Were those stones and shoes raining down? Then Mohit looked over to the side and saw Anshul on the ground next to him, his eyes glued shut, his lips tight in a grimace, teeth chattering, the proud head of center-parted hair intact, but everything under the neck black and pink and partially covered in thick khaki police shirts. The two policemen, with their wobbling, naked flesh, lifted Anshul as he kept chattering his teeth, and then a tall, bearded student came up to one of the policemen and pushed him with his shoulder, and Anshul fell to the ground and the dressing of police shirts fell off and Mohit had to look away from the burned mess of Anshul's chest.

Then Mohit, too, was suddenly dragged to his feet and became aware that he was being led by a policeman; in fact he was happy to be led, he wanted to get out of this madness, and then he was in a police jeep at the periphery of the riots and the engine started, and Mohit said, "It's just my hand," and then he looked at it and fainted.

CHAPTER 79

AS SOON AS KARISHMA HEARD ABOUT MOHIT'S INJURY, SHE rushed over to the hospital. She said to herself, *God, forgive me, I'll stop seeing Laxman, I promise, I'll do anything, let my son live.*

Ever since the anonymous letter and the conversation with Gita, she had been distressed about her affair; and her dissatisfaction with her life had grown; but she had not been able to extricate herself from Laxman, who, after all, was the only thing she had.

Laxman, she had learned, was now above shame. The letter had not bothered him at all. It had only emboldened him.

Brij, meanwhile, had refused to move forward with the construction after the letter. "If you want to keep going to work at Mohanji Balms, then leave me alone," he'd said.

Please God, she prayed again in the auto.

When Mohit had woken up in the jeep, there had been two constables on either side of him. "Bache, what were you doing?" one had asked kindly.

"Sir, I was just saving my friend." He choked up. "Is he OK?"

"You worry about yourself first," the other constable said rudely. "It's an offense to abet suicide."

"But, Sir—I tried to save him," Mohit insisted, bursting into tears.

"Cry, cry, rich boy," the same constable said. "The laws also apply to you."

Mohit was relieved when they pulled up outside Safdarjung Hospital—rather than a jail. He couldn't flex his pink, puffed left hand and felt only a dull pain.

But the doctor in the ICU a few moments later had told him that the lack of pain itself was a bad sign. "Your nerves are gone, bachu," the doctor said in his slangy, stagey upper-class English.

"When you're out of shock, it's going to hurt more than you've ever hurt before in your life, my friend." Mohit lay on a bed, looking at the doctor as a nurse dunked his left hand in cold water. "You got lucky the petrol didn't go anywhere else," the doctor said.

"It was kerosene."

"Yes, and it's all burned up. Sister, put on the gel."

Cold water. Gel. Gauze. Then his left hand was put in a plastic bag and tied with straps and raised.

"We have to keep it up like this, like you're Guru Nanak, for a few days. Then we can start scraping off what's left of your left hand."

Sometime later, his mother, father, and brother were bent around him, and Mohit calmly explained what had happened.

"Your friend has ninety percent burns but is alive," Brij said. "The father is a class-three officer or something." Brij described the scene: how Anshul lay unconscious in a room with a viewing window, pumped with blood and morphine, bandaged from head to foot, invaded by surgery after surgery.

Through a fog of morphine, Mohit wondered silently if *his* intervention, the sacrifice of his left hand, had in fact saved Anshul. But he said nothing.

Brij added, "And why not burn your right hand while you're at it?"

Karishma said, "Be quiet, he's in pain, and we should thank God nothing else happened. He tried to save the other boy! Why are you making him feel bad—wasn't he doing the right thing? And look, Deepak beta, only his left hand is burned, you only bat with your left side, nah Mohit, you don't bowl with it, do you?"

Mohit's pain was ferocious now, as if he had dipped his hand through the sun's surface. The pain crescendoed and then stayed shrill.

Then he heard his mother say something about Laxman Chacha.

"Laxman Papa?" Mohit said, foggily.

CHAPTER 80

KARISHMA HAD MENTIONED LAXMAN FOR A REASON: HE had come to visit his nephew in the hospital but had gotten stuck outside the premises with the TPP leader Santosh Kumar. The students wouldn't let them in.

The TPP was, of course, part of V. P. Singh's ragtag coalition government. But it was also the party of upper-caste Hindus. Much of the TPP's base supported the agitation against affirmative action, as did individual members of the party, like Laxman and Santosh. Yet, at the same time, the TPP didn't wish to alienate the lower castes, which were a huge segment of the population. So they tried to play both sides. "We support the *idea* of reservations," their spokesman had said, "but we don't believe it should be tabled in this manner, without discussions. Economic markers should be used." And in order to not alienate the upper-caste students, the TPP made gestures of goodwill toward the protesters, which is why Laxman and Santosh had immediately driven to the hospital upon receiving news of the immolations—to console and comfort Anshul's parents and to offer them money for medical expenses and, of course, to see Mohit, "my own nephew," Laxman had told Santosh, adding, "So this is the way the movement is dividing entire families."

But by the time they got to Safdarjung Hospital, its grounds had turned into the site of major political theater, another front in the protests. News of Anshul Tripathi's self-immolation—the first of the movement—had spread far. The leaderless protest now had a hero—one who possessed even more moral authority because he lay silent in the hospital, struggling to live, a metaphor for the movement itself.

Hundreds of students were camped outside the hospital in solidarity with Anshul. Opposition leaders started arriving. These politicians' supporters gave free meals and even money to the protesting students.

But when Laxman and Santosh drove up to the hospital in Santosh's official Ambassador, braking to a halt in front of the hospital's main portico, students surrounded the car, chanting, "V. P. Singh! Hai! Hai! Down with the TPP for supporting V. P. Singh."

"We're with you!" Laxman shouted, rolling down a window. "My own nephew is here." But then a rock came sailing through the opening, and he ducked. Stones clattered down from all sides, popping like corn on the top of the car. Thin fractures appeared in the windows and windscreens. Laxman quickly rolled the window back up, and Santosh and he crouched down in the back seat, their hands covering their heads, while the driver, recovering from his initial shock, shouted a stream of obscenities at the students (revealing where his Mandal sympathies lay) and then pressed down on the horn and plowed hard through the knot of protesters, narrowly missing two of them.

In the hospital now, Brij took up the thread for his son. "Laxman Chacha tried to come in and see you, but the students gheroed him." A sadistic smile played on his lips from between his goatee hairs. "I told Laxman, it's a bad idea to play a double game. If you're a party of Hindus, be a party of Hindus, not of caste."

Karishma said, "Laxman said on the phone the students didn't even know who they were attacking."

"But everyone else has entered the hospital with zero problems," Brij reminded her. Then he turned to Mohit. "You were sleeping, but Madhavrao Scindia and even Sonia Gandhi were here to see you. They've offered to pay for your medical expenses, but I said nothing doing, I don't get involved in this politics-sholitics."

"Your chacha really wants to see you; he can help," Karishma said.

As his mother pleaded, Mohit became aware that his parents and brother weren't the only people in his curtained-off cell in the Burns Unit. Four other serious-looking students were conferencing quietly in a corner too. (During this carnivalesque, panicky time, with many upper-caste doctors supporting the striking students, visiting rules had been relaxed—or overcome by force.) The faces of the four students seemed to change by the minute—sometimes they included Neha or Sakshi, the latter of whom, he realized in his haze, he loved; sometimes others whom Mohit did not know. And it was the presence of the students Mohit didn't know—kids who weren't even from his college, who asked if they could bring Mohit or his parents Campa or chai or water or something to eat—that made Mohit realize that he, too, had become a hero of the movement.

What his mother was doing, he saw, was asking him to tell the troops to step aside, to let Laxman Chacha in.

At that moment, Mohit understood why he had thrown himself into the movement with such fervor—instead of simply enjoying the party-like atmosphere of permanent bunking at DU like everyone else … yes, it was to *oppose* Laxman, to oppose his political party.

If he couldn't confront Laxman in person for the affair with his mother, he would do it through politics.

"I'll talk to them about Laxman Chacha," Mohit said to his parents. "But I need you to go outside first." He meant his parents and brother—not the four students.

Brij snorted.

"Just listen to him," Karishma said.

"Bloody crap," Brij said, getting up.

Mohit became tired and queasy as soon as his parents and brother were gone. "One second—water, please," he said to the boys lingering nearby.

Happy to be of service, one of the boys—now Mohit could see his muscles emerging from his Dire Straits T-shirt sleeve—opened the curtain and barked for a nurse.

"Is there anything else you'd like, Mohitji?" he asked politely, turning back to him.

Suddenly, Mohit couldn't recall why he was here with the boys; then clarity trickled back. "So, you blocked Santosh Kumar and Laxman Chopra from coming inside the hospital?"

"Mohitji, it was not our doing."

"No, no, it's the right thing," Mohit said. "Laxman Chopra is my relative, but I don't support his party. Our movement is bigger than these leaders. If anyone tries to let him in, tell them his own nephew isn't allowing it."

CHAPTER 81

MOHIT'S RESPONSE MIGHT HAVE BEEN EMOTIONAL, rather than political, but there was no way for political animals like Laxman and Santosh to interpret it *except* politically. In their minds, the students—who represented upper-caste Hindus—had rejected their presence, thus sending a clear message: *We have lost faith in the TPP, we will go elsewhere.* And with the instinct of politicians, Santosh and Laxman began to plan a diversion. They realized that they would need to torch off an alternative movement to absorb the passions unleashed by the Mandal Commission.

They discussed this in private.

"We need to change the conversation from reservations," Santosh said. "We need a big gesture to show Hindus that we stand for their rights." Then he said, "What about joining the VHP on its yatra?" The VHP's pundits were about to embark on a ten-thousand-kilometer journey through India to rile up Hindus in small towns. They did this every few years, the yatra ending at the Babri Masjid in Ayodhya in the hot northern state of Uttar Pradesh. The Babri Masjid was the cause célèbre of Hindu nationalism. The sixteenth-century mosque was said to have been built on the birthplace of the god Ram and so, for years, Hindus had been agitating to have it demolished and replaced by a temple. For this cause, the VHP collected donations from Hindus all over the world, even baking special bricks for the temple that were consecrated by pundits and stamped with the phrase, "JAI SHRI RAM." The pundits would be carrying these bricks with them on the yatra, for their final putsch on the mosque. But the chief minister of Uttar Pradesh, where Ayodhya was located, supported V. P. Singh and was a secularist and said he wouldn't allow the yatra to reach the mosque, which was anyway under litigation.

"The problem is that going to just a few villages on foot with pundits will not garner the requisite publicity," Laxman said to Santosh.

"Well, let's take a jeep, then," Santosh said.

"Not a jeep," Laxman said. And Laxman now shared his idea, one for which he would be remembered for decades. "We have to create something which people can't attack, which Hindus connect with. You've seen the floats on Republic Day? And Ram's golden rath in the *Ramayan*?" He was talking about the TV show. "We have to make something like that. People have to think you *are* Ram."

Soon, Laxman had sketched out a picture, a van outfitted to look like Ram's chariot from the TV series, with Santosh sitting in the front: the vehicle in which he would make his religious tour of India.

CHAPTER 82

When Mohit's fever subsided after a week, he was taken home. His burns could now be treated simply with ointments and repeated wrappings.

His left hand and arm, however, were still severely blistered, making it hard for him to move, and at home Mohit lay in his old, windowless central room, listening to the radio, reading the paper, staying abreast of the dying movement from afar. Everyone in the country seemed to be tiring of this endless disruption, though it was hard to tell if it was just his mood. Truth be told, he was glad to be done with it: He would never have qualified for the IAS anyway. At other times he told himself that his sourness came from inactivity and boredom, and he perked up when his protesting friends phoned him, calls that Brij and Karishma allowed him to take: After all, what damage could Mohit do from home?

It was there, soon after Mohit returned, that Laxman Chacha came to see him.

Laxman wore a crisp white kurta and a tilak on his forehead, his garb having become more ethnic ever since he had entered politics. Mohit too wore a haggard white kurta, but more out of convenience—the flowing sleeves allowed his wounds to breathe.

"Don't hug so hard, Chacha," he said in the drawing room.

"I would hug you even harder if I could, beta!" Laxman exclaimed. "You're like my own son." Then he said, "Did they treat you OK in the hospital? I called the doctor—"

Laxman was the sort of man who would never mention his failure to get in.

"Yes, Chacha, they were very attentive," Mohit said.

"Good, good, good. Look, Deepak, your brother's famous," Laxman said, turning to Mohit's younger brother, as he mussed up Mohit's hair.

"Chacha," Mohit whined. Even slight movements could make sparks of pain shoot up his arms. The nerves, deadened by the first-degree burn, were randomly coming to life.

"A big hero," Laxman repeated, mussing with aggression.

"Bas, bas, he's not a child," Karishma said shrilly, coming in with a tea-kettle on a tray.

"How's your friend Anshul?" Laxman asked Mohit. "I hear he's better too, thank God."

An image came back to Mohit from the hospital, of a sort of plastic mummy, encased in bandages from head to foot; Mohit had been pushed into Anshul's room in a wheelchair to pay his respects but had found his comrade passed out.

"But poor fellow, he has ninety percent burns," Laxman said, turning to Karishma. "The doctor said he'll need twenty surgeries."

"And the parents looked like such poor types," Karishma added.

"The good thing is that all his expenses will be covered," Laxman said, with a wave of his hand. "Santoshji has told me." Then he shook his head. "Now people are saying it was an accident. And look at all the problems it caused." There had been a spate of copycat student immolations all over the country after Anshul's; the movement had been radicalized.

"It wasn't an accident," Mohit piped up from the sofa, breaking his tense, grimaced silence.

"Beta, but his own parents—" Laxman said.

"Chacha, I was standing right there," Mohit insisted. "It was fully intentional. He had planned to pour kerosene on himself and set himself on fire."

Laxman didn't miss a beat. "Then it's good you saved him!"

"I was also planning to burn myself." Mohit looked sideways at his brother, who sat curled like a monkey on the sofa. Deepak was nodding his head but not listening.

The adults went silent.

Karishma said, "He's talking nonsense—but he did try to save the other boy." Then, to Laxman, she said, "Tea?"

"Two sugars, please," he said.

"Don't take so much," she said to Laxman.

The domestic intimacy between them—everyone noticed it.

"Beta, you shouldn't be taking risks like this," Laxman said. "If you want to get into politics, come talk to me." Taking a sharp slurp of his tea, he said, "You make the best tea in this house, Karishma."

Mohit watched as his mother's expression suddenly turned blank. While Laxman Chacha was always warm and familiar with Karishma in the drawing room—which they had once shared as "roommates"—Karishma, especially in the presence of Mohit and Deepak, often became cold, even indifferent, toward Laxman. Still, everyone could read the studied indifference as a kind of acting.

Everyone knows everything about everyone. This was one of the lessons Mohit had learned as he had grown older. You feel you can suppress the truth, hoard secrets, mask yourself in performance—but forget it: Acting only comforts the actor.

Laxman returned to the subject of the immolations. "Beta," he said, sipping, "it's better to just watch when such things are happening, because the situation is dicey. V. P. isn't reliable, and tomorrow he might tell the police to shoot at all of you—"

"We've been waiting and watching too long. We only did this," Mohit said, "because no politician would take action."

Laxman took another sip and smiled. "Behind the scenes, things are stormy—in a few days you'll see." Now Laxman wondered if he should tell his nephew about how the TPP was planning to force Prime Minister V. P. Singh's hand to make him resign. Instead, he went on, "This government won't last and Mandal cannot pass. The Supreme Court will give a stay." He turned to Karishma. "In a sense, Mohit was right to protest. He acted like a fool, yes, but he was on the right side. V. P. is trying to divide the Hindus."

Karishma scowled at Laxman for validating Mohit's political stance.

Laxman went on, "That's why, beta, we're embarking on this Rath Yatra. To unite Hindus again. And to demand resolution for the Ram temple, which has been stuck in court for years."

"But why won't the TPP just withdraw support for V. P. Singh?" Mohit asked.

"Just see what happens," Laxman said, closing the subject.

Later that day, when Mohit told his friend Sakshi about this development on the phone, she said, "Yeah, they're all worse than the other. The TPP has made building the Ram temple their central plank and they know they can get away with it now. At no other time would this be allowed, except when V. P.'s government is weak. And they're also trying to hide the fact that they didn't openly come out against Mandal. So now they want to create a communal issue."

The interaction with his chacha left Mohit crestfallen. He felt he hadn't been able to say what he had meant—that, in that drawing room, he'd been reduced to the young boy who had accompanied his mother and uncle, on occasion, to the Jeev Sangathan temple.

Now Mohit shut himself up in his room and read a book of poetry that Gita Chachi had gifted him and tried to write with his right hand, entrapping the furious experiences of the past few weeks within rhymes. Yet he felt he was cracking within and couldn't say why. He was on the verge of tears.

Hundreds of students, by now, had immolated; two had even died.

A few days later came the news of rioting and shooting outside the Delhi Boat Club, after a farmers' rally in support of the students.

Mohit listened to the breathless, staticky reporting on the radio. He worried about Neha and particularly pretty Sakshi, with whom he had spoken two times on the phone, though she had not come to visit him despite her promises—who had the time?

CHAPTER 83

KARISHMA WAS GRATEFUL THAT LAXMAN WAS BUSY WITH preparations for the yatra. She needed to think about what she would do about the relationship. She remembered the oath she had made when she had rushed to the hospital—that she would put an end to her affair.

Deep down she felt that her son's injury was her fault. She had neglected her boys for Laxman—who, *despite everything*, was the love of her life, her main project of the last seven years, the sinful act that imparted an equilibrium to the rest of her existence. He had even kept Brij in a harness of money (wherever the money came from—Karishma guiltily imagined Archana being deprived so Laxman and she could thrive). And the air of scandal around the relationship with Laxman had also clarified matters for Karishma in the complex. Trusting no one in the family, she remained equidistant from them, cold in her social interactions—it was enough, after all, to be managing two men and two families; and she knew anyway that Laxman was always waging a bluff public relations campaign on their behalf, cementing his close alliances with his siblings. But, unlike Laxman, Karishma could not bring herself to enjoy the fruit of these alliances or even revel in her role as the family don's mistress. In fact, when she was with his siblings—and especially his sisters, who were all gleefully extra friendly with her—she clammed up, telling Laxman later, "They're being nice to me only because they want more gossip. They have no desire to be friends with me, they never liked me for me, it's just pure curiosity about their own brother."

Now, one Saturday morning shortly after Mohit returned home, she smoothed her clothes and took an auto alone to the Jeev Sangathan temple. There she asked the new, young pundit to organize a private havan for her older son's health. She was reminded, sitting down, of the time she had first come here—after Deepak had recovered from his mysterious high fever: the start of the relationship with Laxman.

The pundit, cross-legged on the floor before the havan kund, said, "Auntie, you should bring your son also for blessing."

Auntie! "Punditji, his health isn't yet good enough for him to leave the house," she lied.

And then they sat there and prayed.

Strange, she thought, praying, the way people can swap their beliefs and opinions—as Laxman and she had. While he had given up coming to the Sangathan altogether, handing over operations some years ago to handsome Mr. Puri and worshipping now at all the great temples and agitating for the construction of *another* temple—she, Karishma, had accepted the self-effacing, self-erasing, self-punishing simplicity of the sect. Given the complications of her life, such simplicity was what she needed. Besides, she liked being dangerously near the epicenter of her sins, always aware of that upstairs bedroom where Laxman and she had acted out their indecent desires. Intoning the mantras now, she scattered samagri into the fire. Some of it blew off in a draft from the open windows. Unlike the previous pundit—who cultivated stuffiness of the nose and of the building—this one believed in aeration, the humid wind of the retreating monsoons blowing in and bringing with it the hope of reviving rain which would cool everything down and bring on winter. October was a deceiving month in Delhi. So was November. Winter only ambled in in December. She shuddered with desire for Laxman as she prayed. Then she tried to focus on Mohit. She was aware at that moment that she was an incredibly, dangerously sexual person, could see her sexuality almost as an entity separate from herself, clarified out from the fire—could see that this was what had drawn her to Laxman in the first place.

She had wanted to abandon herself to him, to recreate the inceptive pleasure she'd felt as a fifteen-year-old, sleeping with an older cousin.

She adjusted the sweaty seat of her salwar and tried to center herself with mantras. Again, she brought Mohit's face and his blistered arm to the fore, the fire of the havan becoming the fire that had scorched Mohit's arm, the fire also burning away sex. To not see Laxman anymore—could that be the end of sex in her life? She chanted loudly, chasing the thought away. But the doubt remained.

At the end of the havan, she asked the pundit if he could show her the rest of the temple. A bemused-looking man with a fine mustache and clear eyes and the palpable discomfort of a young religious man with women, he said, "Auntie, but there's nothing more to see, the temple is just this hall."

"There's nothing upstairs? Punditji, I've come here many times. My family members used to handle the upkeep of the temple. We people founded the Jeev Sangathan." She noted, as she spoke, that the large portrait of SP was gone. "And I'm good friends with Mrs. Puri."

"Ji, ji," he said meekly, and started leading her around, gesturing toward the open door in the back.

"And upstairs, above the temple, there used to be a room," Karishma said.

"It's there even now," he said.

The more panic she sensed in his voice, the more she pushed him.

"But if you want to see it, I can show it to you," the pundit finally said.

Upstairs, nothing had changed. But it was clear to Karishma as she stood in the room that it was now in use by someone unauthorized, perhaps a friend of the pundit: It smelled sweetly of bidis and weed and there were several itchy-looking blankets strewn on the floor, as if multiple people slept there.

"When sadhus pass through, they sleep here—it's like a dharmsala," the pundit explained, in a strained whisper.

"That's a good thing," she said. "I'm coming here after a long time."

"Ji, if you attend the Sunday havans, you'll meet Mr. Puri sahb also."

Karishma looked around the room. It was a terrible crater—a servants' room! Yes, Laxman and she had now graduated to hotels run by TPP members, but even across the gap of all those years, the room's griminess made her feel insulted.

How had she ever consented to come here? She stepped out and shut the door.

CHAPTER 84

A DAY LATER, KARISHMA AND LAXMAN LAY TOGETHER IN A hotel room. Laxman talked heatedly about Muslims, as if winding himself up for the yatra he was about to embark on. "And tell me," he asked Karishma, "if their Prophet's hair vanishes from Srinagar, how would these fanatics respond if we said, 'Can you prove to us it's the Prophet's hair?' They'd loot and kill and destroy—and already they've pulled down fifty-five temples in Kashmir and driven out the pundits, and no one in India has said a word! In Punjab also the same thing happened. But when it comes to Ram—Ram actually being locked up in a mosque at his own birthplace; Ram, who all Hindus worship and even the Musallas look up to, I mean they also watch the *Ramayan* ... for that, the Muslims want us to go to court to prove it! And they haven't even offered namaz at that mosque for fifty years. But it's not actually the mullahs who are obsessed with Babri; it's these pseudo-secular politicians who are trying to appease them. They're the ones who've made a problem out of nothing. In fact, when I talk to Muslims about this temple issue, they say, 'Why have you got us stuck in this? Do what you want there.' They know there are *thirty-five* other mosques in Ayodhya, and probably they were all built on old temples, but no one has touched a brick on those, have they? No, it's these Congresswallahs and OBCs who hate Muslims but will do anything for their votes, even insult Hinduism—" He stopped. "What, you have no comment?"

"Order more food and fuck me," she said, yawning.

Laxman sat up against the wall behind the hotel bed. "You think I'm one of those corrupt politicians too, right?" he said, remembering Mohit's accusations. "But I believe in this deeply, it might be the only thing I've believed in my entire life. Imagine if in the birthplace of Jesus or Muhammad—"

"You're just creating a drama for your party," Karishma said. "And who'll suffer? Young men like Mohit."

"That's where you're completely wrong, completely wrong!" he said. "Why do you think I'm doing this? You think Mohit will get a good job if there's fifty-five percent reservation?"

"He's already in college. He'll become a CA."

Laxman shook his head. "Karishma, your thinking is sometimes so short-term! If Mandal passes, you think these lower castes will stop there? No, the next step is to introduce reservations even in the private sector." He paused. "And try to remember how your son got a seat in the college in the first place."

Now Karishma, too, sat up against the wall. She was no longer yawning in that blatantly rude way of hers. "Yes, you never tire of reminding me," she said.

"Look, I'm going away for a month, we should enjoy this time," he said.

But Laxman could tell something was off. Karishma had agreed to meet him at the Ashoka Hotel but now would not respond to his caresses. Harrumphing back down on her flat pillow, she turned away. Looking past her, Laxman noticed that the silvery thick curtains were stained with ketchup or some other offending red paste; hot beams of sunlight crested through the slits in the fabric. "Is Mohit better?" Laxman asked. "Has he said anything more? I was surprised he was saying he poured kerosene on himself, that's not what I heard—"

"But people like you encouraged him!" she shouted, without turning around.

"Me? How?"

"All your politicking, your influence," Karishma said. "Where else would a stupid boy like that get political ideas into his head, tell me?"

"Sweetie, the whole country is getting this idea."

"Not all the boys are burning themselves," Karishma said.

"But you only told me he was lying about that. And it's a sign of good values that he was helping that other boy. You've raised him well."

"For all I know, he was lying the first time. *I* wasn't there."

"The important thing is he's OK," Laxman said.

"I don't think you'd be so relaxed if it was your son!"

Laxman tensed up, bringing his knees closer to his chest. "I've always treated Mohit and Deepak as ... as my own sons. *More* than my own children. When Deepak was sick ... and even now I tried so many times to come to see Mohit; and Santoshji is offering full coverage of any and all medical costs—"

"And does Santoshji know that right now, there are twenty students sitting outside the hospital collecting funds on behalf of Mohit and Anshul and taking it for themselves and blowing it on liquor?" Karishma asked.

"Show me these boys?" he said with righteous anger. "I'll bloody straighten them out."

"I'm unhappy, Laxman!" Karishma burst out.

He turned off a light, slipped back down onto the bed, and, facing her arched back, stroked her hair. "I understand; you're a mother," he said, quietly.

"You don't understand!" she screeched.

He said, "I wish I could stay with you."

"Then stay," Karishma said, "what does some bloody temple and a statue matter?" She sniffled. "And if you remember, you used to be against all this temple-idol-worship business."

A little return of humor and intimacy; he'd take it.

"But that was centuries ago," he said with a dry laugh.

"I know you can't stay," she said, turning around and putting a cold, placating hand on his. "But I wish you would. I need you now. And now is when you'll be gone."

"It's just a matter of a month."

She nodded. "Chalo, switch off the other light and show me *your* temple."

She felt cleansed after sex and a shower; and somehow, having said what she wanted to say, making love to him, she felt revived.

Yet when she went home and was alone in her bedroom for a few minutes, she began heaving and cried for a long time.

Her eyes were still red when Brij returned from the factory.

Brij asked if she was OK and she nodded and, for the first time in what seemed like years, he came up to her and hugged her.

"I'm just so glad Mohit didn't get badly hurt," she said.

He kissed her forehead. "Me too darling, me too. But come on, let me change out of my sweaty clothes."

CHAPTER 85

IN THE BOYS' TINY BEDROOM, DEEPAK WAS WAITING FOR Karishma to help him memorize paras from his Eco reader.

She held the textbook as Deepak recited the dead words back to her. Each time he flubbed the lines, she said, "No, that's wrong, start again." Yet she was surprised by how minimal her own irritation was. She was better with her boys at this age, when they could almost be her friends; and it was as if, having been with Laxman, she had skipped the most annoying years of their lives, when they were needlessly jumping walls and smashing cricket balls into the windows of parked cars—yes, she had awakened from the dream of her affair to find them grown, smart, independent, manageable: non-fussy boys, boys in her own image, more like her than they would have been had she tried to mold them in a particular way, which would have engendered inevitable revolt.

She went to check on Mohit, who was reading in his parents' bedroom. He lay in darkness; sudden exposure to sunlight could reignite the initial pain, sun coming into contact with its own element. Now Karishma applied cream to his burns; the blisters were clustered like a horrible froth on his hand. He grimaced but didn't complain. Then he lay down flat on his back and umbrella'd the book above his head. Karishma said, "If you read in this posture, you'll hurt your eyes, bacha."

"Just let me live in peace," he snapped.

Karishma had taken temporary leave from her work at Mohanji Pahalwan Balms; Mohit wasn't used to having her around.

"Fine, they're *your* eyes," she said. "But be ready to wear ugly specs like Shilpa your entire life."

She felt unusually flustered.

But the next day, she noticed that Mohit had in fact taken her advice and supported himself with pillows and was reading with the book relaxed against his knees, held at eye level. Despite his participation in the protests, her older son was a better listener now than he had been as a rebelling teenager in senior school. She felt close to him; they were changing together; coming of age together.

But then one day he shouted, "Why the hell are you here all the time? Go back to your job—I was happier when you were gone!" To her surprise, she was not angry but hurt. She retreated to the bathroom attached to her bedroom and closed the door. She thought again of Laxman—now on his yatra—and then she was weeping, clutching at a towel hanging from a nail, crying into that mildewed roughness, the smell of Lifebuoy soap strong around her, Rupvati's bhajans seeping in from under the door, religion chasing you wherever you went.

A rapid rat-tat-tatting on the door made her compose herself.

"Mummy!" It was Mohit's voice.

"Yes, beta, one minute," she said, wiping her eyes. Then she opened the door.

Mohit examined her with a merciless expression. "Deepak is reading a comic again in the other toilet. Are you done with this one?"

The next day, taking a perch in her drawing room, from where she kept an informal vigil over Mohit in his bedroom, Karishma opened up her household account notebook, covered with columns of scrawled figures in her bright, large handwriting, and, wetting the corners with a saliva-moistened finger, found a blank page.

Then she pressed down the rolling, unreliable silver nib of her ballpoint.

Dear Laxman, she began,

What has been happening occurring between us can go on no longer ...

She stopped. It felt like playacting. She missed Laxman. But he had gone off with his tola of politicians, no doubt absorbing the attentions of all the young TPP ladies, with their perfect bindis, sindoor, and saris.

She clawed at the paper in the notebook with her nails—nails she'd painted and manicured for her lover.

Rock music poured out from Mohit's two-in-one in his bedroom.

Getting up from the sofa, Karishma opened her son's bedroom door and stepped in. "Make the volume lower," she commanded Mohit. Deepak was away at the club; only Mohit was in the room.

"Huh?" Mohit said. He was reclining insouciantly on the bed, a notebook on his lap too.

Seeing him, Karishma lost her desire to dress him down. "Beta, do you want something to eat?" she asked.

"No, Mummy, I'm trying to do some work," Mohit whined.

"Fine, fine, I just came to ask a question."

Karishma went back to the drawing room and paced. She was not used to being home like this, watching over her son.

On a whim, she got up again, walked out of her flat, opened Rupvati's door, greeted her, stepped in, and then passed through her room to Sachin and Gita's side.

CHAPTER 86

As KARISHMA CLIMBED THE STAIRS TO GITA AND SACHIN'S bedroom, she realized she had almost never been there, even though their houses lay about forty steps apart. She knocked and heard Gita's voice, saying, brightly, in Hindi, "Come in!"

Gita must have thought it was the servant bringing tea. Without announcing herself, Karishma walked in.

But if Gita and Sachin, who were sitting on their large bed, were surprised to see Karishma at the threshold of their bedroom, Karishma was equally surprised by another sight: Deepak, laid out on the carpet, beached on his stomach, resting on his elbows, watching TV. Deepak looked as if he'd been caught. His hair was wet; he had evidently cycled from the club straight to his chacha and chachi's.

"Oh, I was hoping Deepak was here," Karishma lied, putting a hand theatrically on her collarbone. "These days, with all these protests—one gets worried."

"Come sit, Karishma," Gita said.

Gita lay on the bed, propped up against pillows; Sachin too.

It was Saturday evening. Sachin was in shorts and the A/C was on.

"My God, it's so cold in here, I'm shivering—it's like Shimla," Karishma said, instantly chiding herself for sounding bitchy—why did she act so insincere around Gita? So what if Gita had an A/C and a generator—and she didn't? "I won't sit," Karishma said, even as she plopped herself into the comfortable modular lawn chair made of white plastic, the arms so smooth to the touch they seemed edible, like white chocolate. How much uglier—and yet more comfortable—the furniture was in this house!

"How's Mohit feeling today?" Sachin asked, massaging the underside of his chin with the back of his hand.

One reason Karishma had felt more comfortable making the sudden visit was that there had been a lot more traffic between sides after Mohit's hospitalization—first, Sachin and Gita had braved the enormous crowds at the hospital to visit him; and after that had come over to Karishma's flat, bringing a long imported tube of Toblerone, which Karishma had accepted grudgingly for Mohit, saying, "They're bad for his teeth, he's already got so many cavities," even though, soon after Gita and Sachin had left, she had laid into them with Mohit, breaking off one cone of Toblerone for him and one for herself. "I'm only eating this so you don't eat all of it," she had said. "And for a woman it's good, we need magnesium." She was enjoying time with her son, rued all the years she'd missed. When Mohit teased her about her sweet tooth, she said, "Laugh, laugh, I don't even like chocolate." This was what her bond with Mohit was like: She played the straight man as he mocked her with his increasingly adult smirk. She faltered between being irritated and indulging him, unsure of herself.

How could it be, she'd think sometimes, that one could be self-conscious around one's own kids? Yet this was a consequence of the affair—she was not on a sure footing with her own boys. Her guilt over her absence emerged as uneasiness—an uneasiness that could sometimes be playful (as with the Toblerone ritual) and, at other times, wholly discomfiting.

The key thing was this: Light and dark were mixed together. Both strands of existence were coiled up in each other, and she never knew which one would overpower her on certain days; whether, thanks to darkness, she'd sleep in late after Brij left or pick a fight with him in the evening. Was it guilt? A feeling of being trapped? Of not knowing oneself? Before the affair, whatever you might say about her, she had at least known herself. But love—or sex—with Laxman had changed her. She wanted the old clear-eyed self back even as she could barely recall what that self had been like. (Outwardly, of course, no one could say anything had changed in Karishma's personality; what we perceive as a major emotional seesaw in ourselves might have no import for others at all, might constitute such a minor external behavioral change that, if you were to confess your fears, others would laugh: Change or no change, you are primarily yourself.)

Now, in the room, Karishma filled Sachin and Gita in on Mohit. "Honestly, we're telling him the prognosis is a little worse, so he won't get any ideas. It's so dangerous outside anyway, and because he's a nice fellow he gets pushed around."

"Of course, people are acting crazy these days," Gita said, wondering at how Karishma was talking about the lie in front of Deepak.

"My employee Chandran's car was damaged," Sachin said.

"You mean Sanjay," Gita corrected him.

"Yeah, yeah," Sachin said—he had such a quick turnover of employees in his packaging consulting business that he was always getting their names wrong.

"Has Mohit written more poems?" Gita asked. It was a passion he had picked up while bored in the hospital. "He's very talented, your son."

"Talent-valent, what, he's probably copying from that book you gifted him."

"No, no," Gita said, "he has a real eye for imagery—that poem he wrote about the rivers of Punjab?"

Karishma was uncomfortable around praise for her kids—she felt she had so little to do with their successes and failures.

Gita asked Karishma if she'd like tea—a way of putting the decision about extending the call in the visitor's lap.

"No, I should go," Karishma said, getting up. "I just wanted to check that Deepak was here. And that you all were fine, given the madness that's going on—I know Sachin's work sometimes takes him near DU."

Then Karishma and Deepak left.

"What was that all about?" Gita asked.

Sachin shrugged.

In fact, Gita was glad for the thaw in relations—even if the circumstances weren't pleasant. Though she had become more confrontational with age, confrontation was not her forte, and she had tried, ever since that explosive incriminating anonymous letter, to ingratiate herself with the other women in the Chopra compound—ringing their bells, complimenting their clothes, asking where they got their hair done. But many of the women who had married into the Chopra clan had become Chopra-style bullies themselves. Early on, at a gathering of women in the garden, several of them had scolded Gita for paying her servant Ramesh too much. "If you do that, the other chaps will also start demanding the same rate," Usha had said. "And there's no need to feed Ramesh the fancy food you eat. These guys prefer fat rice." Never mind that Ramesh cooked all the food in the house.

Flustered, Gita had accepted their complaints about the food, doling out miserly meals to Ramesh—only to realize, two days later, that she was being foolish and should do as she pleased. Hadn't Sachin and she caused enough suffering to the servants in this complex?

And so it had gone with Gita—ingratiation on one hand, a blatant refusal to comply on the other.

She wasn't much liked in the complex. But she was respected.

Things with Karishma and Brij, however, remained tense, and so, in the hospital, Gita had taken the opportunity to greet them warmly and gravely.

After hugging Karishma, Gita had turned to Mohit and handed him a Penguin Classics edition of T. S. Eliot's *The Waste Land*.

"You're finally old enough for this, beta," she had said.

"Thank you, Gita Chachi," Mohit responded, smiling through his pain, no longer needing to hide his closeness with his chachi.

And right then, bending over the alcohol-scented hospital bed, Gita was gripped by a thought. *If Sachin and I had had kids, they would be almost this age by now! They would be adults!*

But then she buried the thought down in the graveyard of lost things: Cindy, Hector, kids, America.

Where had that time gone?

In the car ride back, Gita and Sachin traveled side by side in silence, a driver at the helm. They had stopped talking about kids; and no one asked them about children either, which was another kind of death: the death of public pressure, of social shame. So that's what they were now: a "childless couple"—that was how people defined them in a child-obsessed country. Were they doing enough with their lives? Gita wondered. She herself spent the first half of the day in school and the rest of it taking care of the house or visiting her parents, who had both tipped into an early senility. Her father, in the throes of oncoming dementia, had made a foolish decision about his savings, alienating Gita's brother, who was now on frosty terms with everyone in the family.

What if coming back, Gita wondered, made you not closer to everyone—but farther? What if distance was really what enabled love?

She looked over at Sachin. He was focused on the road.

CHAPTER 87

SOON AFTER VISITING GITA AND SACHIN, FEELING GUILTY and torn, Karishma decided to quit her job permanently. Walking into the Mohanji Pahalwan Balms office, she had a heart-to-heart with Archana, who, after listening, said, "But, dear, you're just shaken up and tired—when Mohit is OK, you'll want to come back."

The two women were still friends. But, over the years, as Karishma had grown painfully thin, Archana had acquired prominent love handles. She was now a hull of flesh, the flesh like an armor between her and the cruelty of the world. She ate non-stop, downing liters of supersweet tea a day, not to mention ladoos, barfis, supari, matthees, and murukkus, and yet she hadn't become diabetic or a heart patient, though she complained about her knees. It would have been clear to anyone who hadn't experienced her swelling as a gradual transformation that Archana was eating herself to death. Yet she had crafted such a jolly aura around herself—always joking and laughing, sometimes smoking openly now—that it was easy to forget this and think that (like one of those women who is glad to be rid of a nasty husband) she was happy.

Now, in the office, she munched on salty roasted daal as she proffered advice to Karishma.

Karishma said, "I just feel, after what happened—I need to supervise Deepak more, so he studies. You know, this Mandal Report will probably get passed—the court will rule in its favor—and then getting a college seat will become even harder."

"But, yaar, Deepak can't study all day," Archana said. "And, believe me, teaching him yourself won't be so easy—get him tuitions."

"But who wants to handle the tuition guys? They all come and demand food and cold coffee, and then Brij gets angry with them. And that really smart one, the maths guy who came a few times? He had a gambling problem and always wanted a loan. 'Ma'am, can I get an advance of a thousand rupees, five hundred is fine also.' He was totally shameless—if Mohit got even ten marks extra, he'd ask for a loan. Luckily Prabha told me his gambling is well-known, he's one of those genius types, can get you ninety in the boards but is dead drunk and gambling the next day—no, that's not the kind of influence I want to expose Deepak to, not that Brij will tolerate it, anyway, you know him."

"I can talk to Laxman about giving you a higher salary," Archana said. *How strange*, Karishma thought. *She's as addicted to this arrangement as I am.* Karishma tried to will herself into feeling bad. But one look at Archana's face dispelled it. *How does she hope to keep a man when she looks like that?* Karishma thought contemptuously. Over the years, she had convinced herself that *this* was how Archana had looked when the affair had started; and for this reason, Karishma would be shocked when, at home, idly browsing over the side table in the drawing room, she sometimes picked up a silver framed photo and glanced at the picture of all four of them on a houseboat in Srinagar, nearly two decades before.

From the correct angle, with all that kohl and that tart twist to her mouth, Archana was even prettier than Karishma, or more sexual and knowing, whereas she, Karishma, was always dead-eyed in photos, staring into the heart of the flash.

Photos of herself frightened her much more than looking into the mirror did. In a mirror, like most people, she could modulate her expression to make herself acceptable. But photos revealed something she sensed was true: A part of her was dead. The part that pitied and loved, that cared deeply for others. The part that would have cared for the kids and Archana, if not for Brij. That could look beyond the present to the future. That *cared* for the future. But when she glimpsed these photos, she recoiled. In them, she was always unsmiling and trapped, her brows knitted tightly, a teardrop-shaped depression of skin above her anguished brows—a person surprised at the misfortune of being born in the first place, of having a body that men had always coveted but that she had felt was not truly hers till the affair with Laxman. And then, too, only intermittently.

"A higher salary won't solve it," Karishma said, laughing girlishly, trying to bring the old ghost of their relationship to the surface. "Brij controls whatever funds I get, anyway—you know how these Chopra men are."

"Each one more fateecher than the other," Archana said, throwing a fistful of the salty daal into her mouth, before remembering to push the bowl toward Karishma. It was a cheap black wafer-thin wooden Tibetan dragon-patterned bowl that Karishma had gifted Archana from the Tibetan Market in Dalhousie, in the early days of their friendship. They had been entwined with each other for so many years.

Karishma said, "I would have discussed this with Laxman, but of course your husband is out gallivanting with his political friends."

"Yes, yes, we've lost him to politics," Archana said proudly. "And what will Brij say if you stop working?"

"He doesn't care," Karishma lied. "Anyway, the business is so slow right now and there will be one less person on the payroll. And what do I do here anyway? Just sit here and eat your snacks. I can show you the accounts—you'll learn it in fifteen minutes."

"It won't be the same without you," Archana said.

CHAPTER 88

"THE PERSON WHO SHOULD RESIGN IS LAXMAN," WAS ALL Brij said to Karishma when she told him of her decision. "When was the last time he was in the office? He hasn't come to the factory in months. Politics has completely swallowed the man up and he acts like he's a senior sleeping partner or something. His entire director's salary goes straight to that Santosh Kumar fellow."

Santosh: Laxman's other mistress, Karishma thought. Sleeping partners indeed.

This was how the structure of Laxman's affair was dismantled even as he toured India in a Toyota truck on a pledge to dismantle the mosque built on the birthplace of Lord Ram.

The first phase of the yatra, in the western state of Gujarat, near the Somnath temple, was a success. Thousands swarmed the sides of the Toyota truck, which had been carefully dolled up to look like Lord Ram's chariot from the *Ramayan* TV show, while Santosh and other party apparatchiks stood on a wooden platform built above the drivers' cabin. An "Om" was emblazed on the forehead of the protruding canopy of the wooden float, with TPP painted on both sides in cooling blue letters. A painted portrait of Santosh—his mustache a bit bushier, a long tilak on his forehead—hung from the back of the truck, so that one could technically feel the man gazing down at you from both sides. False wooden chariot wheels half covered the actual rubber tires.

Riding in the float with Santosh, Laxman was proud of the quality of the craftsmanship. He had hired the set designers of the *Ramayan* TV show—the most-watched show in India's history—to build it.

Now, a month into the yatra, winding south through Hyderabad, Laxman stood at the front of the crawling rath with Santosh, half in shade, two loudspeakers angled off on either side. With them were a couple of minions who served as tireless barkers of angry messages when Santosh was exhausted from his eighteen-hour days of travel and waving and accepting shaguns and tilaks of blood—when Santosh wished to retreat to the covered part of the rath, where a soft A/C wind blew, powered by the kerosene generator mounted on the back. And with them, too, was a TPP operative named Raghav Shroff, who would often hold forth on history. "Santoshji, as you know," Shroff said one day, "even for the Dandi March, Gandhiji did what you're doing—he informed the press the world over, and villagers were told ahead of time, that marchers were coming, and not only that—he also picked the *clothes* the marchers would wear. Even Gandhiji was aware that politics is primarily theater."

"That's very good," said Santosh, too tired to speak. Laxman held a glass of rehydrating solution to his mouth, which Santosh sipped and then gestured away. Fainting was common in this drenching, desiccating pre-winter season.

"And your idea of starting from Somnath," Shroff went on, turning absently for a second to wave at the crowds, "was the right one—even Gandhiji gave his blessing to have that temple rebuilt."

"Is that so?" Santosh asked, surprised that Gandhi, that lover of Muslims, had been so openly pro-Hindu. "We must make an entry about it in our Ram Mandir pamphlet."

Laxman, his eyes concealed behind large aviators, listened to this conversation. Who was this Shroff fellow, and how had he insinuated himself into the yatra in this way? And what kind of name was Shroff, anyway? Laxman suspected a Muslim influence here or some kind of craven Anglicization.

When Shroff spoke again, Laxman said, "One minute, let Manohar make his announcement—"

Manohar's voice shrieked from the loudspeaker: "*Mandir waheen banega*! The temple will be built! Which government is bold enough to stop us? Jai Shri Ram!" The rath had entered an old part of the city. The crowds pressed together in the narrow lanes around the trundling truck, the truck itself led by two state-government-provided police jeeps in the front and followed by a canvas-covered truck of policemen in the back, not to mention TPP men flitting around the vehicles on scooters, like flies circling dung. The men and women in the crowds occasionally dove toward the (fake) wheels of the sacred chariot as it passed, trying to scoop dust from them and smear it like ash on their foreheads. And on all sides, as Laxman looked down, he witnessed an effusion of Hindu pride: angular upright warrior-like sadhus; dark men with heads tightened in saffron headbands and turbans; khaki-clad RSS regiments quick-marching together with blade-tipped staves balanced like rifles on their shoulders; young girls in traditional garb carrying coconuts on silver plates on their heads.

The loudspeaker of the rath charged the tiny lanes of this mostly Muslim area of Hyderabad's old city with menace and excitement ...

Laxman had felt, on this trip, that he was seeing India anew—seeing just how powerfully connected Indians were across states by their devotion to Ram. Ram—not V. P. Singh—was India's prime minister, its true hero. Even Gandhiji (*I wonder if Shroff knows this!*) had invoked Ram's name at his prayer meetings and had sung "Raghupati Raghav Raja Ram," and no one, not even the Musallas, had blinked an eye—so why make a fuss about the Ram temple now?

Along the way, on the yatra, Laxman and Santosh and their entourage worshipped at many ancient temples strewn across the ten-thousand-kilometer path; and at each temple Laxman was filled with renewed fury at seeing how Muslim invaders in the fourteenth and fifteenth centuries had scratched away the faces of the gods carved into the walls of the temples; or, worse, lopped off the heads and arms of these gods. It wouldn't have been easy, Laxman knew, at the time, to defile stone—and yet, even on their tours of plunder for gold and diamonds and women, these Muslim invaders had taken the time to enact a religious assault, to sow insults, to show Hindus that they and their nation were coming under the blankening boot of Islam.

In Rajasthan, at a temple near a dizzying stepwell that looked like an inverted pyramid sunk into the ground, Laxman actually wept when he walked along the enclosing inner walls of the courtyard. The faces of the statues of the gods were violently slashed away, the noses cut and the eyes scratched out in a frenzy—a double blinding of already blind stone. He felt now that he understood the inner passion that had driven men like his father—and so many other great men—to throw away half their lives on the quest for India's independence: Beneath the British Raj, there lay an even greater sense of humiliation, of having suffered at the hands of invaders, of having been passive peace-loving people for too long. Yet even then, during the Independence movement, Hindus had not been able to shed their love of peace and tolerance. First there had been the nonviolent expulsion of the British; then the quiet appeasement of the Muslims—*yes, yes*, the founders of India said, *we Hindus will be the majority here, in this country, but to show you what wonderful, moral people we are, we won't punish you Muslims for the bloodshed of centuries and Partition and the perfidy of Pakistan—so, instead, we'll drown you in constitutional favors, we will be the greatest forgivers on earth, we'll meet the bloodshed of Nadir Shah and Babar and your rampages during Partition with the embrace of reservations.*

And where had that brought the nation? Laxman thought now, as he descended the black, ancient, mossy stones of the inverted ziggurat of the stepwell, getting closer with each step to the sherbet-green pool of water at the very bottom, the water so hot and algae-choked it had become a symbol of thirst rather than relief—yes, where this Muslim-love had brought India was into the doldrums, to a place where violent Mohammedans were running amok in Kashmir, handing down death sentences to famous authors, enjoying the cushion of reservation at all levels of education and government, and brainwashing their children in government-funded madrassas, even as Hindus struggled to obtain permission to have even *one temple* built.

Yes, Laxman thought, descending, the top of his head burning, perhaps there had been a time and place for nonviolence, but that time had passed; Gandhi's "experiments with truth" had failed. It was time for the Hindus to grasp who they were, where they were, to see how they'd been humiliated for centuries, to understand that the final step of independence was *mental independence*.

As he arrived at the bottom of the stepwell, clouds closed over the parching sun, and it was at once cooler; and when he looked into the small pool of surviving water in the defunct stepwell (no larger than the pool of a dead fountain in a municipal park) he saw a curtain-parting of clear water in the algae and, at the bottom of that, a bed of tossed thin coins. He had an urge to wash his face with this water and, bending down, he saw, reflected in the pool, not himself but a soldier who had alighted on the cause that he would fight for till death. Looking at himself, he felt a flat curiosity about who he was, how he had become this person—how the flailing and under-confidence of the years before had laid the foundation for this grim determined face, with its jowls and whitening tufty mustache: a man with a cause, a wife, kids, a mistress, a job, a future.

On all sides, other members of the Rath Yatra were descending the high steps of the well, with that hesitant, wobbly motion with which out-of-shape people first peer down steps and then stiffly advance one leg, land it with a thud, and then bring the other foot down too. When Laxman looked up from the bottom of the well, he had the dizzying sense that what he had descended was not a stepwell but a gigantic havan kund; and that what lay at the bottom was not clear water but a film of ghee; and that he and the other descenders were samagri offered to the sun god who would set them all alight.

CHAPTER 89

THIS, IT TURNED OUT, WAS THE HIGH POINT OF THE YATRA (even though it came at the bottom of a well).

A few days later, the entourage stopped at a circuit house in Samastipur, in Bihar, 450 kilometers from their target in Ayodhya. Laxman slept well that night, but in the morning was awakened by shouts. Following the source of the sound, he ran into the next room, where Santosh was sleeping.

Four policemen were standing over Santosh as he lay in his mosquito-net-canopied bed, eyes foggy without specs. As Santosh propped himself up on his elbows, the inspector grasped Santosh by the wrist and said, "For the crime of inciting communal violence I have to take you into custody."

"Please show me one bit of evidence that Santoshji had any role in this?" Laxman growled, though of course there had been small outbreaks of violence against Muslims all along the rath's journey.

But his voice was lost in the commotion as Santosh was led out to a waiting jeep.

"Sir, I'll come straight to the police station," Laxman said.

Santosh smiled weakly. "I was expecting this."

As the jeep drove off, Laxman realized he was lucky not to have been taken into custody as well. The chief minister of Bihar was an OBC and an enemy of the TPP; he was out for revenge.

Laxman stayed in Samastipur for three more days, constantly on the phone with apparatchiks, parlaying with the press and issuing warnings to local bureaucrats. Then he managed to post bail for Santoshji and flew back with him to Delhi. "It wasn't that bad," Santosh said gently on the plane, stroking his chin nostalgically. "Much better than the accommodations they gave us during the Emergency, when we were true nobodies. Now our star has risen!"

Still, the Rath Yatra was over. It never made it to its destination: the Babri Masjid in Ayodhya.

But many of the Hindu devotees or kar sevaks did make it; and as if to prove it wasn't Santosh but History itself that was inciting violence, they unleashed a full-scale assault on the mosque with hammers and stones and tridents. They were met by a phalanx of policemen, who began to shoot. The kar sevaks retreated into the alleys of Ayodhya, attacking Muslims where they could.

The world was on fire again, Laxman thought, reading the news in Delhi, or rather it was as if the fire that had started with Mandal—the fire that had nearly consumed his own nephew—had spread and been redirected into all the tiny gullies of the nation.

And yet Laxman was sad that they had not made it to their final destination. Things would have turned out differently had they been present in Ayodhya. Despite the Uttar Pradesh chief minister's pro-Muslim leanings, the police would have hesitated to fire on a TPP leader and his convoy; and if the crowd had indeed revolted, descending on the temple, the mass of people would have been so huge that no police shooting could have stopped the mob from swarming over the mosque and bashing in its thin mullah skull.

CHAPTER 90

SANTOSH'S ARREST GAVE THE TPP THE EXCUSE IT NEEDED: IT withdrew support from the government. The PM, V. P. Singh, resigned after losing a vote of confidence in Parliament. Soon after, a new tottering government came to power, supported from the outside by the Congress. Laxman and his party were once again marooned in the opposition.

At home, an exhausted Laxman learned from Archana that Karishma had also resigned from the balm business. "Is she asking for a bigger salary?" he asked. They often spoke about Karishma in front of their kids; it was a way of maintaining a fiction that no affair was going on; or at least creating doubt about it; and he appreciated that Archana was party to this.

Now, unable to see Karishma at the office, Laxman dropped in one evening when Brij was at home. In the drawing room, in the early November dusk, Karishma sat with a bored look on her face on the sofa chair, her posture perfectly erect and hands folded in her lap. Brij quizzed Laxman about the current political crisis. Then Laxman said to Karishma, "And what's this I'm hearing? You're leaving our joint partnership?"

Karishma offered a few formal words about the boys' studies. Schools and colleges had reopened, she said, and both Deepak and Mohit were back in their classes, and she needed to be around in the afternoons to supervise them.

"That's the right thing to do, since admissions are so competitive," Laxman said. Then, turning to Brij, "And now that I'm back, and our dear government has fallen, I can pick up all my duties as well."

Earlier, Brij had complained about Laxman's non-participation in the business to Karishma. But both Brij and Karishma had known that Brij would never have asked *Laxman* to resign, for the simple reason that Laxman's political connections brought in a steady stream of orders for balms.

Brij asked Laxman if he would stay for dinner.

"We haven't made much," Karishma said.

"Is this the way to talk to a guest?" Brij asked.

Laxman declined the offer. Dinner, he said, was already awaiting him at home.

It became impossible for Laxman to see Karishma. No matter how much he tried, phoning her or accosting her in the driveway, she would make an excuse and, with zero emotion, shrug him off. He was irritated. For once, after the tiring political fallout of the last few months, he needed her; and she had turned icy. One day, when Laxman was alone in the front garden, he waved to Karishma in the driveway as she returned from an errand. She smiled wanly and vanished through her front door. A few seconds later, Laxman rang the bell. Jatin let him in and he went up the enclosed staircase.

Archana was visiting a relative on the other side of the city, Brij was at the factory, and Mohit and Deepak were at college and school respectively.

Karishma sat moodily in the drawing room the entire time Laxman spoke to her. At first, he was formal, as he always was in Karishma's flat, conscious of being surveilled (Rupvati was just next door, and the servant might step in at any time), but soon he ditched the pose. "Did I do something wrong?" he asked. "You know I had to go with Santoshji."

Karishma released another ghostly smile. It reminded him of one of the first times they'd spoken at the club, when she had suddenly chosen to confide in him about Brij's posting—why had she done it, then? Had she already liked him; had a premonition of the affair? But he'd never asked her about that incident, didn't wish to know the truth, didn't want any of his illusions of mutual affection to be shattered—didn't want to learn the affair was just another mountain he'd sweated his way up.

He had not seen this version of Karishma for seven years.

"It's nothing like that," she said. "Why would you even think that? I made time to see you, no?"

This infuriated him. "I want to discuss with you in private." He gestured to the bedroom.

She gave a high, girlish laugh, which he understood was a refutation of his crazy proposition.

"You think I'm putting myself in harm's way, just like Mohit did," Laxman said, remembering how she'd reacted to his risky patrolling of the colony during the 1984 riots. "But this is very different. It was all preplanned. It's theater. Lalu made a show of arresting Santoshji, but he was treated like a king in jail. Do you think anyone can do anything to him? To me? If they do, they'll upset all the Hindus in this country. Therefore, we all believe it was a minor setback. We'll do another yatra in a year, and this time, we will win. And whatever violence happened was anyway worse in the Congress states—"

Karishma said, "I'm not disagreeing. I think you're on the right path. I always wanted this for you. I told you your talents were lost on these small committees and businesses. It was right that you left the Sangathan, even though you feel bad about it." She glanced at her watch. "I better tell Jatin to heat food for Deepak. Where's Archana?"

By now, Laxman had gotten up and was taking powerful strides toward her. She too stood up, holding her left wrist loosely with her right hand, a weak circuit of protection.

As he came closer, she tried to slip by him, but he grabbed her shoulder and then her left hand and twisted it behind her.

"What are you doing!" she shouted.

Laxman didn't care. Moving swiftly and with force, he frog-marched her to the always musty dark-paneled single-windowed bedroom, pushed her to the bed, and, before she could recover, closed the latch on the door. She jumped off the bed and ran toward the other door leading to her sons' room, only to find that it was latched too; and by the time she reached for the rusty, unoiled tower bolt, he had pulled her from behind and pushed her back on the bed, where he climbed on top of her and held her wrists down as she wrestled back, fuming and spitting.

"Relax, darling," he said. "Relax!"

And then he did what he'd wanted to do.

CHAPTER 91

AFTERWARD, LAXMAN SAT IN THE MOHANJI PAHALWAN Balms office in a state of great confusion.

At the end of it, she *had* been subdued; and she had loved him back. But he felt again that he had perhaps done something wrong to engender such coldness in Karishma; and anyway, he had gone too far in using physical force, as if she were one of those Gharam farm girls from his teenage years ... hadn't he left that self behind, learned to love? But from under the placid surface of your present self, other drowned selves were constantly surfacing, troubled upward by unknown forces. He rocked back in his office chair, removed the towel from the back of the seat, and used it to wipe his face. Was it time to shut this all down?

Laxman told himself to be calm. This aloofness from Karishma might only be temporary. And yet, beneath everything, he felt the churning of powerful forces. Despite the mega-events unfolding in Indian politics, the real shifts, he felt, were happening in his personal realm—an individual rotation of stars that would, by affecting him, possibly *also* affect political matters.

In three days he was supposed to set out to Patiala—near the Chopras' ancestral village—to meet with local politicians; and he made up his mind that he would, on that visit, drive farther to Samana to consult the astrologer Shyam Trivedi, the son of SP's astrologer (and the grandson of the astrologer who had exiled SP when he was a few hours old).

On a cloudless Wednesday, having completed his meetings in Patiala, he took a Maruti Van taxi through the dusty road to Samana, feeling carsick the entire time, despite the cleansing cold of winter. The driver, his face wrapped in a muffler (within the larger atmospheric muffler of car fumes), made hair-raising turns and said that there hadn't been snow in the hills this year.

Along the way, Laxman stopped at the ancestral village of Gharam and paid a brief visit to his eldest brother, Rattan, who continued to live the life of a widower country squire in the ten-bedroom mansion in the village. Rattan had, by now, at the age of sixty, developed some kind of mental illness; and when Laxman sat with him in the heavily carpeted drawing room before a struggling fire, Rattan, dressed in a tan sweater over a white kurta, smiled wildly and gesticulated with his walking stick; he repeated nonsense rhymes and kept shouting for the servant to bring repasts of fresh veggies from the garden, even though the season for cucumbers had long passed. Laxman stayed the night, and in the early morning made a tour of the family orchard. He sampled fresh mosambis at dawn on the orchard caretaker's veranda, and even took a brief dip in the paved hot spring bath his father had constructed, performing dubkis while pressing his nostrils closed between his thumb and forefinger. He was happiest in these rural surroundings, so redolent of his father and his family's zamindar beginnings. He walked to the dispensary and the primary school that SP had built and offered sweets to the little girls who followed their teacher out of their two-room school building to greet Laxman, the big man from the big family.

Laxman was painfully tired from the exertions of the yatra; his head hurt, but he was confident that these climes would work on him like a tonic, massaging the old Laxman out of his worn carapace. He was grateful to have time to think.

He stopped to talk to the village headman in the headman's ramshackle yard, with its tied-up goats and abandoned plow, the plow's yoke beaked into the ground and its rump raised in the air on its heavy wheels. And it was then, absently petting one of the headman's cows, admiring the headman's expanding rural house with its attractive cascading slate roof and packed mud walls, the air rich with the smell of burning wood and dung, that the headman's wife came by, chasing a goat toward pasture. Seeing Laxman, she instinctively pulled her pink sheer dupatta tighter around her head and glanced at him with a shy sideways smile of hello. A stud shone in her nose. Like so many of the women in this area, she had fresh, fair, unblemished skin, and an upright gait and posture. Listening to the headman speak, Laxman glanced at her again and realized with an inner shock that he knew her: She was one of the girls he'd frolicked with in the fields behind the Gharam house years ago, when they would have both been in their teens; and as he tried to keep up with the headman's throaty Punjabi, he saw that the woman's chasing of the goat, now given up entirely, had been a pretext to appear before Laxman, to flash her face at him.

The arrogance of it! Laxman was blasted awake from his mental slumber.

"Come here," he said to the woman.

"She's my wife," said the headman, by way of introduction.

"Your name?" he asked her.

But now the woman's tart defiance, the open offering of her face, crumpled. She was again a shy village woman, scanning the ground as she answered questions; and though she was gaunt and fair, Laxman saw the lines of age swarming her throat, the veins in her scrawny neck exaggerated by the way she was pressing her head down, as if she were a sheep being examined by its owner for slaughter.

"Pinky," she said.

"Pinky," Laxman echoed. "Pinky, did you do any schooling?"

"What schooling," the headman said, speaking for her. "We're poor people, we're worried about putting rice on our plates."

"I'm third pass," Pinky said.

"And your daughters?" Laxman asked.

Laxman was beginning to remember what it would have been like to sleep with such a woman. The unquestioned physicality of it all; the unwashed but fresh smell of her skin; the strange lack of hang-ups that exist in young people who have grown up watching animals casually fornicate around them. He remembered how tangled and matted this woman's hair had been at thirteen and how his hand wouldn't flow through her tangles. "Go and apply some oil next time," he'd admonished her, stuffing a few rupees in her hand afterward.

And then, unbidden, came another memory: Laxman, as a married adult, worried he'd developed a venereal disease and sitting in the filthy room of a shady VD and sex doctor who, examining Laxman's penis, said he couldn't see the white discharge Laxman had been describing.

Laxman didn't think such diseases could exist in this verdant countryside. These were city problems.

"Ji, I have two daughters," Pinky said, looking up at him for a second with the abashed yet passively confident eyes of the girl he had lain with.

"The older is tenth pass," the headman added.

"The young one, her heart isn't in studies," Pinky said. Pinky had a soft, wheezy, asthmatic voice, which came through the sieve of the thin dupatta she held before her mouth. Laxman was always amazed by how few layers these people wore in winter.

"Where is she?" Laxman said. "Call her."

"She's gone to fetch water," Pinky said.

"Oh ho, just call her," the headman said to Pinky. The headman was in his forties but his hair was fringed with white. He had buckteeth and a gray whiskery mustache that seemed to highlight rather than disguise his ugly teeth.

Pinky walked away and appeared a few minutes later with a bug-eyed and apple-cheeked thirteen-year-old girl with a tomboyish hunch, her shoulders raised toward her neck. Her hair was brownish and soft-looking under the scarf she had wrapped around her head; it ran to a braid in the back. The young girl reached down and—she hadn't blinked once yet—touched Laxman's feet.

"Bas, bas, beta," Laxman said.

Then this girl stood up and, puffing out one side of her mouth, as if blowing a bubble inside it, spat sideways. From all around them came the frank morning music of people clearing their noses and running hand pumps, almost as ways of rousing themselves. The girl, with her broad face and bulging eyes, was deeply uninterested in Laxman. She wore, even on this school day that she had evidently bunked, her reddish school jacket. "What's this I hear about you not studying?" he asked.

"She'd rather watch TV," Pinky said. Her maternal tone had desexed her too.

Laxman said to the girl: "Just remember, nothing is more important than your studies. Everything else in this world can be taken away from you—except knowledge. I traveled all over the country, and what I learned is that there is no progress without education. And look, all over the country girls are becoming doctors and engineers—don't you want to be a doctor? Then you can cure your own dadi." (The headman's mother, who was inside the house, was suffering from stomach cancer.) Laxman reached out and took the girl's soft chin in his hand. "From now on, none of this nonsense of missing school." He let go. "Chalo, your goat is running away, go catch it."

When she was out of earshot, he said, "What a sweet girl. Put her in the DAV School. I'll pay for her notebooks and uniform and shoes." He was relieved that he was not attracted to her; that he had only liked thirteen-year-olds when he was a thirteen-year-old himself.

"You're too kind," said the headman, with absent gratitude, clasping his hands above his head in pranam and exhaling his smoky breath in Laxman's face.

Pinky, Laxman noticed, was haughtily looking away.

"Jai Shri Ram," said Laxman before leaving.

CHAPTER 92

IN THE EARLY AFTERNOON—FEELING A LITTLE BIT AS IF HE had expiated his sins by fulfilling his father's legacy of uplifting the villagers—Laxman drove the family jeep to go see the astrologer, forty minutes away. The gears of the jeep were hard and familiar from his first youthful attempts at driving, and he stopped a couple of times to buy aam papad and to inquire at a kirana village shop about whether someone could organize a little tea for him.

The astrologer's wife welcomed Laxman into the dimmest house Laxman had been inside in these parts. No windows in the inner rooms, or perhaps all the windows had been shuttered; and of course this made the house even colder. The astrologer met Laxman with a smile in a long, windowless room, one wall of which was taken up with garlanded portraits of ancient gurus and men that Laxman assumed were the astrologer's ancestors—some of these men would have even been in his superstitious grandfather's astrological retinue. The floor on this side of the room had been cleared of furniture, as if to create a corridor in which one could stand and contemplate and freshly garland these dead men; and on the other side of the room lay a torn, thin, dark carpet (apparently possessing the same thread count as stone-washed jeans) on which a seating area had been devised: a sofa with frayed arms and a plastic chair that faced it.

The astrologer planted himself on the chair, rubbing his hands for warmth, and beckoned Laxman to the sofa.

Shyam Trivedi wore a woolen cap on his head and a sweater with large plastic buttons that were only tentatively inserted in their eye holes.

Laxman gifted Shyam a small carton of oranges from the orchard and then, having been offered nothing to eat or drink in return, asked, "Can I get some chai, please?"

"Of course, of course," Shyam said.

Laxman realized suddenly that the astrologer, who was in his fifties—with a tired, brushy Hitler mustache and glaucous eyes—might be intimidated by Laxman's presence. The Rath Yatra had made Laxman famous; his name was often in the news as a leader of Hindus, a man who had conceived the idea of a chariot that would move at modern speeds, that would arouse in people not only memories of the *Ramayan* TV show but of Ram Rajya itself.

Laxman didn't attempt to put this tall, stingy man at ease. Getting older, Laxman was learning the benefits of holding back and was also realizing how much of his earlier personality had been formed by a fear of silence: Nothing had been more frightening, for a boy born into a family of nine kids and many cousins, than silence. Silence only arose in the household at times of death. So perhaps comfort with silence was also a mastery over death. You sit across from another person, both of you staring into a conversational void, and eking out your own meaning from it; and the one who is more afraid speaks first.

But then the motor of Laxman's heart started up again and he said, "I thought I'd come and see how all of you are doing here."

"Laxmanji, will you run for office against your own brother's party?" the astrologer asked. He meant Bhagat, whose former constituency was in this part of Punjab.

"What kind of question is that, Shyam Trivediji?" Laxman said. And shouldn't he have known, being an astrologer?

"He's Congress, you're TPP," Shyam explained, "and as you're aware, everyone here was very supportive of the Rath Yatra."

"Nothing like that," Laxman said. "I had some work here—and I have my role in the TPP, and I'll run from where they tell me to. And though Bhagat Bhaiya is in the Congress, I have nothing but the highest regard for him. We don't let such matters come between us. He's blessed and encouraged me at every turn. He also agrees that the condition of Hindus is bad but his hands are tied, you see—he's been friends with the Gandhis for many years, and he's a loyal person—"

Shyam's wife came in with tea, which, as Laxman had feared, was cold and weak.

Shyam said, with a self-pleased smile, "You know, it was written on your janmpatri that you would come here today."

"Is that so," Laxman said.

"Yes. I have the patris of everyone in your family, and I spent all morning looking through yours. Usually, I see one person in the morning and then another in the afternoon—but I canceled the morning consultation so I could focus all my energies on your patri, since I sense what will happen with you will also affect the fate of the whole nation. Besides, I'm an old man now, and this work tires me. Before I could see four people a day"—Did he really have that many clients? Laxman wondered—"but now two, and I'm exhausted."

"Was my visit also written in *your* patri?" Laxman asked with a conspiring but mocking smile.

Shyam took a slurp of his tea, acting as if he were pleasuring his tongue with a hot, reviving liquid. "It's like this, ji," he said, "as astrologers, we are not allowed to see our own patris. That's a vow we take. If you ever meet a jyotish who says he knows his past or future, distrust him. That, and if he tells you the date you will die. It's not our business to meddle in life or death that way. That's up to the creator," he said, throwing a pious glance over his shoulder at the gallery of portraits.

Laxman thought, *And what about your grandfather, who told my grandfather he'd die if he didn't instantly exile his baby son? Or your father, who told my father he'd die in a city that began with "K"—which he did?* Laxman was tired. His temples were throbbing.

"You're having some irritation of the eyes?" Shyam asked, pointing. "We've just had the place painted, that's why it might be happening." The room had been coated a dim yet glossy grayish blue, a color you saw on the exteriors of certain commuter trains, the color of late dusk devoid of moonlight.

Laxman said, "Yes, that must be it." Then, he said, "I've come to ask you a question about an important friendship in my life."

"Your niece?" Shyam asked casually.

Laxman sat up, alert. How did he know? "Say more."

"She is your enemy and she is seeking to destroy you," Shyam said, speaking into the ground. Tensing up, Laxman wondered,

How does he know about Karishma? Is this how far the rumor has flowed? Inwardly he cursed his talkative sisters. Had one of them come to see the astrologer? Had *Karishma* sought Shyam out?

Or was Shyam talking about Gita?

Laxman felt he was in the grip of an uncanny power, and he hated it.

The astrologer continued, "You have powerful connections with people who share your blood, but those who don't have your blood—and claim to be your friends—could be your enemies." Before Laxman could interject, Shyam said, "Let me finish. I knew you would visit now because a big change is coming in your life that will unleash all your powers and energies—and, believe me, you possess much of the same power as your father. But with every powerful arrangement also come opposing forces. Still, it's nothing to be worried about. Each man has to follow the line of his fate the way water courses through a riverbed. Each man is a manifestation of God's will, his billions of thoughts. We are *all* God's thoughts; and just as each thought in our minds has a different color and consistency, so does each of our lives. Our job is to accept our life and not fight fate. Let me finish," he said, irritably, still talking at the rutputty brown carpet erupting with white threads, "when I said 'destroy you,' I simply meant there will be an attempt, and you need to be aware and work toward defusing it."

Now he began to talk about the gemstone Laxman ought to wear on his ring finger as a remedy; how he ought to feed one-tenth of his weight in greens to cows in his colony (every morning, if possible); and how he should chant the Gayatri Mantra one hundred times first thing upon waking. "We can't defeat past karmas," Shyam went on, "they're always with us, but we can create new, positive karmas. Help others who are under threat of being destroyed, have compassion for them, and the Almighty will have compassion for you."

Laxman asked the astrologer if he'd have love till the end of his life.

The astrologer said, "The real question is whether *you'll* love others. The love of others for you is guaranteed."

Laxman didn't like that the man was speaking in riddles. How to directly bring up Karishma? "Why did you mention my niece?" Laxman asked.

"Because your chart shows you're a person who cares for the extended family. Which is your strength and your weakness."

"Should I not take care of my in-laws?" Laxman said.

Shyam said, "There are two clear paths laid out for you. But they diverge here. You must meditate to discover which path is the true one for you. But remember: The path of love is not always the path of love; the path of hate is not always the path of hate." Then he said, "You take too much tension, Laxmanji. That's one difference between you and your father—he didn't worry." Then he said, "By coming here, you have chosen a new path for yourself, though you don't know it."

Laxman drove back to Gharam. From there, the driver took him to Patiala, where he caught an overnight train to Delhi. It seemed to him now that the astrologer's message had been clear. End things with Karishma. But then, the message could have also been about Gita, who was his enemy and had likely spread the rumors about his affair in the first place.

He did not know then that, at this exact moment, his niece-in-law, the one he loved, was having her own fateful encounter with a train.

CHAPTER 93

After Laxman had left her flat that day, Karishma had sat up on the rumpled bed in a state of hysteria and despair. Laxman's actions had reminded her of the terrible reality of the affair, that things were not as much in her hands as she'd thought.

And she had welcomed him into her home. She had not resisted him as loudly as she could have.

She moved from the bedroom to the drawing room and sat on a sofa. Her forehead was burning, as if she were coming down with a fever, and she muttered to herself.

The next day, she didn't put on makeup or iron her clothes.

Mohit noticed the change in his mother when he returned from college but said nothing. He assumed his father and mother had had yet another fight—possibly over the fact that she was no longer working. Besides, Mohit was consumed with worries of his own, upset about the turn student politics had taken after Mandal. Anshul, out of the hospital, his face pinkish and puffy, pushed around in a wheelchair by two lackey political types, had been elected president of the student union, but Mohit's heroism in trying to save Anshul had been minimized; it was almost as if Anshul were embarrassed around Mohit. And because it was colder now and Mohit was wearing full-sleeve shirts and sweaters, he couldn't show off to his fellow students the extent of the burn on his left arm.

Anshul had, however, apologized once to Mohit. "Bhai, I'm sorry I was the cause of your injury."

"What are you talking about, boss, I was just doing what anyone would do."

But some part of Anshul continued to look away from Mohit. Perhaps Anshul felt that Mohit had absented himself while Anshul was fighting for his life in the hospital; how could Mohit explain that he himself had been immured in his house by his parents?

Whatever the reason, Anshul did not volunteer Mohit for positions in the cabinet of the student union.

Later, Mohit bitched about this state of affairs to Sakshi, with whom he had started going steady. She was a short and surprisingly husky-voiced girl who always looked off to the side as she made sly comments about everyone, even those she liked. She told Mohit that Anshul was suffering from paranoia.

"Arre, you have so many fundas about everyone," Mohit said. "That's why I'm glad I'm going out with you."

"Don't think that'll save you," Sakshi said, turning her brown eyes on him.

Karishma was now trapped in the flat with Mohit, who had just taken the bus home from college. She wanted to go to the temple but couldn't bring herself to do so. She wanted to see Archana—but were they even friends? She thought about confiding in Gita and realized just how crazy a notion that was.

She had no friends in this complex, in this colony—except Laxman.

Her afternoon was empty and she had too much time to think. When would Laxman return from his Patiala trip? She sank into the sofa chair and bit her nails until her thick, dumpling-like fingers were bald stubs.

Her period was delayed, and almost idly, she wondered if she was pregnant. Then she worried that the temperature, the period, the moodiness—that these were signs she was coming to the end of her life as a sexual being. She had always felt less like a woman (she thought) than the other women she knew—women for whom femininity was a natural cloak. As a teenager, she'd sprouted hair in all sorts of places—cheeks, chin, arms—and her mother had laughed at her: "The curse of the Saxena women!" But Karishma's mother herself had had a smooth rage-polished face; and even today, with that teenage growth behind her, Karishma painstakingly checked her body every morning for stray hairs, plucking them out sharply. She had never understood why her body conspired against her. That was why her husband's comments through their marriage about her mannish posture had stung so much—there was an element of truth to it. And with Brij, in bed, in the early days of their marriage, she had felt embarrassed by his outpouring of love and sentimentality rather than relishing it; she would snicker in his face and turn away.

Laxman's guiltless style had been better for her. It allowed her to be frank and bawdy in response, to be as shameless as God no doubt intended her to be.

She had often told Laxman what to do, and he had followed. Such direction had been impossible to impart to Brij, who took forever to ejaculate and often got frustrated with her for not turning him on faster. He would really only get turned on *after* he had exploded in rage—his true ejaculation—and hit her, gaining an erection as she cried.

When she was dying, she knew, she would not think of Brij. She hadn't loved him for a single day of their marriage and never would. Her life had ended the minute she had disobeyed her own instincts and accepted the proposal. But what choice had she had? He came from an excellent family, he was handsome and sharp-chinned, and her mother was overjoyed at the match. "All the difficulties you've given me in life will be undone now," she had said. "This gives me another reason for living." The "difficulties" her mother, Alka Devi, was referring to consisted mostly of the time Alka had walked into a vacated storeroom with a charpai in it and had seen Karishma kissing her slightly younger cousin Subhash on his lips. Both of them were in their teens and balanced on their knees on the bed as they faced each other, and Karishma had placed her hands on the back of Subhash's head and guided it toward her. Alka had shouted and separated them, giving them both tight slaps. When Subhash left the room, Alka turned to her daughter. "I know you're the one who did it, you shameless whore." And what had been amazing was that she was right. Karishma had in fact lured Subhash into the room and forced him to play husband–wife, and if Alka hadn't burst in, they would have gotten to the stage where Karishma would have shown him how babies were made ... she had been precocious ever since an older cousin had taught her these things. Since then, she had felt she was on the same wavelength as men, a wavelength other women didn't comprehend.

Was she more of a man than a woman? Or more irresistible than other girls? She walked now to the dressing room, but the mirror on the Godrej only rewarded her with a gaunt, lined face; sun-darkened skin—she had not been eating the last few days. If her son could participate in a hunger strike, so could she. She heard the distinct sound of the old door to the house grinding on the floor. She came out quickly and went to the drawing room in time to see Mohit about to slip out. "Where are you going?" she asked. It was mid-afternoon.

"Mummy, just going for a college meetup. The Wordsworth Society."

"And when will you study?" she asked.

"Mummy, this is college, not school. Only the finals matter. And this literary club is good if I apply for a PG abroad."

How quickly he had returned to normal.

"Chalo, good, then go," she said. Then she quickly ran up to him and raised herself on her toes and gave her tall boy a kiss on the head. He had become much more involved with college activities since Mandal. It was as if the burning had been the prelude to a blossoming.

When he left, Karishma went back to her bedroom and sat on the edge of the bed. Deepak was staying back in school today for football practice, Brij was at the factory. Archana was likely munching snacks in the office, and Laxman was in the countryside of Punjab.

Sighing, Karishma slung a purse on her shoulder. She pushed open the door, ducked her head into the kitchen, and told Jatin she would be back from an errand shortly.

She walked out of A-19 in a daze of short breath, the green of the colony fading around her into wintery beige. Then she turned toward the main road. Dodging cars, she crossed the wide highway and entered the north side of the colony, which was even richer, cooler, and more enclosed than the south side. It was four o'clock; too early for walkers. The only people on the streets here were servants wheeling toward markets on bicycles or municipal workers in their khaki uniforms striding into parks with large brooms thrown over their shoulders. Self-conscious about her purse and about being on foot, Karishma followed a small road between two mansions and came to the train tracks that ran behind the colony—the one disfiguring aspect of this otherwise regal and quiet enclave. Commuter trains plied these tracks every thirty minutes or so, honking wildly and belching steam. Almost casually, Karishma walked onto the tracks, standing between the rails and the wooden planks on a depression of gravel. The smell of piss was vivid around her and she dug her fingers into her purse absently, as if looking for something.

A minute later, a train was racing toward her, hissing and hooting. She thought about moving. But at the last minute, when she tried to lift her foot, her chappal got stuck in a plank across the track and the train mowed her down.

CHAPTER 94

LAXMAN WOULD LATER LEARN HE HIMSELF HAD BEEN ON A train when she was killed—or when she had killed herself.

It was an image he never let go of. The feeling that it was *his* train, *his* journey, that had plowed her down, that she was a casualty of *his* life, that—as the astrologer had said—his journey to the countryside, which he had chosen, had sealed her fate.

He had abandoned her and she had killed herself.

At the cremation, which Laxman played a role in organizing—insisting on covering all the expenses: "We're not just family but also partners," he told Brij—he was stoic, directing the pundit and the boys and even Brij as people swarmed around the bier that held Karishma's small sheet-covered body, her smashed jaw having been reset and the blood having been scrubbed from her skin. Then the body was fed into the metal maw of the electric crematorium.

After that, he spent much of his time at home, supporting a weeping Archana, who said, "She was my best friend, what a noble person, why did she do this, she had so many years to look forward to, but I knew something wasn't right when she left the job, she had some tension in her mind, maybe with Brij, but she wouldn't tell me." Laxman patiently stroked Archana's hair as she wet his shoulder in the bedroom. He had just returned from the police station, where he had convinced the inspector (via a contact of his in the police) to file the death as an accident rather than suicide—to avoid scandal.

He could not cry himself. The kids—who had joined them in the bedroom—were not crying either. "You don't feel sad about your chachi?" Laxman asked Shilpa and Vaishnavi, looking up.

Vaishnavi, eighteen and thin as ever, rubbed her nose—a strange habit she had developed—and then let her shoulders droop.

Shilpa said, "Papa, it was a suicide, no?"

"Quiet," Laxman said. "No one knows anything."

It was only in the privacy of his bathroom, while bathing, that Laxman wept.

Gita, for her part, couldn't believe Karishma was gone. For all her opacity, Karishma had projected vitality. Though she might look away or through you, she was always on the go: cooking, working, playing bridge, knitting sweaters, visiting her parents, fighting with Brij, rotating into Laxman's orbits during parties. Her sudden death contradicted all this even if the way she had chosen to go—its ugly violence, staring a brutal machine in the face—didn't.

Then rumors began to spread.

A Congress-leaning Hindi paper published a story titled "Death on the Tracks." It asked why this woman, the mistress of a TPP politician, had been dressed up as if for a rendezvous when she had been found dead. And wasn't it convenient that the TPP politician himself was out of town? Had she been privy to some dangerous political secret? Why hadn't she left behind a suicide note?

From there the story leapt into the English dailies, which everyone in the Chopras' circle read. Soon after, the new (non-TPP-supported) government at the center directed the head of police to investigate whether Laxman, a leader of an opposition party, might have been involved in disposing of his mistress.

Gita's bell rang. It was 3 p.m. Bells ringing in the afternoon or early evening were an ominous sign. This was a time when gardeners and sweepers knew not to puncture the memsahib's post-school afternoon slumber and when Ramesh, the servant, was downstairs in his room taking a nap as well.

A bell in the afternoon could only mean an annoying salesman—perhaps coming by to stiffly sing the praises of a new Aquaguard or inverter for power cuts—or … a relative.

It was the latter.

It was Vibha.

"Oh, Bua, come, come," Gita said, smoothing back her hair and correcting her anti-bell-ringing scowl and leading Vibha to the small sitting area that was their drawing room. The rest of the house was quiet, dark, and cold; the marble under her feet held the day's chill.

"I can bring the heater," Gita offered. "It's upstairs."

"No, no, it's fine, I'm wearing thick socks and it won't take too long," Vibha said. Then Vibha relaxed into a stiff wooden chair with a ridged, cushioned back and said, "Gita, there's an issue I want to discuss with you."

It was at this point that there was a sudden banging sound near Rupvati's room—a door slamming, a husky shout of alarm from Rupvati: "Brij, beta! Brij! Stop!" Gita and Vibha looked up to see Brij, dressed in an argyle sweater and khaki trousers, emerging with a stick in his hand.

"Brij, hello," Gita said instinctively, even as she realized with a shock that the stick was actually a long, polished rifle.

Vibha leapt to her feet but Gita, for some reason, remained frozen in her cane chair.

Brij kept coming toward Gita and Vibha, his face distended. "Bloody, my own sister-in-law, is this how you treat us, I'll fucking show you what murder is. What right do you have to say these things?" Brij raved across the room, past Vibha, holding the gun at his side, the barrel pendulating above the floor.

"Brij, I beg you, put the gun away," Vibha said. "I've come to speak to Gita about this only."

It dawned on Gita that they were blaming *her* for seeding rumors of the affair in the papers. She got up.

"You sit down!" Vibha said to Gita. Then, turning to Brij, "Brij, put the gun down. We're family—"

"And where's family when she bloody goes and spreads calumny to the newspapers?" Brij shouted. While talking, he pointed and shook the heavy gun at Gita, as if it were an accusing finger. "My sister-in-law has had it bloody out for us ever since she built this place."

"Brij, I promise I said nothing!" Gita said.

"Quiet, Gita!" Vibha said, turning around.

Suddenly, Brij sat down on a chair. He placed the gun next to him and stared at the ground.

Vibha walked toward him and said softly, "Brij, please don't do this—go back to your house and put the gun away. Think of what your sons will say."

"It's not loaded," he said between heaves.

"Still," Vibha said. "Just go and I'll talk to Gita, OK?"

Brij got up, turned around, and shouldered past Rupvati, who was standing at the threshold of her room. Then he vanished into his house.

"Rupvati Chachi, I hope he didn't touch you," Gita said, bringing the paunchy old lady into her drawing room by the hand.

"He gave me a little push," Rupvati admitted, eyebrows rising past her owlish clear frames.

Gita then locked the door that led into Rupvati's room—the passage to Brij's house. "You see what we live with, Vibha Bua," Gita said, sitting down.

Vibha said, "The men of this generation—their tempers."

"Should I call the police?" Gita asked.

"What will that solve?" Vibha said. "No, if you call the police, the press will just have more masala."

"Bua, if you had a madman living next door—" Gita said.

"He's grief-struck. You stay here with Rupvati Chachi," Vibha said, "I'll go talk to Laxman. He can take Brij's gun away."

"I don't feel comfortable alone, Buaji," Gita said.

Vibha looked at her balefully.

Gita went on, "I don't know what I have to tell you to convince you that I didn't do it. I'll swear on Chachiji's head. I'll swear on my own mother's head."

"There's no need for that," Vibha said.

Then Vibha went over to the digital MTNL phone lying near the dining table and punched in a number. "Please come and control him," she said on the phone, clearly, to Laxman—who must also have been the instigator of Vibha's visit to Gita. "Yes, Brij threatened me—and Gita—with his rifle. Does he even have a license for it? Please come right now."

Vibha returned to the sitting area. "Laxman is the only one who can handle this."

Gita scoffed.

"You should have a little more trust in the family, Gita," Vibha said.

"Bua, you yourself just saw," Gita said.

"But even if there are problems, we handle them inside."

"With all due respect, Buaji," Gita said, "no one said this when Laxman called the MCD on us. And maybe there *should* be a police investigation."

When Vibha rolled her eyes, as if to say, *There was no proof*, Gita went on, "You saw my brother-in-law. You don't think such a man could kill his own wife?"

Vibha decided to treat Gita like a person in shock. "It's OK, it's OK, Gita, I know it's painful, but it was a suicide. It's the press that's spreading this nonsense."

"Then please go shout at the press," Gita said.

CHAPTER 95

GITA INSISTED THAT VIBHA NOT LEAVE TILL LAXMAN HAD disarmed Brij. Gita then phoned Sachin in his office and let him know what had happened.

"That fucking bastard," Sachin said. "He's full of bluster but I know he's not capable of actually doing anything."

"You should have seen it—if Vibha Bua weren't here," Gita said loudly, to win points with Vibha, who was scolding Rupvati now for talking too much.

As Gita, Vibha, and Rupvati waited for Sachin, Vibha shook her head, repeating, "Brij is grief-struck. He was never good at showing emotion. He'll cool down."

"He pushed Rupvati Chachi," Gita reminded Vibha. "And he used to hit Karishma all the time."

"That's correct," Rupvati said.

Vibha said, "No, no, it's all politically motivated—the National Front is taking revenge on the TPP for withdrawing support." She grimaced. "Laxman was such a good friend to Karishma and Brij. No one helped them more at the cremation, no one helped them more when they relocated to Delhi. That's the sad thing about this. But luckily, Laxman wasn't in Delhi when Karishma's ... accident ... happened. So the tamasha will die down soon. There's no evidence at all."

Maybe she came not just to scold me for the leak, Gita thought, *but to firmly warn me against speaking to reporters or the police in the future—from saying anything. And to convince herself of her lie.*

Gita said, "Why do you think Karishma took her own life?"

Vibha jumped her eyebrows up at the door where Brij had appeared like a furious genie. "I think we saw," Vibha said with a sigh.

How loyal Vibha was to her brother! Gita thought, as they waited in silence for Sachin and Laxman.

The explosion of the affair into the newspapers would have come as an affront; Vibha had to tamp it down for her own sanity.

In order to do so, she had to blame Laxman's enemies. The person who committed adultery and drove his lover to suicide was not the guilty party; it was the person who went outside the mafioso knot of the family. Loyalty—adoration of the family name—was what mattered most.

Where are you, SP? Gita thought now as she called Ramesh up from his room to make tea for all of them. *How is it that you amassed such greatness for yourself—and left behind such a dry bed of pettiness, meanness, violence, squalor?* SP was like a tycoon who dies surrounded by admirers, with the children realizing only later, when they open the almirahs and checkbooks, that he was bankrupt and left them nothing. But instead of exposing the patriarch, the family closes ranks and thinks there must have been a mistake. Ashamed for themselves, they shout his greatness from the rooftops till they believe it too—till it becomes their only form of wealth.

CHAPTER 96

SACHIN ARRIVED.

From the tall windows, Vibha spied Laxman walking into the courtyard. Then Vibha bade goodbye to Gita and Sachin and Rupvati. She went down the stairs, greeted Laxman, and vanished with him to Brij's house.

Sachin took Gita's hands in his own and said, "It'll be OK, he'll calm down."

A few minutes later, they heard it: a flat boom—a gunshot.

It would be narrated afterward by Vibha to the entire family.

How, when Laxman and she had gone to Brij's flat, they had found Brij sitting in the drawing room, oiling his gun with a rag, with Deepak and Mohit milling about awkwardly. Entering the flat, Vibha told the boys to go outside; they obeyed. Then a curious wick of a smile played on Brij's face. He namasted to Laxman and Vibha, lifted the gun, and—still sitting—shot Laxman in the chest.

Vibha screamed.

Laxman angrily moved toward Brij and then collapsed, at which point Brij shot him again—twice. Brij put the gun aside, namasted to a shocked Vibha again, and walked down the stairs.

At this point, Vibha ran over to Rupvati's and to the door that led to Sachin and Gita's—but it was locked. She started banging on it.

Hearing her panicked voice through the door, Sachin opened it and ran to Brij's flat with her.

And so it turned out that Sachin was the one who drove a bleeding Laxman—laid out on the back seat of Sachin's red Maruti Van—to the hospital with Vibha.

And Sachin was present at Aruna Asaf Ali Hospital when Laxman was declared dead an hour after he had arrived.

CHAPTER 97

THERE WAS NO NEED FOR A MANHUNT OR AN INVESTIGATION. Brij had not run away but had rather driven himself to the Modern Colony police thana, where he had confessed what he'd done. Brij's deed had another effect: It sealed off the need for an investigation into Karishma's suicide, since Karishma's would-be murderer, Laxman Chopra, was dead. So even in death, Gita thought later, Laxman had absolved himself, become a martyr: Encomia flowed in not just from the TPP but from the entire political spectrum. Laxman was remembered as a youthful, active, intelligent figure; a true nationalist; a son of Punjab; a devout Jeev Sangathani; the man who designed the rath but was also a voice of reason in a fascist party: "Were it not for his intervention," one journalist wrote, "the death tolls from rioting along the rath route would have been much larger. He diverted the rath from certain communally mixed areas where the casualties would have been greatest." Laxman's role in bailing Santosh Kumar out of prison in Bihar was also recalled. Santosh, in fact, was interviewed about Laxman on television. "He took his nephew Brij under his wing and was like a father figure to him," Santosh said. "But Brij resented this. He wanted a ticket to enter politics, but, as you know, our party is not nepotistic like the Congress, so he was forced to deny Brij this wish. Therefore, Brij, driven mad by his wife's suicide, looking for someone to blame, turned on Laxman. It is a very sad and premature end to what would have been a brilliant career in national service."

Sachin told Gita he would not help his brother. "He's on his own," he said. "He came and threatened you with a gun. Let him rot."

But then Mohit and Deepak visited to ask for their chacha's advice and Sachin felt he had no choice: They were just boys!

He accompanied them to visit Brij in his piss-perfumed lockup and together they watched as Brij sat against a wall with his head in his hands.

Sachin offered Brij a tiffin of home-cooked food, but Brij refused.

Sachin had not seen his brother weep this way since their father's death, the mustache of his goatee slashed with snot.

"He's sad about your mother," Sachin said to the boys on the ride home, unsure of what to do, but also angry at Brij for this display. "We'll do our best."

Gita, meanwhile, watched over the boys in their home, supervising their meals and studies.

Initially, Rupvati Chachi had also been put in charge of the kids. But whenever Gita went over to see if the orphaned boys needed anything, she encountered Rupvati standing in the drawing room with her hands on her hips, bellowing for the boys through their closed bedroom door. Rupvati also came to Gita with complaints about the boys—they weren't eating when she demanded they should, for example.

"Chachiji, their mother has died, their father is in jail," Gita said. "Of course they aren't going to eat. Don't force them."

The two boys were unfailingly polite to Gita. They didn't show much emotion. Mohit's girlfriend, Sakshi, a short, peppy girl, was often over—she seemed almost to be living there—but Gita did not ask her to leave and was in fact grateful for her pressure-relieving presence, the girlish way in which she would defer to Gita and ask if there was any way she, Sakshi, could help. "No, no, you sit," Gita would say. "Ramesh is making you all some food."

"I love the design of your kurta, Auntie—is it from Ritu's?"

Surreal conversations to have in a time of unbearable pain. And a few minutes later, when Ramesh would bring the food, the boys would heartily lay into the tandoori chicken Gita had specially ordered for them. They were ravenous; they refused to eat only when Rupvati Chachi forced them.

Gita was furious about how the rest of the family—so close to Laxman and therefore, by connection, to Brij and Karishma—

had abandoned the boys. Rupvati Chachi was angling for Brij and Karishma's old room. Karishma's parents and cousins came over only a couple of times, and soon Gita realized they too were more interested in pilfering from Karishma's Godrej than looking into the boys' well-being. Gita finally took the keys to Karishma's almirahs and hid them in her own flat.

Gita drove to Ghaziabad one day to update Karishma's parents on the case. There, she also made a small plea for funds for Brij's defense—mainly so the boys could have a parent again. "Funds for the man who drove my daughter to suicide?" Karishma's father said, adjusting his woolen tartan golf cap—his signature accessory—over his bald head. "Never." The lower-middle-class dank sadness of the house. Not just a poverty of things but of emotions. A massing of odiously white British crockery on side tables—the Punjabi love of floral designs, paintings of English women in long skirts carrying umbrellas, windup clocks with gold edges.

Gita realized that she had come not just to update them but to experience the world Karishma had emerged from, to understand why she had been driven into an affair with the worst man in the family.

CHAPTER 98

BRIJ'S CASE GREW COMPLICATED—MAINLY BECAUSE BRIJ, despite his weeping, wouldn't cooperate with Sachin or the lawyers. When Sachin tried to convince him to plead "temporary insanity," Brij said, "And give everyone the pleasure of saying he's always been mad, therefore Karishma had the affair? Forget it." So he was openly talking about the affair now. At other times, he'd say, "Are the boys OK? Good. I taught them to be real men. Tell them to keep their chins up. Their father will be out soon. What was this that the lawyer said about insanity?"

Sachin repeated that it was a normal thing to plead during such cases of murder. He reminded him what the lawyer had said: Though insanity could be hard to prove, with the burden to establish insanity being placed on the accused ("as if being insane were not burden enough haha," the lawyer had said), Brij's case was stronger than most others because (a) his wife had just committed suicide and he was obviously grieving; and (b) he had been driven to rash action by the terrible rumors vomited up by the heartless, politicized press. "Brij, think of your boys—life in prison."

"You tell me," Brij said, with tears dotting the semicircles under his eyes, "was she or was she not having an affair?"

Sachin found this hard to comprehend. Had he really not known? Or was he rewriting history so he could mitigate his reputation as a complicit Chopra cuckold? He thought of his own wife, of her affair with Hector. His anger at her for this would never go away. Yet—he hated to admit this—it made him feel more attracted to her. "I don't know, man," Sachin said. "I was too busy with my own work."

"Ask your wife, then," Brij said. Then: "I don't like that lawyer. There's something ... shady about him." Then: "What I don't want to do is plead insane and *then* be sent to jail. Imagine—I'll be a laughingstock!" Brij's eyes bulged.

But of course he *was* insane! Sachin thought. How quickly he had suppressed what he had actually done—killing another man! His friend and business partner of years! Sachin felt that, watching this tragedy unfold, he was beginning to understand his brother's personality. Madness is its own kind of opacity. If Karishma had been passively opaque, Brij had been madly opaque. Together, they had cloaked their marriage in unknowability.

"The other option," Sachin said, "is pleading guilty and going to jail for life anyway."

Sachin suddenly felt he was fully back in India, as if the US had not existed.

Brij looked down between his legs. "I didn't mean to kill him. Just scare him a little."

The shots—three of them—belied that.

"I know, I know," Sachin said. "Remember that your confession—no matter what the press says—is inadmissible in court. You just have to play the legal system correctly."

Brij laughed. "You know, I wanted to shoot that bastard for years. On some level, he always treated us like children—like he was doing *me* a favor by starting the bloody balm business! He forgets I have years of service in the Indian Air Force—one of the only people in this family to go into government service after Grandfather, not like these buggers living off the fat of the land." Sachin noticed that his brother had unconsciously slipped into present tense when speaking of Laxman.

"Anyway, the lawyer will come and explain more to you," Sachin said. "Just relax. We'll get you out."

Brij laughed bitterly.

CHAPTER 99

GITA WAS AMAZED BY SACHIN'S FEALTY TOWARD HIS brother. At night Sachin drank endless cups of instant coffee and sat at the dining table reading up on past murder cases from a book he had borrowed from the library of a lawyer friend. He also spoke to Gita about the case, and Gita and Sachin felt closer to each other than they had in years.

For Sachin, Brij's case became a canvas on which he could project his own masked and messy emotions.

"You know, he wasn't always like this," Sachin told Gita one evening in their bed. "He used to be really sensitive—artistic—sweet. Very loving toward Mummy. And afraid of Daddy, though of course Brij loved him too." Sachin scratched his neck under the single flickering sconce, one shaped to look like a British streetlight from the 1800s. "But going to the air force and marrying Karishma, something changed—"

Gita listened, picking at a flap of skin on her thumb.

Sachin said, "He wasn't cut out for the defense services, frankly. He was more of an intellectual type." Sachin smiled now, looking up at the ceiling. "I used to try to hide my school marks from him. He always said I'd had a much easier time since, unlike him, I didn't have to move in senior secondary because of Partition, and because I wasn't forced to do the NCC."

"He was always an irritator," Gita said.

"But you have to understand the source: He was much more exposed to the extended family. Daddy would send him for the entire winter to Gharam; I had my cricket camps in Allahabad, so I only went when Daddy and Mummy went. And Brij would come back from these family gatherings much angrier, wilder. For a few days he'd be very rough and aggressive, and then he'd forget. Daddy would notice this aggression but he wouldn't stop him. I think Daddy somewhat enjoyed Brij being wild. He'd clap and laugh when Brij chased me around, trying to pull my pants off. It reminded Daddy of home." Sachin went on, "You know, I told Brij to come to the US so many times. I told him I'd find him a job, I'd sponsor him. He refused. He was too proud. He hated that paper mill, but he still refused. Think of how different his life would be now—" Sachin's voice cracked.

"People's personalities don't change."

"Why do you always think the worst?" Sachin snapped. "Is there any chance the affair—was it just a rumor? You know how conservative our society is."

Then Gita said, "Laxman raped me."

CHAPTER 100

SHE WAS SURPRISED THAT SHE SAID IT, SURPRISED THAT IT came out.

Looking away, still ashamed, Gita told Sachin about the incidents with Laxman at the wedding and the gurdwara. Those incidents were now frighteningly clear in her mind; she recalled them with a ferocious precision she could bring to few other memories of her life; and she was both enraged and relieved to be reliving them in this manner, when neither she nor her husband could raise their voices at the perpetrator.

"But I had no idea!" Sachin said, clutching his head. How had he understood so little?

"How could I tell you? We had so many other problems." She let out a small sob.

"But then you told me to invite him to Midland," Sachin said.

"I didn't—you did!" she whispered.

"But you didn't stop me," Sachin said. "The balls of that asshole."

"He didn't have any balls," Gita said. "He knew exactly who to target. And when I went and complained to Vibha Bua—I thought it was better to settle it in India only and not involve you—that's when she said that she and Laxman had discussed getting me pregnant. That *fool* was going to get me pregnant. No one is a bigger fan and defender of that asshole than her." She realized then just how much she hated Vibha. "Even after all this, she ran to accuse me of spreading rumors. Sometimes I wish I *had* spread them. She's right. I had a motive."

"Why didn't you stop us from living here?" Sachin said.

"I didn't want us to back down—and I knew it mattered to you."

Sachin said, "I'm sorry, Gita. Why is life so hard? I could never imagine our lives would turn out like this." Then, "I was a bad husband."

Gita put a hand on his wet cheek. “You weren’t. You were a great husband. You were young. And stressed with work.”

He went on, “You were so depressed for such a long time.”

“He *made* me depressed.”

Sachin said, “I’m glad he’s gone.”

“But think of all the damage he did while he was on earth,” Gita said.

It was not the end of the damage.

In two years, in December 1992, Laxman’s 1990 Rath Yatra would finally bear fruit.

In a reenactment of 1990, frenzied mobs of kar sevaks gathered at the barricades around the masjid and then jumped over the fences and stormed the structure and tore it down with makeshift hammers and tridents. This time, a TPP government was in power in the state and the CRPF and police made no attempt to stop the violence. Santosh Kumar, Laxman’s mentor, observed it all from a nearby mound. He claimed to be “saddened” by the destruction but didn’t condemn it.

Gita and Sachin watched the news, like many others, with a mix of horror and fascination. But one interview particularly stuck with Gita. It was on Newstrack and featured a kar sevak wearing a band of saffron around his head and a cast on his arm. “I did it all for Ram,” he said. Then, after a pause, “And for the great warrior Laxman Chopra.” But that wasn’t all. He added that, when he had clambered up to the first dome of the mosque with a rope and attacked the structure with a hammer, eventually falling through fifty feet of air to the floor (from where he was rescued from the rubble and rushed to the hospital by other sevaks), at that moment of half-consciousness, his head and arm bleeding, the face of the blessed martyr Laxman Chopra, the designer of the original rath, had flashed through his mind like a deity.

CHAPTER 101

BEFORE ALL THIS, THERE WAS THE COURT CASE.

The story of the sensational murder continued hogging the front pages of the newspapers.

Much to everyone's surprise, Brij's case was growing stronger and stronger. There was the temporary insanity defense, which he had finally agreed to—the insanity brought on by his grief. But the lawyer had also planted the idea in court that Brij, suspecting that his wife had been murdered by Laxman, had reason to worry that Laxman would kill him too—especially after Laxman and Vibha, on their visit, asked the kids to leave. Brij had therefore acted in self-defense, out of "grave and sudden provocation." Laxman, the lawyer said, had made insulting comments about Brij's wife. Also the weapon had misfired. It was a blizzard of utmost nonsense but it distracted from the most damning piece of evidence against Brij: that he had had the presence of mind, after the shooting, to leave his house; drive his car around Delhi for an hour or so; stop at the Krishna Bhagwan Mandir to pray; and then turn himself in to the local police thana, where he had confessed everything in clear, precise English, though there was no audio recording, just a written statement, which was inadmissible in court.

Meanwhile, the rumors that Laxman had murdered Karishma kept circulating in the pro-Congress papers; and Sachin wondered who was involved in spreading them.

The old pundit of the Jeev Sangathan Mandir came forward and told a reporter that he had often seen Karishma and Laxman at the temple. "They would arrive together for pujas," he said, leaving the rest unsaid.

The family hit back strongly at these allegations. Archana was quoted at length in an article. "It's well-known that the pundit was fired by Laxman for skimming funds from the mandir. And, yes, Karishma and Laxman went to the temple—to pray for *her* children's health. I was also invited for these pujas. The boys also went. One wonders why the pundit allows himself to imagine the worst things happening in the house of God."

Archana was becoming more and more vocal in the press. The murder had awoken her after years of emotional slumber, though she continued to eat her way through life at an astonishing pace: Her teeth were now rotting and red with paan, and she chain-smoked in the complex without shame. She was indignant on behalf of her dead husband. Her reputation—and her children's—rested on her ability to resurrect Laxman.

On a warming March morning, before Sachin had left for his office, Archana walked over to Sachin and Gita's flat—the first time she'd been there in years. When Gita came down to greet her—looking dazed—Archana said sternly, "Please, I want to speak to your husband."

"Fine," Gita said, throwing up her hands and going back up.

Seated at the dining table, Archana complained to Sachin about the pundit's insinuations about the affair.

Sachin said, "I'm not even involved. I'm just doing my duty as a brother—making sure he has funds—"

"All of which were loans from Laxman!"

"I'm paying out of my pocket too," Sachin said. "We'll settle whatever loans he has. Right now, I'm just worried about whether his boys are OK." Then, "But I don't think Brij is spreading these rumors."

She snorted. "He's always been a destructive force."

Sachin said, "Can you get the pahalwan to speak on Laxman's behalf?"

"Already all of the TPP is on his side."

Sachin said, "Then don't worry. Justice will be served."

Gita asked Sachin, "Is there a chance he might get off scot-free?" What would they do if that murdering monster returned here?

"The odds of that happening are one percent," Sachin said.

But neither he—nor anyone else—could have predicted the intense effort Brij put into saving himself. His gloves came off. And Mohit, too, became a disciple and soldier of his father, visiting him often at Tihar Jail and helping him prepare his defense.

Brij, on the stand, his beard shaved, showed no restraint in smearing Laxman. He said Karishma had been murdered by Laxman because she had turned down Laxman's advances. He suggested that Laxman had wanted full control of the balm business too, and that his demands grew more strident after Karishma turned him down.

The whole story Brij narrated about Laxman acting vindictively, Gita realized, was actually the story of how Laxman had treated *her, Gita*.

Then Gita herself was called up as a witness in court, having been the first person that Brij had waved a gun at that day. On the stand, she agreed that Brij had been grief-stricken and looking for someone to blame. Then, to her shock, Brij's lawyer asked, "Did Mr. Laxman Chopra ever make a pass at you?" The government lawyer objected, but the judge deemed it pertinent and asked Gita to answer. Gita hesitated. Then she said, "Yes, when I was first married. He was rough with women and didn't take no for an answer." This single line of truth, uttered in public, after years of silence, finally snapped her ties with the rest of Sachin's family forever. It also freed Gita.

In the end, after a trial that lasted a year and a half, the judge found Brij guilty of culpable homicide *not* amounting to murder. Brij was led away by a policeman who held his hand.

He would spend the next twenty-five years in prison. But this was a victory: Under ordinary circumstances, a murderer like Brij could have been executed.

CHAPTER 102

GITA AND SACHIN'S GUARDIANSHIP OF THE BOYS STRETCHED into the foreseeable future.

Gita had always wanted children but now, between her nephews and her students at St. Xavier's, they were practically raining down on her.

Gita constantly checked on Mohit and Deepak, even if it irritated them, asking how their school studies were going, saying that their papa had requested that she guide them. "We can organize tuitions for you," Gita said to Deepak, who was in his final year of school.

"Papa doesn't like them," Mohit said. He was now an adult, almost finished with college.

"Have you thought of what you'll do after graduation?" Gita asked him.

"I'll do a PG. Or take the CA exam. I'm also interested in journalism."

But it seemed he had his eye on none of these things. He had been sucked into the world of student politics. He was now campaigning on behalf of a local Congress politician.

In fact, the case had been a turning point for Mohit's career.

The opposition parties had taken an active interest in trying to smear Laxman and had therefore extended its support to Brij's case. Anshul, now the Delhi University Student Union president and a leader of the Congress Youth Wing, was, in fact, the one who had approached Mohit and asked him how the Congress could be of assistance.

Anshul was permanently confined to a wheelchair; he had wheeled himself up to Mohit in the college courtyard. His face was scarred;

the area under the jaw had turned to pink blubber. His stubble grew in uneven patches, though the proud mustache had returned.

Mohit explained that his chacha and chachi were handling the case and providing the funds. "But who knows how long they'll want to do that? There might be years of appeals."

"That's why we're there," Anshul said. "Rely on us. We can give you strength."

It was as if the murder had allowed Anshul to cast aside the mutual embarrassment and pain that had marred their friendship since the day of the immolation.

When Mohit asked how his health was, Anshul said, "There's still risk of sepsis. My organs could fail. Life is short. I want to do what I can in that time."

So Mohit had accepted Anshul's help; and soon his involvement with the Congress grew. But because of this, he never considered other options for his future.

One day Mohit paid Gita a visit. In the bedroom, he asked if he could speak to her in private, and they went down to the dining room. Mohit was a man now—of middling height, a bit heavy in the buttocks, wearing a puffy button-down shirt and baggy tan corduroys.

"Chachi," he began, "I'm worried that Deepak's studies are being affected."

"I'm also worried," she said.

"He doesn't listen to me, Chachi. And his friends—" he paused. "I'm worried he's falling into the wrong company."

"But he's such a sweet boy—you want me to talk to him?"

Mohit twisted his palms together, as if he were unscrewing a bottle. "No matter what happens, his father is a known murderer." He paused. "I was lucky—I got into college before all this nonsense, but ... I don't want his future to be jeopardized. And now with these economic problems—and everyone feels Mandal will be passed by the court." He went on, "Chachi, I know you've done a lot for us—but I wanted to ask you and Chachu if there's any way you can help

Deepak go to the States. I talked to Sharad Chacha. He said that Deepak can come live with them in Houston; they'll sponsor him, and after doing one year of school, he can join a community college. Only issue is that we need money for his ticket, so I was wondering if Chacha can give a loan—of course we'll pay it back—"

"And Deepak wants to go?" Gita asked.

"It's the only thing he's excited about! All his favorite bands are there," Mohit said, laughing. He accepted a teacup in both hands from Ramesh before settling back into the chair. He blew into it.

Gita thought, a difference of two and a half years, and yet how paternal Mohit was toward his brother! Love is born out of necessity.

"And you don't want to go abroad, beta?" Gita asked. "For your PG?"

Mohit shook his head. "Someone has to be here for Papa. And the property."

"And you're getting involved in politics, I'm hearing," Gita said.

"That's just time-pass, Chachi. They're all matlabi and corrupt. I learned that during my time in the hospital. All these party guys were collecting money for Anshul and me—and they just kept it."

"How is your friend Anshul?" Gita asked.

"Oh, his health is very bad, Chachi. He has to spend many days just resting at home. But he's brave and—despite being in a wheelchair—has become the DUSU president. But it's not clear how long he'll live. He himself says it. All his organs were badly damaged."

"Poor fellow, does he regret it?" Gita asked.

"Regret!" Mohit folded up his face in an emphatic expression he had learned from his theatrical father. "No, I mean he's gotten so much attention from it." *Something slightly cruel and jealous there*, Gita thought. *A new callousness about pain.*

They sat silent, not touching on the subject of Mohit's own burns.

CHAPTER 103

When Gita talked to Sachin later that evening about the possibility of Deepak immigrating to America, he sighed. "It's good. You have to be a self-starter there. Here they fall into being lath-sahibs."

"And Mohit seemed to imply Deepak's taking drugs," Gita said. "He's very obsessed with his hard rock."

Sachin said, "You know the case has drained our accounts."

But both were thinking: *With Deepak gone, our responsibilities will lessen too.*

On one of his bimonthly visits to Tihar, handing Brij a tiffin full of hot, cooked food in the meeting area, Sachin said, "I've heard Sharad has invited Deepak to live in the US?"

Brij's eyes hooded over. "Yes, my older one is very desperate the younger one goes. Probably to corner the property for himself." He smiled a little.

Sachin ignored the provocation. "Given all that he's been through here, it might not be a bad idea. We're willing to pay for his ticket and his first year's upkeep. If we had been in the US, he would have come and stayed with us, so it's not such a big—"

"It's a miracle you came back," Brij said. "No one thought you would. Till the last day we were making bets you wouldn't. We were all shocked." He smiled again as he rolled a bit of roti against a piece of pulverized gobi in one of the tiffin compartments. He looked like a boy frantically rubbing an eraser on a piece of paper. His eating, previously controlled, had grown fast and dexterous, an animal instinct to preserve his tiny spoils. "Do you regret it?" Brij asked.

"Why would I?"

"The house, your work, *this* jail, the court business," Brij said. "You'd be a rich bugger if you were there, not sitting in Tihar!"

"Gita's happy to be near her parents," Sachin said.

Brij said, "But your good wife would be happy anywhere. Are you?"

Sachin tried to ignore it.

"It's OK," Brij said. "You don't have to answer it right now. Think it over." He smirked.

Sachin felt humiliated and angry. He thought: *Why am I helping this bastard—and his son?*

Brij said, "It's not like I'm in the world for twenty years. So if Deepak wants to go, let him go. The coward couldn't come and ask me directly; his brother had to do it for him. Do you know that he's not come once to visit me? Fine, he can go—just inform him that he shouldn't expect anything from me. The property's going to go to Mohit when I die. Let Deepak enjoy himself in the US." Then he gazed up at Sachin. "Don't look so shocked. He'll make plenty of money in that country." He laughed. "So, it's going to be you and me all over again, isn't it? Younger son in America, older one here, taking on the family responsibility." He threw another bite into his mouth and burped. "History repeats itself."

Sachin told Gita, "I don't want to help that bastard or his fucking kids. If I talk to him again, I'll lose my fucking mind."

But they went ahead anyway.

On a winter night full of dense clouds but no rain, they saw Deepak off at the airport. He still looked like a boy; he had worn the very formal clothes of the first-time international flyer (a button-down shirt and slacks); a Walkman bulged from his pocket; he had a backpack and one large suitcase. Gita cried as she hugged him, more for the pathos of the overall situation than from any emotion emanating from the boy, who looked slightly glassy (like his mother) and bemused by affection, wavering like a blade of grass as Gita held on to him and mussed his hair.

Then Mohit and Deepak embraced. Gita watched the tears stream down Mohit's face. Deepak didn't cry but hugged his brother tight.

And with that, Deepak vanished into the garishly overlit airport.

CHAPTER 104

THE PARTING AT THE AIRPORT—MOHIT CRYING AS HE hugged Deepak goodbye—was one of the last times Gita saw Mohit acting nakedly emotional. After that, he always seemed embarrassed around her—and smiley and distant—and rarely came over for lunch and dinner, claiming he was busy with his political work. He was also spending all his free time writing.

Gita saw he was growing thinner and gaunter; the weight he had packed in his buttocks had melted.

She talked with Sachin about whether they should ask him to see a counselor, but Sachin told her that he had already asked Mohit and Mohit had refused.

When, on a visit to Tihar, Sachin expressed his concerns to Brij about the wayward direction Mohit's career was taking without parental supervision, Brij responded, "Let him do what he wants—I also wanted to be a writer, remember? And Gita's grandfather—what a fine man—he was a poet. There's no one I respect more than poets."

"He should at least do an internship at a newspaper," Sachin said.

"We all saw how great the newspapers are," Brij said, with pursed lips. Once he had been convicted, he had turned against the news as an industry—even against those papers that had happily spread rumors about Karishma and Laxman on his behalf.

Sachin noticed a change in Brij during these visits. He seemed … content? Never respected in the free world for his curtailed air force and paper mill career, in prison he had turned himself into a drillmaster of the younger Hindu criminals. "I show them how to properly do push-ups. Then I make them march around the courtyard for an hour every day. Then yoga and meditation. Next time you come, bring some more of my Mohanji balms—even the warden likes them, and the inmates dilute them with water so everyone can share them for strength. And I've been talking to the maharaj about his cooking—he needs to add more herbs." He sighed. "Many people in jail are quite sad. I tell them—look at me!—I'm almost fifty and I've developed a routine. It's all about routine if you want time to pass."

"Some of them must be there for life," Sachin said.

"Even more important, then." And now Brij continued his report on prison life as if it were the only life he had ever known, as if throwing himself deeper into it would make him forget the world outside, the way the world outside had forgotten him.

Soon after this, Gita and Sachin went out for a stroll in the local park.

They had been so involved with the case and with Deepak's and Mohit's futures that they had not spent any leisure time together.

It was now spring—a season in which trees in Delhi shed their leaves again—and Gita and Sachin held hands as they walked over a yellow neem drift.

It was how they had held hands when they had first roamed the streets of Queens together, conversing through the private language of fingers.

Gita said, "Could you have imagined, when we left America, that *this* is what our lives would look like?"

"We knew there'd be more drama," Sachin said laconically.

"Do you think we made the right decision?" she asked.

He said, "You know what's strange? After I made the decision to return, I never questioned it."

She held his hand tighter. This was what she admired about Sachin: He did not vacillate.

That night they made love.

It was a lovemaking shot through with mutual relief, and for the next few days, they made love every night.

Gita still did not get pregnant.

But afterward, when Sachin asked, “Should we look into adoption?” Gita nodded.

A few months later, having commenced the long adoption process with its painstaking paperwork and home visits, they moved out of the death-tainted complex and into a large apartment in an adjacent colony. From there, Gita and Sachin rented out their flat in A-19 to family friends. Predictably, the Chopras of A-19 were incensed. They complained that the complex was only meant for Chopras. But then, unable to block Sachin and Gita, they too began to see the enormous financial possibilities of their position as landowners in an exploding city. In a few years, many of them would cede their flats to outsiders, beginning the process of the dissolution of the complex at A-19.

But that was later. Gita and Sachin, in any case, were not thinking about the complex. Instead they were focused intently on the dazed-looking chubby six-month-old baby girl they had brought home one summer day to their drafty flat. The girl was colicky and napping poorly. They were forty-two and forty-four, and like all others who have desperately wanted children but now have to deal with the anarchy of child-rearing, were overjoyed and flummoxed and tired at once. *This* is what they had wanted so badly all these years? Then they kissed the girl’s inky, spiky hair and their doubts evaporated.

They called their daughter Akanksha—“anticipation” or “desire.”

Unlike the other Chopras, she never lived in the complex.

CHAPTER 105

"SO WHO CAUSED MORE DAMAGE LONG-TERM—MY brother or me?" my father asks me, indicating the sewer outside A-19 filled with plastic bottles.

My father is a free man. He wears a white ponytail tucked into the back of his white shirt.

I never finished the email to my friend Lev.

Then he looks up at the complex. "It hasn't changed at all," he says. "Not even one improvement. And my name is still on the board?"

It was never removed, I say.

"One has to bless the loyalty of this family," he responds.

I nod. Then we walk back together into the rest of our lives.

THE END

THE FAMILY OF SP CHOPRA

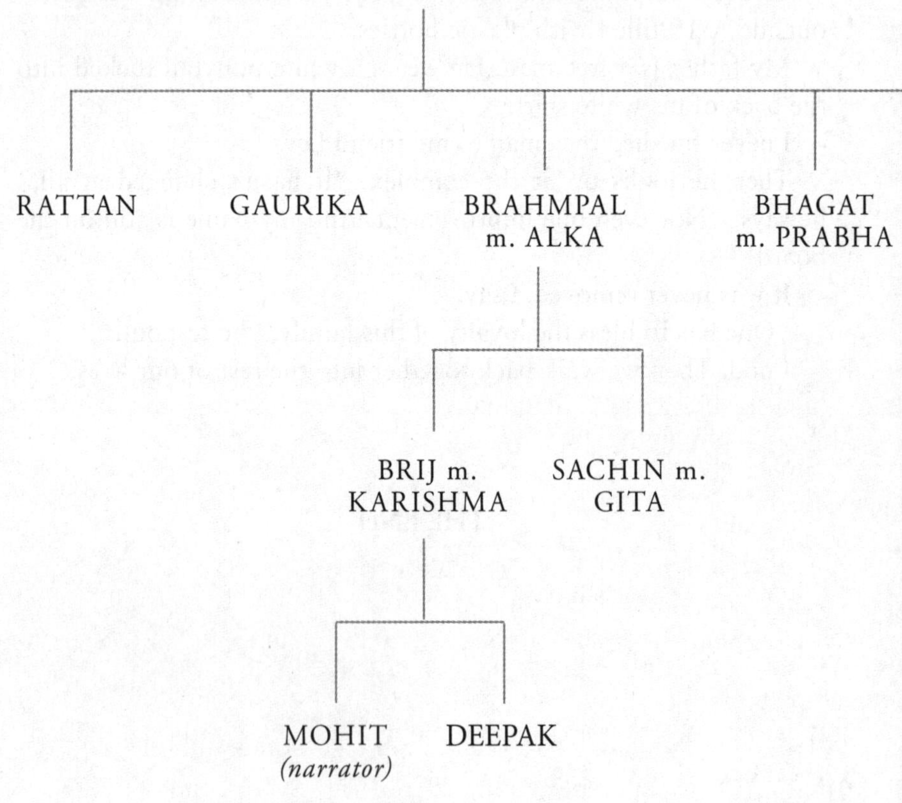

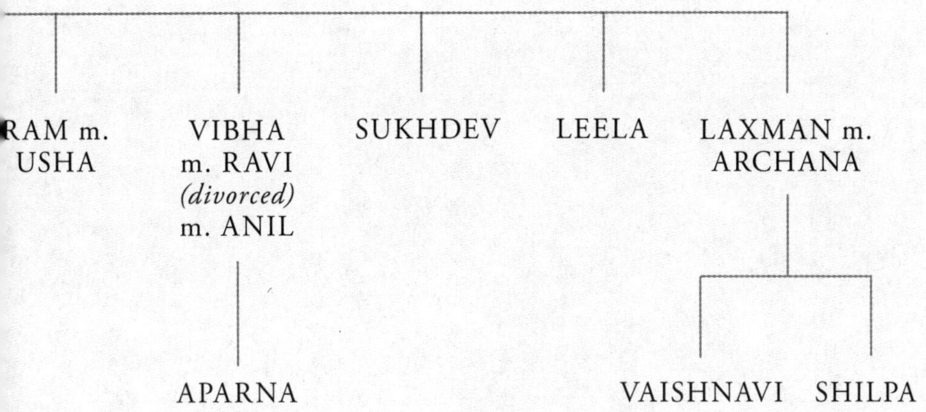
RAM m.
USHA
VIBHA
m. RAVI
(divorced)
m. ANIL
SUKHDEV
LEELA
LAXMAN m.
ARCHANA
APARNA
VAISHNAVI
SHILPA

ACKNOWLEDGMENTS

I WOULD LIKE TO THANK THE FOLLOWING INDIVIDUALS:

For reading (often multiple) drafts: Marisa Silver, Ross Perlin, Laura Davis, Vauhini Vara, Francesca Mari, Aatish Taseer, Nilanjana Roy, Nicholas Casey, Shiv Mahajan, Zubin Shroff.

For their generosity in answering my questions: Antonio Ruiz-Camacho, Prerna Singh, Vidya Vara, Shazia Iqbal, Chitra Ramcharandas, Kamalnayan Agrawal, Donald Levi, Heidi Levi, John Peterson, Kathy Peterson, Shreyas Mishra, Srishti Agnihotri, Tvisha Asrani, Karthika V. K., Ajitha G. S., Debashish Mukerji, Arun Shourie, K. Satyanarayana, Akshaya Mukul, Sohail Hashmi, Vatsala Shrangi, Sayeed Mohammad, Romila Thapar, Megha Anwar, Sarover Zaidi, Anish Vanaik, Ashutosh Varshney, Meera Nanda, Proteeti Banerjee, Anamika Mukherjee, Sharmila Rudrappa, Pulkit Sharma, Miranda Featherstone, Chelsea Finkbeiner, Shayan Sengupta, Indrani Sengupta, Sarah Herman.

For friendship, encouragement, advice: Fatima Kola, Tory Stewart, Brooke Holmes, Maya Jasanoff, Anthony Ha, Lexy Benaim, Tony Tulathimutte, Alice Sola Kim, James Yeh, Annie Wyman, Anna North, Gabe Winslow-Yost, Adam Johnson, Tom Meaney.

For financial support: The Cullman Fellowship, with special thanks to Salvatore Scibona, Lauren Goldenberg, and my cohort. The Bard Prize, especially the committee and Irene Zedlacher. My department at Brown University. Daniel O'Mahony at the Brown University Library. The Corporation of Yaddo. Disquiet International. The Dobie Paisano Fellowship and the late great Michael Adams.

For their endorsements: Karen Russell, Madhuri Vijay, Manu Joseph, Nana Kwame Adjei-Brenyah, Nilanjana Roy, Raghu Karnad, Sonia Faleiro, Tony Tulathimutte, Vauhini Vara, Vivek Shanbhag.

And deep and continued thanks to: Jin Auh, whose honesty I could not value more. Allison Lorentzen, for her steadfast vision and excellent suggestions. Dharini Bhaskar, for returning sharp edits in record time. Willing Davidson, for publishing an excerpt in *The New Yorker*. Sonia Gadre, Camille Leblanc, and Abram Scharf, for their editorial support. Ananth Padmanabhan, Udayan Mitra, and David Ross, for their enthusiasm. Jennifer Bernstein, for foreign rights.

And thanks most of all to my parents and my brother; and to Francesca Mari and Vidya Lena Mari-Mahajan, the latter of whom was born during the creation of this book.

ABOUT THE AUTHOR

KARAN MAHAJAN is the author of *The Association of Small Bombs*, which was named one of the Ten Best Books of the Year by *The New York Times Book Review*, won the Muse India Young Writer Award, and was a finalist for the National Book Award, the Crossword Book Award, and the DSC Prize for South Asian Literature, among other honors. His debut novel, *Family Planning*, was a finalist for the Dylan Thomas Prize. He has been selected as one of *Granta*'s Best Young American Novelists, and his writing has appeared in *The New Yorker*, *The New York Times*, *Vanity Fair*, *The New York Review of Books* and other publications. Originally from Delhi, he now teaches at Brown University.

HarperCollins *Publishers* India

At HarperCollins India, we believe in telling the best stories and finding the widest readership for our books in every format possible. We started publishing in 1992; a great deal has changed since then, but what has remained constant is the passion with which our authors write their books, the love with which readers receive them, and the sheer joy and excitement that we as publishers feel in being a part of the publishing process.

Over the years, we've had the pleasure of publishing some of the finest writing from the subcontinent and around the world, including several award-winning titles and some of the biggest bestsellers in India's publishing history. But nothing has meant more to us than the fact that millions of people have read the books we published, and that somewhere, a book of ours might have made a difference.

As we look to the future, we go back to that one word—a word which has been a driving force for us all these years.

Read.